Newton
Monument

Riddells

of Concord

Roman Amphitheatre

Arcadian Valley

Neptune's
Temple

Grotto

Lime Walk

Palladian
Bridge

Wilderness

Monks-Unmentionable

Temple

Jubilee Field

Arc de Triomphe

drawn by RAYMOND M'GRATH

MISTRESS MASHAM'S REPOSE

By T. H. White

THE SWORD IN THE STONE

THE WITCH IN THE WOOD

THE ILL-MADE KNIGHT

MISTRESS MASHAM'S REPOSE

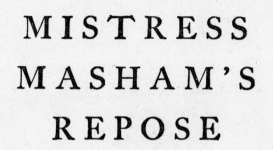

MISTRESS MASHAM'S REPOSE

By T. H. WHITE

ILLUSTRATIONS BY FRITZ EICHENBERG

G. P. PUTNAM'S SONS

NEW YORK

Printed in the United States of America
By H. Wolff, New York

FOR AMARYLLIS VIRGINIA GARNETT

"I took with me six Cows and two Bulls alive, with as many Yews and Rams, intending to carry them into my own Country and propagate the Breed. . . . I would gladly have taken a Dozen of the Natives. . . ."

—*Gulliver's Travels*

MISTRESS MASHAM'S REPOSE

CHAPTER

I

MARIA was ten years old. She had dark hair in two pigtails, and brown eyes the color of marmite, but more shiny. She wore spectacles for the time being, though she would not have to wear them always, and her nature was a loving one. She was one of those tough and friendly people who do things first and think about them afterward. When she met cows, however, she did not like to be alone with them, and there were other dangers, such as her governess, from which she would have liked to have had a protector. Her main accomplishment was that she enjoyed music, and played the piano well. Perhaps it was because her ear was good that she detested loud noises, and dreaded the fifth of November. This, however, with the cows, was her only weakness, and she was said to be good at games.

Unfortunately she was an orphan, which made her difficulties more complicated than they were with other people. She lived in an enormous house in the wilds of Northamptonshire, which was about four times longer than Buckingham Palace, but was falling down. It had been built by one of her ducal ancestors who had been a friend of the poet Pope's, and it was surrounded by Vistas, Obelisks, Pyramids, Columns, Temples, Rotundas, and Palladian

Bridges, which had been built in honor of General Wolfe, Admiral Byng, the Princess Amelia, and others of the same kidney. Maria's parents had made a desperate attempt to keep the grounds in order. They had been killed in an accident, however, and after that there had been no money left, not even enough to live on respectably in a boarding-house, somewhere else. The Rates and so on had used up all the available income, and nobody could be persuaded to buy the place for a school nor for a hospital. Consequently she and her governess had to sleep in two bedrooms which still had a bit of roof over them, the governess using one of the smaller drawing rooms to live in, and they had a cook to look after them, who dwelt in the kitchen. It is literally true that this cook had a bicycle in the basement corridor, which she used to ride along the corridor, when she had to answer the bell.

The house had 365 windows, all broken but six, 52 state bedrooms, and 12 company rooms. It was called Malplaquet.

Maria's governess was a Miss Brown. She had been appointed by the local vicar, who was Maria's guardian. Both the Vicar and the governess were so repulsive that it is difficult to write about them fairly.

The Vicar was 5 ft. 7 ins. in height, and looked as if he were fifty years old. His face was red, with hundreds of little veins of a purple color, because he suffered either from blood pressure or from a weak heart or from both. It was difficult to see his eyes, partly because they were of the same general color as the rest of his face, and partly because he wore thick spectacles, behind which they lurked like oysters. His hair was parted in the middle and brushed flat. He had rather pouting bluish lips, and he walked upright and slow, giving a faint humming noise from the back of his nose, like a bee. He had been a housemaster in a public school before he got the job as Maria's guardian, and his only pleasure then had been in caning the boys—but he had not been able to do so much of this as he would have liked to do, owing to his heart. His name was Mr. Hater. He was a bachelor. It was suspicious that he had a Rolls-Royce, and spent much of his time in London, while Maria had to live in the ruined house on sago and other horrors.

Miss Brown had been Mr. Hater's matron at the public school. She must have had some mysterious hold over him, for it seems impossible that he could have chosen her freely, considering what she was. Her nose was sharp and pinched, with a high bridge, but the rest of her was podgy. When she sat down, she spread, as a toad does on one's hand. Her eyes were pebble-colored and her hair was yellow. It was drawn in a tight bun. She wore rimless pince-nez. She was about the same age as the Vicar, but a good deal shorter. She was cruel in a complicated way. For instance, when Maria's last uncle had been alive, he had sometimes remembered to send the child a box of chocolates for Christmas. Miss Brown's arrangements for any such parcel had usually been fixed in stages. First, Maria had not been allowed to open it when it came, "in case it had germs." It had been sent down to the kitchen to be baked. Then Maria had been sent for, to the Northwest Drawing Room, in which Miss Brown resided, and the ruined parcel had been placed before her to be undone. The next step had been to claim that Maria had dirty hands, untruly, and to send her back to the kitchen, a ten minutes' walk, to wash them. When she had got back at last, agog with expectation, and the poor melted chocolates had been unstuck from the brown paper, Miss Brown used to condemn them as improperly packed and throw them into the nearest lake with her own fair fingers "for fear they would make the child ill."

It is difficult but important to believe that this precious pair may have been trying to do the best they could, considering the kind of people they were.

Maria had two real friends, the cook and an old professor who lived in a distant part of the grounds. She was sometimes very unhappy and sometimes very happy, because people fly between wider extremes when they are young. Her happiest times were when the Vicar was in London and Miss Brown was in bed with a headache. Then she would be mad with pleasure, a sort of wild but earnest puppy rushing about with the slipper of her imagination, tearing the heart out of it.

It was on a summer day such as this, with her tormentors well out of the way, that she decided to visit the Quincunx. to try some piracy at sea.

The Quincunx was one of the lakes at the foot of the lawn on the South Front. It was overgrown with trees, huge alders and beeches and wild cherries and sequoias and cedars, all planted by the numerous acquaintances of the poet Pope, and its surface was matted with water lilies, and there was a decayed wooden boathouse with a punt in it, which leaked. In the middle of the lake there was a small island choked with brambles, and, on the island, there was a plastered temple in the shape of a cupola, or rather, to give it its proper name, of a monopteron. It was a dome like the top of an eggshell, raised on five slender columns, and it was called Mistress Masham's Repose.

But nobody had ever reposed there since the death of Queen Anne. Nobody had cleared the nettles from the little island, nor swept the deep leaf mold from the marble steps, nor cut back the laurels and rhododendrons and blackberries which crowded round the forgotten temple, even seeming to climb the pillars. All the dainty elegance which had once been made so carefully, by hands which had intended it to stay elegant, had been abandoned in the March of Mind. The lake itself was silted with weeds, because there was no money left to cut them, and the island had become a sort of Atlantis, lost in the seas. Maria was the only person who knew the weed lanes by which it could be reached. She had never landed there, however, because of the tangles.

It was a glorious day in June—for that matter, it was the Glorious First of June—and the sun was resounding on the great, green sweep of the lawn. The farmer who rented the land was chasing his sheep about, with a hot-buttered face, waving a bottle of lotion for maggots; the gray squirrels were chattering and cursing in the Chestnut Avenue; the bullocks in the Jubilee Field, safe on the other side of the Quincunx, were flicking their tails and occasionally thundering off elsewhere, because the clegs bit them; cuckoos were changing their tunes; the insect world was humming in the wilderness of shining evergreens; there were rabbits, and long grass, and small birds, and Maria was as brown as a berry.

She lay face downward in the punt, looking over the stern into the deep water. Her knees, and most of the front of her, were green with slime; the water from the bailing scoop had run up her sleeve. She was happy. When the boat dawdled to a stop, she gave it a stroke to keep it going. Under her nose, she watched the mare's-tail and other flora of the ocean floor, as the prow edged its way between the water lilies. Dragonflies, like blue needles, and damsel flies like ruby ones—the husband keeping his wife in order by gripping her tightly round the neck with a special pair of pincers on the end of his tail—hovered over the surface. By going gently, she could sometimes pass above a flight of perch without disturbing them. Or rather, they would raise their spiky fins, blush out the dark anger of their bars, and make mouths at her. Once or twice, she passed a pike, only six inches long, basking under the flat green leaves, and once she came close to the meeting place of the tench—who made themselves scarce with a loud plop. They had been lazily scratching their backs on the lilies, like a school of elephants.

The lakes of Malplaquet were, in fact, a wonderful place for coarse fishing. In the old days, before they were weeded up, the Northampton Anglers used to go there twice a year for competitions. The tench ran big, up to five pounds or more, which was practically the record weight, and there was sometimes taken a pike of twenty pounds. The perch were fair, but not impressive. There were also some small roach.

When she had come abreast of the little island of Mistress Masham's Repose, she began to feel piratical. Swouns and Slids, she said to herself, but you could stap her vitals if she did not careen there, and perhaps dig up some buried treasure while about it. She felt that she could do with a couple of skellingtons, or with a cross marked in dry blood on the wrinkled parchment of a map.

The island had lilies all round, mixed with frogbit and water crowfoot, so dense that it was difficult to push against them.

She paddled round, looking for a place where she could shove through. She laid her matchlocks handy on the thwart, first blowing on the priming so that the rum in her breath nearly caught fire. She loosened her hanger in the scabbard, and paced the poop.

The only place for landing was a fallen larch—which had dropped there as a cone since Lady Masham had died ennobled, had grown to its full stature, rotted, and blown down. It lay outward from the isle, bridging the worst part of the lilies. Some of its branches still tried to dress themselves in green.

Maria laid her bark alongside the end of the larch, and tied it up so that it could not drift away—an Inconvenience, as Gulliver tells us, which all prudent Mariners take special Care to provide against. Then she took off her shoes and stockings, thinking that she would climb more easily in bare feet. She boarded the tree bole, brandishing her cutlass, and swarmed ashore with the battle cry of à Maria, her spectacles twinkling fiercely in the sun.

CHAPTER

II

T HE island on which she found herself was about
the size of a tennis court. It had been carried there
on boats, when the first duke had been beautifying
his park, and it had risen from the water two hundred years
before, an artificial emerald of green grass, crowned by the
white dome of its cupola. There, perhaps, the Mistress Hill
who was to become Mistress Masham—or even Mistress
Morley herself, had sat in silks and laces, in the summer
weather, drinking tay. If Mistress Morley had been there,
she probably enjoyed a dash of brandy in the smoaking
Tyde.

But now the island was tangled with every kind of briar.
It had a boma round it, an outer ring of blackberries and
nettles, choking the jungle of the shrubbery which faced the
visitor. There seemed to be no way of reaching the little
temple without pain, for the nettles were ready to sting and
the briars were ready to prick, and what she really needed
was a machete—or any similar instrument used by Indians,
in cutting their trackways through the Bush.

If she had been a gamekeeper with thick clothes and
leather leggings, she might have been able to push her way
through; if she had been a farm laborer, she could have
cleared a path with her brish-hook; as she was neither of

these, but a determined person all the same, except for cows, she bashed her way with the punt scoop. When she had beaten down a bramble, she trod on it reluctantly; when they caught in her dress, she stopped and took them out—sometimes; when they scratched her face, she swore the appropriate oath; and so, slowly but surely, she burrowed her way into the forest belt. She tore her skirt in three places, and scratched the brown legs horribly, until she had to go back for the shoes.

The tanglewood stopped suddenly, several yards from the steps of the temple, and the intruder came to a halt with a blackberry branch in her hair.

Where the brambles ended, the grass began: the same neat, artificial grass which Lady Masham must have known. It was still kept as short, or even shorter. It was as smooth as a bowling green.

Indeed, the place was like a bowling green. It was hedged with the thicket, as such greens often are with yew. In the middle, there was the beautiful, sun-drenched temple, rising airily on its pillars.

But what was strange—and here Maria's heart went Pat, she knew not why—the strange thing was that everything was neat.

She looked everywhere, but not a soul was to be seen. Not a leaf stirred in the little amphitheater, nor was there any trace of a hut to live in. There was no shed to hold a lawn mower, nor any mower standing on the lawn.

Yet somebody had mowed the grass.

Maria took the bramble out of her hair, disentangled herself from the last branches, and went forward to her doom.

The plaster inside the dome had fallen in some places; but the wooden slats, which were visible in most of the ruined

17

ceilings of her home, were not exposed in this one. It looked as if the roof had been repaired from inside, with clay or paper, as if it had been done by wasps. Also, and this was strange again, there was no plaster on the floor. It had been cleared away.

Everything was so clean, so different from the wasteland which she had come through—so square and round and geometrical, just as it had been when first erected—that her eye was drawn to details.

She saw: first, a square opening, about eight inches wide, in the lowest step, which she took to be the ventilator of a damp course—but there was a path leading to it, trodden in the fine grass, a path for mice; next, she saw a seven-inch door in the base of each pillar, possibly also connected with the damp course—but, and this she did not notice because they were nearly as small as match heads, these doors had handles; finally, she saw that there was a walnut shell, or half one, outside the nearest door. Several walnuts grew in the park, though none were very close. She went to look at the shell—but looked with the greatest astonishment.

There was a baby in it.

She bent down to pick up the cradle, which she took to be some kind of toy, a toy made more beautifully than any she had ever seen. When the shadow of her hand fell across the baby, which was nearly an inch long, it wagged its head on the minute cushion of moss, put out its fists in both directions, pulled up its knees as if it were bicycling, and gave a thin mew, which she could hear.

She did not snatch away her hand when the creature mewed. On the contrary, she grabbed the walnut. If there were one thing now in all the world which Maria was inclined to snatch, it was the baby.

She held it tenderly in the palm of her hand, not breathing for fear of spoiling it, and examined its wonderful perfection as well as she could. Its eyes, which were as small as a shrimp's, seemed to have the proper marble-blue for babies; its skin was slightly mauve, so that it must have been a new one; it was not skinny, but beautifully plump, and she was just able to distinguish the creases round its fat wrists—creases which looked as if the thinnest hair had been tied round in a tight bracelet, or as if the hands had been fitted, on the ball-and-socket principle, by the most cunning of all the dollmakers there had ever been.

It was truly alive, and seemed to be fairly pleased at being picked up, for it held out one hand toward her nose and chuckled. At least, by listening to it like a watch, with her head on one side, she was certain that it made a noise.

While Maria was in a rapture with this windfall, she felt a sharp pain in her left ankle, as bad as if she had been stung by a bee.

Like most people whose ankles are stung, she stamped her foot and hopped about on one leg—a useless procedure, so far as bees are concerned, because it only annoys the others, and the first one cannot sting again.

She held the cradle with the greatest care while she hopped, clapped her spare hand to the hurt ankle, and confronted her assailant from a safe distance, standing on one leg.

There was a fat woman, about five inches high, standing on the marble pavement of the temple, and brandishing a sort of harpoon. She was dressed in rust-colored stuff, like the breast of a robin, and she was wild with rage or terror. Her little eyes were flashing, her hair had come down at the back, her bosom was heaving, and she was shouting in an

19

unknown language something about Quinba Flestrina. The harpoon, which was as sharp as a needle, had a steel head half as long as the baby. Some blood was trickling between the fingers of Maria's spare hand.

Now in spite of the homicides or other torts which she might have committed as a pirate, who was partial to the Plank, Maria was not the kind of person who bore malice for injuries, and she was certainly not the kind of kidnaper who habitually stole babies from their heartbroken mothers, for the mere cynical pleasure of hearing them scream. She guessed immediately that this was the mother of the baby, and, instead of feeling angry about the harpoon, she began to feel guilty about the baby. She began to have an awful suspicion that she would have to give it back.

Yet the temptation to keep it was severe. She would never drop on another find like this, she knew, not if she lived to be a thousand.

Think to yourself, truly, whether you would have returned a live one-inch baby to its relatives, if caught fairly in the open field?

But Maria did her best.

She said: "I am sorry if this is your baby. Please, I have not done it any harm. Look, you can have it safe.

"And really," she added, almost tearfully, "it is a beauty."

She leaned forward to put the cradle at the mother's feet.

The fierce little woman was either too hysterical to listen, or else she did not understand English, for she slashed at the huge hand with her weapon as soon as it came within reach, and cut it across the thumb.

"Oh, you would, would you?" cried Maria. "You little viper!"

So, instead of giving up the baby, she wrapped it in her

20

handkerchief, cradle and all, and put the bundle in the pocket of her skirt. Then she took a second handkerchief out of the other pocket, waved it in the face of the mother so that she fell on her back, dropped it over her head, flicked away the fallen harpoon, and gathered her as well. She so seldom had two handkerchiefs, or one for that matter, that she felt that the hand of the Lord must be upon her. Then, hearing a kind of hum in the pillar beside her, like the hum of a hive, she felt also that it would be wiser not to tempt the Lord's hand further.

Stuffing the larger bundle into the other pocket—it was kicking as hard as it could—she made for her passage through the brambles. When she got there, she turned round for a last look at the temple. She saw a group of three men struggling at the pillar door. Two of them were holding the third by the arms, to keep him back, and he was fighting them to follow her. He was a splendid fellow in a fur tunic, made of moleskin, and well over six inches high.

CHAPTER

III

WHEN she had pushed off the punt and paddled to a safe distance, she laid down the scoop and took the larger package from her pocket. The woman had been kicking all the time, with fluttering skips and flops, so that it had felt like a small bird trying to get free. As soon as Maria had unwrapped and set her down on the slimy bottom of the boat, she stood panting, with a hand pressed to her heart. It was like a carving in ivory. Then she ran for the side, as if she were meaning to leap into the water, but checked herself, and stood glaring at her captor, the very picture of a wild thing fallen into human hands. Maria produced the other bundle and laid the baby, still in its cradle, not far from the mother's feet. This brought her back from the side. She ran to the cradle, snatched the baby out of it, and began talking to it in a foreign language, examining it all over to see if it were hurt. It was clear that she was telling the baby that it was Mammy's Wazzums Oodlums, and did a nasty female mountain try to steal it then, the precious pet?

Maria licked her wounds, washed them in the cool water of the lake, dried them with the handkerchiefs, and kept a tight eye on the maternal scene.

It was getting on for teatime, and she had a lot of things

to fix. She was determined never to be separated from her treasures—or at least, not from the baby—but she knew perfectly well, on the other hand, that Miss Brown would refuse to let her have them. Either she would confiscate them, and keep them in a box with Maria's penknife and sixpenny compass, or else she would take them for her own use, or she might even arrange to have them drowned, as she used to do with the favorite kittens. None of these things was going to happen, if Maria could help it.

Where could she hide them? Miss Brown was constantly peeping about for faults, and there was not a private place in all the palace of Malplaquet which our heroine could call her own. There were no longer any toys in the toy cupboard, so that to keep them there would only call attention to it. Her bedroom was ransacked once a week.

"I will put them," she said, "in the little drawer of my dressing table for tonight at any rate, since Miss Brown's headache will prevent her from interfering until tomorrow."

This time she made a bag from the wet and gory handkerchief, and, after cornering her captives, she put them both in this together, loose. She tied it round the top with string—for she was a handyman who generally carried string, having been told by her professor that efficient people always had a penknife, a shilling, and a bit of this useful article. She kept the cradle separate, thinking that it would be a bruising thing to be with, if one were bumping about in a bag with a baby. Then she made for the boathouse, put up the punt, and hurried home for tea.

She looked in as she passed the kitchen, which had ovens, spits, and ranges suitable for serving a twelve-course dinner to one hundred and fifty persons—but now they cooked on a primus stove—and inquired about Miss Brown from Cook.

"Lawks, Miss Maria, them stockings! And, glorious me, them rents all over the dress!"

"Yes, I know. I was wondering if Miss Brown. . . ."

"You won't see her tonight, my lamb, and for which we may thank our tender stars. You run up to your room now quiet-like, and bring me back them stockings when you have 'em changed. You'd best put on the dressing gown, until I mend the skirt."

"Is there anything for tea?"

"Yes, Miss, there's strawberries.

"Seeing as She," continued Cook, tossing her head, "was took bad-like, as we might say, I presumed the little liberty for to beg a pound on 'em from your professor, and this, with just a touch of condensated milk, which we was asaving of for Christmas, should make a dish, however humble, as might be savored by the Mistress of Malplaquet."

It is needless to explain that Cook was an Old Retainer, who bore with Miss Brown as well as she could. She lived her life in the gloomy kitchen, with nobody to love but Maria, except for a fat collie dog who had been left to her by her deceased husband, and whose name was Captain. He used to fetch the newspaper from the village every morning, in his mouth, and sometimes he went shopping with a basket.

Maria said: "Cook, if you are ever captured by pirates, or surrounded by Indians, or if you should fall into the sea and be chased by a shark, I will see to it that this day's work is not forgotten, if it costs me the last drop of my blood."

"Thank you, Miss Maria," said Cook, "I'm sure."

She climbed the Grand Staircase and trotted down the Ducal Corridor, mounted the Second Best Staircase and passed the Corridor for Distinguished Strangers, plodded

24

up the Privy Stairs in Ordinary and tiptoed down the Third Best Corridor Once Removed. At the end of this, where part of the main roof was still sound, there were the two small bedrooms in which she and Miss Brown were accustomed to sleep. It used to take Cook about three-quarters of an hour to get there from the kitchen, because she had Bad Legs, and Captain panted dreadfully as he padded up the stairs behind. But Miss Brown made them do the bed for her, all the same.

She peeped in at the open door.

There lay the tyrant on the bed, with her nauseous nose erect. She was reading a mauve book with a stuffed back, like a cushion, which was called *The Daily Light*. In her other hand she held a handkerchief soaked with eau de cologne, and with this she occasionally fanned *The Daily Light*, and occasionally patted her nose tip, which had grown pink and polished under these attentions.

Miss Brown's personality lay about her. There, beneath Maria's fearful eye, stood the thirty pairs of pointed shoes, sharp as builder's trowels, wrinkled at the toes, dressed in a neat line under the dressing table. There, on top of the wardrobe, stood the gray toque hats with pins in them. On the bedside table stood the range of books which Miss Brown considered delightful: the *Journal* of George Fox, *Holy Living* by J. Taylor, and *The Pilgrim's Progress*, about which Huckleberry Finn once remarked that "the statements were interesting, but tough." In a corner of the room there was a cupboard, containing the fichus and frills with which Miss Brown adorned her bosom; the dressing table was covered with sharp things or hard things; and the whole place smelled of unused purses locked away in lavender or naphthalene.

25

On the window sill there were some instruments for spying; the telescope with which she watched from the window, and the magnifying glass with which she looked for dirt.

Her pupil went down on hands and knees. She crawled past the bed, below Miss Brown's line of vision, and reached the window unobserved. She put the magnifying glass between her teeth, where pirates keep their cutlasses, except when drinking. She crawled back to the door, dropping a drawing pin, which she kept handy for such occasions, into one of the shoes while passing, and regained the corridor without mishap.

Then she hurried to her room.

In the bare room, where all the furniture was made of

iron, she took the precious bundle out. She opened it upon the bed. The little woman lay like a suffocating frog, still clutching her baby, and Maria examined them at leisure, with the glass.

The dress was poor. It was a simple garment, tied at the waist like a monk's, and it seemed to have been knitted from silky wool. It was raveled in some places and worn, but serviceable. The woman's face was red and healthy. The baby, as she had suspected, had blue eyes.

Maria put them in the small drawer when she had finished, made a bunch of her own spoiled clothes, and tiptoed down to tea.

CHAPTER

IV

BUT when the Mistress of Malplaquet got up next morning, she was not feeling happy. Not a scrap of the strawberry and cream had been touched, though she had left a saucer in the drawer, and she could get nothing from her prisoner but scowls. It was out of the question to play with her.

"Cook," she said at breakfast, "do you think Miss Brown's headache will be better today?"

"No, Miss Maria," said Cook.

"She has left me some mathematics to work out, before dinner—it seems to be about Algebra."

She twiddled her spoon nonchalantly, and looked from the corner of one eye.

"I wanted to see the Professor."

"Run along and see him, luv. If Somebody wakes up, I'll tell her as how you'm busy with them Algerians, whatsoeverashowsobe as which she might inquire."

"Cook..." began Maria.

"Yes, luv. You told un about the sharks."

The Professor was as poor as a church mouse, and he lived by himself in one of the Ridings, in what had once been a gamekeeper's cottage.

All round the ruined palace there were immense avenues, stretching in every direction, down which the departed

28

dukes had been accustomed to drive in state when they had felt like an airing, or when the Comte de Paris and Queen Victoria had dropped in for the week end. These avenues had developed into Ridings which had once been thought the finest pheasant coverts in Europe, and in them King Edward had often popped away. Finally, when the carriage roads had vanished altogether, they had become green fields between the woods, long and thin, which were hired to grazing farmers by the solicitors who represented the Estate.

Such was the Riding in which the Professor lived.

He was a failure, but he did his best to hide it. One of his failings was that he could scarcely write, except in a twelfth-century hand, in Latin, with abbreviations. Another was that, although his cottage was crammed with books, he seldom had anything to eat. He could not tell from Adam, any more than Maria could, what the latest quotation of Imperial Chemicals was upon the Stock Exchange.

In the daytime, he used to chop wood and cut some slices of bread and butter. In the evenings, having lighted the choppings, he would sit before the fire and quaff a glass of liquor, pondering the remarks of Isidore, Physiologus, Pliny, and similar people. His tipples were Cowslip, Dandelion, Elderberry, and sometimes Gooseberry Wine, which he brewed himself. Inflamed by these, in the kind glow of the green ash, he would dream of impossible successes: imagining that the Master of Trinity had referred to him by name in a lecture, or that Dr. Cook had offered to mention him in a footnote to Zeus, or even that one of the poorer colleges had given him a sort of supernumerary fellowship of the lowest class, carrying a stipend of about five pounds a year, so that he would no longer have to cut his bread and butter.

On the second of June, the Professor had got up early to pick dandelions. He was wandering up and down the

Ridings with a sack, nipping off the yellow heads with his fingers, and popping them inside. He did not notice Maria's figure stumping up the avenue.

"What ho!" she cried. "Avast! Belay!"

"Go away," said he promptly.

"Do you know who you are talking to?"

He straightened his aching old back, adjusted the spectacles, and examined her with care.

"Yes, I believe I do. It is Black Maria, the Terror of the Tortugas."

"Then you had better keep a civil tongue, and know your station."

"Why?"

"Because."

"Because what?"

"Look here," she said. "I can't indulge in childish argument. I came on business."

"If you mean that you have come for breakfast, I fear that I have nothing left but half a pound of mustard."

She put her hand on the bottle-green sleeve and made him drop the bag. The reference to breakfast had touched her, for she knew he seldom had enough to eat. She put her arm, a little shyly, round the creaking waist.

"I have found something."

"What sort of thing?"

"I can't show it here. I have brought it, but it might escape in grass. I want to show you in the cottage."

He said: "Dear me, Maria, well, dear me. I must say I am glad to see you. Come in, come in. I hardly noticed it was you at first. Certainly you may come inside my cottage, although I ought to tell you that I have not done the washing up."

She put the five-inch woman on the kitchen table, in the

30

bread crumbs. The only tea cup was full of ink. She told the story and explained her difficulties—how Miss Brown would be against it, how there was nowhere safe to hide the mannikins, how they would not eat, and the rest of the trouble.

"H'm," said he. "Let me see. It is one of these modern writers, I believe. Martin or Swallow or ... Yes, yes, dear me, it must have been our Dr. Swift. He was conscious of the similarity himself. Indeed, his nickname with Ld. Treasurer was Martin, if I have my facts. Yes, yes. Now Dr. Swift was at Malplaquet, as we know, in 1712. He came here straight from Twit-nam, with the poet Pope. But that was long before the *Travels*. H'm, h'm, h'm."

"I don't..."

"Please hold your tongue, dear girl. It interrupts the flow. Now what more natural than this, that the immortal Dean should finish off the *Travels* here for Motte—could he have come again in '25?—and what place could there be more suited to the toils of literature than the cool, quiet arbor on the Masham Isle? No doubt he left some Lilliputians there behind him, by mistake. We know that authors suffer from the absent mind."

"*Gulliver's Travels?*"

"Gulliver! The very name! This will be an addition to the annals of Malplaquet, to know that *Gulliver* was finished here, and that they left the people too. Excuse me while I look it up."

She dangled her legs on a soapbox, keeping a good lookout to see that the supposed Lilliputian did not run away, and the old gentleman brought down one first edition after another, with grunts and puffs of dust, but always with tender fingers. His findings were a disappointment.

"It distinctly says that not one single citizen was carried

31

off. Gulliver brought 'six Cows and two Bulls alive, with as many Yews and Rams.' One of the sheep was eaten on the voyage by a rat, and he gave one cow and one sheep to Captain John Biddel, who brought him home. H'm, h'm.

"Wait a bit," he added hastily. "It says that Gulliver left Blefuscu, in his rowing boat, on the twenty-fourth of September, 1701. He was picked up at sea by this Captain Biddel, on the twenty-sixth, in latitude thirty degrees south. Mark you, it was only two days later. He told his story to Biddel—he even gave the pair of animals to prove it—and, on their return to England, he was able to sell the remaining cattle for six hundred pound!

"Believe me," continued the Professor, taking off his spectacles and pointing them at her, "in those days, six hundred were six hundred. Why, Stella herself contrived to live in genteel comfort, with a capital of little more than twice that sum.

"If you," said he, "were a captain who had picked up such a castaway, within two days' rowing of a known latitude, carrying a dozen cattle worth six hundred pound, old style, what would you do?"

"I should go back to search the latitude."

"Then?"

"I should bring back plenty more. My goodness, I should bring back men!"

He shut the book with a bang, which he immediately regretted, wandered off to return it to its shelf, and began to think of something else.

"All the same," she said, "even if this creature—this, er, little lady—even if she did come originally from Lilliput or Blefuscu, I don't see how it helps."

"No?"

"She won't eat."

"No?"

"She won't do anything."

He put his hands behind his back, shuffled on the floor, and scowled.

"She isn't any fun."

He stuffed his beard in his mouth, rolled his eyes, and glared. Then he unrolled them, liberated the whiskers, and looked haughtily upon his visitor.

"Why should she be fun?

"Why should she do anything?

"Why should she eat?

"Is she yours?"

Maria twiddled her fingers nervously, but he sat down on the soapbox and took her hand.

"My dear neighbor," said he, "there is one thing which I promise, and that is that I will not say, How would *you* like to be wrapped up in a handkerchief? I am aware that it is not a question of you being wrapped up in one, but of this person. I will, however, make a suggestion. As we all know, I am a failure in the world. I do not rule people, nor deceive them for the sake of power, nor try to swindle their livelihood into my own possession. I say to them: Please go freely on your way, and I will do my best to follow mine. Well then, Maria, although this is not a fashionable way of going on, nor even a successful one, it is a thing which I believe in—that people must not tyrannize, nor try to be great because they are little. My dear, you are a great person yourself, in any case, and you do not need to lord it over others, in order to prove your greatness."

"I would not do her any harm! I would not lord it!"

"But would she do the harm to you? Think what may happen, for a minute. Suppose you managed to tame her, suppose you even managed to tame all the other people from the Island of Repose. No doubt there are several more. You would be a Big Bug then, however kind you were, and they would be little bugs, without the capitals. They would come to depend on you; you would come to boss it over them. They would get servile, and you would get lordly. Do you think that this would be good for either of you? I think that it would only make them feeble, and make you a bully."

"I wouldn't bully them!"

"No?"

"I would try to help."

"But God helps those who help themselves."

She produced her battered handkerchief, and began to twist it into shreds.

"Then what am I to do?"

He stood up stiffly, went to the cobwebbed window, and stared out.

"It is not for me to say."

"What would you do, Professor?"

"I would put her on the island, free, with love."

"But not have People any more?"

"No more."

"Professor," she said, "I could help them, if I saw them sometimes. I could do things for them. I could dig."

"No good. They must do their own digging."

"I have nobody to love."

He turned round and put on his spectacles.

"If they love you," he said, "very well. You may love them. But do you think, Maria, that you can make them love you for yourself alone, by wrapping prisoners up in dirty handkerchiefs?"

CHAPTER

V

SHE sculled the punt toward the island with a heavy heart. Once there, she tied it to the larch and produced her bundle, feeling as if she would like to drop, as she did so, an unpiratical tear. She put the captive on the tree.

The small lady of Lilliput stood for a moment, clutching the baby. She was creased and rumpled from her adventures. Her hair was in disorder and her mind confused. However, when she had at last got her bearings, she did do one thing which made up for much. She curtsied to Maria. Immediately afterward she spoiled the effect, by turning round and running for dear life.

Our heroine paddled round the island despondently, noticing that the path, which she had broken down, had been blocked up. The brambles had been pulled into place again, and woven together, to make a screen.

"After all," she thought, "it is my own island. I did discover it, and I have as much right to look about it as anybody else. Even if I have to turn them loose, I don't see why I should be warned off from my own island."

So she tied to the larch again, and sat there meditating. She wanted to go ashore, to explore the temple, for she felt certain that there would be interesting things to find, even if the people stayed in hiding.

While she was meditating, she looked at the tree, and, while she looked, it struck her more and more that there was something queer about it. The roots were still on dry land, and the larch lay outward into the lake until its top was under the surface. The straight bole gradually rose from the water at a gentle angle; the branches which stuck up with their small cones had put on a summer green: and there was a greenness along one side of the bole also, a misty curtain, like the bright strands of the larch itself, which hung into the water. It was like a camouflage net.

Maria scrambled to the other end of the punt, which brought her close enough to lift it. Underneath, in a dock between the net and the tree trunk, dozens of canoes were moored. They were the best kind of canoe: the kind in which, because they have a water-tight deck, the Eskimos can button themselves and turn somersaults in the water, without sinking. The only difference was that these Lilliputian boats, which were about eight inches long, had collapsible outriggers on both sides. She examined them closely —they were folded back, for convenience in mooring—and, by fiddling with the nearest one, which she took from the water, she discovered that the outriggers ran in a slot. By pushing them forward and down, they could be made to fold astern like the wings of a gull; by pulling them back and up, they were locked into position outboard, like the legs of a "water boatman." She did not know this at the time, but these boats were used for fishing on the lake, and, by throwing the outriggers into position, it was possible to play fishes of a pound or more, without being upset.

She put the canoe at its mooring again and dropped the net.

For all I know, she thought, there are things like this all over the island. For instance, what about the sheep and cows? Evidently the People defend themselves by hiding. The barrier of brambles is to keep stray humans off. I bet the bowling green was full of cows when I arrived—that was why it was cropped short—and, while I was hacking my way through the blackberries, everything was driven away.

37

So far as that goes, what about the square door in the bottom step, the one with a path leading to it? I shouldn't wonder if the cattle were driven into that. Perhaps the step is hollowed out, for cowsheds. Yes, and I suppose the cradle got left behind in the hurry, and then naturally the mother came to defend it. If it hadn't been left, I should never have noticed anything.

They must have sentries, continued Maria. If I wanted time to hide things on the island, I should post a sentry. Then, if I saw myself getting out a punt, I should be able to warn myself that I was coming, with plenty of time to spare. I bet they were hiding things from the minute they saw me climb into the boathouse.

The best place for a sentry, she thought, looking at it, would be the top of the cupola.

There was something on the top. Very small, not easy to see, perhaps lying flat on its face, there was something not much bigger than an acorn. It might have been the sentry's head.

Maria shook her fist at it cheerfully, for she had suddenly seen her future plain before her. She paddled off, feeling happy once again, to consult the Professor for the second time that day, before Miss Brown's headache got better.

He was translating some remarks by Solinus, and, when he saw her, he merely raised his eyebrows thus:

?

She nodded.

"Good."

"I came about the language."

He pointed to the table.

On it, laid open at the title page, was a beautiful octavo volume in brown calf, which was dated 1735. It said:

A General Description of the Empire of Lilliput,

from its first Erection,
through a long Series of Princes,
with a

Particular Account

of their Wars and Politicks, Laws, Learning & Religion
their Plants and Animals,
their peculiar Manners and Customs,
with other Matters very curious and useful,
to which is added

A Brief Vocabulary

of their Language, together with its English
Correspondencies

By Lemuel Gulliver, first
a Surgeon, and then a
Captain of several
Ships.

"It's rare," said the Professor, modestly. "In fact, I don't suppose there are any other copies in existence. You will find it mentioned in the *Travels*."
She turned to the vocabulary:

Quinba, s., f., a female
Quinbus, s., m., a male.
Ranfu-Lo, s., m., no sing., the breeches.
Reldresan, s., n., a secretary . . .

"It is not very easy to learn a language from a dictionary."

"It is all we have. There are some idioms at the end."

So she sat down beside him, and, while he muttered about Solinus, she muttered "the correct Modes of Address." She was surprised to find that the idioms were not the usual ones about "Have you (got) some cheese?", "Is my aunt in the shop of the barber?", "Please give my pen to the greengrocer," and so on; but were about such matters as "Pray order me a Dish of Coffee," "Odd-so! I have broke the Hinge of my Snuffbox," "Come, Gentlemen, are you for a Party at Quadrille?" and "Madam, the Chairs are waiting."

CHAPTER

VI

MISS BROWN'S headache had left her worse than ever. She questioned Maria venomously about the Algebra, cross-examined Cook, and even sent a sharp note to the Professor, on suspicion, requesting him not to interfere with the education of her Little Charge. It was because Maria had looked happy, which made the Governess think that she must have been doing wrong. She confided this fear to the Vicar, who agreed that hers was a truly Christian attitude, but luckily they did not discover anything which they could punish.

For the remainder of that week, it was nothing but exercise books and knuckle-rapping, with Miss Brown's quick pounce of the ruler, like a toad's tongue catching flies. Several new tortures were invented. One was that Maria had to lie down for two hours every afternoon, with the blinds half drawn and nothing to read, for the sake of her health. This was called "having a rest." Another was that whenever Miss Brown pronounced the grass to be wet, which was always, she had to wear an enormous pair of football boots, which had been bought in a jumble sale by the Vicar. They were too large for her, and made her feel ridiculous, and on Sunday she had to walk up the aisle in them, wishing that the earth would swallow her. Miss Brown knew that children are conservative about their clothes, and dread to seem outlandish, so she had invented this ingenious torment in order to take advantage of Maria's shyness. While she was clumping up the aisle she felt that all the choirboys would be thinking that she was too poor to have proper boots, and Miss Brown knew this also.

There were no more strawberries for tea.

All the same, Maria was far from miserable. She had a secret life of her own now, thinking about her plans for the conquest of Lilliput, and at night she stayed awake for hours, reading under the bedclothes with Cook's electric torch. The Professor had kindly lent her a first edition of *Gulliver's Travels*, as well as the phrase book, and she was learning the language. She had a faraway look of private content, which drove her governess half mad. On the Monday they had a scene about Ingratitude, in which Miss Brown stated that it was sharper than a serpent's tooth to have a thankless child, and this brought on a new headache, sooner than was expected.

Maria hurried down to the lake next morning. She went by the Professor's cottage on the way, to pick up some articles which he had bought for her, by secret arrangement through Cook.

The passage past the brambles had been plaited up, but she forced her way for the second time, and stood in the middle of the empty cupola with a beating heart.

"Glonog," she said, furtively consulting a piece of paper, though she had been repeating the sentence since the night before, "lumos Kelmin pesso mes?"

She said this three times, in a loud, uncertain voice, hoping that the construction would be right. (It was meant to mean, "Please, will you swear a peace with me?")

42

Almost immediately, a small man was pushed from one of the column doors. He was dressed in shabby clothes, and had an agitated, determined look, as if he were sure that he was due to die for his country.

"Glonog," shouted the man, in a high, clear voice, as you would do if you had to hail somebody three or four times higher than your house, "advuntos!"

She hastily produced the Professor's vocabulary, and was already looking up "glonog" when she realized that she had said it herself. Come, thought she, we are not getting on so badly if he begins with "please." So she began looking up "advuntos" and was not long in finding it: "ADVUNTIN-TIMMY, v.i., intrans., To go away, Get out, Remove oneself."

"You horrid little pig," she cried. "Why should I get out, when it's my own island?"

The little man grew pale, but stated firmly, in good English: "It has been our Island, Ma'am, Y'r Honor, Miss, during the Course of nearly thirty hundred Moons."

"I don't care how long it has been your island. It was my ancestor, the first duke, who built it. It said so in a book in the Library, before the books were sold."

"Indeed," said the little man, looking interested for half a second—he was middle-aged and fattish, as if he might have been a lawyer or a member of parliament, if he had owned some better clothes. "It has long been a Topick for Speculation among our Sages, to determine the Origin of so prodigious a Structure."

"You talk English!"

"It has remain'd our second Language, Ma'am, since the Exile under Captain John Biddel."

"Then the little woman must have understood...."

43

At this point their conversation was interrupted by an urchin, about three inches high, who was pushed from the pillar, and ran to the spokesman with a message. There was some brief whispering, and then the urchin went back with a dignified pace; which failed him, however, at the end, for he ran the last few inches in a panic.

"In short, Ma'am," said the spokesman coldly—he had evidently been told not to gossip with giants—"I am instructed by my Countrymen to desire your Complaisance in leaving these poor Territories forthwith."

"Well," said Maria. "I see. Please don't be frightened when I move. I am sitting down."

She seated herself carefully on the bottom step and leaned her elbow on the top one, which brought her head fairly close to his, and saved him the trouble of shouting. The messenger drew back.

"Now," she said, "I have been talking about this business to my Professor. You people are hiding on the island—why? Evidently because you are afraid of being captured by human beings, and the Professor says he doesn't wonder. He says that you are only protected by secrecy, for you could never escape us if the secret were to leak out. But it has leaked. What is the good of ordering me off, when I know it already? The Professor says that Accident Has Delivered You Into My Hands, and it is no good Shutting The Stable Door When The Horse Has Bolted. He says you may just as well make friends with me now, so that I won't tell anybody else. In fact, he says it is your Only Hope."

"Ma'am . . ."

"And honestly," said Maria, "I won't tell anybody. I won't even tell Cook."

"The Accident, Ma'am . . ."

44

"Listen. Please go and explain what he says, inside the pillar. Tell them that I will Defend The Secret With My Life, whether your friends are kind to me or not. The Professor says I am not to Threaten With Discovery. He says that the secret must be kept in any case, and that any Decent Person must leave the rest to you."

"The Professor, Ma'am. ..."

"Your little woman knows about him. I bet she didn't miss a word. Now go and talk it over, please, and the Professor says that I must Walk About Politely while you do."

The messenger looked as if he were going to say several things at once, but he pulled himself together, thought it over in a muddled way, remembered the Topick which he would have liked to discuss, opened his mouth, shut it, glanced at the pillar door, bowed, and withdrew. At the door, he turned, opened his mouth again, shut it, and disappeared.

Maria went round the green, with her eyes skinned, but without making any discoveries. She did find that there were four stone walls, about three inches high, which divided it into fields for the cattle. On her other visit she had taken them for drains. They looked as if they had been made of rubble from the inside of the temple, which, as she was beginning to suspect, was probably hollow. Ants, she knew, would sometimes eat away the furniture from inside, in tropical countries—or perhaps it was termites—and it looked as if the People had been doing the same thing. At any rate, there were no houses or other buildings of any sort, which might have given them away.

When she had finished with the green, she went and sat on the steps for nearly half an hour, but there was no sign of the conference in the cupola having come to an end. So she went round the green for the second time, visited the

45

camouflaged dock for canoes, and took a look at the shrubbery. There was little to discover. It did seem that the lowest parts of the tangle, what we might call the undergrowth of the forest, had paths in it, leading in various directions toward the shore, but only a rabbit would have noticed these. One thing she found, and that was a robin caught by a noose of horsehair, on one of the higher branches. It was dead. Maria did not mind this, as she had no illusions about the habits of robins, and she saw that it had evidently been caught for somebody's dinner.

After these trips she sat on the steps again, for still another half hour, and wished very much that the Parliament would rise.

When it did rise at last, the original messenger came out alone, looking pleased, important, and slightly out of breath. He bowed politely, mopped his brow with a small handkerchief, and announced that the Professor's case was won! If she would kindly sit here, at a safe distance from the cowsheds, the People were prepared to show themselves.

She sat where she was told, holding her breath with excitement, and the messenger stood beside her, as if she were his private discovery. Wonderful things began to happen.

First the gate in the lowest step was opened, and out of this the cattle came, each one led by a cowman holding a rope, for fear that they should bolt on seeing Maria. They were black cattle, like Friesians, and, curiously enough, they showed no sign of being afraid. Probably she was too big for them to notice. They took her for a tree, and left it at that. The sheep came next, all baaing, with their lambs bleating and frisking. When the lambs had a drink, their tails went round like propellors, and this could be distinctly seen. The cattle were about four inches high, the sheep about an inch and a half. There were some small sheep dogs,

like something out of a Noah's Ark, which ran round the sheep and yapped in squeaky voices, evidently enjoying the performance very much.

When the farm animals had been promenaded round the green and driven back for safety in the step, there came a procession of fishermen from the same entrance. These marched round, peeping sideways at the Giantess, carrying paddles for the canoes, harpoons like the one with which she had been attacked, small gaffs, and minnow rods with horsehair lines complete. They had leather thigh boots, tanned from the skins of mice.

While the fishermen had been making their parade, the population of the island had been coming from the doors in the five pillars, without being noticed. She turned round when the last fisherman had disappeared, and there they were on the top step of the temple, in hundreds. (She found out later that there were more than five hundred. This was a greater number than could be supported by the green, but they lived by fishing and hunting and also by using secret pastures on the mainland at night, as we shall see.) When she turned round, all the People said with one voice: "Ooo!"

They were in rags.

It was not exactly rags, when she looked closer, but poor working clothes made of knitted wool from the sheep, and from moleskins or mouse skins. Some of the women had sewn themselves capes, from the breast feathers of small birds.

They all stood gazing at her with their mouths open, and the mothers held their children tightly by the hand, and the men stood rather in front, in case of emergency.

Nobody knew what to do.

Finally she remembered her instructions. She called out

47

that she was going to stand up, so they must not be afraid. When she did stand, there was another "Ooo!" She told them to stay where they were, as she would be back in a minute, and then she rushed to the punt to fetch her package. When she got back, she warned the crowd to stand away from the middle of the pavement—some of the babies began to howl—and laid the package in the center, only staying to undo the string.

She stood off gently, being careful to look behind her for fear of treading on somebody, and said: "See what it is."

The lawyer, or whatever he was, was the coolest person, for he had already passed his own fears, so he called up a team of fishermen, who pulled back the brown paper under his directions. Maria was interested to see that they did not tear the paper off, but treated it with care and admiration. Indeed, a piece of thick cardboard covering about half an acre seemed to them a useful article. When it was off, the People began to come forward slowly, hesitating between curiosity and suspicion, and the lawyer—he was the school-master really—looked at her, to find out what was going to happen next. She pointed to him, to spread the presents out.

It was the silk handkerchiefs which did the trick. When the women saw these, they came quickly to finger them, and to love the bright, smooth colors. There were six three-penny ones, from Woolworth's, of artificial silk, the thinnest kind, for ladies, very gay.

They did not pull them about. They spread them reverently on the step. They were the loveliest things they had ever seen, since their forebears had been carried off from mighty Lilliput, two hundred years before.

Then there was the packet of needles. The men fingered these weapons, trying their temper and their points, with wagging heads and learned comment.

48

Twopenny worth of nails were dragged aside by one party, evidently smiths, and these rang every bar of metal with a hammer, lifting separate nails and dropping them with the smallest clangs, pointing out their beauty in thoughtful tones.

A packet of razor blades, the useful kind with only one edge, so that one does not cut one's fingers when sharpening pencils, proved a puzzle to undo. But, when they had been undone, and their greasy paper stripped, there was a universal cry of admiration. For those two hundred years and more, there had been no metal for the People, except the rusty nails holding the laths inside the plaster dome: only these, and six cutlasses which had come with them from Lilliput, but which were now harpoons.

The final glory was in a paper bag. Maria opened it herself, the People standing back in wonder, and laid the contents out in rows. It was a shilling's worth of chocolate creams.

She had gone through a tussle with the Professor about these. He, with his giant's obsession about choosing small things for small people, had wanted to buy an old-fashioned sweet which was sometimes used on cakes, called Hundreds and Thousands. They were tiny pellets of hard sugar, colored pink or white or blue. Maria had insisted on full-sized chocolates. Which would you have preferred, then: a hard piece of sugar about the size of a toffee apple, or a chocolate cream the size of a pram?

There was no doubt about the kind which the people of Lilliput admired. Half the chocolates were quickly cut into slices with one of the razor blades, and in a minute everybody was nodding his head, smiling at his neighbor, rubbing his waistcoat, and taking another bite.

It was a pushover.

49

But suddenly there was a movement of dismay. All the eaters stopped eating the slice in their hands, all the ladies dropped tears on the silk handkerchiefs, everybody went off into a corner of the pavement and began to argue with the Schoolmaster. Maria watched them with a worried eye.

Presently the Schoolmaster came back.

"The People, Ma'am," he said awkwardly, "have call'd to Mind, that Transactions of this Complexion were carry'd out for Currency among the Nations of the civilized Globe. Four hundred Sprugs, Ma'am, Y'r Honor, Miss, were all the Treasure ever brought away from our unhappy Country, and these we have retain'd as old Mementoes of our former Greatness. . . ."

Maria knew about sprugs. She had been reading the famous *Travels* madly, ever since she had found the People, and she knew that these were the golden coins of ancient Lilliput—each about the size of a sequin or spangle.

"Goodness me," she said. "But this is a present. Nobody has to pay. I robbed my money box, and the Professor bought them, and when Miss Brown finds me out she will take my life. We bought them for you freely, with our love."

"A Present, Ma'am," said the Schoolmaster with unexpected pathos, shedding a tear like the smallest dewdrop on a spider's web into his right sleeve, "a Gift of such Magnificence, Ma'am," he shed three more, "is, after all these Moons, is, Ma'am, Y'r Honor, Madam, Miss, is . . ."

And the poor fellow dissolved completely. It was from having too many shocks in one day.

Maria, very sensibly, turned round and left them to recover.

CHAPTER

VII

MISS BROWN'S headaches sometimes lasted three days, one in getting them, one in treating them, and one in recovering from the treatment. Consequently our heroine was able to pay the island a third visit.

It was a different affair from the others.

She had scarcely tied at the larch, noticing that the brambles had been trained across her avenue, when the branches began to lift of their own accord. The passage had to be closed when she was away, for fear of other humans, but the People had secured a number of horsehair ropes to the trailers, and on these a picked gang of engineers was hauling lustily. In a minute, there was a clear road.

She bowed to the engineers and proceeded toward the temple, only to stop dead as she reached the green.

The People were drawn up on three sides of the pavement, perfectly silent. Some horsehair cables had been stretched from pillar to pillar, fluttering with little wisps of red and green and yellow bunting. In the center the Union Flag was flown, which she was able to recognize as the standard of England, although the red stripes were missing on the diagonals. The real Union Jack did not come in until long after Hogarth's time, although Maria did not know this fact. Under the old-fashioned flag, a band of music was arranged. It was a queer, eighteenth-century band, with flutes, violins, and drums. When they saw her, the fat bandmaster waved his arms excitedly, and the music struck up. They played "The British Grenadiers!"

She stood still, while the whole tune was played twice— the tiny horsehairs sawing away at the mouse-gut, the reeds, and they were really rushes, twinkling gaily under ivory fingers, and the acorn drums rolling across the square. Then, at the last note, with an inspiration from the memory of the female Lilliputian whom she had first captured, Maria dropped a curtsy, with all the skill at her command. She remembered to do it slowly, and, as this was the first one which she had ever wanted to make, she did a beauty.

When she lifted her head, there was a scene of wonder. All the little women had curtsied too, and were still down! All the little men had put forward their left feet, placing the other foot behind at right angles, and were bowing to her, or, rather, as they used to say in the old days, were "making a Leg."

Then, when they had recovered themselves with a gentle rustle, the bandmaster whirled his stick in several compli- cated parabolas, the drummers gave some terrible bangs, and the whole band countermarched to the tune of "A Right Little, Tight Little Island," revealing the Surprise which had been laid out behind.

It was a cask of wine with the top broached, about the size of a tumbler; a complete bullock roasted whole, or buc- caneered, and placed on three green laurel leaves; six loaves of grass-seed bread, each one as large as a walnut; and one of her own chocolates kept on purpose, though they would have dearly loved to eat the rarity themselves.

They had invited her to dinner.

She was so charmed that she did not know what to say. So she curtsied again, a smaller one, mounted the steps in a stately manner, and knelt down to her repast.

The wine was elderberry, better than the Professor's; the bullock had nearly as much meat on it as a young partridge; the loaves were newly baked and were delicious. While she was eating, the People stood round in tense silence, not missing a thing, but remembering carefully not to say Ooo, and not to make Personal Remarks about the size of teeth, etc.

She had scarcely finished, and was just wondering whether she ought to say grace or to stand up, when the Schoolmaster, who had been waiting officiously to see that everybody behaved, waved to her to keep kneeling. A party of ladies was trying to make its way from the back of the crowd with a heavy bundle, about the size of a ship's sail. It was a ship's sail, as we shall see. Maria remained where she was, and the bundle was laid before her knees. A dozen willing hands unrolled it.

It was a handkerchief.

The People had been as anxious to choose something coarse for her, as the Professor had been anxious to choose something small for them, so that this handkerchief was not so fine as an ordinary linen one would have been. It had more the texture of cheesecloth. But the charming thing about it was that a motto had been worked round the border, in cross-stitch, like a sampler, with the finest green and yellow wool.

The motto said:

A Humble PRESENT to Our FEMALE MOUNTAIN +
From the CITIZENS and BOROUGH of LILLIPUT
IN EXILE + With Hopes of Continued HEALTH
AND PROSPERITY + GOD Save The KING +

They must have been working all night to have finished it.

Maria found that she was afflicted with the Schoolmaster's weakness. She said: "Oh, what a lovely handkerchief!
Is it to blow my nose?" And, without further ado, for fear
that they would notice something like a tear, she put her
nose in the middle of it and blew.

It was a great success. Everybody clapped respectfully—
they had never heard such a blow—and a little boy who
began to howl was promptly smacked.

"The final Motto," explained the Schoolmaster, "has been
preserv'd in our Archives, since the Days of Captain John
Biddel. He taught our Ancestors to pronounce it, Ma'am,
to entertain your Countrymen, and this particular Circumstance caused us to feel the Hope that it might prove acceptable."

"How kind of you," said Maria, wiping her eye, "how
kind to think of something which would prove acceptable
to me.

"And, of course," she added, blowing her nose again,
"the King will be delighted too."

When this tender scene was at an end, the Schoolmaster
explained that he had been chosen to be her guide. He had
leave to show her anything she wanted to see, or to explain
anything she wanted to have explained, and he trusted that
their simple Oeconomy would prove to be of Interest, however Rude. Maria replied that she would endeavor to merit

54

their Confidence and Esteem—goodness, she thought, I have begun to talk in capitals too—and she repeated to the crowd that she would keep their secret. They looked hopeful but wistful when they heard this from her own mouth, not knowing Maria well enough, as yet, to be sure that her word was her bond. However, they were willing to make the best of it. To tell the truth, the thing which had impressed them most about her had been her curtsy. However small they were, they liked to be treated with respect, even by a Mountain, and the politeness of their new giant had created a favorable impression.

The first thing was to show her the national treasures. These were few and simple, and were housed in the highest room inside the cupola. (Maria's only regret about the wonders of the island was that she could never see the actual rooms in which the People lived. They had feared to build a town for themselves, because of the danger of discovery, and were compelled to exist in crowded conditions inside the shell of the temple. Her Schoolmaster told her later that she was missing little by not seeing the interior, for he said that it was like a tenement house, cold and dark and drafty, but it was the best that they could safely do. The three steps were hollowed out, so that they were like a squat, three-storied house, and there was a staircase leading up the inside of each pillar. There were 240 steps in each stair. Inside the dome itself, there were other rooms, and a flight of eighty steps led to the tiny platform on the summit, where the sentry stood. All these rooms and staircases were only lit by small air holes through the joints of the stone, or through the plaster of the dome, and the whole of the lowest step was kept for cowsheds, granaries, storehouses, and the communal kitchen. They used charcoal for cooking, and to warm the rooms in small pans, so that there would be no smoke to give them away. The charcoal was got by burning laurel bushes on the mainland, in a part of the grounds which was known to Maria as the Wilderness. The only decent room they had was the highest one of all, directly under the sentry post. It was circular, and was used for the Parliament room, or for dances, though the floor was slightly curved, and it was in this that the national treasures were preserved.)

Six porters carried them down, one by one, and displayed them in front of Maria, like the assistants at an auction. The greatest was the ancient portrait of the Emperor of Blefuscu, full length, which is mentioned in *Gulliver's Travels*. There was also a chest containing the two hundred sprugs of gold. Maria would have loved to own just one of these, but she did not like to ask—so that she was charmed when they did give her one of their own accord, on her next visit. To complete the humble list, there was a collection of the original clothes worn by the captives of Captain John Biddel, when he had been exhibiting them round England. They were threadbare, but not moth-eaten, any more than your clothes would ever get owl-eaten, and they consisted of a few skirted coats of blue silk, white pantaloons, white stockings, buckled shoes, three-cornered hats, and ladies' dresses. Most of the musical instruments used by the band were also national treasures. They had been made to Captain Biddel's instructions, and his prisoners had been forced to play upon them, to amuse the crowds.

When these articles had been shown, the Schoolmaster told Maria the history of the People, since the days of Gulliver. The bystanders listened politely, being pleased to hear their own story, however often it had been told.

56

"A Student of your Talents, Ma'am," said the School-master, "and One who has become acquainted with the earlier Annals of our Race, besides mastering the Elements of our mother Tongue, will be aware that the Empire of Lilliput was visited by a Man Mountain nearabout three thousand Moons ago. The Occurrence took Place during a Period of Hostilities between that Empire and the neighboring Realm of Blefuscu, from which two Nations our People here is indiscriminately sprung.

"Little may the Man Mountain have suspected, Ma'am, throughout the Course of his subsequent Travels, and indeed to his dying Day, what Calamities were brought upon our Ancestors by his Visit! For no sooner had he quitted the sister Island in his majestick Vessel, which, you will call to Mind, had fortunately been discover'd by him in a derelict Condition, floating with its Bottom up, than the Emperor of Lilliput was pleas'd to declare a War against his Cousin of Blefuscu, alleging the hostile Conduct of Blefuscu in allowing the Man Mountain to escape from those Realms, contrary to an Embassage particularly sent from Lilliput to restrain him, of which Island the said Mountain was a Subject, a Nardac, and a discover'd Traytor.

"The Campaign, Ma'am, which follow'd the Declaration, was exasperated by the old Bitterness of the Big-Endian Heresy—a Topick of Dissension, which I am happy to say we have since resolved by a Determination to break such Eggs as we are able to find in the Middle—and, no Quarter being ask'd or given by either Schism, the War was signalized by Atrocities and Inhumanities hitherto unexampled in the Legends of our People.

"Corn Fields were burn'd, Cattle were driven away or slaughter'd, the Cities were subjected to a Number of Sieges which reduced the Inhabitants to Starvation, and the Emperors of both Realms died by each other's Hands, in single Combat outside the Walls of Mendendo. The Anarchy which subsequently prevail'd among the Leaders of the rival Factions, each of whom sought to draw the Power of Direction into his own Controul, reduced the Hopes of Reconciliation still further; and it was therefore upon a Civilization already tottering from its Foundations, Ma'am, that Captain John Biddel descended, after a Lapse of seventeen Moons, all of which had been devoted to Rapine and Destruction.

"For such was the secondary Effect of our Visit from the Man Mountain, whose Name, it was later discover'd, had been Culliver or Gulliban. He, Ma'am, Y'r Honour, Miss, unlike Y'r Honour, had made no Efforts to conceal our Whereabouts from the greater World. He had committed the Indiscretion of confiding the Whole of our Oeconomy to the Mariners who convey'd him Home. He had presented a Pair of our Cattle to the Captain of the Ship, the said Captain Biddel; and the Latter, premising the extreme Value of their Fleeces owing to the Fineness of the Wool, had return'd to Lilliput for his next Cargo, without finding any Difficulty in raising the Island, by running down the Latitude.

"Captain Biddel, Ma'am, according to our Annals, was a Seaman of his Æra and Country, neither better nor worse than others of his Rank. To him, Ma'am, and, I must beg Leave to add with honest Gratitude that we have found no Occasion as yet to notice such a Disposition in Yourself, to him our broken and distrackted People were Creatures not possessed of human Rights, nor shelter'd by the Laws of Nations. Our Cattle were for his Profit, because we could not defend them; our very Persons were an Object of

Cupidity, for he had determined to show us in his native Land, as Puppet Shews and Mimes.

"Ma'am, Y'r Honour, Miss, we fled, such as could still flee, from the Pyratts of his monstrous Vessel. We conceal'd ourselves in Rocks and Woods, breaking off the internecine, fratricidal Strife too late. Our few remaining Herds stampeded, some finding their own Destruction in the Sea, others falling into the Hands of these unprincipled Mariners, who joyfully collected them into Enclosures or *Corrales*, made from the grog-barrels of their ship. The capital City of Mendendo was ransack'd for the last Time, in Search of Slaves, but, such had been the Desperation of the People, even before the Arrival of Biddel, that only thirteen Refugees were found surviving, and these promptly empanell'd into the Possession of their future Master. Lilliput, Madam, and Blefuscu, ceased at that ill-fated Epocha from their Existence among the Nations of Antiquity."

There was a sigh from the listeners when the Schoolmaster had got to this, and he himself looked inquiringly at Maria, as if he were ready to hear some apology. After all, Captain Biddel had been a mountain like her.

"Was nobody left?" she asked.

"That, Ma'am, is a Question, which has agitated the Speculations of Lilliput in Exile. Naturally, however, we have no Means by which to reach a Determination. Our Philosophers have hoped, Y'r Honour, perhaps deceived by the delusive Dreams of Hearts which could not wish to be entirely cut off from the remember'd Home of their admired Progenitors, that some small Remnant of our Consanguinity survived, and that perchance, on the old Latitude, there still exists a Lilliput Redivivus, rebuilt, by them, in Splendour suited to the Genius of our Kind."

"When I am rich," she said, "we will buy a yacht, and go

to find them. The Professor is making a translation of the *Hexameron* of Ambrose, which will make his fortune when it is published, and then we will all go together."

The People sighed and looked away—they knew nothing about the commercial demand for St. Ambrose—and the Schoolmaster continued his story. ("Fetch the Lock for the Receptacle," he said to the porters. "We shall have Occasion for it shortly." Later, when he was talking about the captivity, it was displayed before her—a cheap, pewter lock with an expression which said: Well, you won't undo me.)

"The Captives of Mendendo," said he, "included Flimnap the Treasurer and two Gentlemen of the Rank of Snilpall, beside seven Women and three men. These Persons, the Ancestors of all here present, together with the Flocks and Herds collected by the Pyratts, were taken to the Vessel. Captain Biddel weigh'd Anchor with a favorable Wind; and proceeded for the distant Shores of his own Land, well satisfy'd with future Hopes of Advancement and Prosperity.

"How miserable, Madam, was the Condition of our Countrymen, cut off from all Recourse to the Cradle of their Fathers, disillusion'd by the long Series of Disasters which had attended the War of Eggs, surrounded by Beings out of all Proportion incompatible with themselves, and convey'd, in an insanitary Box, to the Servitude of a foreign Clime!

"For Captain Biddel had caused the Ship's Carpenter to construct a single Receptacle, whose Lock you see, for Man and Beast, in which all together were assembled promiscuously; and there they were kept on a Diet of Ship's Biscuit crumbled in Water, which had previously been found to answer with the Cattle carried off by Surgeon Gulliban in former Moons.

"Madam and Y'r Honor, I need not distress your tender Susceptibilities, by describing the Hardships of the Voyage, during which the greater Number of the Cattle were lost of a Murrain, nor even by dwelling upon the Indignities to which our Forbears were subjected, after they had landed on the alien Shore.

"Captain Biddel made Sale of his Command, anticipating a larger Prosperity from the Exhibition of his Captives among the Fair Grounds of the Kingdom; and, in this Manner, for more than fifteen Moons, the High Treasurer of Lilliput, the two Snilpally, and the eight surviving Commoners, two of whom had died on Passage, were shewn about the Wakes and Ales of Neptune's Isle.

"Musical Instruments, Ma'am, which you have heard already, were constructed to the Directions of their Master. The English Language, to them excessively difficult owing to the Inequalities of Pronunciation, was ruthlessly impress'd upon them by the insatiable Avarice of their Proprietor. The ancient Skills of Lilliput, such as Leaping and Creeping, or Dancing upon the Strait Rope, were exploited for the Entertainment of the Vulgar. And all the Performance, for which the miserable Captives were rewarded with no other Guerdon than the Lash, their Tyrant being by then accustom'd to punish Misdemeanors by a Flogging with a Sprig of Heather, was attended by no other Prospect of Amelioration, than the Amelioration of the Grave. Madam, it was under these Conditions that the Exhibits were taught to cry: God save the King! It was under these Conditions, Madam, that the Banner of St. George was flown—a Climax, as we learn, to the Spectacle promoted by the Mariner Biddel.

"These Facts, Y'r Honor," continued the Schoolmaster

61

kindly, "are mention'd not from any Thought of Bitterness toward yourself, but merely as a Measure of our own Respect; for we were willing to return your Kindness with any Exhibition calculated to divert the Species."

Maria bowed.

"Captain Biddel," he went on, "was satisfy'd in his Expectation of Profit. Numerous Crouds were collected on every Fair Ground by the Reputation of his Shew; and the Exertions of the People, constantly urged forward to greater displays of their gymnastick Abilities, soon added a handsome Fortune to their Master's Pocket. Captain Biddel, Ma'am, insufficiently educated to the Temptations of a comfortable Station, and passing his Time, as he was forced to do, among the Gin Shops of the country Fairs, now grew addicted to the Bottle. Perswaded as he was that our People fear'd his Race too much to seek Escape among them—and indeed, beside the Annoyance of their Breath, our Ancestors were much terrify'd by the vast Faces which crouded about on every Occasion, by the Stink of their Persons and by the bucolick Covetousness which they exhibited—Captain Biddel had grown remiss in locking the Receptacle at Night, particularly on those Nights, now becoming imperceptibly more frequent, during which he had amus'd himself with Licquor.

"The People, Ma'am, suffer'd, however, in an even greater Measure from their Master's Tyranny, the more his Constitution was exasperated by the Effects of this Debauchery. The aged Flimnap, forced to perform his dangerous Acrobaticks on the Rope, dreaded an Accident with more Reason every Day. The others, long dejeckted by the Toils of their Performance and by the Menace of the Heather Whip, were accustom'd to consider, more and

62

more anxiously, whether Death itself, if attended by the least Chance of Liberation, might not be preferable to the Miseries of their Condition.

"It was at this Stage in our History that the Captain was summon'd to the Palace of Malplaquet, in order to demonstrate his Puppets before the Household of the reigning Duke.

"Captain Biddel, Ma'am, dined at Northampton on the Night before the Exhibition, with more than customary Indulgence. Proposing to himself a handsome Remuneration from so great a Patron, attended probably by a valued Recommendation to the World of Fashion, he celebrated his Fortune in several Bowls of Grog. Then, calling for his Horse and for a final Bottle as a *Vade Mecum*, he set out for Malplaquet, where he was to sleep that Night.

"A Bridge, Ma'am, spans the Torrent, four hundred Blustrugs to our West, below the Other Sea."

"H'm," said Maria. "That would be the Oriental Bridge, I suppose. It is the one on the Northampton Avenue, at any rate."

"It was at this colossal Structure, Madam, or so our Histories relate, that Captain Biddel fell Victim to Intoxication, and dismounted from his Nag to seek the Safety of the *Terra Firma*, on which he instantly composed himself to Slumber.

"The People, in their horrid Receptacle, which was strapp'd, as usual, to the Horse's Crupper, and whose Lock he had omitted to turn, came out upon the Saddle to survey the Night, the Horse meanwhile being content to graze at Ease beside its Owner. It was a moonlit Eve. The Torrent could be plainly seen, issuing from the Other Sea, and all about the Land appear'd deserted. The Resolution to escape was taken on the Spot, all solemnly asseverating their desperate Intention to perish by their own Hands, rather than submit to Capture.

"Cables were rapidly made fast, the Strait Ropes of their Exhibition proving suitable. The Sheep and Cattle, slung from these, were quickly lower'd to the Ground. And the Receptacle itself, being unstrapp'd with Difficulty, was also taken down. It was the Plan of Flimnap to transport his little World by Sea, until some Refuge on the further Shores could be discover'd.

"I will not, Madam, tire you further with the Tale of our Migration. Towing the Receptacle against the Stream, the Torrent was surmounted. The quiet Waters of the Other Sea permitted the driven Cattle to be embark'd within it, and all together made their Way by Navigation to the eastern Bank; where, as the Morning dawn'd, the Expedition was conceal'd beneath the overhanging Branches of a prodigious Tree. Some slight Attempts at Search were noticed during the Hours of Daylight from this Refuge, but without Commotion. It was conjectured that the bemus'd Biddel, having been addled since his Setting Out, might not retain the slightest Recollection of his Actions, and might retrace his Steps at least toward the Tavern where he dined, still seeking the Receptacle along his Way. Next Evening, shelter'd by the Darkness, our Ark, as we may call it, having been hoisted with incredible Pains along the Cascade to the Upper Sea, a Scout, who had been sent ahead in Order to survey the Country, return'd with Informations about the secret Island where we have ever since continued, and on which, Y'r Honour, Madam, Miss, you stand today."

CHAPTER

VIII

MARIA could not help feeling relieved when the History was over. Her head was buzzing with capital letters, and she secretly thought that it was more fun to ask questions, instead of listening to lectures. She was also doubtful about being called "Ma'am, Y'r Honour, Miss," knowing that her proper name was Maria, and she was determined to keep the proceedings on a less formal level. The best thing would be to get away with the Schoolmaster, so that they could talk to each other sensibly, instead of being a public meeting.

On the other hand, she saw at once that there would be a difficulty about exploring with her guide, since even the most versatile human would find it complicated to go for a walk with a person who did not reach much further than her ankle. For one thing, there was the problem of taking steps. One step of hers would have covered about twelve steps of his, so he would have been forced to run very fast, to keep up. But she did not like to suggest the idea of carrying him. There was something babyish about being carried, and she did not want to humiliate him; for she had a certain amount of good taste, in spite of being only ten. She was also afraid of holding him, for fear of squeezing too much, and she guessed that he would be afraid of being dropped.

Maria had finished her elderberry wine while listening to the History. She now suggested that, if he were going to show her round, he might prefer to stand in the barrel, as seamen do in the crow's-nest of a man-of-war, while she carried it in her hand. He was delighted with the scheme, which saved him from being mauled by the big fingers, and which left him his dignity. While she washed the barrel in the lake, and dried it with the remains of her handkerchief —not the new one—he dispersed the crowds in a short address, advising them not to stare, and not to get trodden on.

With the Schoolmaster in the barrel, there was a good deal more to see as they went round the green, and of course there were a number of questions to be asked.

One of the things which she had not discovered before was the underground rat stable, hidden by a part of the shrubbery.

No horses had been brought from Lilliput. Gulliver had not troubled to do so, and Captain Biddel had not been able to obtain any, because the final wars had almost destroyed the breed, in cavalry battles. The people of Lilliput in Exile had therefore been forced to turn to the rats of their adopted country, which were used for farm work at harvest times and for carrying urgent messages on the mainland. They were swift, but not stayers, when ridden; for farm work they were strong and intelligent. The Schoolmaster said that they were not vicious when taken young or bred in captivity, that they were cleverer than the other domestic animals, and that they were not dirty when properly groomed. They were fed on the scraps of the community. Several were brought for her inspection, and promenaded in a circle on the lead rein. They were always ridden on short leathers, as jockeys do for flat races nowadays, because of the shortness of their legs.

She wanted to know about the food of the People: about the way they lived, their enemies and dangers, and about all the other things which her guide insisted on calling Oeconomy.

One thing which interested her was that they ate a good many insects, and that they kept the green fly, as the ants do, for syrup. The difference was that the ants thought of these creatures as cows, while the Lilliputians thought of them as bees. She did not like the idea of eating insects, at first, but when she remembered that the Professor had told her how a lobster was practically an insect, she began to see that there was not much difference. The Schoolmaster told her that his people used to boil wood lice just as we boil lobsters, and that they turned red when boiled, and gave people bad dreams.

As for keeping the toy cattle and getting food for five hundred people on the green, she learned that the colony owned a proper frigate as well as the canoes—he was taking her to see it—and that, in this, they carried cows to pasture on the mainland every night. Indeed, the whole life of Lilliput was really a night life—he explained that talking to her in the daytime was like staying up late for them—and they gathered their harvests of Yorkshire Fog or Rye Grass or Cock's Foot, for flour, by cutting them in the Jubilee Field, under a harvest moon, and bringing them back in the frigate. They also fished at night. In the winter the frigate was used as a whaler, to catch pike, because the winter was the main season for living on fish. This also was done at night.

The Lilliputians had trappers. These brave men would go off on long treks into the Park, sometimes being away for a moon, and would come back with stores of furs or salted meats. They trapped voles, shrews, mice, and even live rats, but were in constant danger from cats and weasels. Every year, one or two of the bravest hunters failed to return. Many of them had been able to snare rabbits; but then they needed to be in bands, to carry back the meat.

One of the foods which they valued most was the leg of a frog, which was eaten, like turkey, for Christmas.

The grass snakes, which are perfectly harmless and beautiful to us, were dangerous to the Lilliputians, because, like boa constrictors, they were inclined to eat any animal the size of a frog, on the rare occasions when they were hungry. On the other hand, they were good to eat themselves.

In the winter, when times were hard, the trappers sometimes caught wild ducks on the lake, by leaving baited hooks firmly secured, and of these they often had mallards, tufted duck, pochard, and teal. The coots and dabchicks gave bad meat. Even in the winter, the difficulty of the season was relieved by the greater length of the nights, which left more time for hunting.

Maria's Schoolmaster told her that an interesting experiment had been tried in the lifetime of his father. It had been nothing less than to use the birds of our world as airplanes. A young jackdaw had been found, too young to fly, and had been kept alive with difficulty, on insects and sliced worms. It had grown up tame, though snappish, but had at first refused to fly at all. They had been forced to starve it, and finally to drag it to the top of the cupola, with its wings brailed, and then the man who usually fed it on a lure, as falconers do, had waved the lure energetically from the ground. Finally somebody had pushed it off, and it had flown to be fed. When it had grown accustomed to flight, and had got some power in its wings, a strap had been fitted round the base of each wing, and under and over the breast, and the daring aeronaut had sat on its back for some time every day, gripping the strap, which had loops, like stirrups, for the feet. Of course, it had been kept tethered all the time, except for meals. The aeronaut had been forced to pad himself, as people do who are teaching Alsatians to be police dogs, because it was inclined to peck at him, over its shoulder. In the end, he had flown on it several times, from the top of the cupola, but the experiment had collapsed on the question of navigation. They had found that it was possible to make the bird fly in circles, or to left or right, by means of a bridle in its mouth, if used with a light hand. But they had never discovered a way to make it start flying, or stop flying, when wanted. So all flights on it had been in the nature of balloon ascents, which might come down anywhere, and the enterprise had been dropped.

In spite of Maria's efforts to keep him talking about the jackdaw bomber, which was an idea that interested her, the Schoolmaster seemed to be ashamed of it, perhaps because it had been a failure, and was more anxious to lecture about his politics.

There were few laws, he said, but a good deal of public opinion, and there was no death penalty. There were no wars, owing to the fortunate circumstance that there was nobody to have a war against. Writers and bards and musicians were rightly regarded as mechanics, like carpenters, and were valued, like carpenters, for the soundness of their work. There was no revealed religion, because it had been destroyed by the War of Eggs. The mothers were considered to be the heads of their families. They believed that the most important thing in the world was to find out what one liked doing, and then to do it. Thus the people who liked being hunters, were hunters; those who liked fishing, fished; and anybody who did not like doing anything at all was supported by the others with the greatest care and commiseration, for they considered him to be the most unfortunate of mortals.

They had three meals a night. They went to bed at dawn and rose at sunset. Their children were never taught a word about Algebra, but were, on the contrary, educated in the various sciences of life: that is to say, in Natural History and in their own History and in Oeconomy and in anything else which dealt with being alive. They were never told that their elders were better than themselves.

70

Maria could not help feeling that these things sounded wonderful, but she wanted most of all to see the frigate.

The usual way to reach it was along one of the secret paths through the undergrowth of brambles. Unfortunately, it was a path which she could not follow. So they went down to the punt and sculled round the island, to reach it from outside.

It was beautifully hidden.

The channel leading to its harbor was covered with the leaves of water lilies, just like the other lilies round the island, but these leaves were without stems. They were merely flat plates floating on the water, and were renewed once a week. When the frigate was to sail, they were dragged aside.

At the end of the channel there was a bluff of land which masked the dog-legged entrance to the harbor, and the bushes grew above. She had been round the island many a time without discovering it. It was only after following the channel, under her Schoolmaster's directions, that she raised the harbor mouth.

There lay the frigate in her quiet pool. She had gun ports but no guns, no foundry nor gunpowder being available on the island; her cordage was of plaited horsehair stolen from the horses in the Jubilee Field; her canvas was the same as the presentation handkerchief; her Admiral was the tall young husband who had tried to chase her when she first secured his wife and baby; and all the sailors, as a compliment, had gone down by the other path, to man the shrouds.

CHAPTER

IX

I
T was a week after seeing the frigate for the first time that Maria was invited to witness a grand whale hunt, at night. It was not only safer to go by night, when Miss Brown was in bed, but also it was more natural to see the Lilliputians at this season, because they slept by day.

Maria waited in her bedroom, in a fever of impatience to be gone, but she knew that her governess and the Vicar were sitting in Neptune's Temple, over an after-dinner cup of coffee. She could see their motionless figures in the moonlight through her window, two small dots squatting under the silver columns, for the Temple had been built to finish one of the Vistas from the palace itself. What made it worse was that the whales of Lilliput were pike, and these fish would only take the bait at mysterious periods, which they chose for themselves. One of these periods had been reported to be passing that evening, for the People had noticed the small roach skipping from the water to save their lives, which was an infallible sign that pike were feeding. They had promised to catch a big one for her, if they could, for there was a famous monster of twenty pounds, which had been seen in the deepest hole. She walked up and down the linoleum of her bedroom, afraid to lie down for fear that she might go to sleep, and wished her pastor and mistress at the bottom of the lake.

The Vicar was a constant visitor at Malplaquet, generally for tea. In the afternoon she would meet him in the grounds, humming his way from the Vicarage, his body stiff, his hands behind his back, moving at a slow and steady pace with his lips pursed up in disapproval. It was a mystery to discover why he came, for he seldom spoke to Miss Brown when he was there, and did not enjoy what he ate.

At tea they would sit on either side of the fireplace in the North-northwest Drawing Room, with one of those pagoda-like cake stands between them, and a low table with the silver tea things. Sometimes they said nothing. At most they said eight sentences: "This bread is cut too thick," "I will speak to Cook," "More tea?", "Thanks," "Cake?", "Thank *you*," "The child was late for luncheon again today," "Inconsiderate." Miss Brown used to eat three cream buns greedily, with a fork, but the Vicar used to choose the nastiest cake on the pagoda, apparently to spite himself. After tea, he would walk mysteriously for hours through the palace rooms.

So there they were on the steps of Neptune's Temple, in the lovely moonlight, while the precious time was slipping away. It was the famous Temple in which Dr. Johnson had written the fourth stanza of his immortal *Pomphoilugop-paphlasmagoria*, the one which begins "Ponder the aweful Hippopotamos"—but little they cared for this. It was June and the nightingales of Malplaquet were in full voice. They did not hear them. Six fluted columns rose on either side, bearing the pediment on which Neptune, in high relief, was awarding a wreath of seaweed to Viscount Torrington, after the battle of Cape Passaro, amid the applause of several dolphins. They had never looked at it. Before them, on the silver sward of the Arcadian Valley, the thousand wild rabbits of Malplaquet were nibbling and hopping forward

73

and nibbling again, while the owls hunted food for their babies, gliding with soundless feather. The Vicar and Miss Brown stared out with oyster or pebble eye, to where the towering pillar of the Newton Monument closed the sweet curve of the valley with its slender finger, glittering like salt under the moon; but they did not see this either.

They were thinking about Maria, just as she was thinking about them, and they had reason to do so. There was something which they did not want her to find out, but which they wanted to find, or rather to alter, for themselves. They did not like the idea of her talks with the Professor—who was an authority on ancient laws and enjoyed nothing better than a good bout of *nolle prosequi*—because their mystery was connected with a missing parchment, concerning the inheritance of Malplaquet. The Vicar was humming softly.

"It is a question of *mort d'ancestre*," he said at last.

"No child could understand it."

"She will come of age."

"Not for many years."

"But by talking to the old man, Miss Brown?"

"I shall forbid it."

"M-m-m-m-m."

"More coffee?"

A long time afterward the Vicar said: "You should watch her." Then he stood up heavily, and paced off sullenly to bed.

Maria crept down the moonlit corridor, as soon as her governess was safely asleep. Down the various staircases she went, creaking on the bare boards of the less important ones, patting on the bare marble of the company ones, passing from one bar of moonlight to another. On the

ground floor she took a short cut through the Grand Ballroom, where her feet shuffled in the fallen plaster from the
Adam ceiling, and the three-ton chandeliers, too big to sell,
gave out a mysterious note of crystal; through the Third
Duke's Library, which had a monstrous plaster Garter on
the ceiling, in gold relief, in celebration of the Order of the
Garter which that duke had at last obtained after twenty
years of chicanery—and which he had subsequently worn
round his neck, even while bathing at Brighton; through the
Main Dining Room she went, which had once housed a
mahogany table exactly as long as a cricket pitch; through
the Little Drawing Room, where the two Grinling Gibbons
mantelpieces had been wrenched from the walls to sell,
leaving caverns which looked frightening at night; and

75

through the Absolutely Insignificant Morning Room, which was a room with only one fireplace, and that was plain marble. Maria passed from dark to light, from light to dark, down the rows of shuttered windows, until she began to look like a cinema film, flickering badly. She went too slowly for the Persistence of Vision. At last she came to the great double doors which led to the South Front, hauled them open enough to let herself through, and appeared in full moonshine between two colossal stone caryatids, with an antique frieze, stolen by the Fourth Duke from Herculaneum, thirty feet above her head, and the forty-five marble steps which led to the Terrace stretched below her feet.

She had been thinking.

Whatever the Professor says, she thought, I don't see why I should not give presents to the People, since they give presents to me.

She had found out that the silk handkerchiefs had been distributed by tickets in a lottery, since there had only been enough material to make dresses for about twenty women. The rest had been forced to go without.

If I were rich, she thought, and could afford to live in some respectable little cottage with a bit of money in hand, how I would like to dress them all! I would give the men old-fashioned dresses like the ones their ancestors had: blue coats and canary waistcoats and white breeches and silk stockings and tiny swords! And the women should have flowered gowns of the same century, and I would get coaches made for them which the rats could draw, or even sedan chairs, and all would look as bright and beautiful as a bed of flowers....

Alas, Maria only had three shillings and ninepence half-

76

penny left. It would not even buy enough handkerchiefs to dress the other women.

One thing, she thought, cheering up, is that I can scrounge things for them from Cook. An old saucepan with the handle broken off might be of value to them, as a boiler for the farm animals. I must think of all the broken things which are of no more use to humans, but which might be treasures to the People: things like used toothbrushes, for brooms, or jam jars for barrels, or even an ounce or two of salt and pepper, which would go far and scarcely be missed. But the three and ninepence halfpenny must be kept, for a special present, and what is that to be?

Presents can be of two kinds, she decided, flickering once more as she trotted down the chestnut avenue: Either they can be useful, or else ornamental. How I wish I had some real money, say a pound!

She was still considering as she sculled the punt toward the Repose, and had only got so far as this: A useful present would be to buy them a pair of guinea-pigs to breed draught horses, or even for meat, while an ornamental present would be to purchase Christmas cards—so long as they were not sloppy, but showed pictures of sailing ships, or of eighteenth-century coaches in the snow, or of anything else which the People could recognize from their Annals—and to frame these in passe partout, so that they could be hung round the walls of the council room. In the middle, they would hang the ancient portrait of the Emperor, with his *Austrian* lip and costume partly *Asiatick*, party *European*. They might look grand by rushlight, hoped Maria.

And then she thought again: Or I could teach them to grow potatoes, like Sir Walter Raleigh. You could probably get plenty of potatoes for three and nine.

77

The People were relieved when she arrived, for they had almost given her up.

The frigate was on the lake—how beautiful she looked, too, with her white sails spread in the silver light—and the sailors were at their stations, and they were only waiting for their guest to let the expedition begin.

The sad thing was that she could not go in the ship. It was hardly five feet long. However, they advised her to stand in the punt at the end of the larch, to watch from there, and the Schoolmaster offered to be carried in the barrel, so that he could explain the maneuvers.

The Quincunx was so overgrown that it was only in the deepest parts, near the middle, that it was free from weeds—for most water weeds, except duckweed, need roots in the bottom, and these cannot grow below a certain depth. It was in the largest of these holes that the big pike lived, and it was consequently to these latitudes that the frigate sailed. When she had got there, a live bait with the appropriate hooks was thrown over from the bows, and the frigate herself sailed to the nearest lilies, where she anchored in deep water. The live bait was on an eight-ply cable of horsehair, which came in through a hawser in the bows and went over a drum which could be braked.

She had scarcely anchored, and the poor live bait was still wriggling in a baitly way, when there was a snap and swirl in the water. The drum was allowed to run out while Maria's Schoolmaster excitedly counted ten; then the brake was thrown into gear and the drum crew rapidly began to wind against it, to drive the hooks home. After a dozen of these turns, they put her out of gear and used the brake.

The whole frigate went ahead two or three feet from her moorings—the Schoolmaster said that it was thirty-five

glumgluffs—and began yawing one way or the other as the monster tugged. It was given a freedom on the brake when it struggled too hard, but at any sign of weakening the brake was increased, while, if it lay motionless for a moment, the crew began to wind.

The Admiral directed from the poop.

It was a ticklish business in many ways, for the pike was really being played, not from the frigate, but from her anchor. There were two holds which needed attention, instead of one.

After the first minute, the Schoolmaster said sadly that it was not the big pike. He had been able to tell from the splashing, to some extent, for the big one would have been more sullen, and also from the working of the ship. He added that he thought she would prove to be of about four hundred snorrs, or nine pounds, at which weight they were usually fierce.

The real danger was that the pike's teeth might cut the cable. They needed a metal cable at the end, like a fisherman's trace, but there was no suitable wire to be found in the Park. The barbed wire used by the farmer who rented the land was much too thick.

When the monster had been played for about two minutes, it began to give in. It was towed slowly to the ship's side, made one more dart to get away when it saw its captors, was brought in again, and this time actually rolled right over in the water before it lay on its side, looking vanquished. It was far from being so. Pikes have great vitality, with which they live for hours even after they are on the bank, and the real difficulties of whaling were only beginning.

As soon as the gleaming body was stretched beside the

79

frigate, five picked harpooners set to work. The harpoons were driven deep into its back at intervals of six inches or so, and, by means of the ropes attached to these, it was drawn firmly to the ship's side. Then the Admiral came down from the poop—he always took the last hazard himself—and went over the side on a rope ladder with the sixth harpoon. His business was to drive it through the backbone, near the head.

Now the pike had grown furious as each harpoon drove home, threshing with a great clap on the water at each thrust. If the Admiral could find a joint in the backbone at the first blow, its spinal column would be cut and the danger would be over. If not, there was a good chance of his being thrown into the water by the commotion, where he would run the risk of being snapped up by the pike itself, for these ferocious creatures would grab at food even as they were dying, and would sometimes seize the bait again, if they had escaped from it.

He chose his place and thrust. The huge body, more than half the length of the ship, bent like a bow, opening its wide jaws, with row on row of skinny teeth. Then it lay slack.

Three of the harpoon cables were drawn up on either side of the vessel, and the sinking body was secured by these, under her bottom, before she sailed for home. The passage of water through its gills made the fish lively as she sailed, but the severed spine prevented it from making a flurry. All it could do was to clash its jaws, which, as the Schoolmaster told Maria, was often felt through the ship's fabric.

In the meantime, the cables were sent ashore. A team of rats, and twenty men on each cable, dragged the still gnashing body through the shallow water to the bank, where the flensing could begin. The Admiral drove his rapier, tempered from one of the cupola nails, into its brain.

Maria paddled round, to see the capture brought in. She wanted to help with the victory, and was so excited that she nearly trod on the haulers, as the rats strained wisely at the seven ropes, under whips which cracked with a noise she could have made between her finger nails. She cried: "Here, give it to me! Let me pull! I can get him out!" She snatched several of the cables to tug, and each one broke in her hand. She was too big for them. The many small fists could control the horsehair, which only snapped in hers. The dead fish sank heavily beneath the water-lilies, and was lost. The precious harpoons would have to be dived for. She stopped when she saw what she had done, and the People tried to be polite.

CHAPTER

X

MARIA'S misfortunes with the Island of Repose dated from the night on which she had interfered with the whale hunt. Although she was decent, as was shown by her offer to carry the Schoolmaster in the barrel, she was still young. The more she adored and wondered at the doings of her six-inch People, the more she wanted to take control of them. She wanted to play with them, like lead soldiers, and even dreamed of being their queen. She began to forget what the Professor had said, about not being an owner.

But the Lilliputians were not toys. They were grown up, however short they were, and they were civilized. Lilliput and Blefuscu had been countries of high civilization; and so had England been in the eighteenth century, when they had been brought to it by Captain Biddel. They had painters, who did wonderful formal pictures of old-fashioned shepherds and shepherdesses in pannier skirts and ribbons, painted on stretched puff-ball skins. They had poets who still wrote the original meters of their native land. These latter had found the heroic couplet too cumbrous for them in English, so they wrote the smaller verses of the other language: a highly polished form of poetry. The first words of the line rhymed as well as the last ones, and, as there were seldom more than two words in a line, or four lines in a poem, it was not easy to write. This was one of their love poems:

> Mo Rog
> Glonog,
> Quinba,
> Hlin varr.

It meant: "Give me a kiss, please, Miss. I like your nose." Other writers produced Tragedies of five scenes, which observed the Unities, and these were acted by the opera company in the top room of the monopteron—where there was a miniature harpsichord in the orchestra, sounding like the ghost of a ghost, which had been made to the order of Captain Biddel. Still others were famous for their Essays, which were seldom more than two lines long, and generally on a moral subject. "Nothing fails like Success" was one of the Essays; another was "Narclabb meeting an Ass with a fortunate Name, prophesy'd Success. I meet many Asses, but none have fortunate Names."

In short, although, as we shall see later, the People lived hardy and dangerous lives, they were cultured, and could not possibly be treated like lead soldiers. For that matter, they had hidden on the island to escape this very fate.

However, Maria lost grip of herself, and she now proceeded on the road to ruin with the speed of a Rake's Progress.

The first mad thing she did was to make a favorite. This was a beautiful but silly young fisherman, who was too stupid to mind being carried about all day, to the detriment of his fishing. He felt distinguished when chosen to be the man in the barrel, and did not dislike being used as a toy, because he was a vain fellow in any case. (The School-master, on the other hand, had gone on strike soon after the incident of the pike flensing.) Maria devoted herself to the new favorite, began carrying him in her hands instead of the barrel, and even carried him in her pocket. She took him with her everywhere. Once she took him to sleep in the small drawer of her dressing table, which was dangerous so far as Miss Brown was concerned, and bad for his character also, because it made the other Lilliputians look down on him. She would sit for hours in the pasture field on the other side of the Quincunx, inventing exciting stories and making him act them for her. Occasionally she kidnaped one or two others, to act with him, which annoyed them, although it flattered him. She began to grab and snatch like a rough baby greedy for toys, which generally get broken in the process, saying, "No, no. Do this. Do that. You be the conquered enemy and I will be General Eisenhower. Give it to me. I will be the Queen and you can be my subjects."

There were no more welcomes when she visited the island. The People began to have a worried look, and to hide when she came.

The next craze which she got into her head was for toy airplanes. She had been so delighted by the story of the jackdaw bomber, in spite of the Schoolmaster's diffidence about it, that she borrowed twopence from Cook and per-suaded the Professor to buy a model for her in Northamp-ton, with a propellor worked by elastic. It was a cheap and nasty one, having cost only 3/11½, but it looked as if it would carry the fisherman. She just had sense enough to realize that it would need ailerons, tail plane, and rudder, but there was an old copy of the *Illustrated London News* in Miss Brown's drawing room, which had a diagram of

84

these controls. She helped herself to this, and called a meeting of the reluctant Lilliputians, to plan the conquest of the air. She flew the model for them several times, with the usual stall and crash landing on its propellor, and explained how they would have to make the ailerons according to the diagram, as the work was too fine for her fingers.

The Schoolmaster refused to help. He pointed out that an elastic which lost its power after forty seconds was useless for practical purposes, as it would scarcely take the machine across the lake; that there would have to be a gang waiting after each short hop to wind it up again; that the fisherman did not know how to use the controls in the picture; and finally that it was a conspicuous object, while their whole mode of life in the Repose depended on concealment.

Maria said that she was bigger than they were, and that it had to be done.

They were flatly refusing, when the young fisherman said that he would do the carpentry himself. He felt the importance of a favorite, and the grandeur of flying in an airplane had gone to his head. The others had to give in. But they avoided Maria completely after that, leaving her and the poor coxcomb to arrange the affair in their own way. The Schoolmaster made one awkward attempt to read her a lecture—but she laughed, and would not listen.

It was only because she was inexperienced and had not thought, not because she was a bully. Besides, she was on fire with her dream of a tiny airplane really flown, and she scarcely noticed the reactions of other people.

The fisherman made the new controls beautifully, using horsehair for the wires and sailcloth stretched on twigs of silver birch to make the various flaps. When it was finished, it looked like the first flying machine built by the brothers

Wright, except that it was a monoplane. He had to sit on this plane, as the Wrights did, with his legs stretched nearly straight in front.

The great day came for flying it, and the pilot was ready to win immortal fame. Both of them were too enthusiastic to think.

It would not rise from the ground, because of the long grass in the Jubilee Field, but ran in circles, buzzing and skidding on its wings, before it turned upside down. Fortunately the propellor missed the pilot as he was thrown clear.

They tried the controls anxiously, wagging them with the control column, and the horsehair to one of the ailerons had snapped. This was replaced. They chattered as they worked to fix it, agreeing that Maria was to launch the next flight from her hand, as she had done when showing how it flew.

"Are you ready?"

"Yes, Y'r Honour."

"Are you sure you will be all right?"

"Yes, yes!"

She let it go, and he was off.

It went straight for the ground at her feet, pulled out of the dive when within an inch of crashing, skimmed along faster and faster less than six inches from the grass, with its port wing down, rose with a great zoom when it was twenty yards away, and, at an altitude of twenty feet, turned upside down.

The pilot was still falling, a crumpled mass like a shot partridge, when a gust lifted the starboard wing. The machine slewed sideways and down with a sickle swoop,

86

landed on its wing tip, shed the wing, and lay there thumping feebly as the elastic tried to turn.

He meanwhile had been falling a-sprawl. Before the airplane struck, he had hit the ground.

To a man who was six inches high, one of Maria's human feet represented twelve. Twenty of her feet would have been two hundred and forty of his. That was the fall he had.

Her heart rose to her neck, turned over there, and plunged into her stomach. Her blood began to fizz and her fingers to tingle and the bones vanished from her legs. She started to run, wishing she could turn back time, wishing she could unhappen the awfulness of now.

She had not marked him, and could not find him in the grass.

She ran round searching madly, beating the scutch with her hands; then stood still in agony, realizing that she might have trodden on him. When she was still, she could hear him groan. He was stretched beside a tussock with only one leg! Or with his other leg twisted under him horribly! His face was white, but oh, he must not be dead!

If he had been a human, even from twenty feet, he might have killed himself; from two hundred and forty, he certainly would have done so. But bones are made of much the same material, whatever one's size is, and this is why the small creatures like rats and cats can fall from greater heights than we can. They have less weight to fall, and so the bones are stronger in proportion.

Maria knelt beside him, not knowing what to do, or how to bear the pathetic noise he was making. He had certainly broken his leg, even if nothing else was broken. She tried to remember what little she knew about first aid. People who had broken their backs ought not to be moved, and fox hunters who had broken their legs, she remembered, were sometimes carried home on gates. She felt that she could not dare to decide. Suppose his back were broken? How was she to find out without moving him? All the time, in another part of her mind, she was trying not to let it have happened.

They had told her not to, but she had insisted. She had let the game run away with her, not noticing that it was growing rougher; and now she was awake from the mad dream, with one of the beautiful People broken, perhaps killed. It came over her like doom.

The responsibility and the distress were too much. She

began running back to the lake, to get help. After a few yards, she feared that she might not remember exactly where he lay. She went back to find him, knelt again, and touched him with her finger.

The touch cleared her head. Whether I am guilty or not, she thought, I must get him within reach of aid as quickly as I can. His leg ought to be set, but I could not do it daintily enough, nor could I make small splints, nor even, she added with a sob, make any. I must not sob, but I must carry him to the Repose without jerking him. If I keep my hand quite flat and steady, it will do for a gate.

The horror of lifting him to the palm of her hand and of straightening the leg as he groaned unconsciously, for he seemed to have concussion; the nightmare walk to the lake, like some dreadful egg-and-spoon race; the paddling of the punt with one hand to the island; all these were got through somehow.

There was nobody in the Temple.

She called, deathly white, but nobody would answer. She was sure he was dying. She found a large rhododendron leaf for a stretcher, and edged it under him. She made a mattress by folding her handkerchief and laid the stretcher on it, under the middle of the dome. "He must be helped," she said. "You must come."

The Schoolmaster did come, from one of the pillar doors, and pointed silently for her to go. She went, and as she disappeared the stretcher party came to carry off the murdered man. Halfway across the lake, she laid her paddle down to howl—then sculled away, looking exactly like a retrieving puppy which had eaten its pheasant instead of retrieving it.

THE Professor was busy with Camb. Univ. Lib. Ii.
4.26, and was stuck on the first leaf with 𝕿𝖗𝖎𝖕𝖍𝖆𝖗𝖎𝖚𝖒. He had looked it up in Lewis and Short,
to no avail, and had also tried to verify it in a charter-hand
manuscript called Trin. Coll. Camb. R. 14. 9 (884), where
he had found 𝕿𝖗𝖎𝖚𝖒𝖕𝖍𝖆𝖗𝖎𝖔𝖓, partly scratched out. This
had made confusion worse confounded.

He motioned the retrieving puppy to his soapbox ab-
sently, as it slunk into the cottage with its tail between its
legs, and observed: "It says 𝕳𝖚𝖏𝖚𝖘 𝕲𝖊𝖓𝖚𝖘 𝕿𝖗𝖎𝖕𝖍𝖆𝖗𝖎𝖚𝖒
𝕯𝖎𝖈𝖎𝖙𝖚𝖗, but the trouble is that a part of the line seems to
have been erased."

"I came about something terrible."

"Murder?"

"It might be," said the puppy, blushing all over.

"Whom have you murdered? The Vicar, I hope. The
word has evidently proved a stumbling block to other
scribes, who either evade it by omitting the sentence, or
make wild guesses, or, as in this case, resort to some erasure
and to complete obscurity.

"He was an unpleasant man," he added. "I never liked
him much."

"It is a man from Lilliput that I have murdered."

"Indeed! Just fancy! 𝕿𝖗𝖎𝖕𝖆𝖗𝖙𝖎𝖙𝖚𝖒 is a possibility, of

course, but one hardly cares to divagate so widely from a lucid script."

"The People are arranging never to see me again."

"So long as they will arrange it themselves," he said kindly. "One has so many calls on one's time, so many little annoyances like this stupid *lapsus calami* I was telling you about. I suppose I shall have to write to Sir Sydney Cocker-ell or to Dr. Basil Atkinson. Even perhaps to Mr. G. C. Druce."

"But you must help!"

"No," he said firmly. "I cannot spare the time. On any other day, my dear Maria, but not just now. What with Ambrose and Ctesias the Cnydian, one scarcely knows which way to turn."

She pulled herself together, took away his manuscript, and put it in one of the bookshelves, upside down. He winced to see this done.

"Do you know what I have been talking about?"

He took off his spectacles and looked at them painfully, with watery eyes. He did not know at all.

He said: "I can remember every word. You were telling me that you had murdered the Vicar, and a good job too. How did you dispose of the body?"

She told her story carefully from the beginning, how she had ruined the whale hunt and bullied the People and prob-ably killed the fisherman in her wretched bungee airplane.

"Dear me," he said, when she had finished. "But this is very inconvenient."

He considered for some time, then went over to the book-shelf and turned his manuscript the right way up.

"You know," he said, "it could easily be some monkish mistake for 𝕿𝖗𝖎𝖇𝖎𝖆𝖑𝖎𝖘, a common species, except that they seem to have attached particular value to lions—the sentence

91

refers to lions—owing to their association with the gospels. The maddening thing is that I have mislaid Du Cange."

Maria burst into tears.

"Good heavens!" he exclaimed when he heard the noise. "What ever is the matter? My own Maria, anything but this! Allow me to lend you my handkerchief, a dishcloth, a towel, one of the sheets. Have a glass of cowslip wine. Have a sniff of some burned feathers, if I can find any. Have anything, Maria, but do not weep!"

"You won't think!"

"Think!" cried the Professor, bashing himself on the head with Lewis and Short, which looked as if it could weigh about ten pounds. "Think! Great Powers of Pedantry assist me now!"

After a bit he sat down calmly beside her on the soapbox and waited for the sobs to subside.

"Would you object," he asked humbly, "to repeating the subject which we were just discussing?"

She repeated it with hiccups.

"I think we may depend upon it that the pilot was not killed. If he had broken his back or his neck, you would have noticed it when you moved him, by seeing that he was hinged in the wrong places. No, no. He has only broken his leg, and richly he deserved it. You should take him some fruit every now and then, with magazines to read in bed. We shall find that he recovers in no time."

"I hope he will!"

"Even if he does, you will still be at loggerheads with Lilliput."

"They sent me to Coventry!"

"Yes. I see. Now Maria, you must try to look at this from their point of view. It is an exceedingly curious situation. You are a child, but very big; they are grown-up, but

92

very small. Just imagine what you would feel, if you were
a grownup whose head was bothered with the affairs of a
family. Suppose you were off to catch the London train,
with your umbrella well rolled, to see a solicitor about
some mortgages, and just as you were getting near the station a little girl who was forty-eight feet high stepped over
the hedge and carried you away to a distant field, in the

wrong direction, where she put you down and told you to be a German, while she was being General Eisenhower. Think how exasperating it would be, as you heard the train puffing off without you."

"But I only played with a few of them!"

"All the same, they could see the tendency of the position. If they had given in to you, they would never have been able to call their souls their own, and their economic life would have been upset in order to play at queens and subjects. However nice you were to them, it would have been intolerable."

"I used to help them. I spent all my money buying chocolates and airplanes!"

"But they did not want the airplanes and they could not live on chocolates. They had a living to earn."

"I suppose . . ."

"You see, Maria, this is a problem which has only once occurred before, and that was when the small man Gulliver was in the keeping of the huge girl Glumdalclitch, in the land of the Giants."

"They got on very well."

"Exactly. But it was because she did not paw him about. Don't you remember how disgusted he was with the other young ladies who tried to make him a plaything? He hated being mauled and messed, and he was grateful to Glumdalclitch because she only behaved as a loving attendant and helper. This is what you will have to do, if you want to make it up with Lilliput. You must never, never force them to do anything. You must be as polite to them as you are polite to any other person of your own size, and then, when they see your magnanimity in not exerting brute force, they will admire you, and give you love.

"I know it is difficult," he added gently, "because the

94

trouble about loving things is that one wants to possess them. But you must keep hold of your emotions and always be guarding against meanness. It will be very difficult indeed."

"The Schoolmaster pointed for me to go away. He meant I was not to come back."

"I think you may go back once, if it is to apologize."

"But I don't see why I should apologize! I was only trying to help them fly."

"They asked you not to."

An obstinate vanity made her stiffen.

"I have tried to help, and I never struck or forced a single one of them. I *won't* say I'm sorry."

The Professor got up to fetch his manuscript, dismissing her from his mind.

"Very well, Maria. Certainly I am not going to force *you*. Meanwhile, if you will excuse me, there is this little matter of 𝕿𝖗𝖎𝖕𝖍𝖆𝖗𝖎𝖚𝖒, which I must elucidate as best I may."

She could not get another word out of him, and went away in the sulks herself, feeling twice as guilty as before.

It took her two days to swallow the lecture which she had been given. Sometimes she protested to herself that she would rather die than apologize to a set of miserable hop-o'-my-thumbs. Sometimes she thought how disgusted the Professor must be feeling with her. Sometimes she swallowed a small piece of the lecture at a time, thinking that perhaps it *had* been a bit annoying for the People, but all the same they ought to have been more grateful. I could have killed the whole lot of them, she thought, if I had wanted to, merely by stamping my feet, and I could have told Miss Brown their secret. Yet they order me off my own island, and won't even speak!

After two days she had swallowed the lecture success-fully—a meal of something nasty like cold porridge, taken with rests between the spoonfuls and finished in the end.

She sat down to write a straight and manful letter, in her smallest handwriting. It said:

Dear Sirs,

   I am young but tall. You are old but short. I am sorry and will be better. I hop he is getting better.

Yours sincerely

with Tons of love

from Maria

Then she persuaded Cook to boil a large snail shell for her—there were some *Helix pomatia* in the park, which was very rare for Northamptonshire—and bored two small holes with a pin when it was clean, so that she could give it a handle of thread. This made it into a kind of shopping bas-ket. She found a couple of wild strawberries in the Ridings, put them in the basket, and tore one of the middle pages out of Miss Brown's *Pilgrim's Progress*, which was all she could think of for a magazine. She folded her letter as small as she could, stamped it with a patch of paper like confetti, and set off for the lake.

When she reached the island, she found that the brambles had been woven across her path. She did not beat them down, but left the letter and the comforts for the invalid in one of the canoes.

For three nights Maria went with an aching heart, carry-ing her fruit and magazines, but on the third night the brambles rose of their own accord. There was the School-master waiting to welcome her with a beaming smile, and they flew into each other's arms.

CHAPTER

XII

THE People gradually recovered confidence as they saw that their child mountain intended to do her best, and the pilot began to get better, as the Professor had foretold. But Maria was careful from then on not to make favorites, and she never again mentioned the subject of indiarubber airplanes. She blushed to think of queens.

She used to visit them for an hour or two every midnight, because the days were devoted to Algebra and threatened by telescopes.

It was true that she felt sleepy in the mornings, and Cook said that she was beginning to look peaked; but Miss Brown did not notice anything, as she was busy puzzling about her plot with the Vicar.

Maria cast away dull care and enjoyed herself to the top of her bent. She loved stealing out at the dead of night, with the dangerous journey past her tyrant's door. She loved the wonderful summer moonlight, silver and velvet black. Above all, she loved being with the old-fashioned People, and wondering at their minuscule Oeconomy.

One thing which she discovered was that it was a mistake for giants to choose small presents for dwarfs. The proper thing for a giant to do was to choose the largest present which a dwarf could possibly use, while the dwarf

97

had to choose the smallest or finest thing which could be of use to the giant. The Professor, with his Hundreds and Thousands, had been astray. For instance, her most successful present—for she tried to take something with her every night—had been the saucepan with no handle. It had been just what they needed, a wonderful farm boiler, which could boil for a week at a time, and, though she had taken it shyly, for fear that they would be offended at the poverty of the gift, she had never been thanked so heartily for anything else. They said it was "compleat."

The People found this out as well.

Instead of using a ship's sail for the next presentation to Maria, they decided to make her a spider-web scarf. The silk was taken from the webs of the garden spider, the brown one with a white cross on its back, and it was treated with the juice of gorse blooms to get rid of the stickiness, which also made it yellow. Then it was knitted in thin strips by a team of volunteers, for they had no looms, and the strips were finally sewn together. Maria was allowed to watch the process, and she had the satisfaction of seeing, in the course of it, one of the things which had interested Lemuel Gulliver. She saw a little woman threading an invisible needle with invisible thread.

It made a wonderful scarf, and the curious thing was that it was as strong as good linen, or stronger. It was resilient, like elastic, and she could stick her finger into it without breaking it, although she could see through. Many years later, she wore it as part of her wedding dress; but meanwhile she had to hide it under a floor board in the Duchess's Powder Closet, for fear of Miss Brown.

She suddenly realized why, whenever she brought the

98

Lilliputians a present, they tried to give her one. It was because they did not want to be possessed.

Another thing which she discovered was that the People lived a dangerous life, although they did not complain about it. In spite of the fact that there were no wars, they had other dangers. For instance, there had been a family of magpies some thirty moons before, who had taken a fancy to young Lilliputians, and had carried off a dozen babies before they had been mastered. Magpies were wily, and had good memories; so, when two of them had been wounded with arrows, they had finally given it up.

The bows and arrows were interesting. The wood of our gigantic trees, when it was in twigs sufficiently thin for a Lilliputian bow, had not enough snap in it. So they used the spines from the pinion feathers of large birds, farm hens if they could get them, strung against the curve. The arrows had metal tips, forged from the nails in the cupola, but these were inclined to be soft.

By the way, the ancient Lilliputians were accustomed to use poisoned arrows. But in England they could not find the proper poisons—which had perhaps been fortunate for Maria. They did use the formic acid from bees; but they could not get enough strength on the tip of the arrow, although they boiled it down, for any work more formidable than killing insects.

When they raided hives for the poison, and for honey, which was important to them because they had no sugar, the raiders wore a kind of plate armor made from the wing cases of beetles. The scales were sewn to a mouse-skin foundation, overlapping; but of course they generally raided the nests in frosty weather, and used smoke.

99

Another danger was owls, worse than the danger of magpies. There were three main kinds of owl at Malplaquet: the barn, the tawny, and the Lilford, who also hunted by day. Horned owls were rare, though they did come sometimes. These creatures were braver and less wily than the magpies, and they had never learned to keep away. Also, instead of merely pouncing like the crow tribe, they came down vertically like dive bombers, and it was impossible to slay them. There was no time. Consequently the sentry on the cupola had to do night-watching for owls, and, when he spotted one, he rang a bell. Maria, when she found out about it, realized that she had heard the bell often. But there are such a lot of noises in the country, queer noises like donkeys braying and so on, that we neglectful humans do not properly attend to them. The bell made a deepish tonk-tonk-tonk, and Maria had always thought it was a carrion crow. When the bell was rung, the only hope was to stand still without looking up. If they moved, the owl saw them; if they looked up, it noticed their white faces under the moon. If they stood still, looking straight in front of them, it nearly always passed over.

In the daytime, when they were not so much about, there were kestrels. The procedure was the same for these.

As for the mainland trappers, their lives were in their hands. A fox was about as big as the National Gallery to them, and, as it could easily pounce across Trafalgar Square, there was nothing to be done. The worst of it was that it could also smell. It was no good shooting at it with their poor arrows. It was no good hiding in the grass, or standing still, because it had a nose. Many ideas had been tried for dealing with foxes, ideas like making a loud noise or a nasty smell, but none of them had been successful. A famous trap-

per, three hundred moons before, had blinded a fox by shooting an arrow into each eye. Ordinary people could not be expected to have the nerve for that. The common reaction was to stand still and trust to luck, if surprised, but, above all, to keep a weather eye open, and particularly a nose, in case foxes should be about. Even a human, with nostrils as clumsy as two fireplaces, can usually smell a fox. The Lilliputians, with their fine noses, had better warning. Then they had to climb trees.

It was like living in a world full of dinosaurs and pterodactyls, or even bigger creatures, and they had to keep their wits about them.

A result of this, which biologists will understand—and if you are not a biologist nobody cares a fig for you—was that the ladies of Lilliput had begun to have twins. They often had triplets, and were delighted when they did.

Maria wished that she could help them in these dangers. If she had been rich or grown-up or any of the other things which seem so desirable until one gets them, she could have bought a shotgun to shoot the owls, and could have cleared them out like that. Unfortunately, she was not. She did, however, make sensible suggestions. She said that, if they would show her the fox earths all over the Park, she would put tar in them at the next breeding season, or anything else that was unpleasant, whatever the Master of the Malplaquet Hounds might think. She said that with their local knowledge, and her bigness, there were probably several things which could be done. "For instance," said she, "I can get some petrol from the Primus and put it on the wasps' nests, if you will show me where they are. I could even smash up the nests of owls, once you had spotted them."

The People of the Island were grateful for her kind

thoughts, and decided that she was not a bad Mountain after all.

One pearly night toward the beginning of July, with the owls hooting and the twigs cracking and the paw-feet rustling and the great moon reigning over all, Maria crept up the silver stairs to bed. She passed the door of the square eighteenth-century chapel, where the plaster cherubs with fat cheeks like amoretti looked down from the flaking roof between the Royal Arms and the Ten Commandments; passed the much more than full-length portrait of the Fifth Duke, by Romney, which was unsalable because it covered half an acre of canvas, and also the water color of Naples with Vesuvius by Moonlight, equally unsalable because it was fifteen feet long, the biggest water color in the world; passed the cold busts of the Main Library, not the Third Duke's, where Sophocles and others looked down with beards like twisted tripe upon the empty shelves which had once housed the Malplaquetian MSS.; passed, with a special tremor, the lofty bedroom in which the Empress Amelia had breathed her last, and also the Duchess's Chamber, where her own ancestors had been brought into the world, in the presence of twelve doctors and any members of the Privy Council who had happened to be disengaged.

Maria was an educated person, and for her the Palace was full of ghosts. She knew where the Wicked Marquis had condemned the two young poachers to death; where the Mad Earl had played the violin at midnight, to Lola Montez and the King of Bavaria; where the Impetuous Viscount had blown off his whiskers with a six-shooter, on discovering that he had sold his Honor to the Jews; and where the nasty little Honorable had lighted his Nannie, to see if she would burn.

102

She turned up the last corridor and opened the door.

"Good evening!" said Miss Brown smoothly, sitting on the bed. "So here is our little vagrom, returned from her clandestine tour."

"Yes, Miss Brown."

"And what has tempted her to brave the inclement airs of night? What horns of elfland, if one may so express oneself, have summoned the tender cheek to leave its downy pillow? Eh, Maria?"

Miss Brown moved her hand on purpose, and there was the painful ruler which was used at Algebra.

"I went for a walk."

"The midnight ramble. Yes, indeed. The moonlit constitutional, to coin a phrase. And why this promenade among Diana's minions?"

"I wanted to go out."

"Exactly. So explicit. And yet, to some ideas, the time would scarcely seem conventional?"

"It was the moon."

"The Moon! How true! How sweet the moonlight sleeps upon this bank, et cetera.

"And these," added Miss Brown, opening the other hand to show the spider scarf and the handkerchief and the other presents, which she had discovered by tracking her pupil to their hiding place, "and these delicious trifles, fairy fragments as one might designate them if devoted to the Essay Form, are these as well, Maria, nothing but moonshine and Titania's dreams?"

There was nothing to be said.

"Where did you get them?"

"I got them."

"She got them! Lucid explanation! Where?"

"I won't say."

"Will not say. The elision is so vulgar, is it not? She will not say. And yet, suppose she is made to say, you ask?"

Maria said distinctly, with some surprise at finding that she was speaking the truth: "The more you hurt me, the less you'll hear."

"Indeed?"

"Yes."

This put the Governess off her stride. One of the best ways to deal with tyrants is to tell them the truth, and to face them, and to let them see how much you hate them plainly, so long as you can make them understand that you will hurt them if you can. It frightens them away.

Miss Brown gnawed her fingers.

"The child's recalcitrant," she said complainingly. "Ungrateful...."

And, with a sudden swish like a cobra's, which made Maria duck, she was out of the door. She slammed the same triumphantly, and turned the key.

Five minutes afterward, however, she changed her mind; for Maria was surprised to hear the key turned back again quietly, and to know that she was at liberty after all. Why?

CHAPTER

XIII

NEXT morning was bright and breezy, and there were two expeditions from the ruined palace, in the hours which ought to have been devoted to Irregular Verbs. Miss Brown made an expedition to the Vicarage, while Maria seized the opportunity to visit the Professor.

She found him searching mournfully for his set of Du Cange—which is a dictionary of Mediaeval Latin, in case you don't know—but this was an almost hopeless task in the chaos to which he had reduced his cottage. There were books in the shelves, which had been filled some fifty years before. Nearly all the floor, except the part around the tea chest on which he used to sit, was taken up by piles and piles of mildewed volumes. Also, alas, as he had been verifying quotations and things of that sort since the turn of the century, and as he was one of those unfortunate people who leave the book open at the quotation in some accessible place, all the window ledges, oven-shelves, mantel-pieces, fenders, and other flat surfaces were stocked with verified quotations, which had long been forgotten. He had left a narrow path to each door. But the steps of the stairs had proved to be tempting flat surfaces, so it was difficult for the poor old fellow to climb to bed, and the bed itself

would have been denied to him—except that it was fortunately a double one, and he was able to squeeze in somehow between Gesner and the eleven tomes of Aldrovandus,
counting the extra one on Monsters.

The Professor was crawling about on hands and knees,
trying to read the names of the bottom books sideways,
without disturbing the piles. He was sick of erudition and
only too glad to listen to Maria.

She told him how Miss Brown had found the artifacts of
Lilliput, perhaps by tracking her to the Duchess's Powder
Closet with the magnifying glass, and how she herself had
refused to tell where she got them. He was interested.

"Well, now, my dear child," said he, sitting down absent-
mindedly on a stack of books, which happened to be the
missing set of Du Cange, "have you ever noticed that when

something unusual turns up, you are immediately confronted with a moral problem? For instance, if you were to find yourself in the unusual position of Alice in Wonderland, who was able to make herself large or small at will, nothing would be easier than to rob the Bank of England. You would simply have to go in small, say about the size of a pin, and come out extra large, through the skylight or somewhere, with a few million pounds in your pockets. Moral problem: shall I become a burglar? Or if you found yourself in the unusual position of the Invisible Man, by my young friend Mr. Wells, nothing would be easier than to introduce yourself into the boudoirs of your acquaintances, in order to earn a handsome competence by discovering their secrets. Moral problem: shall I become a blackmailer? Now it is certainly unusual to discover a colony of people six inches high, and so you were immediately confronted with your moral problem, about being their Queen. Shall I interfere with Lilliput's proper freedom and become a tyrant? But, dear me, Maria, this is becoming a lecture. I fear I bore?"

"Not at all," she said. "It's quite fun."

"So now we have your governess on the track of the unusual, with her own moral problem straight ahead of her. How will she solve it?"

"Solve what?"

"About interfering."

"If Miss Brown can interfere," said Maria bitterly, "she will."

"How?"

"I suppose she will just forbid them or something."

"Much worse."

She looked at him anxiously.

"She will sell them," he said.

"But, oh, she couldn't! They are real! They are People! She couldn't sell them like . . . like hens!"

"Nothing is more likely. Don't you see that they are tremendously valuable? Any big circus would pay thousands and thousands of pounds to get them, perhaps millions. They are the only things of their kind in the world."

"But . . . But . . . She *couldn't*. It would be *too* beastly. It would be . . . it would be *slaves*."

"So now you know, Maria, why they did not want to give away their secret."

"I'll never tell her. She can kill me first, but I wouldn't tell. The beast!"

"Dear me. Yes. But the question is, my dear young lady, whether she would have a right to sell your Lilliputians after all? Just let me think."

He tottered off to one of the bookshelves, where he had just noticed some brown volumes which might have been Du Cange, but which were not, then wandered back refreshed.

"You see, Maria, the whole situation is wrapped in such unusualness that it is difficult to consider it clearly. For instance, are these creatures human or not? What is the legal definition of a human being? Does he cease to be human when he is six inches high? If they are human, presumably it would be illegal for your guardians to sell them, as there are laws in England against slavery. But again, if they are human, what is their nationality? Should they accredit an Ambassador to represent their interests at St. James's? Will they be regarded as British Subjects By Birth, and as being Domiciled in England for the Purposes of Income Tax? Certainly the latter, if what I hear about the

108

Inland Revenue is true. And then, on the other hand, if they are not human, are we to regard them as *ferae naturae*, wild animals which become the property of the landlord? If so, you are the landlord, but, as you are a minor, Miss Brown and the Vicar could sell them on your behalf."

"I don't know what they are," she said sadly.

"Whatever they are, they only have four hundred sprugs in gold. It seems inevitable that if they are to escape being sold, once your governess has found them, they will have to go to law about themselves, and four hundred sprugs, Maria, is not enough. They could never brief a reliable counsel with such a sum, and, under the due forms of suit and countersuit, I fear that they would be liable to get the thin end of the Law."

"We won't let her find them then."

"Last but not least," said the Professor with a deep sigh, "here we are talking about their future as if it depended on us. But they are reasonable and civilized beings who must decide their future for themselves. I blame myself for this. I am becoming a barbarian. I must not."

He patted one of the nearest folios secretly, to cure himself of barbarism, and looked at Maria over the top of his spectacles.

"Personally, I have found that the best way to deal with a dangerous situation is to face it, and to make it happen, and to go through with it, rather than to keep it hanging over one's head. If I were a Lilliputian, I believe that I would prefer to be discovered, and to go to law, and to bring the matter into the daylight of some kind of certainty, rather than to creep about in dangerous hiding, under the shadow of discovery."

"You said they wouldn't get fair law."

"It is what I fear."

"Why," said Maria, "can't we just prevent Miss Brown from finding them at all?"

"The question is, whether you can. Children are under dreadful disadvantages compared with their elders. If your governess made up her mind to discover where you got your sprug and the other things, she could nag for weeks on end, she could send you to bed without any supper, she could keep you on bread and water or tog you out in football boots, and I daresay that a person of her caliber might do worse."

Maria's heart sank at the thought of what Miss Brown might really do. She knew that she was perfectly capable of beating her, and her womanly little heart shrank from the prospect, not only because of the agonizing pain but also because of the humiliation and beastliness. For a few dreadful moments she saw herself as she was, and doubted whether it would be possible to keep even the most important secret under such conditions. However, she said bravely:

"I don't mind if she does."

"You may think you would not mind, but suppose she kept it up for months?"

They went on debating the problem for more than an hour, without making it much clearer, until it was time for the Conquistador of Lilliput to go home.

Incidentally, talking of Conquistadors, the Professor got mixed in a digression toward the end, and insisted that she should take away two books about Conquest by Prescott. He said that they would show her what human beings were liable to do with newly discovered Peoples, when they happened to be valuable.

Meanwhile, in the Vicarage, a different kind of discussion had been going on.

The hold which Miss Brown had over Mr. Hater was this. She was a very distant relative of Maria's, and was the only living one. You remember about the missing parchment concerning the inheritance of Malplaquet. The Vicar believed that if it could be found, and altered slightly, a vast sum of money which ought to have been Maria's could be gained for Miss Brown, by means of a suit of *mort d'ancestre*.

This was why he always wandered so much about the palace, looking for hiding places. Had he been able to find the parchment, and to do the necessary forgery, he would have married Miss Brown for her money, although they hated each other. They would have been bound together by the crime. His knowledge and her name were needed to bring it about.

You may think that Vicars are not usually forgers, and sometimes indeed they are not; but the heart of man is a strange mechanism, my dear Amaryllis, and it is astonishing what even Vicars can bring themselves to believe, so long as it is in their own interest. Somehow or other, by strange and crooked by-paths of special pleading, Mr. Hater had convinced himself that there would be nothing wrong in altering the ancient title deed, if he could find it. For one thing, he had worked hard, searching about like a sulky old vulture in the British Museum and the Public Record Office, to discover the existence of the deed, and Maria had not worked at all. In any case he was that kind of person. There are people who will just doggedly avert their minds from wrong-doing, and do it.

The Vicar was like this, and it did not make him preach

any the less cruelly, about darksome sins, in his shoddy little church on Sundays.

So the conversation in the Vicarage that sunny and windy morning was not about Lilliput. Neither of them was cultured enough to associate sprugs with Gulliver, nor to draw any conclusion from the name of Lilliput which was stitched upon the handkerchief. They had not enough imagination to believe in six-inch people. If you had mentioned *Gulliver's Travels* to them, they would have said: "Oh, that's a children's book, isn't it?" They had a few instincts about money, and about appearing respectable, but for many and many years they had not had any thoughts on real ideas at all.

They had decided that Maria's three treasures, the sprug, the eighteenth-century handkerchief, and the silk scarf of such fineness as to be obviously of value, must have been found in some secret robing-room of the by-gone Dukes. They thought that the sprug was a sequin from a Duchess's evening dress. Their sagging cheeks were shaking with greed, when they realized that if Maria had really discovered a secret strong room full of valuables, then probably their missing parchment would be in it.

Usually they were mumchance villains, but the excitement about the discovery made them chatter.

"Such a difficult child," deplored Miss Brown, "obstinate and untrustworthy. She refused to say where she had found them, Mr. Hater, in so many words, though I thought it wiser not to make a fuss. Punishment would have only made her still more obstinate."

"But why should she refuse?"

"Out of naughtiness."

"This is ridiculous, Miss Brown. We have a right to

know of assets at Malplaquet, as a matter of business, as the child's guardians. How can we administer the estate with the extent of it concealed? You must talk to Maria at once, and bring her to reason. You are her governess. Surely you ought to have her under better control than that? You must talk to her seriously, this very afternoon."

"I will indeed."

The Vicar looked away and mumbled to the gothic mantelpiece:

"We must think how much depends upon it."

XIV

"COME here."

Maria went and stood in front of Miss Brown awkwardly, looking at the hard rings sunk in the fat fingers on the spreading lap.

"I have decided to overlook your conduct last night."

She said nothing. It was never possible to tell whether her governess was going to be cruel or kind, for her face wore the same quelling look in either case. She waited to see where the catch was.

"I have been talking to the Vicar about the hidden strong room which you have discovered."

This was Greek.

"You know, of course, for I have told you dozens of times, that you spring from a long line of wasters, who only considered their own pleasures, and who thought nothing of going bankrupt, to the ruin of poor tradesmen who had trusted them."

"My great-grandfather," said Maria proudly, "was the Prime Minister of England."

"I'll thank you not to answer back. You know that Malplaquet has been ruined by your ancestors, and that you yourself are practically supported out of Mr. Hater's pocket, a charity brat."

This was untrue, for the Vicar drew a salary as guardian, and was also stealing most of the money which ought to have been paid into the estate, against Maria's coming-of-age. That was why he had the Rolls-Royce.

"I thought the debts were being paid."

"So they should be. Would they not be paid the quicker if the ill-gotten gains of your forbears could be brought from this secret chamber which you try to hide from us?

"There was the Coronation coronet," pursued Miss Brown cunningly, peeping shrewdly at her victim through slit eyes, to see if there was a reaction, "which went astray in 1797, with the black pearls in it. There was the insignia of the Garter which were never returned to the Sovereign, and the diamond-hilted sword presented to the Second Duke by Catherine the Great. Where are these?"

Maria began to be filled with unholy joy for Lilliput, as she partly understood how far her governess was going astray.

"I don't know anything about a secret chamber."

"There would be papers in it too, parchments, deeds, which you are too young to understand. You could be sent to prison for keeping such things back."

"Children don't get sent to prison."

"Hold your tongue, Maria. Be careful what you say."

"But I tell you I haven't found a secret chamber."

Miss Brown searched out her pupil's eyes and fixed them with her own. She had a pleasant trick of staring Maria down, which is not so difficult to do when a child expects to be punished.

"Very well," she said at last, "you shall go straight to bed this minute, without your supper, and there you can think it over by yourself."

It was horrible to be sent to bed on a summer afternoon, when all the park was calling her to be out-of-doors, but she made the best of it. There was the wonder and glory of Lilliput to think about nowadays, and that made up for much.

If only one were rich enough to own a grouse moor, thought she to distract herself in the dreary bedroom, it would be much more suitable for the People. The stems of heather would be natural trees to them—for heather is more like a gnarled and stunted tree than anything I know, a coniferous, not a deciduous one—and there they could live in their small forest, with proper glades, and bog holes for lakes, and all the tiny mushroom things which you can see, if you lie on your face. There would be millions of insects to hunt in the summer, and they could build themselves real towns, and it would be to scale.

The trouble would be, she thought, that it would be impossible to protect them. The moment they were found out, on their moor, all the big humans would try to catch them, for circuses and so on, just like Captain Biddel and Miss Brown.

On a moor, you see, it would be impossible to keep them hidden. Somebody would find them, walking across it, and then the game would be up.

Even if you put a fence round it, with enormous walls, this would only make people more inquisitive than ever. You would get twice as many trespassers, trying to find out what it was about.

And if you paid an army of guards to stand round the boundary with tommy guns—well then, the trespassers would get half mad with inquisitiveness, and so would the

116

guards for that matter, and the whole thing would be discovered at once.

What you want, she thought hungrily, for tea-time was past, is some island off the west coast of Scotland or of Ireland, some uninhabited island with a watchtower, so that if anybody approached in a canoe the People could hide. It would have to be a heather island. It does seem a shame that even on that you could not give them proper houses on the surface. They would still have to live underground, for fear of visitors. I wonder if you could make houses that would sink into the ground when you turned a handle, like a bucket in a well?

If I were rich, I would buy some island like that, and we would live there safely with ourselves. But what about when I died? I suppose I should have to tell my eldest daughter when she was twenty-one, like the Secret of Glamis. But suppose she turned out to be a pig like Miss Brown? The best thing would be to buy a large model submarine, like the liners which the shipping companies put in their London windows, and then the People could always sail away in search of Lilliput, if they wanted to go. It would be a terrible dangerous voyage....

No, I would not. If I were really rich I would buy some big, shallow loch in Scotland or in Ireland, so long as it had plenty of tiny islands. I mean tiny. As soon as an island is as big as an acre, the humans take an interest, and try to make some money out of it, with a sheep or something. But there must be millions of islands in lochs and in Clew Bay and in places like that, which are not so big as a tennis court, or even smaller. They would be useless to humans. I daresay there are islands in Lough Con which no human being has set foot on for a hundred years, simply because they are too small to pay. Well then, I would buy this loch with the uninteresting islands in it—they would need to have heather—and, do you know, I would not try to keep it a secret at all? I would buy doll's houses and toy trains and Japanese plants and all that, quite openly, and I would set them up on my islands. I would even have a public day, Friday, when anybody could visit them on paying a shilling to the Red Cross. I would get people to think: There is that funny old Miss Maria, whose hobby it is to make sort of Japanese gardens in her loch. And all the time the People would be living there safe. It would have to be a big enough loch to give them proper warning, so that, when a boat set out from the banks, they would have time to hide themselves in the man-raid shelter. They would be warned from the watchtowers. And, of course, they would have to keep an extra lookout on Fridays.

Everything would have to be hidden. They could leave the houses and gardens standing, or anything which I might be supposed to have made myself, but no slops or half-cold cups of tea or telltale details of that sort.

We should have to hold raid drills.

When I came out by myself, they would still have to hide, until I blew a certain whistle. We should have to be strict about it. If I ever found a fire burning or a bed rumpled, I should call the magistrate at once, and show him the evidence. Then the culprit would have to be punished, really punished, not to punish him, of course, but to prevent it happening again.

The trouble about punishments, she thought, is that people enjoy giving them. We should have to stop that sort of thing in our islands. I think we would hurt the culprits on their feet, like in China. Nobody feels shy about their feet. And we would not have executioners at all, but it would be done by a machine. All the punishments for all the mistakes would be invariable, just as fire burns when you put your finger in it, and everybody would know what they were.

Well then, I would show the rumpled bed to the magistrate (but I must be careful not to be the queen), and he would show it to the lady who had made the mistake, and she would say, "Oh, dear me, I forgot," and he would look it up in the Retribution Book and say, "It says three turns of the machine on the soles of your feet," and she would say, "Drat!" I think we would have the machine in a room by itself, so that the criminal could go in without anybody to see, and put her feet into the holes, and press the button for herself. I daresay there would be nervous ladies who would prefer to have an executioner, and there would be a public service to supply one, if asked. I can imagine sympathetic executioners earning quite high fees. "Oh, Mr. Globgruff, I do *hope* you will be able to see me through my execution tomorrow. I always tell my husband there is *no* executioner in Lilliput with a machine-side manner like yours."

And what about murderers?

Well, no doubt the People have their own rules about that, and I would not like to interfere with them. But if they did ask me, considered Maria hopefully, I would advise them to keep a special island for murderers. There would be nothing nasty about it: It would be quite as comfortable as any of the others; but everybody on it would just be a murderer. We would tell them: "We don't want to make you unhappy, but we others cannot trust you any more, so you must live with the dangerous people. If you murder each other, it can't be helped, there it is; but you must keep away from us."

And we would take away any babies they had, to be brought up on the sensible islands. That would be the worst of it for them, poor dears.

There would be Murder Island and Swindlers Island— what a hard time they would have, swindling each other— and Cruel Island, for people like Miss Brown. All the others would be Happy Islands, and we would only give weapons to the people on them, for fear of wars....

"But oh," cried Maria dolefully, out loud, "I do feel hungry, however much I think!"

CHAPTER

XV

THE reason why Maria felt peckish just then was because honest old Cook had come hobbling up the stairs with Captain, carrying a bowl of soup with which she hoped to relieve the siege; so that the smell of soup came through the door. But Miss Brown had evidently been lying in wait, for there was a sudden scurry in the passage outside. There was the sound of a door banging, and then Maria could hear poor Cook being given notice on the spot.

"Without a character!" screamed Miss Brown down the corridor.

"Any character of yours, Mum," said Cook superbly, "is what I'd not besmirch my own possession of which with the application of."

The door shut again more gently, the footsteps died away, but the smell of soup remained.

It was growing dark in the shabby little bedroom. The evening breeze had dropped to nothing and all the summery trees of the park stood silent, without moving a leaf. The twilight hush had impressed the birds and beasts. You could hear a rabbit nibbling twenty yards away. The distant coots on the lake gabbled in undertones.

Maria spotted patterns in the darkling wallpapers,

drummed on the counterpane, practised whistling, pulled feathers out of the bolster, and listened to the sleepy birds outside the window.

I shall have steamboats, she thought, to ply between the islands: the kind you can buy in toy shops, which are worked by methylated spirits.

One of the islands is sure to have gulls on it, those black-headed gulls who breed on islands in big lakes and murder each other's children. It will be unsafe to use that island for the People, at least during the breeding season, for I am sure that no black-headed gull would think twice about snapping up a Lilliputian, considering how they treat their own nephews and nieces.

On the other hand it might not be a bad idea to play a joke on those same birds.

At the time of the year when they were not breeding, we would go to Gull Island in force, and set about a bit of engineering. We would dig shallow pans among the pebbles all over the strand, like saucers, or like the depressions which are made by the ant lion, and we should put a trap door at the bottom of each saucer in the earth. Each trap door would lead into a narrow passage, and the passages would communicate with a central chamber underground, in which I would probably bury a large earthenware crock for isinglass. Then, when the next breeding season was due to come round, a picked gang of Lilliputians would set off for the tunnels of Gull Island, with their necessary provisions, and there they would live like puffins, underground, for the whole season. Every time a gull laid an egg, it would of course roll into the bottom of the saucer, and the gull would sit down on top. This would ring a bell—we should have to put in electric batteries, and one of those indicators which the Master of the Malplaquet Hounds has in his kitchen—and two of the People would immediately run down the corridor, open the trap door, and let the egg fall through to the cellarage, where it would be wheeled off to the isinglass for storage. After a bit the ridiculous gull would set up, look between its legs, say, "Goodness me, I thought I was sitting on an egg," and settle down to lay another. By this means we would not only be able to keep down the number of black-heads, but we would be able to provide egg powder for Lilliput.

We would need a factory for dehydrating the eggs, or whatever it is called, because one egg would be enough to feed a family for a week, and thus it would not be an economical size to cook. But if we turned the eggs into powder, the stuff could be used in small quantities, about the size of a salt spoon, and this would be a blessing in the kitchens....

Or else, thought Maria, beginning to yawn, we could hatch them out in incubators and eat them as day-old chicks, or we could ring the parents from underneath for the purposes of Research, or we could train the young ones up for seaplanes....

Soon she was far away in a sky of dreams, where jet-propelled white seaplanes folded their wings on landing, or stretched them at an angle of incidence of forty-five degrees, when they wanted to take off. It was because she had been short of sleep for the last few weeks. Her hands were together under her cheek; her dark pigtails strayed on the pillow; the mysterious shadows under her eyelashes were quiet gates into a secret world where things went on which nobody could fathom.

Just before she dozed away, she thought she could hear,

half in her dreams, that Miss Brown and the Vicar were talking on the terrace.

She woke in the dark, feeling wide awake at once. She was healthy and happy and alive, and a most delightful thing was happening.

Like a spider on the end of its thread, a six-inch man was dangling lower and lower from the gutter outside the window, in the moonlight.

The fact is that if there are five hundred pairs of bright eyes all round your pleasure ground, fixed steadily on you from under clumps of dock leaves and thistles—if there are five hundred pairs of ears like tiny shells, straining to hear behind the green blackberries and wild parsley—well then, if you will walk about on the terrace telling the Vicar that Maria has been sent to bed without her supper, this development is liable to be discussed in the metropolis of Lilliput before long.

So it had been, and the little People were not the kind who left their friends to suffer. Arrangements had immediately been started. Ropes from the frigate had been spliced together, transport had been organized, and the other needs of the moment had been put in hand. By ten o'clock they had started the journey, and had come to the South Front an hour before Miss Brown went to bed. They knew which the two inhabited bedrooms were, from seeing the windows lit of an evening.

A well-known steeple-jack, who generally did the outside repairs of the Temple of Repose, had gone up inside the nearest drainpipe, using it as mountain climbers use a chimney. That is to say, he had put his back against one wall of the pipe and his feet against the other, and had walked up slowly like that, in a sitting position, by pressing his back

124

against the walls. His rope had been too short for the immense length of the pipe—he could not have carried enough —and so he had been followed by a second climber, with a second rope, who had spliced the two together when he was halfway up. Then the top climber, who was by now on the roof gutter, had drawn up certain other tackle that was needed. The second climber had joined him to help.

They had thrown down the long rope outside the drainpipe, and willing hands below had been ready to tie it to a stake which they had driven on the edge of the lawn. Now there had been a thread of plaited horsehair stretching from the gutter to the grass. The next thing had been to pass this through a metal loop, forged from a nail, and to tie a second rope to the loop. This had made two long ropes, the fixed one, which was to act like the overhead wire of a rope railway, and the other, which could pull the metal loop up or down on it. It was a bit like a funicular.

When this had been arranged, and Miss Brown was known to be snoring, the steeple-jack had begun to let himself down on a short cord to Maria's window sill.

She opened it stealthily.

"I am so glad to see you!"

He said in a low voice: "Tie the End of this to your Table, Ma'am, or somewhere inside the Room. Speak softly, or we shall be smoak'd. We have a Pulley at the Top. Do you desire to see the Schoolmaster?"

"Yes!"

"In one Minute, then."

And he vanished like a tiny monkey, leaving her to fasten the bottom end.

The next thing to arrive was the Schoolmaster, in a breeches apparatus.

He whispered: "Good Evening, Miss."

"Good evening, Sir," she said, in heartfelt tones, "Your Honour, Mister! You are the best thing I have seen today, and don't I mean it!"

"Your Servant, Miss. Allow me to present the Victuals."

And there they were, coming down slowly on the pulley: three roast oxen, two barrels of elderberry wine, four dozen loaves of grass-seed bread.

She said: "Oh, dear!"

She could have squashed him flat.

It was a regular deputation. Apart from the roast bullocks and other blessings, there was the Schoolmaster and the Admiral and the steeple-jack and an aged town councilor, carrying an illuminated address, all of whom had come to visit her on the principle that invalids and captives needed to be cheered up. They told her that it was past Midnight already. Then, while she consumed the dinner on her face towel, which she spread on the window sill for a table cloth, they watched her gobble it up.

"I shall eat you out of everything," she said with a blush.

"We were sent to convey an Address of Gratitude, Miss, for your Constancy in shielding the People, which has been subscrib'd by the entire Borough of Lilliput in Exile."

"And by the Navy," said the Admiral firmly.

"It is me that gets shielded," she said, overcome with shyness as the address was presented. "At least we are in a horrid muddle. I have such a lot to tell you. I can't help talking with my mouth full. And please excuse me if I read."

While she was reading, they looked about politely—more politely than she had looked about the island. Her room was as strange to them as the island had been to her, but they tried not to stare.

126

The Address was written in black-thorn ink on a pre-pared vole-skin parchment, as thin as Indian paper, and it explained how present and future Generations were to know that the Female Mountain had kept her Word to the People through Famine and Incarceration, etc., etc. It was a splendid testimonial to have, and, as she did not know how to thank them for it, she folded it up and placed it tenderly over her heart (in her pajama pocket). Then she went on eating.

She said, when she had finished: "Thank Lilliput for my good dinner."

"Your Servants, Miss."

She noticed that they were no longer calling her "Y'r Honour," but "Miss," which was the proper eighteenth-century address for girls, and this made her feel pleased. She did not know why.

"Don't go away. Wouldn't you like to see my things? I have not much to show."

They admired the texture of the sheets, because they had no looms of their own, and gazed over the vast expanse of polished oilcloth with respect. Miss Brown was too mean to let her have a carpet, so there was nothing except this wintry oilcloth, and one cheap woolen mat. The furniture, as we know, was cast iron.

Maria did the honors as well as she could. She found that they were more amused by the looking glass on the dressing table than by anything else. She tilted this backward till it lay level, and they stood on it, admiring themselves upside down. The Admiral did a hornpipe, fascinated by his toes.

Afterwards it was time to tell them the whole story of how the sprug had been discovered, of the Professor's views about Law and Slavery, and of Miss Brown's wild-goose chase after the secret room. The Schoolmaster did not seem so pleased as she expected when he heard of the false trail. He, like the Professor, saw at once that the safety of the People now depended on the endurance of one young girl, and, though he did not like to tell her so, he was beginning to think that his countrymen had better migrate while there was still time to do so, and without revealing their destination even to Maria. All he said, however, was that he would have to think things over.

When it was time to part, they kissed the tip of her little finger in turn. The town councilor was put in the breeches apparatus to go first, and all were bowing, smiling, or waving good-by—when the thunderbolt fell.

The key turned in the lock with a sudden click, the door slammed open on its hinges, and there, in the doorway, stood Miss Brown with a candle, in her flannel night dress.

Everything began to happen so quickly that the scene seemed to go slow. There was Miss Brown, who had heard talking, first ready to be angry; then amazed and not believing what she saw; then, for the briefest moment, half impressed, half wondering whether she ought to be polite to visitors; then guessing, then realizing, then seeing plain the opportunity to catch some of them, to appropriate them to herself, to make her fortune. And at the same time there was Maria crying "Escape!" and there was the deputation tumbling over itself to be gone, the old councilor being bundled into the breeches apparatus and the Admiral drawing his new sword, forged from one of the Woolworth pins, to defend the bridgehead like Horatius.

Miss Brown ran to grab them. She got a dig with the pin which went right through her finger. (The good sword stood a hair's-breadth out behind the Tuscan's hand.) It

128

stopped her for a second. (She reeled and on the mantelpiece she leaned one breathing space, then, like a wild cat mad with wounds, sprang at the Admiral's face.) She got hold of him by one leg, but Maria charged at the same instant and bit another finger till she felt the flesh turn on the bone. There was a scrimmage free-for-all, with the breeches apparatus going up twice. There was the Admiral climbing hand over hand. There was Maria thrown panting into a corner, like the oak on Mount Avernus. And finally there was Miss Brown left triumphant, with the Schoolmaster in her podgy fist, nearly squeezing the life out of him.

CHAPTER

XVI

THE most famous of the trappers was called Grad-gnag. He was a wiry man with gray hair and a taciturn disposition, who seldom spoke to anybody, but could call birds by note. For many moons he had been planning the longest of his treks. He was a kind of Allan Quatermaine, and now he had reached the hinterland of a continent, which he had been exploring all his life. It was King Solomon's Mines to him, for the legends of Lilliput in Exile talked of a mysterious house, beyond the vasty borders of the Park itself, from which there could be got a wondrous breed of piebald mice. The skins were of fabulous value, for only one existed on the Island of Repose, and that was used as a part of the communal regalia. It was said that this skin had been taken, three hundred moons before, by the legendary trapper who had blinded the fox and passed into history as the greatest of his trade. Blambrangrill had been his name: a dreamer of strange horizons and of epic deeds; and Gradgnag, although he never talked, had caught the dream.

The arrangements for the trek had taken many days. He always traveled light and alone, living on the country, but it had seemed wiser to arrange for caches as an emergency store, spaced out at intervals of four hours' march. He was

130

a methodical man. Then there had been the scouting for direction, which had extended not only over days but over moons, because, although the mouse-house was fabled to lie some way beyond the western boundary wall, the compass bearing was not fixed. On many and many an expedition he had climbed that monstrous wall by cunning footholds, to stare out with his pale blue eyes across the Great Unknown. He had added one fact to another. He had read the archives relating to Blambrangrill, including the bloody parchment with crosses on it which had been found beside his mummified body in a crevice of that very wall, where he had crept to die of his wounds, while the cat waited outside.

Now Gradgnag himself was there. He had crossed the wall, the ditch, the giant road shining like malachite. He had seen horseless coaches, one hundred and twenty feet high, thundering past with the noise of stampeding elephants; gargantuan men innumerable, like trees walking; dogs thirty feet tall. He had hidden and scouted and pondered over tracks. By day he had sat philosophically at his minute fire, cooking rashers of rat. Now he had found the Eldorado. He was at the House itself. He was tucked up comfortably in his sleeping bag on a branch of Virginia creeper on its wall, beside a pointed window, and six piebald mouse skins were his pillow.

It was the Vicarage.

Thirty years before our story, in the time of the previous incumbent, this inconvenient mid-Victorian house had been full of happy people. Then no wheezing disapprover had hummed along its red-tiled corridors, but a merry old hunting parson had bustled to send port wine and jellies to anybody who had the faintest stomach ache in all his parish. Then about a dozen tumbling children, covered with mud from head to foot, had pursued in it the numberless delights of childhood. The eldest son had been a falconer, the second a stamp collector, the third, a tramping botanist, the fourth had owned a puppet show, the fifth had been a carpenter, and the sixth, a very young one, had kept white mice.

Even now, in the attics which Mr. Hater never visited, there was a jumble of dusty fishing rods and of stage props and of cabinets with well-set butterflies and of falcon's hoods, and heap on heap of shredded paper, which the mice —the once white mice who had escaped and mated with the gray ones—had used for generation after generation in their nests.

Gradgnag's sleeping bag was outside the study window. By craning his head, he could see Mr. Hater, and the room in which he sat.

The study was a gloomy place with wallpaper the color of mildew, and one small window, imitation Gothic, in the thick wall. The Vicar's hood, gown, and surplice hung on the door under his scout's hat, which he wore when he took the choirboys to their holiday camp in the summer, at a featureless and wind-swept beach on the East Coast. On the wall beside the door there was a group photograph of the Vicar and friends, at Sidney Sussex College, where he had been a high light in the Student Christian Movement. There were also two photographs of Pompeii and of Trajan's Column. The desk at which he was writing his sermon was of soap-colored wood, and the sermon pen was shaped like an oar, with the arms of Sidney Sussex on the blade. On the mantelpiece there was a china tobacco jar, with the same arms. Over the mantelpiece there was a picture of Sir Galahad, who had conducted a cart horse into a bramble bush, and gone broody there. The seating accommodation included two cane armchairs, which gave a bamboo roar at sitters, and a horsehair sofa which was so slippery that anybody who sat down immediately began to slide off. It was kept for the Confirmation Class, and caused them acute embarrassment.

Gradgnag was accustomed to all this by now, and would have settled to sleep, so that he might be fresh for the mouse hunting that evening, if he had not seen Miss Brown, on Cook's bicycle, come floating up the drive. She was an inhabitant of the Park, whose appearance was familiar to him, so he edged round to the window sill, to see what she was after.

Miss Brown waddled into the study without a word. Mr. Hater looked at her with suppressed hatred, for he disliked being disturbed in the mornings. She put a strong cardboard boot-box in front of him, on the desk. It was tied with several lashings of string and had holes in the lid as if for transporting caterpillars. She undid the string and lifted the lid cautiously, ready to slam it back. Gradgnag was high outside the window and could see into the box. There, pressed against the side in a corner and looking upward, was the rumpled and miserable Schoolmaster, helpless, scared, captive, uncertain whether to risk a smile.

The Vicar sat motionless, looking at the exhibit from behind his glasses, which reflected the light and hid the eyes, and the wrinkles on his thick neck gradually went brick red. He poked the Schoolmaster with his sermon pen, to make him move. He put back the lid with trembling fingers. He tied it up again. He produced a bottle of Ruby

Wine which was kept for the Bishop, from a cupboard, and
gave Miss Brown a whole glass.

The window was open at the top, so that the Trapper
could hear what they said.

Miss Brown related how she had surprised the deputation
late at night, when they had gone to relieve Maria, and how
she had missed several of them, and how she suspected that
there might be many more. She mentioned that these creatures were probably of fabulous value, better than any
treasure chamber, and that in any case the supposed treasures must have come from them. She suggested that Barnum
and Bailey, Lord George Sanger, or the Circus at Olympia
would offer many thousand pounds apiece, if they could
catch such oddities.

Mr. Hater breathed one word: "Hollywood."

They thought it over slowly, sipping the Ruby Wine.

"The money would have to be held in trust for Maria."

"There would be nothing to prove that the creatures had not been found at the Vicarage."

"If they are human it may be illegal to sell them."

"They are not human."

"Not one word must be breathed about this discovery, Miss Brown, for fear of competition. Nothing must be mentioned until they are safely trapped."

"The child refuses to say where they live."

"Perhaps we can get the information from the midget you caught."

"He will not answer questions."

"I hope you did not...punish Maria?"

"Although she bit my finger most savagely, Mr. Hater, positively like a wild animal, I never raised my hand to her."

"Very wise."

"It crossed my mind that as she knew where they were..."

"M-m-m-m. You have not locked her up?"

"She is in her room for the time being..."

"But can be set at liberty."

Miss Brown suddenly opened her bun face and let a kind of cackle out of it. It might have been the first time she had laughed in her life, and had a startling effect. Even the Vicar gave a wintry twinkle with his glass eyes.

"How fortunate," he said, "that she should visit them at night! The cloak of darkness, Miss Brown. She will never notice that she is being followed."

So they hurried off to Malplaquet, to arrange about Maria's liberty. But first Mr. Hater took the Schoolmaster

135

from the boot-box, which did not look too strong, and locked him in a metal cash-box which was used to store the offerings for the Society for the Propagation of Christian Knowledge.

Gradgnag only had to climb the creeper a little higher and to let himself down by the blind-cord. The key was beside the cash box. He was able to force it round. Miss Brown and the Vicar had scarcely reached the bottom of the village before their captive had been liberated. They were not at the North Front before the Schoolmaster and his deliverer had started the long trek home. Unfortunately, it would take them a couple of days.

Maria, meanwhile, was surprised to find that she was not to be punished for biting. She was more than surprised, she was astonished, when they gave her the favorite pudding for luncheon (chocolate custard) and said that Cook need not be sacked. When they told her at tea-time that she was a good girl and might visit her "dear little fairy friends" whenever she pleased, she was more than astonished, she was deeply suspicious.

When one comes to think of it, Miss Brown and Mr. Hater were pathetic creatures, not terrible ones. It was so long since they had forgotten about being young that they were powerless in Maria's hands They were in the strong position of being able to bully her, of course, but their weakness was that they had no idea that she was twice as bright as they were. "Parents," says the immortal Richard Hughes, who wrote the best book about children that was ever written, "finding that they see through their child in so many places the child does not know of, seldom realize that, if there is some point the child really gives his mind to hiding, their chances are nil."

136

"I wonder," said Maria to herself, several times that day.

For dinner they gave her lobster *à l'Americaine*, and a *bombe glacée*, after which she pretended that she was ready for bed.

Miss Brown retired early.

At midnight, Maria rose from her deceptive couch. She had lain on it religiously, to save up her energies, and was now in the pink of training. She went past Miss Brown's door, with a bit more noise than usual, and made her lengthy way to the Chestnut Avenue. At the bottom of this, she paused and turned round for a look, knowing, like a good Indian, that she would have a dark background for her own body, while anybody who followed would be outlined against the moonlit sky.

There they were, sure enough, actually in black cloaks.

Maria grinned and went her way.

The Wilderness had been a Japanese garden, or something of that sort, two hundred years before. It was now a labyrinth of rhododendrons, laurels, and assorted shrubs, with several useful features. One of these was that the original paths had become overgrown by the evergreens, but not entirely squashed out. There was generally a track of some sort, often as much as four feet high in clearance, like a tunnel, however much the leaves and branches met above that height. A person of ten could get along them fairly quickly, by shielding her face, while a person of later years was confronted by a swishy barrier from the chest up. Another advantage of the Wilderness was one which was shared by all jungles, and that was that a single traveler could get about in it more easily than two. When two people forced their way in single file, the branches, swinging back from the first of them, whacked the second in the face. There were other attractions. For instance, on account of the place having been abandoned to growth and wildness, it needed an expert to know which way the ghosts of paths were leading. It was like the Maze at Hampton Court, but worse: worse because the top of it was grown across with whipping branches.

Maria waited till she was sure they could not miss her trail, then plunged into the rustling gloom.

She did not go too far. After five minutes she sat down, and pricked her ears.

It was pleasant, listening to Miss Brown and the Vicar, as they fought each other among the dark and oval leaves. "Hush!" "There!" "This way!" "That way!" "You crackle." "No, I don't." "Which turn?" "M-m-m-m."

Half an hour later, knowing that they were soundly lost, Maria slipped away to bed.

In the morning she was as fresh as paint. Miss Brown, who turned up for breakfast looking pale, with a scratched eye and twigs in her hair, asked for a bowl of bread and milk. The Vicar, who called in time to say their grace, asked hollowly for brandy neat. Maria, thanking them for all their kindness, begged for permission to take out her lunch in sandwiches, and to go exploring. They rolled their watery eyes, grinned horribly, and wished her joy.

She went by Malplaquet-in-the-Mould to Maid's Malplaquet, turned left through the parishes of Gloomleigh, Marshland, and Malplaquet St. Swithin's, cut across the Northampton road for Bishop's Boozey and Duke's Doddery, skirted the famous fox covert at Monk's-Unmentionable-cum-Mumble, doubled back from Bumley-Beausnort to Biggle, and ate her sandwiches in the gorse patch on the

138

round barrow at Dunamany Wenches, overlooking the drovers' road to Ort.

Here she saw the sleuths go by.

Staggering with fatigue, quarreling about the route, red-eyed from lack of sleep, Miss Brown and the Vicar tracked her doggedly on. Miss Brown had blisters on both feet, and the long heel from one of her shoes had become detached, causing her to roll as she walked, like a ship of the line in the famous gale of 1703. The Vicar, who had corns, limped behind her in dejection, humming out at intervals that they ought to have turned left at Dumbledum-Meanly. Miss Brown, with her nose in the air, refused to listen, and Mr. Hater could be seen planning things he would like to do to her.

Maria finished her sandwiches and enjoyed the summer weather. All the farmers of Dunamany Wenches were saving their hay. All the farm laborers of Dunamany Wenches were doing the same thing, criticizing the judgment of the farmers. All the iron spikes were charging up the elevators in endless squadrons, carrying the captive grass to the ricks. All the swarth turners were crig-a-rig-a-rig-rig-a-rigging round the edges of the fields, throwing up their bow waves of hay. All the horse rakes were threading the swarths, giving a stately clang each minute, as they delivered the rakeful to its place. All the headmen, who did the difficult part, were swishing the great mounds which they had collected in the arms of a thing like a snowplow, to the right position. All the publicans in the Green Man at Muddle, in the Malplaquet Arms at Pigseaton, and in the Duke's Head at Biggleswesterleigh were tapping innumerable casks of bitter, which they knew would be required for the evening. Everybody everywhere was keeping a tight eye on His Majesty the Sun, for fear that He might take it into His head to thunder.

The sun, so far as that went, was in a tyrant's mood. He was burning so hard that Maria could almost see him twinkle, could almost see the javelins of radiation being hurled out in all directions, as he jingled and hammered away like a Siva with a thousand arms, on the cloudless anvil of the sky. She nearly panted as she lay there, on the sheep-nibbled grass, and her pursuers panted in good earnest, as they pottered off through Idiot's Utterly, High Hiccough, Malplaquet Middling, and Mome.

When they had disappeared, Maria dropped her nose into the thyme-smelling grasses; watched a stinking beetle, with wriggly tail and aromatic scent and shining armor, as he scuttled his way under some bird's-foot trefoil; and was shortly fast asleep.

In the afternoon, she woke in time to see them return. They were fifty yards apart, no longer on speaking terms, and this time the Vicar was in the lead. She hailed them and ran down the hill, to join the march. Somehow they did not seem too pleased to see her. They had to do their best to look delighted. She rallied their shattered energies with bright inquiries about their walk, and led them briskly home to dinner.

After dinner, which was of fresh salmon followed by ices, Maria left them spread out in the drawing room, and rested on her own bed until dark. But as soon as Miss Brown had retired, she got up and trotted past the door. She could hear the tyrant groan aloud as she went by. She found the Vicar hiding behind a statue of Psyche in the Assembly Room, where he had taken his shoes off and gone to sleep on sentry-go, and she had to cough to wake him up. Then, while he creaked with exhaustion at the effort of getting his swollen feet into the shoes once more, she set her course for the North Front, for a change, and went by the Beech Avenue instead of the Lime one.

This led her up the Arcadian Valley to the Newton Monument, which was a thing like Nelson's Column in Trafalgar Square, except that, instead of having a statue at the top, it had a small glass observatory with a broken telescope. A staircase led up the inside, which, being in memory of Newton, had exactly the same number of steps as there were days in the year.

Maria turned the rusty key, entered the darkness of the little hall, and hid behind the stairs.

Her detectives arrived soon after.

Gasping and hissing from their various corns and blisters, weaving with exhaustion, leaning against each other to keep upright, the Vicar and Miss Brown edged the door open feebly and stood whimpering at the stairs.

"How many steps?"

Three hundred and sixty-five, point two five six four."

"Civil?"

"Sidereal."

"Come," he said finally. "Excelsior! They may be worth a thousand pounds apiece."

"Excelsior," agreed Miss Brown. They tottered up the stairs.

When they were well away, Maria let herself out, locked the door behind her, and went back to bed.

In the morning, after an excellent breakfast of kedgeree,

she took a circumbendibus through the Wilderness, as it was important not to be visible from above, and reached the Newton Monument before noon.

Miss Brown was at the top of it, waving a petticoat out of the observatory window on the end of the telescope. The Vicar was at the bottom, hammering on the door and whining for help. As the park lands of Malplaquet were about twenty-five miles in circumference, and there was nobody left inside them except Cook, they had little hope of rescue. Horace Walpole had once described these grounds as "that Province which they call a garden."

Maria waited for some time, then carefully wriggled her way to the door, hidden by arches of rhododendron. She unlocked it softly, while the Vicar was still banging, and snaked into the shrubbery, to watch.

The Vicar and Miss Brown continued at their tasks till luncheon. Then, suddenly growing maddened beyond endurance, the former seized the door handle to shake it, as a punishment for its contumacy. Of course it opened at once. His hum of fury brought Miss Brown stumbling down the stairs.

Both prisoners assumed immediately that the door had been unlocked all the time. Each of them accused the other of not having tried to open it properly. When they at last dispersed in passion to their beds, they had determined to sleep it out till Doomsday, if necessary, whether Maria visited the hidden mannikins or not.

That will teach them, she thought, to let young children out of bedrooms, so that they can track them to the secret places of their friends.

CHAPTER

XVII

THESE matters were fun for Maria, and no doubt they were good for the characters of Miss Brown and of the Vicar, as well as being good for their physical training. But Maria had made the mistake of letting her amusements run away with her.

She had forgotten her outposts, a thing which no general ought to do.

The People were in a worse muddle than the Vicar was, because she had failed to explain what she was at.

They did not know where their Schoolmaster was—they thought he was still a prisoner in the palace—and, from the few glimpses which they had caught of Maria's wanderings, they had got the idea that she was trying to escape her persecutors, but that she had been followed and brought back.

Maria ought to have gone to the island to explain, so soon as she knew that her pursuers had given in for the sake of rest; but she had been tired too. She rested, pleased with the lesson which she had given.

In the evening, when Miss Brown and the Vicar had partly recovered, they sat before the fire in the North-northeast Drawing Room, with Maria sitting between them on the sofa. They were determined to keep her with them all the time, so that she could not snatch a rest between times on her own. The Vicar was showing her his photograph album.

It contained several photographs of the Lake District, together with picture postcards of Wordsworth, Ruskin, and other worthies, with "A Present from Skiddaw" printed underneath. The portrait of Wordsworth had small views set round in panels, depicting a field of daffodils, forty cows feeding like one, etc., etc. There was a view of the Vicar and Miss Brown halfway up the Old Man of Coniston, and there was a photograph of some ladies bathing at Ramsgate in 1903 with the horizon at thirty degrees; but he hid it. All the pictures which were not of Wordsworth had their names and dates written under them in white ink: "Noodles, Pribby, Poo-Poo, me, and Mr. Higgins. Ambleside '36," or "Nurse Biggleswade (and dog). Kendal '38."

On the other side of Maria sat Miss Brown, knitting. She had long, sharp, metal needles, which clicked.

The fire was a small one, because it was summer. It was for ornament, not use. The room was comfortably furnished. The electric light shone cheerfully on the deep chairs and the coffee things, for it was after dinner, and the Vicar kept turning his pages with a rustle. He told them which was the window of the bedroom in the hotel which he had slept in, as if he had been Queen Elizabeth.

They were at Keswick when the noise began.

Outside the window, the acorn drums started to roll, the pipes began to shrill, and hundreds of clear, high voices began to sing together boldly.

> "And shall the Schoolman die?
> And shall the Schoolman die?

Five Hundred Men of Lilliput
Will know the reason why."

They had come to the rescue of their countryman, whatever the odds against them might be.

The moment the Vicar heard the song strike up, he grabbed Maria by a pigtail. Miss Brown grabbed the other one.

The window was behind them.

There she sat, unable to look round, and, from outside, the rescuers could not see that she was held. The back of the sofa hid everything except her head.

The Vicar rose to the situation.

He said, between his teeth, without looking round: "Miss Brown, please rise to your feet in a nonchalant manner, and saunter to the door. When you are out of sight of the window, you might peep from behind the curtains. Remember that the electric light is behind."

She gave him the other pigtail, and slunk off as instructed, on her mission.

It was a wonderful scene which she described.

The army was lined up, where the bars of light fell from the window across the terrace. There were the infantry in mouseskins standing at attention, their officers, in beetle breastplates, standing three paces to the front, with swords unsheathed. There were the cavalry, with the Admiral at their head—waving his saber and dressed in one of the ancient dresses of Captain John Biddel, so that he looked like Nelson. As with all Admirals, he sat his rat badly. There also were the archers, with their left feet forward as if they had been at Agincourt. Behind these, in orderly ranks, stood the Mother's Union, the Ladies Loo Club, the Bluestockings, and other female organizations, all singing lustily and waving banners, which stated: "Votes for Maria," "Down with Miss Brown," "No Algebra without Representation," "Lilliput and Liberty," "No Popery" (this was for the Vicar), or "Schoolmasters Never Shall Be Slaves." The A.D.C.'s were cantering up and down with messages; the bugles were blowing; the drummer boys were beating to quarters; the regimental standards were uncased; the band had changed over to "*Malbroock s'en va-t-en guerre*"; the swords and pikes and harpoons were flashing in the golden light; and, even as Miss Brown peeped, a flight of arrows was discharged against the window "as it had been snow." "Huzza!" cried the infantry. "Death or Glory," cried the cavalry. "The Admiral expects..." cried the Admiral, but when one of the A.D.C's had whispered to him behind his hand, he quickly changed it to the better phrasing: "Lilliput Expects That Every Man This Day Will Do His Duty."

Poor little forlorn hope! They lacked the wise counsels of their kidnaped dominie, who would certainly have shown them that the odds against them were too great, but it was brave of them to come to save him all the same.

After the Governess had described all this from her spy hole, the Vicar said: "M-m-m-m."

"I will trouble you," said he later, "to extinguish the electric light.

"And now that we are in the dark," he added, "you will kindly shut and latch the window."

When this was done, they sat down on either side of Maria, each gripping a pigtail, and Mr. Hater hummed.

"This time," said he, "there must be no mistake."

"No confusion."

"Our object, I presume, is to impound as many of these
146

minnikins as possible, for future profit. How shall we set about it?"

"Might I offer a suggestion?"

"What?"

"The minnikins, as you so ably dubbed them, are, as I know from sad experience, armed with such minnified weapons as, though fragile, can make a painful puncture."

"The fact had not escaped me."

"Grabbing by handfuls, if we leave aside the fact that hands when full would hold but few at best, might seem an occupation comparable to catching porcupines?"

"M-m-m-m-m."

"But with a broom, rapidly brushing all before us, they tumbling upside down and separated from us by a lengthy handle, we might roll up a regiment or two without mishap, and clap a bucket on them?"

"Bravo, Miss Brown! We find these brooms and buckets, creep out by different routes, you west, I east. We take the line in flank, one at each end, and sweep toward the middle. Their limbs, though bruised, will not be permanently harmed by bristles. They, in confusion, tumbled up and over, will prove unable to deploy their weapons...."

"We with our brooms and buckets...."

"Saucepans...."

"Anything with lids...."

"Collect our spoils! And sell 'em! But first, the child must be disposed of."

They winked at each other for some time over Maria's head, which she had to keep down because they were pulling her hair so, and made wide mouths or big eyes or complicated gestures, in their efforts to discuss the plan. Finally they nodded agreement.

147

"Our cherub," said the Vicar sarcastically, summing up the winks, "must be conducted to her chamber, there locked in. I will assume this pleasant duty. You, Miss Brown, shall look for suitable receptacles, me being absent. Come, dear child, your arm."

He was dragging her out in the dark, still by the pigtails, when Maria opened her mouth to yell. It was her last chance to warn the people about the brooms.

But the Vicar could see in the dark, like a cat. Before she could make a sound, his puffy hand was clapped across her mouth. They went in silence.

In the bedroom, her captor proved to be a thoughtful scoundrel. He threw her on the bed with a wheeze, and stood in the middle of the linoleum, tapping his teeth with one blunt fingernail.

"Our pet," said he, "is not without intelligence, indeed resource. Merely to lock the door would be to leave her practically at liberty. Now, let me see. Firstly, the troops are camped before the window, although some stories down. We therefore shut the window, so, and to secure the catch, m-m-m-m, we bend the metal with this poker, thus, using a grown-up's strength, and still remembering to remove the poker when we leave. Just so. No child will shift it now, especially without the poker. Next we pause, consider. For instance, a resourceful maiden, m-m-m-m, standing well lighted at a window, though unopened, might by some sign or gesture warn our quarry. We therefore draw the electric bulb from out its socket, thus—the merest twist removes it—and we find: why, that the room's in darkness! No amount of clicks upon the switch, manipulated by those childish fingers, will now illumine Lilliput. What more? Locked in, unlighted, windowless, high up....I think we may withdraw. Sleep well, Maria."

148

She listened to the key being turned in the lock, and waited tensely while the Vicar chuckled out of hearing. Then she leaped off the bed like an arrow, took the water jug from the washstand, and threw it through the window. So far as bending catches went, she was not the fool he thought her.

The glass went outward with a jangling crash, followed, long after, by a thump as the enameled ewer hit the terrace. This thump was in the middle of a tinkling shower of musical meteors, made by the falling glass. There was a thin high shout from all the army down below.

She leaned out from the hole and yelled,

"Go away! They are coming from different doors, with brooms, to sweep you up. Don't go together. Scatter. Everybody go his own way, till you meet at home. Go quick! They are coming now!"

She could hear them shouting back, so narrow a sound, but she could not hear the words.

"Yes, I am safe. Quite safe. I am free. But go! Go at once! Spread! Run! If anybody is followed, don't lead them to you-know-where. Stand still, as if they were owls. They will miss you. But go, run, every way, not all together! I am safe. They won't hurt me. They want to track me till I lead them to you. The Schoolmaster is not here."

"And, by the way," screamed Maria, for they seemed to be fading already, "don't bring me food! They feed me now! And don't expect me in the evenings!"

She ended on a positive shriek, for fear that she would not be heard, just as Miss Brown and her Führer came charging up the terrace.

Too late.

XVIII

THEY came upstairs with livid faces. The Vicar's was plum-colored with rage and with the climb; Miss Brown's was pallid, with scarlet nostrils. They were almost too furious to speak. They had heard what she was shouting through the window. They replaced the electric light bulb and sat down.

"Maria," said Miss Brown, "listen to Mr. Hater."

The Vicar said: "These dwarfs are worth a fortune in cold money. Do you understand? They are worth enough money to make you a rich girl, and to give an old age of peaceful security to poor Miss Brown here, who is always doing her best for you. I do not mention myself. Where do they live?"

Maria looked at him.

"Do you understand that if they could be sold, the shameful debts of your ancestors would be paid off to many a ruined tradesman, and Malplaquet rescued from disgrace?"

"I thought they were being paid from your allowance."

"You are a wicked girl. Where do they live?"

She folded her hands.

"Maria, you are to tell the Vicar where they live."

"I won't."

"Do you understand that it is evil to look God's mercies in the face? You are throwing the gift horse in His mouth.

God has sent these creatures to help us in our difficulties, and by your thankless stubbornness you are giving an insult to God. Where do they live?"

She shut her lips.

Miss Brown stood up and came waddling to stand over her.

"You are a naughty girl. You are impertinent. You had better tell the Vicar, or you will regret it. You know what I mean."

When there was no answer to this, or to anything else, Mr. Hater lost patience. He did not even want to hurt Maria, he was so hot with avarice. He wanted the People.

"If you will not tell, you will be locked up. Do you hear? Locked up without your dinner. And punished. Punished till you do tell. Such obstinacy is sinful, monstrous. It is selfish. You are a naughty, wicked, stubborn, selfish girl!

"Very well," he said, when there was no reply. "She can stay in this room till she speaks, and you, Miss Brown . . ."

The Governess said: "Cook comes to this room, Mr. Hater, and there might be talk."

"Then she must be locked in some other room, where Cook won't come, and we must say that she has gone away."

"To stay with an aunt."

"That will do very well. What room do you suggest?"

"There is always," said Miss Brown most sweetly, "the dungeon."

Everybody ought to know the dungeon at Malplaquet, the one which historians have mentioned in so many works. It was an excavation extending backward in time, far beyond the First Duke, far into the misty past which saw the Tower of London rise.

The Duke's ancestors had been some Nova Scotia bar-

onets, who had dwelt since the days of James I in an ancient
Norman castle, which had once stood on some of the ground
that was now covered by the ballroom floor. They had
fallen out with Cromwell, who had blown the castle up,
and the Duke had used the stones when he started to erect
his palace, pulling down the rest. The only parts which he
had been unable to pull down had been the dungeons,
for they had been down already. So he had left them
for wine cellars, keeping the main one in its original state.
He had thought it a curio, owing to its being Gothick.

It was lit by red light, through a small window which had
crimson glass, in a wall about twenty feet thick. The window was barred, and the effect of the color on the stone
arches of the Norman roof was better than anything in the
Chamber of Horrors.

The furniture, where it was not red, was coal black. It
consisted of instruments of torture, which had not been sold
at the sale, because there had been no demand for them.
The floor was covered with rushes, except where sand or
sawdust were needed, to soak up blood.

In one corner stood the Rack: the improved pattern, per-
fected by the villain Topcliffe. Written on the side of it, in
vermilion letters, were the awful words of the warrant to
torture poor Guido Fawkes:

PER GRADUS AD IMA.

The opposite corner held a German instrument called the
Virgin of Nuremberg, which consisted of an upright coffin,
shaped like a woman. Its lid opened like a door, and was
covered with six-inch spikes, arranged so that they would
run into people at various places when they stood inside
the coffin and the door was shut.

A third corner held the machine known as the Manacles, which happened to be the one on which Peacham had been tormented in 1614, in the presence of Francis Bacon—when he had been examined "before torture, in torture, between tortures, and after torture." Its inscription said:

PAINE IS GAINE.

The fourth corner held the Block. It was black like the others, but covered with a pall of scarlet velvet. When this was lifted, the scars in the wood could be seen, where the ax had bitten deep. The ax itself lay across the pall, a ruby flash of steel, and this was the very one which had been used to decapitate King Charles I. It had been wielded by Richard Brandon—or "Young Gregory," as he had been called, to distinguish him from his father, "Old Gregory," who had also been an executioner. The same sure hand had used the same ax on Strafford, Laud, Holland, Hamilton, and Capel, all lords, and little can these martyrs have paused to reflect how lucky they were, to get the job done by an artist who took himself seriously. For Young Gregory had trained from earliest childhood, by chopping off the heads of stray cats. It was not so with that scoundrel Ketch, who took five whacks to decapitate the unfortunate Duke of Monmouth, and even then he had to finish him off with a penknife.

Next to the ax, in a small crystal casket, there was half the fourth cervical vertebra of King Charles, the other half having been stolen from the King's coffin in 1813, by a doctor called Sir Henry Halford.

Across the casket, somebody had engraved the famous quotation:

In the middle of the main wall, opposite the massy door, there was an enormous fireplace, for heating branding irons. Opposite the window, in the darkest recess, there was a pile of thighbones, skulls, and so forth.

Prisoners had scratched their last remarks upon the walls. The Little Princes, who were finished off at Malplaquet and not in the Tower, had written "Adiew," "Adeiw." A witch had inscribed, before they burned her, "I come, Graymalkin," and some homesick Scot, tired by too much thumbscrew, had suggested: "East, Quhest, Hame Ys Best." An anonymous villein had written: "yis hurte me mo than it hurtës yow."

They dragged Maria struggling to the gloomy chamber, a secure hold which Cook would never dream of searching, and they actually chained her with one of the handcuffs, when they remembered her resourcefulness with the water jug. Of course they did not intend to use the instruments of torture on her, but they did intend to find out where the People lived.

"If," said the Vicar finally, looking at her with a thoughtful hum, "the child insists on being sullen, she must be punished till she speaks. Naughty children should be whipped."

CHAPTER

XIX

THE Professor was sitting at the end of his vegetable garden, under a marble monument to the Tragic Muse. He was chopping wood. The other side of the monument was to the Comic Muse, so that he had two wide mouths above his head, one laughing and the other howling. It was to Congreve, or to somebody of that sort. The Professor was chopping with a sixpenny hatchet from Woolworth's, where he did his shopping, and he had a one-and-threepenny metal hacksaw beside him, counting the cost of blades, with which he had managed to fell a small blackthorn for firing. His head was buzzing with schemes.

The first scheme was to work his passage to London as a bus conductor, where, perhaps, they might be likely to have a set of Du Cange in the British Museum Reading Room. In connection with this scheme, he was certain that 𝕮𝖗𝖎-𝖕𝖍𝖆𝖗𝖎𝖚𝖒 meant either "trefoliated" or else "tripartite"; but the trouble was that the manuscript could bear either construction, with different results.

The second scheme was, to save up until he could afford a penny fishhook, and then to ask permission from Maria to fish in the lakes at Malplaquet. His mouth watered at the thought of the fishes he might catch—perch perhaps—and

156

of how he would eat them grilled, on slices of bread and butter. He could not afford to buy a rod or line, but he was planning to use a sapling of ash, with some string from a parcel which he had once received, tied to the end, and the only difficulty was to save up a penny for the hook. He felt so greedy when he thought of the hot perch that he almost decided to sell one of his first-folio Shakespeares, to get the money.

The third scheme was about making some parsnip wine in the kitchen copper.

The fourth was about touching the Vicar for a testimonial, so that he could go to Buckingham Palace and ask to be made Prime Minister. He felt sure that a person who ruled the whole nation would be expected to be an educated man, and, as he had been educating himself for the last sixty years, he thought that there would probably be a chance of getting the job. He argued that people who had spent their lives leading revolutions, or killing other humans, or howling out lies on election platforms, could have had very little time for education, and thus that his own weary life of study might have put him ahead of them in this respect.

Perhaps the maddest of his schemes was that, when he had been made the Premier, he would choose educated people to be his ministers, just as one chooses a trained dentist to pull one's teeth out, instead of going to the nearest quack at a street corner who likes to scream from the top of a tub that he "opposes toothache." The Professor was silly enough to think that if doctors had to pass examinations before they could cut out his appendix, then members of parliament ought to pass examinations before they could rule his life.

He was well mixed up with all these schemes when the garden gate was pushed open, and Cook appeared. She was dressed in a brownish-gray alpaca dress, with a serviceable hat pinned on, and she carried a Rexine shopping bag which bulged. She was on her best behavior, but determined to do her duty. She had sadly left her beloved Captain at home, with tears on both sides, because she knew that the Professor did not get on with dogs.

He stopped his chopping and hurried along the path between the currant bushes, looking hungrily at the Rexine bag. As he came, he cried out joyfully: "Ah, Mrs. Noakes, good day, good day! You are welcome to the Ridings! Pray do not ring the bell! It does not ring! We are enjoying very seasonable weather! Yes, yes! Some small fault in the mechanism, I believe! I must buy a gong! It is due to the sun being in Aries!"

Cook said: "There now."

"I assure you that I am correct. The Zodiac ... But I am leaving you to stand upon the doorstep without a welcome. We must enter the cottage before embarking on abstruser themes. Let me see. Just so. The door is locked, we notice."

"I only come, Sir, if you please, on account of what I was desirous ..."

"But love laughs, Mrs. Noakes, ha! ha! at locksmiths. I have my own methods, Watson, that is, er, Mrs. Noakes. The pot of geraniums! Whenever I lock myself out of my cottage, I am careful to conceal the means of ingress in a place known only to myself. Now, Mrs. Noakes, if you will kindly look the other way for just one moment, I will extract the key from under this pot of geraniums, where I keep it for secrecy, you see, and we shall be inside the edifice before we can say Tom Robinson. Tom? Perhaps I am thinking of Crusoe. But even then we ought to call him Kreutznaer. The idiom I am attempting is that we are likely to be there in half a Nippy."

Cook said that she was sure she did not wish to intrude upon a gentleman, knowing, as she hoped, what was due to such, and being able from a girl to observe her station. ...

The Professor said that it was no intrusion at all, none, in fact a pleasure, an unexpected pleasure, and that, if she could just wait for a moment or so while he tried the key the other way up, as it was, he feared, inclined to be recalcitrant, there was no doubt but what, with a little humoring—

which he pronounced without the "H"—a favorable entry would be effected....

Cook said that she trusted not to make herself an Imposition, being as how as which it would go just as well outside....

"There! It requires, as you see, a simple sleight of hand. The key has to be inserted *upside down*, and *back to front*, owing to some anomaly in the formation of the lock, and then it all goes as smoothly as, as..."

"Smooth."

"Exactly. And now, Mrs. Noakes, you must step in from the sunlight. You have walked far and fast. Let me see...

"I fear," he continued coyly, "that I am unable to offer you a cup of tea, as I have finished the packet; but there is some excellent boiling water, which can be procured at a moment's notice, by igniting some of these pieces of wood that I have been making, and..."

It was true that he could not offer her the tea, for he had finished the last teaspoon a week before, but it was hardly straight to offer the hot water. He would have had to offer it to anybody else, and he would have done so, but this was not his first visit from Cook. He stood on one leg, looking anxiously at the shopping bag, and continued to say "and..."

"Well, there now, Sir! If I did not fortunately think to bring..."

He sighed happily.

"...knowing your 'Abits..."

And Mrs. Noakes vanished into the dirty kitchen with her bag, while the Professor peeped through the crack of the door in an agony of anticipation. The whole thing was whether she had brought bloaters or sausages. She always brought one or the other, and today he felt like bloaters. He knew that she would make some tea, out of a screw of paper, and that she would have remembered a bottle of milk and six lumps of sugar, with two buns baked by herself. These were delicious. But, afterward, she always left behind a packet in greased paper, which was either bloaters or sausages, as if she had forgotten it. The Professor never mentioned the packet any more than she did, nor thanked her for it: either because he was too proud, or too shy, or too grateful to thank her properly. He just ate them next day. Meanwhile, he wanted badly to know which it was; but he did not like to ask, could not see through the crack, and was rather ashamed of peeping. So he went back to sit on the soapbox and swallowed rhythmically, because his mouth was watering.

When Cook had made them an excellent cup of tea, and they had eaten their buns, sitting side by side on the box, she mentioned the reason for her visit. It was that here Miss Maria, Sir, on account of which she was anxious of, being as how there was neither sign nor parable of her to be seen these two days, as which the one what he knowed of, to wit, Miss Brown, though not accustomed to name names, the same what she had referred to notwithstanding, had, though not in the 'Abit of discussing her employers with the Gentry, as the Professor might be sure, on account of her having been bred at Malplaquet from a girl under Mrs. Batterby that was housekeeper to the late Duke, seemingly, if uncharitable to Nourish Suspicions yet Truth will shame the Devil, provided some haction against her, the poor mite, as might be detrementious in a manner of speaking.

The Professor, who had begun to think of other matters while she was talking, noticed from the silence which followed that it was his turn to say something. He observed resourcefully: "Just fancy!" He had a secret plan for conversations, which consisted in saying either that or else "You don't say so!", both of which were foolproof, and could be used in answer to any statement whatever.

Cook said it was a rare shame, and she had been in such a taking since Friday morning as how she scarcely knew which way to turn, what with the goings on and all, and that here Vicar, for you can't make a silken purse out of a sow's ear, not though the Archbishop of Canterbury were to lay his hands on, which she doubted, so it had seemed best that morning, while she was a washing of the dishes, to put the matter before them as was a gentleman born, which you could see was what the Professor was of the stock of, as she would say and had said to any that miscalled him, and to leave the matter in his hands, being as how as which he would surely know what was rightful for to be done.

A sudden suspicion darted across the Professor's mind. Cook had been saying ... Surely he had heard ... Something about ...

"Where is Maria?" he demanded.

"That's what I'd give a deal to know. I hant clapped eye on her this two days."

"Good gracious!"

"She's gone, Sir," said Cook tearfully. "My Maria. And I always tried to help her little ways."

"My dear Mrs. Noakes, but this is most extraordinary! A serious business. Gone? Clapped eye? She cannot have become invisible. Could she be in bed? Under the bed? Up a chimney? At the seaside? Lost? Mislaid somewhere or other? Can she have gone to London? To the British Museum?"

"That Governess of hers give out that she were gone to visit with an auntie, but no auntie has she got."

"And what do you suspect?"

"She's in the Palace, yet, Sir. That I'd swear to. But hid. Locked up. She's in her durance vile."

"Dear me. You will, of course, have searched?"

"There's rooms, Sir, more than mortal man has counted. I done me best, a-bicycling along the corridors and ringing of my bell."

"Well, Mrs. Noakes, you rightly came to me. I will assume the search at once. Some matters are best relegated to the sterner sex. Dear me, dear me! Our poor Maria scotched. Wait till I fetch my hat."

The old gentleman hurried upstairs, and returned after some time in a tweed ulster smelling of camphor, with a curious bowler which he had worn as a dandy in the nineties. It had a curly brim. He had to wear the ulster when visiting, however hot it was, in order to cover the holes in his clothes.

"We will attack," said he, "this governess in her den. You, Mrs. Noakes, had best return in front of me, using some other path. It would be wise if I might seem to come by chance, inquiring for Maria. We must be exceedingly politic."

He bustled her outside the cottage, promising to give her ten minutes' start, and pushed her off, along the Riding. Two minutes later, he had caught her up.

"Oh, Mrs. Noakes, excuse me for a moment. You would not have, about you, that is, at your home perhaps, a set of Du Cange?"

"Well, no, Sir. That I hant. There's Beeton . . ."

"You refer to the second archbishop of that name, no

doubt. Certainly not the Cardinal. The others were un-clerkly, as we know."

"It's cooking, Sir."

"Indeed? An ancient and a noble art. A continuator of the Goodman, I daresay. But still, you have no volumes of Du Cange?"

"Not that I know of, Sir."

"A pity. Well, well, well, we can't have everything. But I am keeping you. Good-by, good-by."

After another minute he had caught her up again.

"The word," he said hopefully, "is 𝕿𝖗𝖎𝖕𝖍𝖆𝖗𝖎𝖚𝖒. You have not come across it in the course of reading, I suppose?"

"Not as I recollect, Sir, no, I haven't."

"No. Ah, well. We must possess our souls in patience, Mrs. Noakes. The '𝕴,' of course, is optional, as scribes would use their vowels more or less to fancy. '𝕿𝖗𝖎𝖕𝖍𝖆𝖗𝖎𝖚𝖒,' with a '𝕯,' would do as well?"

"There's tripe . . ."

"Tripe," cried the Professor angrily, "is a Gaelic word. Nothing to do with tripe at all. Good day to you. Good day."

And he stalked off in a huff, until he remembered the parcel in the kitchen. This made his anger melt, and he turned to wave to his kind friend if he could, but she did not look back. Then, to give her the start, he hurried back to investigate the parcel itself. It was bloaters, as he had hoped!

He forgot about Maria and began looking up "bloaters" in a dictionary, to see if they were derived from the Swedish word "blöt," which they were.

CHAPTER

XX

AN hour later the Professor tried to scratch his head, found that the hat was in his way, and wondered why he had put it on. He made several attempts to solve this problem, by free suggestion and self-analysis, finally deciding that he had put it on because he was going out. He therefore went out, and looked at the sky. It did not seem to have any message for him. So he went in again, found a piece of paper, and wrote on it the first word which occurred to him while concentrating on hats. This was 𝕿𝖗𝖎𝖕𝖍𝖆𝖗𝖎𝖚𝖒. He tore it up and tried again, getting RATTO, which he thought was probably something to do with Bishop Hanno and the rats. So he tried HANNO and got WINDUP, tried WINDUP and got CAPE, tried CAPE and got ULSTER. He discovered that he was wearing his ulster, and was delighted. This was followed by a longish tour through the provinces of Ireland, the Annals of the Four Masters, and so forth, which brought him back to 𝕿𝖗𝖎𝖕𝖍𝖆𝖗𝖎𝖚𝖒. He tried this, and got BLOATERS, which he connected by now entirely with Sweden, took a short circuit through GOTHENBURG, SWEDENBORG, BLAKE, and GUSTAVUS ADOLPHUS, and suddenly remembered that he was pledged to find Maria. So he balanced the bottle-green bowler still more carefully upon his head, and trotted off to do his duty.

It was a basking day.

The trees trapped the heat until the Ridings were long ovens, the ulster was unbearably hot, the bees droned like aircraft in the sticky leaves of the lime trees, the swallows who had built nests on south walls fanned their babies and gasped for breath, the grass snakes were out in force, making life a misery to the frogs, and the frogs themselves were committing suicide by dozens, under the wheels of any passing motor. The Professor toiled away into the distance, a small industrious beetle under the copper sky, getting smaller and smaller as he plodded off toward Malplaquet.

He was not sure what to do.

To search the Palace legally, as he knew from his studies, he would require several writs of *Habeas Corpus*, together with a *De Heretico Comburendo* or so, and perhaps a *Non Compos Mentis*. On the other hand, he also knew that it was possible for two or three people to ramble about in the various corridors for several weeks, without meeting each other; so that there seemed little reason why he should not search in an unofficial way, because nobody was likely to notice whether he was there or not. The easiest thing would have been to find Miss Brown, to face her down, and to demand the release of her pupil. Unfortunately, he had no real proof that Maria was still in the house, and, besides, he was afraid of the Governess. She had once been very rude to him, and he was afraid that the facing down might happen the other way round. He felt unhappy, and tried to cool himself as he went, by waving his hat.

When he had passed the Grecian Amphitheater, and the sixty-foot pyramid in honor of General Burgoyne, the Valley of Concord opened before him, as Capability Brown had always intended that it should, and there was the vast bulk of the mansion at the end of it. Wren, Vanbrugh, Hawksmoor, Kent, and the rest of them had erected its dozen colonnades; Adam, Patrioli, and others had plastered its hundred ceilings; Sheraton, Heppelwhite, Chippendale, etc., had stuffed it with furniture, since sold; and there it lay before the Professor in the evening sunlight, with more rooms than anybody could remember.

He let himself in by a ruined door in the west wing, and began to search.

He searched the Gothick Billiard Room—which had once held a table as big as a swimming bath, and which still had the coat armor of all Maria's ancestors painted on the imitation wooden tracery of the ceiling. The central achievement had been kindly provided by Horry Walpole, and it had 441 quarterings, including the arms of Boadicea and Herod Antipas. All the bends were sinister and all the wives were on the wrong side of their husbands.

He searched the Orangery, where Gibbon had scratched out a semicolon in the famous last paragraph of *The Decline and Fall of the Roman Empire*, before presenting the eighth volume to the Duke of Gloucester—who had observed affably: "Another damned thick book! Always scribble, scribble, scribble! Eh, Mr. Gibbon?"

He searched the Menagerie, where the Earl of Chesterfield had once been locked by mistake for two days as a monkey, and a pity they did not keep him there for good.

He searched the Chinese Parlor, into which Rousseau had suddenly rushed in 1768, when he had indignantly read out an interminable and incomprehensible letter from himself to Diderot, leaving all hearers completely stunned.

He searched the Rent Room, where the Wicked Earl had once run his estate agent through the body—the former claimed during his trial by the Lords that it had been in a duel, but the agent still walked on Tuesday nights, with the hilt of the sword in the small of his back, which was a good argument to the contrary.

He searched the Chart Room, where one of the viscounts, an admiral, had been accustomed to keep his sextant and other instruments, on retiring from the service after having lost Majorca, Minorca, Bermuda, Goa, Simla, Hecla, and Alabama, in a series of naval engagements.

He searched the Gun Room, out of whose window the Duke of Orleans had been accustomed to shoot larks with the corks from champagne bottles.

He searched the Fertilizer Room, where the Master of Malplaquet, who had invented three separate potato grubbers, had been accustomed to store enormous quantities of Hypersuperextrainfraphosphates, for the use of his tenant farmers.

He even searched the State Room, in which Queen Victoria had held the only Drawing Room ever held outside a royal castle, and in it there was the very chair in which she had sat, with a glass lid over the seat, to preserve the royal imprint.

The Professor lifted the lid and sat down himself, for he was beginning to feel tired.

Then he got up with a sigh and went upstairs to the Clock Room in the pediment of the North Front, which had a clock made by Christopher Pinchbeck II, which played "When the Heart of a Man Is Depressed with Cares," in four parts, one at each quarter—people got over it in time, and stopped listening.

His quarry was not there.

The Professor began to lose his head, and to hurry from one floor to another, as the different ideas occurred to him.

He searched the Butler's Strong Room, which had at various times held the Derby, Grand National, and Ascot gold

168

cups, as well as an épergne in the shape of a banyan tree which had been presented to the Sixth Duke by the grateful inhabitants of Bombay.

He tried the stables for 144 horses, the kennels for 144 hounds, the attics for 144 abigails or footmen, and the Card Room, where Charles James Fox had once lost £144,000 in a single night, wearing scarlet heels to his shoes and blue powder on his wig.

He even tried the Armory, which had once housed the accoutrements of the Third Duke's Own Northampton-shire Fencibles—and also a party of visitors who had been mislaid while being shown round the Palace, in aid of charity, by a forgetful butler, in 1915.

His hostage was nowhere to be seen.

The poor Professor sat down on the bare floor of the Armory for a second rest. Then he pulled himself together for a final effort, and searched afresh.

He searched the Pavilion, where an absent-minded Lord Dudley had once invited Sydney Smith to dinner with the remark: "Dine with me today, and I will get Sydney Smith to meet you"—to which Mr. Sydney Smith had courteously replied that he was engaged to meet him elsewhere.

He searched the Colonnade, where the great Pope himself had walked with William Broome, on the night when he was persuading the latter to persuade Tonson to publish a letter from Lintot, signed however by Cleland, and pur-porting to have been written by Bolingbroke, in which Lady Mary Wortley Montagu was accused of having sus-pected a Mr. Green of persuading Broome to refuse per-mission to Tonson to publish a letter by Cleland, purporting to have been signed by Lintot, without the knowledge of Bolingbroke, about the personal habits of Dr. Arbuthnot, under the pseudonym of Swift. (On the other hand, a person named Worsdale, a mere tool, calling himself R. Smythe, was to tell Curll that a certain "P. T.," a secret enemy of Temple, possessed a copy of the correspondence between Lord Hervey and Colley Cibber: with obvious results.)

He went out of doors at last, and searched the fountain which Boswell had once fallen into, to amuse the Great Lexicographer.

He even poked about under the equestrain statue of dapper little George II, seated on a horse with no girths, and for that reason perhaps the very one which had run away with him at Dettingen.

Maria was nowhere to be seen.

In the garden, the Professor observed Miss Brown on her knees, doing something venomous to a bed of geraniums. She was wearing a straw hat, wielding a trowel, kneeling on a carpet mat, and singing bitterly to herself. The Schoolmaster's escape had been discovered.

The Professor took off his green bowler, and said politely: "Excuse me, Miss Brown."

"Oh, it is you, is it. What do you want now?"

"Well...nothing. Thank you. I was just...walking round."

"You have a fine day for it," said she. "The gate is there behind."

"The gate? Oh, yes, I see. The gate for going away from. Yes...

"Well," he continued after a bit, "good-by, Miss Brown."

"Good-by."

"Good-by."

"And none of your Nosey-Parkering."

"What?"

"I said: None of your Nosey-Parkering."

170

"No, certainly not. No."

He turned his hat round several times, and added bravely: "The geraniums are red?"

"Do you want me," cried Miss Brown viciously, swinging round on her knees and pointing the trowel at him, "to set the Vicar on you? Go away. Shut the gate after you. What are you doing here?"

"I was ... calling on Maria."

"Then you can call elsewhere. She's gone away."

"To stay with an aunt?"

"Who told you so?"

"I ... I was guessing."

"She's gone away," said Miss Brown brutally, "to stay with her aunt on Timbuctoo, tee-hee! I suppose you won't be calling on her there? Buzz off, you bluebottle."

The Professor scuttled away while Miss Brown laughed atrociously, and the last he heard of her, as he closed the gate with trembling fingers, blushing all over, was when she settled down to sing some private words once more to her geraniums:

> "Down among the Dungeons,
> Down among the Dungeons,
> Down,
>   Down,
>   Down,
>   Down,
> Down among the Dungeons,
> Let
>   her
>   lie."

Incidentally, Miss Brown was fond of flowers, and would tell anybody who chose to listen that the Dear Little Roses were her greatest joy.

CHAPTER

XXI

T HE Professor walked home with tingling ears, inventing appropriate retorts which he could have made if he had only thought of them in time, and worrying about his friend. He felt certain that she could not have an aunt in Timbuctoo, not without being darkish, and he was distressed by the song which the Governess had been singing. It sounded suspicious, he thought, as if there had been something going on. He began remembering Berkley Castle, and the agonizing king.

All the same, he could not think of anything to do. He could search again tomorrow, of course. There were still plenty of larders, laundries, cupboards, closets, still rooms, coal cellars, outward rooms frequented in his early days by Dr. Johnson, servants' halls, sculleries, harness rooms, pantries, dairies, cloakrooms, storerooms, and so forth, even in the wing which he had already visited, and then there were the other wings as well. Taking cupboards alone, he calculated that there must be at least two thousand. But the danger was that he might arrive too late, however hard he searched. He wished that Miss Brown had not been looking so cruel.

When the Professor got home in the rosy twilight, with a wonderful sunset making the cottage windows flame, and

172

etching one of the obelisks to Admiral Byng in deepest ebony, he went straight to the kitchen and sniffed the bloaters. These cleared his mind, like smelling salts. He saw at once what he would have to do. He would have to get the help of the People. Where one old man might take many weeks in exploration, five hundred searchers working simultaneously, however small they were, would have the advantage.

It was dark when he started once more, for the moon had waned. He was distended with bloaters, at peace with the world, contented with his plan. As it was dark, he did not have to wear the curly bowler. He was thinking about this and that.

Now if the Professor had a vice at all, apart from his glass of dandelion wine, it was the fact that he had never cared for dogs. It was not that he thought them vulgar or mobbish, but rather that he disapproved of them for being dependent. He thought that people and animals ought to be free and wild, like falcons for instance, and he disliked dogs because they depended on their masters, in what he considered to be an undignified way.

It was the same with the People.

He could not see how beings who were only six inches high could hope to be independent, when they were associated with people who measured as many feet. This was why Maria had never been able to persuade him to visit the island. The very thought of going made him feel awkward. He felt, if you can follow the idea, that the fact of his visiting them would be an inroad on their proper freedom, because he was so much bigger than they were. He agreed with what Gulliver felt among the giants, that it would be better to die than to undergo "the Disgrace of

173

leaving a Posterity to be kept in Cages, like tame Canary Birds." In his heart of hearts, he disapproved of their association with Maria. It was, as the same writer has remarked, "upon such a Foot as ill became the Dignity of human kind." His idea was that respectable people ought not to be the masters of others, nor their slaves.

Now if I, thought he, as he pottered down the darkling ride toward the distant Quincunx, if I had my own choice of capturing one of the species mentioned by Gulliver, I would prefer to capture a Brobdingnagian. Think of the glory and the excitement of catching somebody who was as high as a church spire! But I wonder how high they really were? It says in the book that Glumdalclitch, who was nine years old, and little for her age, was only forty feet high. The Premier was "near as tall as the Mainmast of the Royal Sovereign." The horses were between fifty-four and sixty feet. Now a horse of sixteen hands is sixty-four inches high, so, if we do a sum by the unitary method, comparing sixty feet to sixty-four inches, we get the comparison that one inch of theirs would be about equal to one foot of ours. This would make the average Brobdingnagian some seventy-two feet high. Later in the book, it says that a Brobdingnagian on horseback measured ninety feet. That would be about four times as high as my cottage.

But the best comparison, continued the Professor enthusiastically, for at least he knew everything there was to be known about books, is that their largest Folio was not above eighteen or twenty feet long. It would be a Royal Folio, I suppose, which is twenty inches by twelve and one-half inches, and so we get the exact scale of one inch to one foot! They were twelve times as high as we are!

"Now if I were to stand on my own head twelve times,"

said he aloud, to the dark form of a beech tree, while the owls of Malplaquet hooted on every side, "I should be a good deal higher than you are."

The tree rustled.

"Well, then, suppose we wanted to capture one of these Brobdingnagians that was as tall as you, we should need a ship to reach the country (on the west coast of North America, somewhat above the Streights of Annian) and to bring the creature back. I wonder how deep the well is, in an oil tanker? Probably not deep enough to hold a beech tree without bumping its head. On the other hand, I do not think we should need to take the *Normandie* or the *Empress of Britain*. A P. and O. steamer of about twenty thousand tons would be big enough; or, better still, a middling sort of aircraft carrier. The advantage of having an aircraft carrier would be that we could disguise it as a rowing boat more easily, through its not having too many funnels and things, and that is what we should finally have to do.

"I would have to publish my Solinus, of course, to get the money, as they are probably expensive.

"And another splendid advantage of taking an aircraft carrier would be that we could carry an aircraft."

He resumed his journey, feeling pleased.

"When we got near to the Streights of Annian, we would make the aircraft fly away on a reconnaissance, and we would hang about ourselves, out of sight of the country of Brobdingnag, until we heard from the pilot, by wireless as I think they call it, that he had spotted one of these giants in a rowing boat by himself, out fishing.

"The Brobdingnagians do not fish much, because our sea fish are smaller than minnows to them, but sometimes they

175

do go fishing for whales. The giant would think our airplane was a large bird, I suppose, if he saw it.

"Well then, when we had a bearing on this lonely fisherman in his boat, we would clear our decks for action. Everybody would have to hide. We would steam up quietly from behind him, pretending to be drifting. When he saw us, he would give us a hail, taking us for a wherry of some sort, and then, when he got no answer, he would row round us once or twice, trying to make out what we were. We should have to leave an enormous cable hanging over the side, which he would take for a rope. After a bit, he would climb on board."

The Professor began to snap his fingers.

"Now this is where our previous arrangements would begin to come into action. We should have made a big lid in the flight deck, which slid like the sunshine roof on that motor car I once saw, and inside this lid there would be our huge cabin, filling the whole of that part of the ship, fitted up with a chair forty feet high and a table and a bunk to match! Of course, the Brobdingnagian would take the whole thing for the forecastle, or whatever they call it, of the wherry. And on the table we would have left a specially made loaf, twelve feet high, and a bottle of wine to scale!

"So the poor Brobdingnagian would shout out once or twice: 'Is anybody there?' And then he would climb down the outsize ladder, to investigate. He would be inquisitive.

"The moment he was inside, we would push a button—and snap would go the lid!"

The Professor pranced with satisfaction when he got to this; but suddenly he fell into a sober pace.

"We should have to see that this aircraft carrier was solid. He would be bound to bang a bit."

He thought it over for some time, considering how the plates would have to be riveted with bolts that were too small for the giant to move with his penknife, and then went on with his plan.

"After he had finished bumping and yelling, which might go on for several hours, he would begin to feel faint or miserable, and he would sit down at the table, to consider what to do. That would be the time when he would notice the food. So he would suddenly feel thirsty and decide to take a drink. Now here is where our cleverness would come in for the second time, for the wine would be drugged! Then the poor gaint would lie on the bunk, because his head was going round inside, and in five minutes he would be asleep. We should have to use mandragora.

"The moment we had him under hatches, we should have begun to steam away from Brobdingnag, after turning his boat adrift, and the moment he was asleep we should go down with the chains and handcuffs and leg irons. We could sling them from a crane or something of that sort, until he was properly done up. Then we should have to wait until he woke."

The Professor grew moody at this, and began to shuffle as he walked. He did not like the idea of chaining people, even when they were giants.

"Anyway, when he awoke, the captain would have to go down to the bunk, and he would walk up his chest, and he would tell him not to be afraid. We should have to have learned the language beforehand. Perhaps there is a book on it somewhere in the British Museum, like Du Cange ..."

He managed to escape from 𝔗𝔯𝔦𝔭𝔥𝔞𝔯𝔦𝔲𝔪 in the nick of time.

"We would tell him that he was a prisoner for the time

being, because we wanted to be safe ourselves, but also that we would not keep him prisoner forever. We would only keep him for one year, after which we would promise to take him home. And we would explain how we were carrying him to England in order to make our fortunes by exhibiting him, but that he would not be made to do anything undignified, and, if he would be friendly with us, we would be polite to him. All through the voyage we would feed him well, and talk things over in a reasonable way, and then, when we got to Southampton or wherever it was, we would free him enough to let him stand up, so that he could look out from the hatch. Then we would explain to him about antiaircraft guns, as they call them, and we would have one on the jetty, mounted in a lorry, and we would shoot down some balloons for him, so that he could see it work. We would say: 'We are going to free you altogether now. You are in England, thousands of miles away from home. You cannot get back, nor do much harm to us—for, after all, you are only as big as a tree—and we have weapons like this one here, which would do for you in no time. This is why we are setting you free. Now, Giant, if you will be sensible and walk with us to London without any bonds or indignity, we will take the Albert Hall for one year, for you to live in, and we will charge five shillings for a ticket to see you having your dinner every evening. We will not ask you to do any tricks, but only to let the people see you having dinner. Perhaps you will be kind enough to talk to them, in the various galleries, if you feel like it. We will feed you and house you and treat you with respect, and we will carry you home after one year.'

He considered this for half a mile, before concluding: "Perhaps it would be wise to keep the gun pointed at him, from the Gentlemen's Cloakroom or somewhere like that, just in case. We would not tell him about it, of course, for fear of hurting his feelings."

"Also," added the Professor later, still feeling a little uncomfortable, "we would naturally pay him a commission of ten per cent."

CHAPTER

XXII

BY the time these matters had been settled, the old
gentleman had reached the Quincunx, and had remembered there was work to do. He pushed his
way through the reeds beside the boathouse and stood in
an oozy place, where the water quickly climbed his ankles,
looking across the glimmering lake. The more he looked,
the more ashamed he felt. He was guilty about being bigger.

However, he remembered his young friend's desperate
case, and pulled himself together as well as he could. He
clenched his fists at his sides and shouted in a gruff, uncertain tone, which was half a squeak and half a whisper,
because he was unsure of it: "News from Maria!"

Try shouting by yourself, out of doors, in the middle of
the night, in the country, without knowing whether anybody is listening, and you will see how he did it.

He nearly jumped out of his skin when a clear voice near
his right ankle said politely: *"Quid nunc, O vir doctissime,
tibi adest?"*

It meant: "What is biting you, learned man?"

The Professor's shyness vanished. Monkish Latin was the
one language which could have made him forget his unfair
size. It was the Schoolmaster, safe home from the Vicarage
at last, who had spoken, and the latter, of course, had been

brought up in an eighteenth-century way, to talk Latin with educated foreigners. He had known that he was talking to the Professor, from the description given by Maria's captive.

"*Vir eruditissime*," exclaimed the Professor joyfully, "*sed solo voce mihi cognite ...*"

They were sitting side by side on the ledge of the boathouse, jabbering about Pomponius Mela, when the frigate came upon them from the darkness.

The Admiral wanted to know what was the matter, what was the news from Maria? The crew hung over the bulwarks with their mouths open, as if they were to eat it. Even the Schoolmaster remembered that Pomponius could scarcely be the main object of the visit; and the messenger remembered too.

When the story had been told, there was a council of war.

Considering her captors, it was obvious that the prisoner must be rescued at the earliest moment. The Palace was four hundred yards from the Quincunx. To cover this distance with a pace of three inches, the forces of Lilliput would have taken three-quarters of an hour. But the Professor could do it in a few minutes. It was decided, therefore, that sixty men should be disembarked from the frigate immediately, and the Professor was to carry them carefully but quickly, rolled in his ulster like a sack, so that they could begin to search without delay. Meanwhile, the frigate would return to the Repose for more of the men, and for the saddle rats, and for as many women as could be spared. If the Professor liked to come back for a second cargo in the ulster, they would be ready for him. The searchers were to begin in the East Wing for a change, spreading out in parties from corridor to corridor and from floor to floor, as

181

quickly as possible, and working inward from the outside, till all met in the middle. The second cargo would begin in the North Wing, the third in the South Wing, and so in order. Where the doors were shut, they were to look under them if they could; if not, they were to call and listen. Probably their keen ears would be able to hear Maria, even if she were gagged but breathing. If and when she were found, the finder was to go at once to the steps below the clock on the North Front, where a first-aid party would be waiting. People were not to make any noise while they were near the North-northeast Drawing Room. If anybody sent reports, they were to be careful to write the time (in hours) and, above all things, reports were to be copied in triplicate, with capital letters.

One party of desperadoes was willing to wait till midnight, if the worst came to the worst, so that they could try to tie Miss Brown to her bed when asleep, as Gulliver had once been tied in the sleep of his exhaustion. Then they could prick her with pins, until she confessed where Maria had been hidden.

The work of search began.

Meanwhile, in the furnished drawing room, Miss Brown and the Vicar were sitting on either side of the fireplace as usual, two silent images in their evening clothes. The People could see them through the windows and under the door: the Vicar in his black clerical silk, sipping half a glass of sour sherry because he was too mean to take a whole one, and Miss Brown in a violet fichu, eating chocolates with a kind of disdainful greed. They had nothing to say to each other for the time being. They were thinking, perhaps, about the best way to break Maria's spirit, and dreaming

of the vast fortune which they hoped to enjoy when they had sold the little islanders into slavery, for the circus at Olympia or the cinemagnates at Hollywood.

When she had finished the chocolates, Miss Brown went to the piano. She began to play hymns.

Silently and anxiously, while the piano tinkled, the People of Lilliput pattered up and down the corridors, with footfalls quieter than falling leaves.

They peeped under doors according to instructions; they whispered shrilly, "Maria! Maria!" They mounted the big stairs laboriously with scaling ladders which had been brought by the frigate. For going down, they slid on the banisters. In the corridors, they ran, to save time. Outside, in the inky shadow of a pillar on the North Front, the Professor waited with the first-aid party in an agony of nerves. He was afraid that Miss Brown might catch him and call him a bluebottle, but he was still more frightened for Maria.

At last there was a flutter of mouselike feet upon the marble pavement, and the messenger stood gasping. He had forgotten his forms in triplicate, but he had not forgotten the news. He was picked up, together with the waiting ambulance men, and bundled in the ulster. The Professor scampered down the servants' stairs.

Down they went, past empty pantries and broom cupboards; down wooden steps which sounded awfully beneath the Professor's hobnail boots; down into deeper regions where there were stone walls and cobwebs and the smell of mouldy corks. Past wine bins and dusty footsteps, past looming vaults with sweeping shadows in the light of Cook's torch, which he had remembered to borrow, past the heavy safe in which the famous Malplaquet Diamond, 480 carats, stolen by William Malplaquet ("the Great Publican") from the Nawab of Poona, had once been locked in beamèd darkness, past bricked-up arches which might have contained any number of sherry tasters buried alive by Montresor; they hurried along past the heavy doorway of the cellars, which had bolts on the outside but no key, until they reached the last massy door of the dungeon itself. It was shut. A small knot of Lilliputians was standing in front of it, pointing out Maria's footsteps in the dust.

XXIII

THE door was battle-ax proof. It was laid together in two plies of wood, the grain of one ply being horizontal and of the other vertical, so that no ax could split it. In its early days, when it had first been set on its hinges by some feudatory of William the Conqueror's, it had been secured by an enormous bar of wood, the size of a yule log, which had run in two wide tunnels left in the masonry of the wall. When this bar had become worm-eaten, somewhere in the reign of Queen Elizabeth, the village blacksmith had constructed a wrought-iron lock to take its place. This was still there, locked. Miss Brown had removed the key, which weighed two pounds three ounces. There were, from the same period, some handsome iron bolts. These offered no difficulty, because they had only to be drawn, if one happened to be on the outside. Since the days of Elizabeth, various other people had done their best for the security of the hold. Under the Regency, somebody had fixed iron bars, like the bars for windows, but these could be shifted like the bolts. Under Queen Victoria somebody else had put on the kind of chain which people have for front doors. Under King Edward, an expert had come down from the Bank of England, and had provided a circular lock which nobody on earth could open, unless he knew the key word for the combination, which happened to be "Mnemosyne." (One of the dukes had won the Derby with a horse of that name; the bookies had called it "N or M.") Under King George V, an American gentleman had sold the reigning duke a ten-shilling lock by Yale. Under King George VI, the whole affair had been provided with strips of antigas and black-out paper, by means of which it could be stuck together. The door was shut.

Now the ignorant Amaryllis, who probably knows nothing about anything except cricket bats, may have come to the conclusion that our Professor was an inefficient old person. Because he knew so much about everything at large, it may have been thought that he would not have known anything about housebreaking. Well then, to be absolutely frank, he did not. But, and this is where he differed from many well-known cricket bats, he had a brain. He had used it before when discovering the origins of the People. Now, as he stood outside the dungeon, his skull could almost be seen to swell and rise like a football being inflated. His white hair stood on end like a thunder-stricken cat's, when stroked; his eyes sank into their sockets with the effort of concentration; the veins on the side of his temples throbbed like a frog's heart beating; the temples themselves lifted like a cockchafer's wing cases, when about to fly.

The door shook on its hinges.

"Exactly," said the Professor. "Now here we have a door. Pray stand in front, most erudite Schoolmaster, to assist my meditations."

The Lilliputians fell back in awe, not of his size but of his mental powers, and the Schoolmaster stepped forward solemnly to do his best, feeling proud that he had lived to see that day.

186

"When," said the Professor, stroking his beard with
majesty and glaring upon the lock, "is a door not a door?
This is the conundrum which we, among others, and not for
the first time, are called upon to determine. *Hic labor, hoc
opus est.*"

While he was thinking, the People tried to imagine a way in which they could take advantage of their size, in opening it. For instance, if the Professor had lifted one of them up, the latter could have put his small arm into the Elizabethan keyhole, and might have been able to shift the wards, if they had not been too stiff. But there was no way in which their smallness could help them in dealing with the combination lock, which was opened by the secret word, and the Yale lock was also beyond them, because the box part was inside, so that there was no hope of unscrewing it. They were talking these matters over in whispers, when the Professor lifted his hand for silence. He had thought.

"When," he repeated, "is a door not a door?"

"*Tibi ipsi, non mihi*," said the Schoolmaster reverently, meaning "I will buy it."

"When it is off its hinges."

All were struck by the justice of this. The old gentleman might have gone on to point out that most locks and bolts are really a kind of bluff, that fox hunters who are confronted by a chained gate have only to lift it from the other end, and that the human race will generally be fascinated by a padlock as if it were a rattlesnake, instead of going round another way, or climbing through the window. He only said: "Produce a poker."

The hinges were of wrought iron, and had been made by the same blacksmith who had made the ornamental lock. They were T hinges, with hasps like the fleur-de-lis, and they had been put outside the door, so that the prisoners could not get at them. The result was that the rescuers could. They were old and rust-eaten.

Luckily there was an abandoned poker in one of the outer cellars, and the Lilliputians brought it between them, carry-

188

ing it as keepers at the zoo carry an outsize in boa constrictors.

The Professor set to work with bangs and wrenches; the ancient hinges gave out showers of powdered rust; the bolts began to fall off one by one; and the other helpers stood to watch the Titan's effort, with miniscule anxiety.

In the Drawing Room, the Vicar was thinking private thoughts. Why, he wondered, should we only sell the mannikins to Olympia? Once we have caught a sufficient number of them, say a barrelful, I will take half a dozen to London in a cigar box, with holes in the lid. I will go in the Rolls, or at any rate I will go first class, for the Clergy are expected to set an example to the lower orders. Then I will call, not only at the Olympia offices, but also on Lord George Sanger, Barnum and Bailey, and the rest of them. This will be even better than taking them to Hollywood. I will show my specimens and sell the barrel to each of these in turn, without telling the others. After all, they are commercial people, probably of low moral character, and one has to meet guile with guile. It is a sad thing, but there it is. When in Rome one must do as the Romans do. And by the way perhaps it would be wiser not to mention the treble sales to dear Miss Brown? She is a woman, and might not understand; besides, if I do not tell her about them, I shall not need to share. She will have quite enough by getting a share in the first sale, indeed she will have more money than any unmarried woman could possibly want, and I know that her requirements are few. It would be a pity to spoil her simple nature. M-m-m-m-m. Besides, I daresay I might need to leave the country till the fuss blows over, after selling the same article to three separate firms, and it would be useful to leave Miss Brown behind, to handle the business of delivery. She might desire to leave the country also, if she knew about my laughable deception. I understand that women's prisons are extremely comfortable, and I daresay the climate of Bermuda might not suit her. M-m-m-m-m. Palm Beach, Bermuda, Honolulu? I must order travel leaflets from the shipping companies.

Miss Brown was also thinking privately. If, she thought, if—if an accident were to happen to Maria? I don't mean any violence, of course, not premeditated, but if some little accident did happen so that she—well—was very ill—or even —even if she died? Quite by accident, naturally. We should all regret her. And if the Vicar were to be involved in it, so that he felt—well—almost as if he had been guilty of— of a murder? If he should attempt to swindle me of what I've rightly earned? They say that blackmail is a stronger bond than matrimony ... But there, murders never happen nowadays. Such thoughts are merely day dreams. And if we found the missing parchment afterward, and altered it in favor of ourselves?

The Vicar startled her from the reverie.

"Come," said he, finishing his sherry quickly. "We have been patient long enough. Obstinacy is one thing, mere naughtiness is another. We must have obedience: it is written in the catechism. Maria must be made to speak."

"Now?" asked Miss Brown eagerly.

They rose and went downstairs.

The last bolt fell from the top hinge in a little cataract of worm-eaten wood. The Professor took a firm grip of the battered iron and began to heave the door ajar. It creaked and grated on the flagstones, opened an inch or two, then

190

stuck. The ill-treated flanges of the locks on the other edge were bending in their sockets, splintering the old wood of the frame, and shedding screws. He took the hinge again and dragged the door half open. They did not wait to widen it, but squeezed their way inside. The Lilliputians ran between his feet without thinking about being trodden on. They cried: "Maria! You are saved!"

There she was in the beam of the torch, handcuffed to the wall, looking furious. All the thanks they got was: "Why didn't you come before?" Then she said defiantly: "I did not tell." Then she burst into tears.

They found that she was covered with bruises, not because she had been spanked, for she had escaped that last indignity, but because she had struggled so hard in being dragged downstairs that the action had developed into a rough-house. As a matter of fact, if she had not struggled, they quite likely might have spanked her then and there—they were so furious about her feat with the water jug—but the rough-house had put them out of breath. So you see it is always best to go down fighting, and if anybody ever tries to beat you, you should fight them till you die.

She had a splendid black eye.

"Right!" said the Professor. "That's quite enough of that."

He was so angry that he was almost shaking.

They told her how proud they were of her courage in not telling, and how much they owed to her. They found the keys on a nail by the fireplace, and unlocked her chains. They asked if she were really hurt, or hungry, or ill. They begged her not to cry.

"To begin with," said the Professor, "I shall take her to my cottage. Not one night shall she stay at Malplaquet, until this matter has been settled. I shall revive her with cowslip wine and bread and butter. Here, have my handkerchief. And then—"

He raised his fists to the heavens.

"And then I shall get on my tricycle and go to find the Lord Lieutenant or the Chief Constable, I am not sure which, and I will see to it that these monsters are made to pay for their outrage, to the last drop of their inky blood! What a heaven-sent opportunity! Do you realize that with these handcuffs and these bruises we can probably get her guardians removed and actually sent to prison, which is the only hope for the people of Lilliput? Otherwise they would always have had the legal right to sell you, and Maria could hardly have kept your secret forever.

"I must say this is an excellent development," added the Professor, restored to the best of humors by the idea. "I trust you are seriously injured, my dear child? Can you walk?"

"Yes, I am quite safe really. They didn't hurt me."

"Good. We shall walk to the cottage at once. I suppose you wouldn't like to be carried? I learned rather a good lift when I was a boy scout?"

"No."

"Oh, well, you must please yourself. And let me see. Is there anything we ought to arrange with the People?"

The Schoolmaster asked: "Do you intend to call the Constable this Evening?"

"Yes. The sooner the better. The quicker we have these villains under lock and key, the better it will be for all."

"Should she **be** guarded while Y'r Honour is away?"

"No. I will lock the door. I trust that this will answer. I always hide the key under my pot of pink geraniums, a

192

highly secret spot, known only to myself. Yes, h'm. Besides, they will not know that she is gone, or, should they find she is, will not know where to look for her. Forward to safety! But hark, what noise was that?"

They were in the passage, within reach of freedom. The Professor disentangled the torch from his whiskers and pointed it toward the cellar door—the other one, which blocked the end of the passage. Even as he pointed, it was softly closed. Something suspiciously like a chuckle, though muffled by the wood, echoed beneath the vaulted ceiling of the corridor, while on the outward side, the bolts creaked home.

CHAPTER

XXIV

M R. HATER leaned against the outer door with a long sigh, which whistled between his pursy lips as if he were letting off steam. "Got them!" he said. "The floor was crawling with the creatures."

Miss Brown lifted the candle to his face and examined it without a word.

"At least fifty. Say at one thousand pounds apiece. I think we may at last allow Maria her supper!"

She held the candle closer.

"And the Professor?"

"We can let him out as soon as the small people are secured."

"Are you deaf?"

"Deaf, Miss Brown?"

"He has found your ward handcuffed to the wall in a dungeon, and he intends to visit the police. You heard him tell them. The Society of Prevention, Mr. Hater, may have a word to say."

"Well, we cannot keep him locked in there forever. Besides, when we have sold the minnikins..."

"Did you observe that he and they appeared to be acquainted?"

"Good heavens! You mean a prior claim? But no, they

live on our land, not on his. They are the property of the landlord. He has no right, whatever their acquaintance . . ."

"The landlord is Maria."

"But, my dear lady, do I understand that you suggest . . . It would be impossible to keep them locked in there perpetually . . . The difficulty of feeding . . ."

"Why do it?"

"Impossible! We cannot . . . It would be . . . wicked. Unfriendly critics might consider that it was tantamount to murder. Besides, even if we did starve them till they died, what of the risk? It is unthinkable."

"Cook has been told that she is with her aunt, and not one living person knows the whereabouts of the Professor."

"But the dungeon is a room still visited by antiquarians!"

"We can put off their visits, for a month or two."

"Miss Brown, we could not, no, we must not, dream of such a thing. We are Christians. We must not be selfish. Besides, if we kept the big ones locked up, how could we get the little ones out?"

"Sir Isaac Newton bored a hole, to let his kittens through the door."

"Ingenious. M-m-m-m-m. You mean, to bore a hole and place some wire rat trap on the outer side, to catch them. Yes. Meanwhile, the Professor and Maria stay inside. . . ."

"The informer and his evidence."

"It was you who suggested the handcuffs."

"No, it was you."

"It means imprisonment for both, whoever it was, if the Society for Prevention should be set upon us."

"Yes."

"Miss Brown, we must resist temptation. The idea is far too dangerous. Murder will out. Not, of course, that we should be intending murder, for it is not our duty to feed the Professor for the rest of his life; but we must think of the construction which others might put upon it. No, Miss Brown, we must manage things more carefully. We will bore the hole as you suggest, collect the little men, give food and water to the captives through the aperture, and proceed to make our sale. Once we have cashed the checks—that is, the check—we will set off for Florida, or for some luxury hotel among the Azores, by airplane. When there, we can safely cable Cook to let them out. But murder, no! I am amazed that you should mention such a thing."

Miss Brown puddled the hot candle grease with a fat finger while she thought. Finally she said: "You must fetch a brace and bit from the Vicarage, also a rat trap. Or a bird cage."

It was noticeable that she no longer called him "Mr. Hater," in her respectful way, but spoke to him as an equal, or as an inferior.

Meanwhile, in the cellarage, the Professor was trying King Charles's ax on the door. It proved to be of cross-ply like the other, and would not split. The hinges were on the wrong side. They were trapped.

He went back to the dungeon, where Maria was sitting up and taking notice. He had used too much of his brain on the subject of doors and bruises, and was beginning to feel peevish. He wanted to go home and read books.

"Well, here we are."

Maria said cheerfully: "I must say it is nicer than being alone."

"It may be nicer for you, but it is not nicer for me. I like

to be alone. Why did we start this fuss in the first place? Scampering about with axes. I had left a bloater for my supper."

"It will have to keep."

He swung the torch round the walls.

"There must be some way out. Where is the back door? Where are the windows? What an inconvenient house!"

"There is a small red window there, behind the rack."

"Then we must simply break it, and climb through."

"It is six inches wide, and has some iron bars."

"Why?"

"To prevent us climbing through it, I suppose."

"How very inconsiderate! They might have known that we should need it. Nobody thinks of anybody but themselves. And where am I supposed to sleep?"

"Y'r Honour and Miss," said the Schoolmaster, "the Dimensions of this Window, if I may be permitted an Observation, would not preclude the Passage of my Companions, suppose the Glass to be broken. Once liberated, we might make our Way toward the other Aspect of the Cellar Door, and draw the Bolts."

"Dear me. Of course!"

"Even if you can't get it open," said Maria, "you could bring us some food. I have been feeling rather hungry for the last two days. Miss Brown and the Vicar will not want to come in while they know we have an ax, so I suppose they mean to let us starve, unless you can get us something."

"Just let them come," said the Professor.

He gave Maria the torch to hold, and broke the glass with the ax in question, as if the former were the Vicar.

Then the People had to be lifted to the stone ledge, one by one. They went silently and seriously, without looking

197

back, so that the prisoners could see that they had realized the gravity of the situation, and were determined to do their best.

The dungeon window faced a coal shaft, between the Boilerhouse and the Armory. When they had climbed up that, they found themselves in the open air, under the pared fingernail of a moon, which was almost slenderer than themselves.

They sent a party to fetch provisions for the prisoners, while others went to gather the main body, which was still dispersed about the Palace. The remainder started for the bolted door. They collected two of the ladders which had been brought by the ship, together with ropes and spikes. Getting round the Palace was like mountaineering for them, and this was why they brought the gear.

For Malplaquet was a real mountain to the People of the Island. It was a range of mountains. To imagine their difficulties, we should have to think how we would get about in a house that was as high as the downs at Selborne, and more than six miles long. The countless steps on the terrace were, for them, each one as tall as a man. If the doors were shut, they could not turn the handles. The pavements of the colonnades were airdromes. Even the smaller columns seemed to be two hundred feet in height; the greater columns, which held up the pediment, were half as much again. The basins of the fountains were great lakes. The statues were colossi. Eight of them could have dined at ease inside King George's head.

The flat cliff of the South Front towered above them, mat-silver in the moon and starlight, boldly slashed with its deep bars of velvet shade, but half in ruin. It was the ruination that made it possible for them to make their way about.

Beaded and paneled doors, which would have been impassable if sound, drooped on their parting hinges, or hung ajar. Masonry, once too true and square for foothold, gave purchase now that it was crumbled. Windows, gap-toothed with broken glass, opened on the vasty halls. Spider and swallow, bat and mouse, had long inherited the coigns of vantage.

The obstacles which we should overlook were tedious to Lilliput. Gravel paths seemed bouldered beaches, which might turn an ankle in their desert strips. The long grass was a jungle of tripping roots. They moved, climbing and jumping, clambering and toiling, where we should stroll.

The ladders were in a dump at the foot of the steps on the South Front. Now they had to carry them round three sides of the Armory, through an archway, across the Boilerhouse Yard, and down the basement to the cellar stairs. By their measurements, it was as if they had to march three miles; and it was not across easy country.

The first part of it was along what had once been a gravel drive, where the Fourth Duchess, an invalid, had been accustomed to be promenaded in her pony carriage, with a powdered footman at each wheel, and another behind to carry the smelling salts. Now it was a weedy trackway, whose weeds were bushes to the People and whose pebbles were smooth rocks. It was a heartbreaking trail, although it was one degree better than the scrubland of meadowsweet, scutchgrass, scabious, and sorrel which lay on its borders. This part ended at the west corner of the Armory, where an iron gate, fifty feet high, and a stone step as high as a man, led to the Menagerie Path and the Orangeries.

They turned right, along another strip of gravel which was dilapidated like the first, and struggled on. Here there were toads, who swelled themselves up, lifted their back ends stiffly, and made strange moonlit faces at the rescuers as they stumbled past. There was also a chance of grass snakes, who used to go to Boswell's Fountain for the frogs.

To reach the Archway, they had to climb six steps. They had to hold the ladders firm, because the stones were slippery. Above them the great Arch, dedicated to the unfortunate Queen Caroline Matilda and ornamented with the royal arms of Denmark, blocked out a section of the sprinkled stars.

The Boilerhouse Yard was an Arabia of stones, between which the nettles vied with the goose grass, and a nettle sting was like an adder's for men so small.

The bats creaked above them, sharper than kingfishers, as they wove their way between the deadly trees. Outside the yard, beyond the Temple of the Graces, a corn crake sawed across its comb. From an abandoned flower bed the smell of stock was sweet.

The basement door was shut and locked, but its upper panes had once been glass. These were now missing.

They had to tie the ladders together, but even then they were a human foot too short. The steeple-jack had to go up with spikes, which he drove into the wood, like the steps on a telegraph pole, until he reached the open ledge. From that he lowered a rope inside the door, and made it fast. The rest climbed up the ladders, up the spikes, and down the rope. The last man had to help the steeple-jack, while he hauled the ladders up and lowered them inside.

Then they were in the dark in earnest. The basement corridor, four furlongs straight and long enough to stage a modest canter even for us, was gloomy in daylight. By night, with rats about, it was the valley of the shadow. Some

200

of the bats hunted it also, swerving through the broken panes. The dim pipes and the drains above them, and the myriad bellpulls, were no longer lit by the Professor's torch.

However, they were accustomed to working at night. Their eyes were as fine as they were small. After a minute they could partly see.

The flagstones of the basement were as large as tennis courts. They clicked across them silently in skirmishing order, whispers forbidden.

Outside, they could disperse. They could run, hide in the undergrowth, or stand motionless with a concealing background. Inside, within four walls, the case was altered. Suppose Miss Brown were to spring before them, were to step from behind a pillar or to pounce with her candle from a yawning door? How could they hide on a stone floor, or disperse with walls round them, or run away even, when they were locked in, and needed to climb out by ladders? One stride of the pursuer would cover twelve of theirs. Later, when they were down the steps, their retreat would be cut off by a series of cliffs, which Miss Brown could mount as easily as the stairs they were.

So they advanced in silence, like red Indians on the warpath, with their scouts thrown out. They had to peer round corners, reconnoiter, listen, even sniff. Humans have a pungent smell, which is plain as daylight to the animals. The People could distinguish with their noses as clearly.

If a scout were to wind the Vicar, he would squeak like a mouse, three times. All would then turn in silence, and would fade back into the darkness, since silence was their only hope.

But if the Vicar leaped from behind; if he too had managed to lie concealed without being winded, and had cut off their retreat: in that case they would have to run in all directions, giving as much trouble as possible in being caught. While he was trying to kidnap one of them, grabbing to seize the nimble figure without injuring it too much for sale, why then, perhaps, during that time, another would be able to climb a stair.

The door toward the cellars had left its hinges twenty years before. The cellar steps were worn by countless feet—the oldest steps in the Palace, contemporary with the dungeons. They had to lower the ladders, climb down two steps, assemble on the third, lower the ladders once more, and repeat the process.

They passed the strong rooms and the wine bins, under the massive Norman arches. They left minuscule footsteps in the dust. They passed the moldy corks and cobwebs and the bricked-up vaults.

Dimly, through the bolted door, they could hear the Professor and Maria talking. For some reason these two had begun to neigh.

The lower bolt was reached easily from a ladder. A spike was driven in the door, six of our inches behind the back end of the bolt. A rope was tied to the arm of the bolt and passed over this spike. Then, while one of them held the arm up from the ladder, the others heaved upon the rope. It came out sweetly.

The upper bolt was too high for the ladders, even when they were tied together. The steeple-jack had to go up with spikes, which he drove in slantwise until he was six inches behind it, as with the other. Then he had to reach the bolt arm, by three more spikes, so that he could tie a longer rope to that. He had difficulty in raising the arm from its slot, although it was only just inside it. Before he could get it to move, he had to hammer it with a spike. The rope was passed over the pulley-spike and thrown down to the haulers.

They heaved with all their strength, climbing the rope in order to put their weight upon it.

The bolt was immovable.

The door had sagged on its hinges in the course of centuries, and was leaning on the socket. It needed human strength to shift the metal.

XXV

THE Professor walked round the walls with his torch, reading the Latin inscriptions.

"Not a sign of Triparium," he said sadly, "though there is an interesting use of "questeur" by this Pardoner behind the block, who dates himself 1389. I see that Dame Alice Kyteler, the Irish sorceress, was here for the week end in 1324."

Maria was resting on the rack, with the famous ulster for a pillow.

"A month ago," she said, "the People were thinking how much they would like to visit Lilliput, to see if there was anybody there. I said that when you were rich we would buy a yacht, and go to find them."

"A pleasant holiday. Yes. We might pay a visit to all four countries, kidnap a Brobdingnagian, call on the Balnibarbians and take a distant look at all the Horses."

"The Balnibarbians?"

"The people with the flying island overhead, the airy island of Laputa."

"What fun! We could capture it from a Flying Fortress, if we wanted!"

"Why?"

"It might come in useful for something. We could put

it over London in the next war, for an air-raid shelter."

"Unfortunately it will only work over Balnibarbi. It says so in the book."

"Well, we could use it for a health resort. Or for investigating the stratosphere, like Professor Picard."

"Its ceiling was not more than four miles. Airplanes go higher."

"We could..."

"I don't see why you want to capture it in the first place," exclaimed the Professor petulantly. "Why couldn't you leave it to the people who had it? They were perfectly happy."

"But they were silly people. All those old philosophers with their heads on one side, and one eye turned inward, and the servants to flap them when they got absent-minded."

"What was wrong with that?"

"Well, look at the ridiculous things they invented. Look at the projector who wanted to get sunbeams out of cucumbers!"

"Why not? He was only a little before his time. What about cod-liver oil and vitamins and all that? People will be getting sunbeams out of cucumbers before we know where we are."

Maria looked surprised.

He stopped wandering and sat on the block.

"Do you know," he said, "I think that Dr. Swift was silly to laugh about Laputa. I believe it is a mistake to make a mock of people, just because they think. There are ninety thousand people in this world who do not think, for every one who does, and these people hate the thinkers like poison. Even if some thinkers are fanciful, it is wrong to make fun

205

of them for it. Better to think about cucumbers even, than not to think at all."

"But..."

"You see, Maria, this world is run by 'practical' people: that is to say, by people who do not know how to think, have never had any education in thinking, and who do not wish to have it. They get on far better with lies, tub thumping, swindling, vote catching, murdering, and the rest of practical politics. So, when a person who can think does come along, to tell them what they are doing wrong, or how to put it right, they have to invent some way of slinging mud at him, for fear of losing their power and being forced to do the right thing. So they always screech out with one accord that the advice of this thinker is 'visionary,' 'unpractical,' or 'all right in theory.' Then, when they have discredited his piece of truth by the trick of words, they can settle down to blacken his character in other ways, at leisure, and they are safe to carry on with the wars and miseries which are the results of practical politics. I do not believe that a thinking man like Dr. Swift ought to have helped the practical politicians, by poking fun at thinkers, even if he only meant to poke fun at the silly ones. Time is revenging itself upon the Dean. It is bringing in, as real inventions, the very ones which he made up for ridicule."

"What would you do," asked Maria suspiciously, "if we called at Laputa?"

"Hire a flapper there, and settle down."

"I thought so."

"In any case, I do not fully believe in Laputa. I suspect that Gulliver was drawing the longbow a little. So many of these travelers are inclined to be like Sir John Mandeville...."

"Why don't you believe?"

"Do you remember how it was supposed to be kept in the air?"

"It had an enormous magnet inside, and one end attracted the earth and the other end repelled it. If they wanted to go up, they put the repelling end downward."

"Just so. I do not think it would work. Sir Thomas Browne discusses this very question in his *Pseudodoxia Epidemica*, in relation to Mahomet's Tomb and other articles, like the iron horse of Bellerophon, which were said to be suspended in the air by magnets. He says that it cannot be done."

"Why?"

"If a magnet is pulling hard enough to pull you up, it will also be pulling hard enough to pull you upper. The moment you are up, you are nearer, and consequently you get pulled harder. That was one reason. Another one was that, if you hung a thing between two equal magnets, the balance would be so infinitely delicate that the least breath of wind would disturb it, and so the object would fly to one or to the other. By the way, do you remember the size of the flying island?"

"It was on a plate of adamant two hundred yards thick, covering ten thousand acres."

"What is adamant?"

"What is it, then?"

"It was one of the old words for diamond. If you must have a reason for capturing Laputa, Maria, I think that a diamond five miles long and two hundred yards thick ought to be sufficient."

"Gee!"

"I wonder why Surgeon Gulliver did not steal a bit."

"Perhaps he could not break it off."

"Perhaps."

They thought about the huge blue fire scintillating in the air, the light from the waves reflected and refracted from its flashing bottom, as Gulliver first saw it, till their minds were awed.

"Tell me about the Horses."

"What about them?"

"Tell me," she said guiltily, "how they ought to be pronounced."

The Professor threw his head back firmly and began to neigh.

"What?"

"Can you neigh?"

Maria tried, to see if she could.

"How did you do it?"

"Let me see. I kept my mouth shut, and I don't think my tongue moved, and I sort of kept on huffing out a wriggly squeal, through the back of my nose."

"How would you spell a neigh?"

"You couldn't spell it very well, because you do it with your mouth shut. So there can't be any proper letters, really, not real vowels."

"Well, Dr. Swift used a 'hou' for the huffing part, and a Y for the squealy part, and the N's and M's are the part in the nose, Houyhnhnm. It is what a horse says."

"It isn't very easy to pronounce it in the book, not when you are reading aloud."

"It is only a question of practice," said the Professor grandly. "Practice and self-confidence."

He began neighing merrily, saying that he was quoting a passage at the end of Chapter Nine. Maria started also, each thinking his or her own imitation to be the best, and the Lilliputians wondered outside.

"It is a pity," said he, stopping suddenly, "that we cannot visit them."

"Why not?"

"We are Yahoos."

"But I thought the Yahoos were horrid hairy creatures, who made messes and thieved and fought."

"That's what we are."

"We?"

"Dr. Swift was thinking of human beings, my dear, when he described the Yahoos. He was thinking of the politicians I was telling you about, and the 'practical' people, and the 'Average Man,' for whom our famous democracy exists.

Just so. Do you realize that the Average Man probably cannot read or write?"

"Oh, surely . . ."

"If the Average Man means anything, Maria, it means the average human being in the world. He lives in Russia and in China and in India, as well as in England. Less than half of him can read at all."

"But the Yahoos had claws. . . ."

"We have tommy guns."

"We do not smell!"

"We do not smell ourselves. They tell me that a European smells quite horrid to an Asiatic."

"I don't believe it."

"No."

"And anyway, the Horses could not turn us out."

"Why not? They turned out Gulliver."

"Why did they?"

"Because he was a human, like ourselves."

"What cheek!" exclaimed Maria. "I'd jolly soon turn out mere animals."

"There," said the old man calmly, "speaks the young Yahoo. Exactly. There speaks our budding Homo sapiens."

C H A P T E R

XXVI

THE Palace kitchen was rather too small for an aircraft hangar, but its appointments had been praised by Dartiquenave, and the Prince Regent's chef had there conceived his famous Sauce Chinoise—which had been composed mainly of red pepper, as the Prince had by then become incapable of tasting anything else.

In a gloomy corner of the kitchen, with a tallow candle which threw enormous silhouettes of titanic ovens, of spits for roasting bullocks whole, and of braziers for deviling small whales, on a broken rocking chair which she had inherited with Captain from her deceased husband, with her steel-rimmed spectacles slipping from the end of her nose and a copy of *Mirabelle's Last Chance* slipping from her knobbed fingers, with her head nod, nod, nodding, and jerking up straight again, with a bundle of Maria's black stockings on the workbasket beside her and Captain's head upon her knee, old Cook sat snoozing off. It was long past midnight, but she was sitting up to make Miss Brown her nice-hot-water-bottle.

Captain, with his head on the knee, was gazing soulfully at his mistress with his eyes turned up like lollipops, while he gently dribble, dribble, dribbled on her apron. He used to get a sugar biscuit every night at bedtime, and this was why he was doing so. He was also thinking what a charming person Cook was, and wondering how on earth he could get along without her.

Alas, my poor Miss Maria, thought Cook between her nods; alack, my dowsabelle. But Rule Britannia is my motter, and while there is life there is hope. Supposing as which her old gentleman was lucky enough for to lay his hand upon her nest, according to the Scriptures, before them tryons has her imbrangled, which is what we must imprecate the Almighty Powers for the accomplishment of before the expiration of which, I wouldn't be surprised but what there was some of them eternal hope-springs for the deliverance of whom, not with the aid of them Glorious Shiners which we wot of. Dearie me, dearie me. I'm sure I didn't hardly have the heart to darn her little stockings. . . .

She jerked her head upright for the fifth time, looked around with an expression which said: "I wasn't asleep, so there," and laid her spectacles on the work basket.

These saved, the sixth nod brought the tired head upon her chest, and she began to snore.

Poor Cook, thought Captain, I must be kinder to her. She makes a splendid pet. How faithful she is! I always say you can't get the same love from a dog, not like you can from a human. So clever, too. I believe she understands every word I say. I believe they have souls, just like dogs, only of course you can't smell them. It is uncanny how canine a human can be, if you are kind to them and treat them well. I know for a fact that when some dogs in history had died, their humans lay down on the grave and howled all night and refused food and pined away. It was just instinct, of course, not real intelligence, but all the same it makes you think. I believe that when a human dies it goes to a special

212

heaven for humans, with kind dogs to look after it. It may be sentimental of me, but there it is. Poor things, why shouldn't they? For that matter, I daresay there are humans in our own heaven even, for the dogs to make pets of. It would scarcely be heaven to some dogs, if they couldn't take their humans with them. I know I should want to take Cook. . . .

Captain suddenly lifted his head from the knee and looked at the distant door. The hackles rose on the back of his neck, and there must have been some setter blood among his ancestors, for he froze with his tail straight out behind him. His nose went whiffle-whiffle-whiffle.

In the huge arch of the doorway stood the miserable Schoolmaster, holding out a Lilliputian biscuit about the size of a daisy, and saying hoarsely: "Poor Fido, a good Fellow then! A fine Pug, Fido. A Comfit for poor Fido. . . ."

The Schoolmaster was always chosen for difficult missions of this sort. His companions stood in the background, waiting to see how he would fare.

"Fido!" thought Captain with disgust. "Good Lord!"

He walked stiffly toward the door, to examine the intruder.

The poor Schoolmaster held the biscuit in front of him like a weapon of defense, shut his eyes tight, and kept gasping out his store of pacifications for Fido, while he was sniffed all over.

"It is the same shape as a human," thought Captain, "in spite of the size, and it smells the same, too, only less. I think I will keep it for a pet, like Cook. I hope she won't be jealous."

So he picked the Schoolmaster up in a velvet mouth, and carried him to his basket, which stood beside the rocking chair. The Schoolmaster said faintly, "A poor Boy, then, a noble Fellow," as he was transferred. He dropped the biscuit.

Now Captain was an elderly bachelor, and, like many people of this sort, he nourished an unconscious hope that one day he might have puppies. The size of the Schoolmaster must have suggested the matter to his mind, for he sat down carefully on the basket and arranged the Schoolmaster on his stomach. He prodded him with his nose several times, to shovel him into the right position, and the Schoolmaster said indignantly, "Leave me go, you nasty Br . . ."

But, before he could say "Brute," Captain's tongue was slapped across his face like an outsize in custard pies, and, before he could say anything else, he was being given a bath. Captain knew very well that the proper thing with puppies was to lick them all over instantly, and this he proceeded to do, while the exasperated midget kept spluttering about Br-br-brutes. He even punched Captain on the nose, he was so annoyed, but his new mother took all in good part, and held him down with one paw, since he seemed to be fractious.

"Oh, you Creature! Down, Sir! Put me down! A bad Dog, Fido! Leave me down this Instant!"

Long afterward, while Captain snoozed contentedly in a loop, the damp Schoolmaster crawled cautiously from under his chin. He stood on tiptoe by the side of the basket and tugged the great gray curtain of Cook's skirt.

"Yes, dear," said Cook, without waking up. "You shall have it in a minute, my sparrow. Not before bye-byes."

She thought that Captain was asking for his biscuit.

At the second tug she opened one eye.

214

She next opened both eyes, rubbed them, put on her spectacles, looked at the Schoolmaster, shrieked in a determined way, and resourcefully threw her apron over her head. Two minutes later, she lifted a corner, peeped out with the eye which she had used first, found he was still there, and replaced the apron.

"Madam..."

Cook began drumming on the floor with her heels, to show that she intended to have hysterics if he did not leave off and go away.

The Schoolmaster stroked his clammy hair. "The Sex!" he thought wearily. "La! A very little Wit is valued in a Woman, as we are pleas'd with a few Words spoken plain by a Parrot."

He turned his back, so that she could get accustomed to him in her own way, without meeting his eye.

Presently his sharp ears heard the apron being lifted for the third time, but he stood still, without speaking, and waited.

"Lawks!" said Cook.

"Madam, if you will pray compose yourself so soon as may be Convenient, I have the Honour to present myself upon Business of the most pressing Urgency."

"A fairy!"

"A Sylph, Sylphid, Fay, Fairy, Genius, Elf, or Daemon, Madam, which you please, if you would kindly relieve me from the Attentions of Fido here or Shock, whatever the Animal may be named, and deeply oblige."

Cook took her scissors out of the workbasket and lifted the tallow candle.

"I bid you begone," said she, "by the Power of Iron and

by the Might of Fire, forever and ever, by Christopher Columbus, and Whatsobe, Amen."

The Schoolmaster turned round cautiously.

"The Effort to convince you of my Reality, Ma'am, would prove a Task beyond my moderate Powers at present. You will, however, permit me to observe that, whatever my substance, I am the Bearer of an urgent Message from Miss."

"By Snip-Snap-Snorum and High-Cockalorum. . . ."

He stamped his foot with vexation, causing Captain to give a growl.

"The Professor and Miss Maria are bolted in the Cellar!"

"Ladybird, Ladybird, fly away home. Your house is on fire, your chillun . . ."

"What the Devil!" screamed the Schoolmaster, who had, after all, been tried rather high. "Z—ds! D—n the Ladybird! Plague on't, Madam, can't you understand plain English? We wish you to unbolt the Door!"

"Maria in the cellar?"

"Don't you hear me, Ma'am (with a Pox), when I tell you that the Bolt is stiff? Must I e'en be slobber'd to death with Spittle and stifl'd by the filthy Carkass of your Monster, to be deafen'd with the Follies of Domesticks and exorcised under the Appellation of an Insect? Miss is in the Cellar, I say, and the Devil fly away with it!"

The Schoolmaster's indignation was more convincing than any explanation could have been, and, as Cook felt certain that fairies were not accustomed to swear, she began to pay attention to his news. When she realized that it was about unbolting the dungeons for the Professor and Maria, she gave up trying to understand why the visitor should be six inches high. Were he a spirit of grace or goblin dammed, she felt prepared to follow him, if it meant the rescue of her mistress.

She produced the bicycle from one of the smaller ovens, which she used as a garage, and seemed resigned when more and more of the Lilliputians began to filter into the kitchen. They had watched the proceedings of Captain from a safe distance, and now came forward, seeing that the embassy had been safely accomplished. There was a basket on the handlebars of the bicycle, into which she put several of them, at their request.

Captain wanted to carry the Schoolmaster in his mouth, and was dissuaded from this with difficulty. He ran behind when the expedition set off, anxiously watching the basket, for fear that his new puppy might fall out.

Cook pedaled down the Service Corridor at full speed, carefully ringing her bell at the corners. She propped the machine against the wall at the top of the cellar stairs, and hurried down the ancient steps as fast as her bad leg would permit. A crowd of the People were grouped around the bolted door. They had smoky torches, made from rushes dipped in mutton fat.

She was able to draw the bolt.

When the door flew open at last, it was to show the Professor and Maria at the end of the corridor, seated on the rack in the fading light of the electric torch, eating a hearty meal of small sheep and smaller loaves, which had been brought for them by the other party, through the broken window. The Professor was in high good humor, and had forgotten about being locked in.

"Ah, Mrs. Noakes," he cried, waving a leg of mutton. "Come in, come in! Just in time to share our miniature repast! Something quite in your line, Mrs. Noakes, a piece of cookery which would interest the Goodman himself. The mutton positively melts in your mouth. Take a chair. No, there is no chair. Take a block, Mrs. Noakes. Allow me to help you to a couple of these hoggets. You will remember the extraordinary miscalculation made by Dr. Swift, when he was estimating the number of sheep that would be eaten daily by Surgeon Gulliver, on the island of Lilliput. I fear that the poor Dean must have confused himself with his cube roots. Sufficient, he says, my dear Mrs. Noakes, for one thousand seven hundred and twenty-eight Lilliputians. Yet, if a hungry Lilliputian could eat, say, one leg of mutton in a day, one thousand seven hundred and twenty-eight of them would eat the equivalent of two hundred and eighty-eight entire sheep. Do you suppose that you could eat two hundred and eighty-eight of these excellent hoggets in one day, Mrs. Noakes, hoggets, you will recollect, which the Dean himself describes as being of a size with larks, and eaten, as larks were eaten in his day, bones and all? Could you eat two hundred and eighty-eight larks in one day, Mrs. Noakes? No, no. Twenty-eight is more like it. The estimate must be ten times too high."

Cook took no notice of all this nonsense. She rushed to her long-lost Maria, and folded her to the ample bosom.

While the hugging was being done, the Professor trotted off to find a convenient block for his old friend. He was determined that she should sample the mutton, and, after trying various makeshift seats, he fixed on an ancient chest which stood beside the Manacles. When he began to pull it across the floor, the lid opened. It was full of parchments.

"Dear me," he exclaimed. "What a find! Somebody hold that torch. Why, here is a charter-hand script, Maria, which says that your ancestors were seized of the Castel of Malplacé in the thirteenth century! And here is Castellum Male Positum, in a late Carolingian minuscule. But wait! What is this? My goodness, can it be ... I wonder ... Suppose one were to sue out a suit of *mort d'ancestre*, on the basis of this charter, with perhaps just a touch of *praemunire*, but particularly the *mort d'ancestre*, and suppose ... Dear me, this is extremely interesting! I think I will just take the liberty of putting this document in my pocket, Maria, so that I may work it out in full, at leisure."

CHAPTER

XXVII

IT was late at night, and two expeditions were plodding across the province which Maria's ancestors had called a garden. The Vicar was pacing back from the distant Vicarage with his brace and bit, while Maria and the Professor were making their way in the opposite direction, along a different path, to the cottage. What with the rest which she had enjoyed, and the nourishing meal, she had flatly refused to be carried in the Boy Scout lift, to the Professor's grief. He was consoling himself by telling her the names of stars, as they went. The moth wing of the Milky Way was gently glowing above their heads, which he claimed to be really the Milky Wey, except that people had got it muddled.

The time was nearly one o'clock in the morning, so that Sagittarius the Archer was lowly crossing the meridian, and the old gentleman told her how the hub of the Universe was situated near that constellation. They themselves were spinning round the sun, and the sun was spinning round the hub ten thousand times faster than an express train, and the hub at that moment was in its right ascension. Maria felt quite giddy with all the spinning, particularly as she had to walk with her head craned backward in order to admire the zenith. She felt as if she would soon begin to spin herself, till she whirled away in a powdery blue, to join the mealy bloom of nebulae.

At the cottage she was given a good dose of dandelion wine, and put to bed.

The Professor wheeled his tricycle from the coal shed when she was settled, fetched the curly bowler hat and the faded ulster to cover his shabby clothes, locked the front door, and hid the key as he had promised under the geranium. He looked at the window where Maria was already sleeping peacefully, and told himself that all was safe. It was high time to claim police protection on the score of bruises and handcuffs, and to lay an information against the villains of our story. Even if the Lord Lieutenant were in his Garter or his Bath, or in his bed itself, he would have to be waked without delay. "Speed!" cried the Professor, as he pedaled away. "Expedition! A stitch while the iron is hot! Never put off till tomorrow without a hap'orth of tar."

When the Vicar reached the Palace at last, after his double journey, he and Miss Brown went down to the cellars at once, to set about the work of capturing the People. They stood staring at the open door in the light of the guttering candle, and the hum died to silence in the back of his nose.

"Gone!"

First he looked at Miss Brown, convinced that she had double-crossed him. But as she was looking at him with the same expression, each with a face as wicked as the other's, they trusted one another instinctively. They went in hastily, and poked among the instruments of torture. They searched the other cellars. They sat down in the cobwebs on an empty barrel, and were silent for so long that the gray mice crept out once more to scamper through the dust.

Miss Brown spoke first.

"However they went, they are gone."

"And the midgets."

"He has taken her to the cottage, as he said he would when we were listening, and has gone for the constable on his tricycle, to lay a charge against us."

"It was you who suggested the handcuffs."

"Fool," said Miss Brown.

She continued evenly: "The old dolt said that he would lock her in, and hide the key under his secret pot of pink geraniums."

"What does it matter where he hides it? If we are to be arrested, and the dwarfs are lost . . ."

"No need to be arrested."

"How?"

"Nobody knows that Maria was here. She was thought to be away on a visit. We thought so ourselves."

Her pebble eyes challenged him to contradict.

"We thought so ourselves. We told Cook. Yet we find that he has somehow or other managed to decoy her to his cottage. If she were found dead in that cottage, Mr. Hater?"

"I refuse to have anything to do with it! I will not be mixed up in an affair like this. It is too dangerous. It is impossible."

"He locked her in when he left," pursued Miss Brown, "and hid the key under the pot of pink geraniums, *a secret spot known only to himself*. His finger marks are on the key. Suppose the key were in its place when he returned, with the police, and that the cottage were still locked, the key still finger marked? We only need to lift it carefully, in gloves."

222

"I will not help."

"In the locked house, which he confesses to have locked himself, the kidnaped child lies dead."

"It is preposterous."

"He will be judged insane, because he fetched the constable."

"But, Miss Brown, this is a nightmare! There can be no possible reason for killing Maria, no chance of escape for ourselves if we did."

"It is that or prison. If he is sane, there is his charge against us, with her evidence. If he is mad, and she is dead, we are at liberty."

"But the minnikins!"

"You and your minnikins."

She held the candle close to his face again, and the purple veins and the blue lips were pale.

"We could not do it."

"We must go at once, or it will be too late."

"I refuse. It is all too hurried."

"We must get there first, whatever happens. Perhaps we can think of something better on the way."

They stood up simultaneously, and left the cellar.

The dauntless Gradgnag—as usual, like Alan Quartermaine, a dependable Watcher-By-Night—stepped from behind a wine bin when they had gone, and made all haste to climb the stairs. Everything depended on speed. The Schoolmaster and the Admiral would have to be found at once. Plans would have to be made for warning Maria, even for guarding her if possible, since the secret of the geranium pot was out. It seemed beyond the bounds of possibility that they could really mean to kill her, but the

Professor would have to be warned also, wherever he was, and the police protection would have to be hurried.

Fortunately the main body of the searchers were still inside the Palace, for things had been happening quickly. The Schoolmaster was in the kitchen with Cook, where he was trying to explain to her the difference between himself and a fairy, now that the danger seemed to be over.

He took the direction of affairs when the crisis had been reported to him, and did his best to arrange a plan.

Speed was the main object, and speed was a multiple of length. One could not go at so many miles an hour unless one covered the miles. In the first place, owing to the difference in stride, it would be impossible to keep up with the assassins on foot, once they had started for the cottage, and this they had probably done already. They were twelve times faster than the People, by stride alone, and that was leaving out the question of country. What was walking country to them was generally climbing country to the Lilliputians, and, where they could go straight, their pursuers would often have to make a détour. Fortunately there was a cavalry squadron of guards, mounted on fast rats, and he sent a message to these that they were to gallop hell-for-leather to the cottage, where he would join them on one of the rats which were still about the Palace, once he had arranged the rest of the campaign. They were to detail a troop to harry the enemy as they walked, were to wake Maria up and hide her if they should get there first, and, if not, they were to take whatever action they could.

This brought up the question of size once more. Lilliput had none of the aircraft carriers, antiaircraft guns, and other paraphernalia with which the Professor had been proposing to capture his Brobdingnagian. It was a question whether

224

even a squadron of six-inchers could do much against a towering human. The Admiral had arrived while the operations were being arranged, and he and Cook made a kind of defense council with the Schoolmaster, to discuss the difficulty. They could skirmish round the prowlers on rats, charging in like kerns to prod them with the needle swords, and cantering away again for safety, but this might not prove to be more than an annoyance. Their archers could shoot also, but both the Vicar and Miss Brown, like Gulliver, wore spectacles. On the whole, the best hope seemed to lie in stratagem. What form it might take would have to be dictated by the circumstances of the field. By some means or other, taking advantage of whatever might turn up, they might be able to lead their adversaries astray, or to trick them, or to defeat them by cunning. All this would have to be left to the psychological moment. If necessary, if no trick presented itself, they were willing to give them battle, face to face.

The worst problem was how to reach the Professor. It was evident that he would have to be recalled as fast as possible, so that he could bring the police upon whom Maria's safety really depended. The best that the People could hope to do against such desperate characters was to delay them until help arrived. But all the telephones of Malplaquet had long ago been disconnected, in the general ruin of the Family; Cook's bicycle had developed disastrous punctures on the way back from the cellars; and the People themselves had never been outside the grounds. They did not know the way to the Lord Lieutenant's, and could not have reached his home in the time available on rats— for these animals were not accustomed to distances.

It seemed an insoluble problem, and there was no time to think about it properly.

The Schoolmaster seized Cook by the little finger, for he was standing on the workbasket beside her, and squeezed it hard.

"Madam, we must resign these Circumstances to your Sagacity. Some Message, somehow, must be sent. Pray cogitate, Ma'am. Pray rattle your Brains. 'Tis a Matter which concerns her Life and Honour. We leave the Message to you. So, so, a Gallop, a Gallop. Faith, may we come in Time!"

Meanwhile, on the dark Riding, Miss Brown suddenly shrieked with vexation, and clapped her hand to one ankle, as Maria had done before. She was still hopping when the Vicar put his foot in a trap made by tying two bunches of grass together, and fell on his nose.

Indeed, it was a strange sight to see them thereafter, as they blundered up the midnight avenue under the cobalt light of stars, wrangling about Maria. The miniature ratmen were charging unseen, and thrusting with their needles, which the villains mistook for thorns. The glint of small accoutrements flickered in the long grass. Every now and then the giants fell over a grass trap. Every now and then they hopped about. Sometimes they paused to upbraid each other for their clumsiness, sometimes to hiss agreement or dissent about their schemes.

And all around them, in the darkness, there were the smaller and revengeful denizens of the island world. It was like a rodeo, to see them gallop in and out.

Shortsighted badgers, at the din, faded their starlit streak of snout into a deeper darkness. Foxes, with concave eyelights, peeped at them and pondered. Inquisitive rabbits stood on their hind legs, with ears erect, to see them go, and said: "Good Lord, what's the matter now?" The owls of Malplaquet, on silent wing, glided about the center of commotion.

In the doomed cottage, Maria slept in peace. In the vaulty kitchen of the Palace, brave Cook sat writing hard. Her nib was rusty, her ink was only sediment in a penny bottle, and her pink tongue was sticking out. It carefully made the curls that she was turning with her pen.

"Kind sir come back at onct as them as what you knows of sir is up to triks again..."

CHAPTER

XXVIII

THE Professor had found the Lord Lieutenant out of bed. The latter happened to be the Master of the Malplaquet Hounds, the one with the electric bell-indicator which Maria had coveted for Gull Island, and he had evidently been having a Hunt Ball or a Farmers Dinner, for he was dressed in a scarlet tail coat with violet facings, and was wearing the buttons of the Hunt, awarded only For Valor. He had changed into mauve carpet slippers with his monogram worked in gold.

He was a tall man with an anxious expression, and he had a walrus mustache which he had to lift with one finger, when he wanted to eat.

He took the Professor into the Dining Room, and gave him a glass of port, while the latter told his story.

The Dining Room had a polished mahogany table with a sideboard to match, and fourteen chairs ranged round the walls, where the servants had to say their prayers every morning. The wallpaper was dark red and there were oil paintings on the walls. There was a picture of the Lord Lieutenant on a Borzoi-looking horse, by Lionel Edwards, with a lot of hounds wandering about among its legs. There was one of the Lady Lieutenant, on a roly-poly one, by Munnings, and another of some of the little Lieutenants,

228

on anatomical ones, by Stewart. There was a baby Lieutenant, on a rocking horse, and several generations of Grandpa Lieutenants, on mounts called Mazeppa, Eclipse, or the Arab Steed. Some of the pictures were of mares and stallions by themselves, and these included honest creatures by Romney, fiery creatures by Delacroix, sagacious creatures by Landseer, and dotty animals with distended nostrils by anonymous eighteenth-century artists. The only person not on a horse was the Hon. Lettuce Lieutenant, the eldest daughter, who had made the mistake of being done by Augustus John. He had left it out on purpose, out of spite.

The Lord Lieutenant said: "But I say, I mean to say, do you mean to say, old boy, that this vicar of yours and that charmin' Miss What's-her-name have been maltreatin' the gel in the what-do-you-may-call-it?"

"I have been trying to tell you . . ."

"But, good Lord, my dear chap, you can't do that sort of thing in the nineteenth century, or the twentieth, or whatever it is. I mean, you take the first two figures, and add one, or subtract one, I forgot which, for reasons I never could fathom, possibly owin' to these X's which those chaps are always writin' on monuments, and then it is different. Now, take horses . . ."

"Whether you can or can't, it has been done. I tell you . . ."

"My old Granddad, or his granddad, I can't remember which, used to ride a hunter in a long point until it foundered, old boy, died, absolutely *kaput*. Now you couldn't do that sort of thing nowadays, not in this century, whichever it is, without getting the Society for Cruelty to Animals after you. Absolutely couldn't do it. Not done. Out of date. I heard it was the same with dungeons?"

"It may be out of date, but it happened. They locked Maria in the old cellar, because..."

The Lord Lieutenant poured himself a glass of port, inserted it neatly under his mustache, and eyed the Professor warily across a silver horse full of walnuts.

"Did they torture you?"

"No, they didn't. It so happened..."

"There you are, you see. All hearsay. Now, take horses. You are always meetin' chaps who say they know of a horse that trotted thirty miles an hour, but when you ask them was it their horse, they say it was some other chap's horse, and there you are. Now..."

"Good heavens..."

"Here, have a cigar. We keep them in this filly here, for parties. Look, you just press her tail down, like this, and the cigar comes out of her mouth, like that, oh, I'm sorry, and at the same moment her nostrils burst into flame, so that you can light it. Neat, isn't it?"

The cigar shot out of a gold-plated steed, hitting the Professor on the nose, while a musical box inside the creature's stomach played the last bars of "A-Huntin' We Will Go."

"I came to ask..."

"My dear old boy, look here, be advised by me. You drop the whole thing. You've got it muddled up. Perfectly natural, of course; no criticism intended. Anybody could get muddled on a thing like that, I should have done myself. But when you've been a Lord Lieutenant as long as I have, or a Chief Constable, or whatever I am, you'll know that the first thing a Lord Lieutenant has to get hold of is a motive. Can't have a crime without it. I assure you, it's an absolute fact. First thing a criminal must do is get a motive.

230

It's in a book I read. Printed. Now what motive could Miss What-you-may-call-it possibly have for wanting to handcuff young Thingummy in the what's-it?"

"There was a strong motive, but I am not at liberty to disclose it. It concerns the identity of other people."

"Ah, I see. Very proper, I'm sure. No names, no pack drill. H'm, yes.

"It couldn't," whispered the Lord Lieutenant breathlessly, "be dear old Lottie Catamount gone off again with one of the footmen?"

"Certainly not. Nothing of the sort. Maria was aware of the whereabouts of certain people whom Miss Brown wanted to trace, and she maltreated the child to make her disclose it."

"Whereabouts, eh? Gypsies, I daresay. Wonderful chaps with horses. Now..."

"Not roundabouts!" shouted the Professor. "Whereabouts..."

"Here, have some coffee. We keep it in this copper horse here, with the methylated lamp under its tummy. You just twist his near fore, like this, and it pours out of his ear, like that, oh, I'm sorry, and the sugar is strewed about in this silver-plated stable here, to represent bedding. Pretty, isn't it?"

The Professor mopped the coffee off his knees despairingly, while the coffeepot played "John Peel."

"I have a right as a citizen of this country to ask for police protection, and it is your duty, as the Lord Lieutenant, to investigate the grounds..."

"Good Lord, old boy, you can't have police protection here. What's the good of sending old Dumbledum to protect you? Besides, I happen to know he has a lumbago. His wife sent up to borrow a smoothing iron only this evening. And who, may I ask, would stop all the motor cars, and take their licenses and that, if Dumbledum was protecting you all the time?"

"Dumbledum..."

"Here, have a chocolate. We keep them in this china hunter here, for convenience. You just lift its tail, like this, and the chocolate comes out there, like that, oh, I'm sorry, and he plays the 'Meynell Hunt,' only some of the notes are missing. Useful, isn't it?"

The Professor fished the chocolate out of his coffee with fury.

"And another thing, old boy. What about witnesses? That's one of the first things you have to have in a crime, believe me, as a Lord Lieutenant—unless you go in for cir-cumstantial evidence, as we call it, or whatever they call it. Witnesses! It's vital. You can't do anything, hardly, with-out them. Look at that fellow who blew the other fellow up, unless it was himself, in the garage, or the swimmin' bath, or whatever it was, only the other day. He had dozens of witnesses. Blew them all up as well. You see? I mean, you could almost say that you can't do a crime without 'em. And where are yours, do you suppose?"

"I have a witness, Mrs. Noakes."

"And who is Mrs. Noakes, when she's at home?"

"Mrs. Noakes is the cook at Malplaquet."

"Good Lord, not Mrs. Noakes! Mrs. Noakes is Mrs. Noakes? Why, I know Mrs. Noakes as well as me own mother. That's an extraordinary thing, I must say, I mean that she should be her! Well, I remember her quails in aspic, in the old Duke's day, poor fellow, yes, and her oyster soufflé. An invaluable woman. Often we tried to get

232

her to come over to us, but she preferred to stay. Family feelin'. Now, take horses..."

"Not horses!"

"Well, hounds then."

"Not hounds!"

"Yes, hounds. Take hounds. A hound will eat almost anything.

"In fact," added the Lord Lieutenant blushing, "they often eat horses. Boiled, you know. In a sort of soup. Cruel, really, when you come to think of it. But there, it's their nature. So far as that goes, they often try to eat me. Desperate animals. It comes of living in the open air, I suppose. Makes them hungry. And horses too, they eat all sorts of things. Hay and that. But human beings, they want quails in aspic. Makes you think, doesn't it, what, don't you think?"

"I don't think anything at all about horses or hounds, and, once for all, I insist..."

"Good Lord, I believe you're back again on those dungeons. You ought to think about something else, old boy, or it will become a fixed monomark with you, like when the wind changes. Here, have a cigarette. We keep them in this platinum polo pony here, for sentimental reasons. It's an old pony of my own, poor chap. Dead, of course. Must have been dead about forty years by now. You just lift up the polo stick, like this, and he opens his mouth, like that, and out comes a cigarette, oh, I'm sorry, use a napkin, and, as you see, he plays 'Old Faithful.' Sad, isn't it?"

The platinum pony had shot out a stream of about fifty cigarettes, knocking over the coffee and the port into the Professor's lap.

He leaped to his feet, banged the table, and shouted

wildly: "I demand a hearing! I refuse to be pelted with these articles!"

Then he folded his arms and sat down on a comic cushion, which began to play "Boot, Saddle, to Horse, and Away."

"Good Lord, old boy, what are you sitting on that for? You aren't supposed to sit on that. It's supposed to be a sort of trick, to catch people..."

The Professor hurled the cushion on the floor, which made it play again, swept several horses out of the way, and shook his fist under the Lord Lieutenant's nose.

"No good browbeatin' me, old boy. Everybody always browbeats Lord Lieutenants. Doesn't do a bit of good. To tell you the bitter truth, I simply don't believe a word you say. Tryin' to pull me leg. Won't work. Now, if Mrs. Noakes was to tell me all this about dungeons and things, I'd believe her like a shot. I'd believe her if she told me that a mince pie was a ham omelet. But when a chap like you comes along, jabberin' about roundabouts..."

"But I tell you that Mrs. Noakes will corroborate what I say..."

"Produce her, then. Produce your witness. That's what we say, in the Law, you know. Produce your witness."

"How can I produce her when she's an old woman with a bad leg five miles away in the middle of the night?"

"There you are, you see. As soon as we get down to brass tacks, you always say it can't be done. Like trottin' at thirty miles an hour. I say I'll believe Mrs. Noakes, you say you can't produce her. I say I don't believe you, you start chuckin' cushions about. Now, take horses..."

The Professor clutched his whiskers.

"Take horses. You can always believe a horse. I always

say to everybody, Give me a horse, and I'll believe it. If a horse says there is wire in that gap, believe me, my boy, there is wire in it. Or take hounds. I always say to everybody, Give me a hound, and I'll believe it. If a hound says there is a fox in that gooseberry bush, or in that hatbox, or wherever it is, believe me, my boy, there is a fox in it. Always believe a horse or a hound."

The Professor had sunk back in his chair, pulling his hair out in tufts, when there was a gentle scratching on the door.

"That's one of the hounds," said the Lord Lieutenant happily. "Let him in, there's a good fellow. I suppose I must have fourteen or fifteen of them round about the house, in various places. They sit under all those chairs at dinner and wait for biscuits, like dear old Lord Lonsdale. Always believe..."

A footman, however, opened the door, and announced deferentially: "A strange dog, me Lord."

Captain was standing politely on the mat, with a shopping basket in his mouth. When he saw the Professor, he wagged his tail and came in.

The Professor read the letter in the basket and passed it to the Lord Lieutenant.

"Read for yourself."

"Dear me, a letter from the dog. Interesting, very."

He produced an eyeglass from his waistcoat pocket, disentangled the ribbon from his mustache, fixed it in his eye, and began to spell the letter out.

" 'Kind sir come back at onct...' Bad spelling, that. Should be an S in it. However, you can't expect good spelling from a dog. It's not their nature. '...as them as what you knows of sir is up to triks again, namely that here Vicar and his fly by nite'—Good Lord, that will be Miss

235

What's-her-name, just like you said—'and have gorn off'—good heavens—'gorn off to cut Maria's throat'! Poor child, poor child, good gracious, this is shockin'! 'So please to come at onct'—I should think so, too—'as If not it may be two late and Tell His Lordship'—that will be me, I expect—'to bring the Army'! My stars, thank heaven the hound has come in time! Always believe a hound! How clever of him to write it. Must have learned it in a circus or somewhere. Bring the Army, he says. Yes, of course. The Army. Fancy cutting a child's throat like that! Well, we must act. Action. Let me see. Where's Kingdom? Somebody fetch me Kingdom. Oh, there you are, Kingdom. Here, Kingdom, get me some people on the telephone. Get me the Army and the Navy and the Air Force and the Fire Brigade and the Home Guard and the Rural District Council and the St. John's Ambulance Association. Get me. Here, get me the telephone. I'll do it meself."

The butler carried in a telephone in the form of a plastic Derby winner, and the Lord Lieutenant began to shout commands into its mouth, occasionally applying its tail to his ear.

"Is that the Exchange? Where is the Exchange? Why not? Well then, why didn't you say so? Get me Mr. Winston Churchill. Certainly I said Mr. Winston Churchill. Give him to me at once. Who the deuce are you, Sir? I tell you I'm the Lord Lieutenant. No, I'm not. Yes, you are. An imposter? So are you. That settled him. What? My good man, what's the use of Mr. Attlee? Get me Mr. Churchill, like I said."

CHAPTER

XXIX

WELL, they dissuaded him from recalling Mr. Churchill at last. After that, he wanted to have General Eisenhower, Field Marshal Montgomery or Scotland Yard. The Professor cunningly went aside and wrote a message, which he persuaded Captain to deliver, saying that though the Far Eastern Battle Fleet might be very useful, yet they themselves, being on the spot, would be sure to get there sooner. The Lord Lieutenant was delighted by this second example of canine sagacity, and agreed to send at once for P. C. Dumbledum. The posse was collected without further argument.

It set off to the rescue in the early hours of the morning, much excited. The Lord Lieutenant was on a horse, the Professor was on his tricycle, and P. C. Dumbledum was in a wheelbarrow, owing to the lumbago. This was propelled by his wife, a woman of strong character, who was also the village postmistress.

"Faster, Mrs. Dumbledum! Faster, Professor! How can I gallop, old boy and Mrs., when I have to keep up with a wheelbarrow?"

"Faster, me Lord, I cannot go, but ride you on ahead with the gentleman, and Dumbledum shall not be far behind!"

"Faster, indeed! How can anybody go fast with that confounded horse stamping on everything? Have you brought the warrant, the *habeas corpus,* the *de heretico comburendo?*"

"No, no, no. I tell you it will be sufficient for Dumbledum to produce his truncheon. It has the Royal Arms painted on it, dated 1807. How are you, Dumbledum? Can you move at all? Are you still conscious?"

"Oh, me Lord!"

"There you are, you see. He can produce his truncheon. I wish I had a badge to wear, though, or a lassoo or something. Never mind, I can crack my whip. I say! Good Lord! Old boy, I say, can I see something white? Look there, ahead of us! Goodness! Oh, my, do you believe in ghosts?"

"No, I don't."

"I don't either, really. Could we keep closer together?"

"There is something white. I can see it."

"Good Lord! I say, shall we go home? I mean, we could come again in the mornin'. Now, don't tinkle your bell so much. You might frighten it.

"Take horses," added the Lord Lieutenant faintly. "Horses believe in ghosts, you know. In fact, they frequently are ghosts. Headless ones, with hearses and that. Don't you think it would be best if we...I say, do you think it is walkin'? You know, out for a glide? Do stop tinklin' your bell, old boy. I mean, if we could just sort of pass by without lookin' at it, it might go on with its walk, mightn't it?"

"There is a hound with it."

"Yes, I see it. Now, take hounds. Hounds are frequently ghosts also. Headless, of course, with the hearse, and gen-

238

erally black. I say, must we keep talking about hearses? Oh, Lord, do you feel all right?"

"It is Mrs. Noakes."

It was, and Captain was with her, as she limped on valiantly through the long grass, for the second time during that long day. He had returned home at once, after delivering the two vital messages so magnificently.

"Mrs. Noakes! Hurrah! Hullo, Mrs. Noakes! Bless me, you did give us a turn! We thought you were a ghost, only, of course, we don't believe in them. Well, well, well! I think we ought to have a biscuit now, to revive us after the scare. Fortunately, I have brought my biscuit box, which I take with me when I am out huntin'. I keep them in this chromium steeplechaser here, for safety. You just turn his tail to the left, like this, and his saddle swings open, like that, and a kind of machine inside him gives you a biscuit, like this, oh, I'm sorry, never mind, we will have some others when we get home, and of course he plays 'Reynard the Fox.' Convenient, isn't it?"

They left the biscuits where the machine had scattered them, in a wide circle, and hurried on beside the new recruit. They passed by peeping fox and shadowy badger, by inquisitive rabbit and soft-winged owl. The stars of the short summer night began to pale as they went and the small wind that goes before the dawn rustled the treetops with its single sigh. They could already see the outline of the cottage chimney, dark against the dimness, when the second ghost appeared.

It was outside the cottage itself, dancing gravely in the dew. When it saw Mrs. Noakes it gave a shout of joy, and rushed to fold her to its bosom.

"Maria, my lamb! So they ain't cut your throat arter all!

239

Oh, dearie me, I've come all over queer of a sudden, and I can't find me ankercher!

"Who-hoo-hoo," added Cook, weeping happily down Maria's neck, "and you a-dancing in the dewdrops without any shoes on, my cherubim, and in the pore Professor's nightie! Glory hallelujah, is what I say, begging His Lordship's pardon, I'm sure, but such a day as it's been for old bones with this and that is more than some could suffer the endurance of with whatso willingness as they was sustained by whithersoever! And, oh, my precious pet, them villyans that was arter you, they may be still about us notwithstanding!"

"We got 'em," said Maria. "We . . ."

The Professor coughed.

"I got 'em," said Maria, catching on. "I locked them in the cellar. Come and see."

The Professor used to keep his homemade wine in the wooden coal shed, so he hurried the party round to the back of the cottages, to see what damage had been done. There was profound silence inside.

"Now then, Dumbledum. Produce your truncheon. Good Lord, he's left it behind. Never mind, produce your armlet. It has blue stripes on it. Yes, yes. It will do splendidly. Mrs. Dumbledum, tip him out of the barrow. Are you alive, Dumbledum? Good, good. Try to prop him up, Professor. Don't groan so, Dumbledum, or it won't be a surprise. Now then, Mrs. Noakes, you open the door. Unlock it first, of course. Maria, take horses. I mean, take my horse. I mean, hold it. You hold it by this thing here. That's right. I shall stand behind you, Mrs. Noakes, with my huntin' crop, in case they turn nasty. Excellent. Now then, when I say One, unlock it, when I saw Two, throw it open. Then we shall all rush in and overpower them, or they will all rush out and overpower us, of course, since it depends how it happens, and Dumbledum must do his duty. Don't let him fall down, Professor. He is sagging in the middle. That's better. Now, are we all ready? Keep calm, everybody. Don't get excited. I shall begin to count in half a minute, when I can get my breath. Desperate characters. Oh, Lord! On the word Two. One, two, three, four, five, six, seven, eight..."

The door swung open, revealing the silent prisoners seated side by side on a barrel. They had so many expressions on their faces, of anxiety, of outraged dignity, and, yes, of triumph, that their features moved like water with the wind on it, formless. The Vicar's mouth was fluttering at the corner. He could not stop it.

"Now," said the Lord Lieutenant, taking control of the situation, "I arrest you in the name of the Lord. Dumbledum, the handcuffs."

"I protest," said the Vicar. He was husky, scarlet in the face and shaky. "I insist on making a statement. Before witnesses. This barrel contains several hundred people six inches high. Found by me and Miss Brown on our own property. We insist on opening the barrel before witnesses."

"D.T.'s!"

"I am a beneficed clergyman of the Church of England, wrongfully detained in this coal shed, and I insist..."

"Now, now," said the Lord Lieutenant, "none of that."

The Vicar pushed him away with a fumbling gesture.

"But you can't push me, sir! I'm the Lord Lieutenant. You have insulted the King's Uniform. This blue-and-white thing of Dumbledum's. It's an indictable offense. Probably High Treason!"

"We insist," cried Miss Brown in a shrill voice, "on opening our barrel. Our own barrel. We call you to witness!"

They trundled it out with painful care, and knocked the lid in.

It was empty.

"D.T.'s," said the Lord Lieutenant. "Obvious case. Think they see little men wanderin' about. Blue elephants and that. Well, well, sad thing really, I mean considerin'. We shall have to arrest them, of course. Can you move Dumbledum, Professor? That's right. I give them in charge for High Treason, drunk and disorderly, obstructing the police in the discharge of their duties, that's the push they gave me, and for attempted manslaughter of Maria, though that seems hardly accurate, as it ought to be girlslaughter, but perhaps we can think of a better word on the way home. Yes, and everything they say may be used in evidence against us, so you can't say I didn't warn them. Now then, Dumbledum. Shove him along, Professor. Clap 'em in irons. Hanging too good for them. I say, what an exciting evening! Hold up, Dumbledum. Here, give me the handcuffs. I'll do it. Look, you just put your hands in this nickel stirrup thing for interest's sake, like that, and I press this knob, like this, and there must be some sort of machine in it, I suppose, because a kind of bar comes out to lock you up, like that, good Lord, it worked, but unfortunately it doesn't play anything at all. Ingenious, isn't it?"

"You stole them!" screamed the Vicar and Miss Brown, recovering simultaneously, and, already handcuffed together, they clutched each other by the throat.

242

Mrs. Dumbledum removed them in the wheelbarrow, with the aid of the Lord Lieutenant.

In case you would like to know what happened to them afterward, perhaps this is the best place to tell it. Most of the charges preferred by their captor were found to be valueless, much to his annoyance, but the cruel treatment of their ward was proved to the hilt, and it was also discovered that they had been embezzling the little money she ought to have had. They got heavy sentences for these things. The last that was seen of them in the Northampton district was when they were taken to jail in a third-class carriage. The Vicar crouched in a corner seat, holding a two-day-old copy of the *Daily Express* in front of his face, upside down, with trembling fingers.

It was reported some years later that they had married each other, which was about the worst fate that could befall them, and one of the locals who came back from a holiday at Whitby said that he had seen them in that district, being booed by the small boys, refused drinks by the publicans, and made to walk by the bus conductors. The Professor does not think they would really have murdered our heroine, but it served them right for all that, say I.

Maria told the others her own story in the gamekeeper's cottage, over a filling breakfast of boiled water and the remaining bloater.

"The Schoolmaster got here long before they did," she explained, "but you had locked the door and he couldn't reach the keyhole. He managed to scramble up the plum tree to the window sill, but then the glass was too thick for him to break, so he had to go down again for a stirrup, and he managed to smash it, in the end, with that. And luckily the doors inside were all open, and he told me I had got to hide, and we went all round looking for a place, and in the end he said it would be best in the wood. And we were going out when he looked into the coal shed, and he said it was a pity I couldn't hide in a barrel like him, and he went in and knocked the barrels with the stirrup, and one was hollow, and he had a brilliant idea. It was simply brilliant.

244

And we could hear them quarreling near the Byng Monument, and I unlocked the front door, and we put your candle so that it would light the steps, and we opened the cellar door, and I hid behind it. And in the end the People arrived, all skirmishing and galloping on rats, and he drew them up on the step so that they would be seen, and when those two silly asses opened the gate he made them all shout rude remarks and wave their swords like anything! And Miss Brown and the Vicar forgot about me, and they ran to and fro like mad things making grabs, and the People kept withdrawing according to plan, without being caught, and in the end they rushed into the coal shed, and Miss Brown and the Vicar rushed in after them. And I slammed the door, and I locked it, and I danced on the back step. And I could hear them striking matches and cursing. And of course the People had climbed into the barrel, through the bung hole, where they could not reach! And that was the plan. Wasn't it terrific? But I got it better, you know. I found a brace and bit they were carrying, and I went round behind the shed, and I drilled three holes, and it was a three-quarter-inch bit, and they went right through the wall and through the barrel, and the People all scrambled out by the back! Wasn't it a sell? Wasn't it clever of us? As a matter of fact, they are hiding out there in the gooseberry bushes, this minute. . . ."

She got up hastily at the thought of her friends, and went gladly to the window, where she waved the bloater.

From outside, in the golden sunrise there came a tinkling cheer.

CHAPTER

XXX

IT was nearly five months later that a tired old gentleman in a curly bowler hat and a faded ulster was wheeling his tricycle up the Grand Avenue of Malplaquet, in the snow. A tired young lady was sitting on the saddle, clutching an enormous parcel, and the bare trees were thick with icing. The sun was setting in a blaze of scarlet, tinting the white expanse with a saffron tinge between the purple shadows. Various robins hopped about in the correct manner. It was Christmas Day.

They had been long away, staying at a poor hostel in the great metropolis of Northampton, for the Vicar's trial, and now Maria was coming home to the palace of her ancestors, a free girl. She was to have no more governesses or Algebra. It had been arranged that the Professor should teach her instead, at an inclusive fee of sixpence quarterly, which would be of assistance in his housekeeping. They were tired with the excitements of the trial, with the difficult shopping they had done the day before, and with the long trudge from Northampton, taken to save the fare. Also they were hungry from doing without dinner, for they had saved on that too, in order to keep everything for the shopping, and the Professor was footsore, and Maria was cold.

246

"Dear me," he said. "Here is the Triumphal Arch at last. Only another mile and then I can sit down. It looks noble with the sun behind it."

The Triumphal Arch was twice as big as the Arc de Triomphe. It had been put up to welcome the First Duke, when he came back after conquering the Nabob of Ooze, at Marzipan, in 1707.

"You scarcely notice it is falling down, not from a distance."

"No."

"I hope the People will be safe."

"I hope so."

"Do your feet ache?"

"Very much."

"Do you know," said the Professor later, "I fear I must be getting old. I seem to need food nowadays, and a chair to sit on. It would be nice to be able to afford them. Well, well, we cannot have everything. I must say it is nice to have a tricycle. I forget who gave it to me. It was a thoughtful gift. Now you mention it, however, I recollect that I found it in a ditch. There must be several people who have neither food nor tricycles, when one comes to think of it, so one is lucky, really, compared with them. And this new sixpence a quarter will go very far, very far. I shall be able to buy the penny fishhook, and all sorts of luxuries. Quite a plutocrat. Dear me, I believe we shall shortly be able to go freewheel, downhill."

"There is something in the Arch."

"So there is. Bless me, it seems to be barred."

"I think it is something lovely!"

They quickened their lagging steps, to find out what it was.

In the enormous archway there was a banner. It was at least as large as a pocket handkerchief, high enough for them to pass underneath.

It said:

WELCOME HOME!
A LOYAL GREETING FROM LILLIPUT
TO THEIR MARIA!
AND TO HER ERUDITE FRIEND!
VENI, VIDI, VICI!
SIC SEMPER TYRANNIS!

The band was drawn up underneath, dressed in their best eighteenth-century clothes and three-cornered hats, with a lantern on a pole, so that they looked exactly like the Waits in a Christmas card. The flautists had red mittens to keep their blue fingers warm, and they licked their freezing lips so that they would be able to blow. As soon as the travelers were within earshot, the whole orchestra burst out as fortissimo as they could with "See, the Conquering Heroes Come!"

There was the usual illuminated Address, and, while the Schoolmaster was reading it aloud, a party of sailors under the Admiral swarmed up the tricycle to attach a harness of horsehair ropes. If there had been any horses they would have taken them out, but, as there were none, they had to do without. Then, with the Address concluded and the band marching in front to the strains of "Rule Britannia," the haulage party set to work, for the rest of the way was fortunately downhill, and Maria was drawn home in triumph by her devoted tenants! The Professor marched behind with quite a springy pace. He was charmed with the

Latin on the banner, which had been put in specially for him.

When they reached the North Front, the whole of Lilliput was drawn up on the top step, in their furs and comforters, and Cook stood in the middle with a second banner of red flannel and cotton wool, which had been used in the old times when the dukes came home from school. It said: Happy Holidays! As soon as the cortège arrived at the steps, all the ladies of Lilliput produced handkerchiefs and fluttered them, all the children removed their hats, as they had been instructed to do, to give three shrill huzzas for the Squire, and, in the hush that followed, the bells rang out Noel!

A party of musicians had been sent to the Clockroom in the pediment, where they had disconnected the machinery which played "When the Heart of a Man," so that they could use the bells for a Christmas peal.

Most extraordinary of all, there was a blaze of light from the Grand Ballroom. They hurried in, to discover the cause of this, and there was an enormous Christmas tree, a whole spruce in a barrel, with hundreds of rush lights all over it and the Lord Lieutenant lighting them with a cigarette lighter in the shape of a filly, while Dumbledum held the ladder. The People had voluntarily disclosed their secret to these two, so that they could get help in moving the tree, and to have them at the celebration. On the tree there were presents for everybody, made by the craftsmen of the island in their spare time. There was a pair of spider-silk stockings for Maria, for which any film star would have given a king's ransom. For Cook there was a moleskin comforter to be worn round her bad leg. Dumbledum got some snake-fat ointment for his lumbago, which was better. Captain, who followed the Schoolmaster about all the evening, got a new collar made of the softest frogskin beautifully tanned. And the Lord Lieutenant got a carved hound, no longer than his fingernail, which played "Bobby Bingo" almost inaudibly, and threw out a shower of snuff, which made everybody sneeze. The Professor's present was a masterpiece. It was a Medieval Latin Word List (Baxter and Johnson, 10/6), which they had obtained by getting Cook to pawn their sprugs in Northampton. They had then written a letter on a piece of graph paper out of an exercise book of Maria's, enlarged it ten times by means of the squares, traced it on a piece of notepaper, and painted the words with a rat-hair brush. The letter and the money from the sacrificed sprugs had brought back the dictionary, in which the Professor instantly found TRIFARIE, trefoil, and he thereupon danced a coranto with Cook.

Maria dashed out for her parcel as soon as she could, which gave the final glory to the tree. During the trial the Professor had managed to touch the Lord Lieutenant for a fiver, and the whole of this had been expended on presents for the People. There were Woolworth silks galore; the finest threads and tinsels sold by the firms who tie trout flies, together with some Greenwell's Glories (size ooo) for the ladies to wear in their hats; hack-saw blades for felling timber, and also fret-saw blades; wire traces for the fishermen; ant eggs for bait, but of course these were really pupae; plenty of pins and needles; plain horn buttons without holes for plates; silver thimbles for drinking toasts on state occasions; a packet of mixed seeds of the smallest rock plants; for the children such things as the charms from plum puddings and some preserved currants, one each; for the grownups edibles such as whitebait, caviar, small beer, and snipe; medicines such as Carter's Little Liver Pills; a toy yacht for taking pleasure cruises; a toy telescope for looking at Maria through the wrong end of, in case anybody developed an inferiority complex; a Penguin book called *Elizabethan Miniatures;* some white mice and a pair of guinea pigs for farm stock; and a little crystal set with earphones, which would do for loud-speakers. No sooner had the presents been distributed and hugged, than the ringers in the Clockroom pealed out "God Rest You Merry, Gentlemen," and the doors of Miss Brown's dining room were thrown open, suddenly to reveal the Banquet.

There were hors d'oeuvres of small sheep, a fish course of the twenty-pound pike, done by Cook so that it tasted like salmon, entrée of deviled bullocks, pheasants trapped in the grounds, plum pudding provided by Mrs. Dumbledum, and a savory of sticklebacks on horseback for the Lord Lieutenant. Dumbledum had carried down the Professor's barrels in the wheelbarrow, and the Lord Lieutenant had brought some bottles of port.

Afterward they had healths. The Lord Lieutenant proposed Mrs. Noakes, Mrs. Noakes proposed Dumbledum, Dumbledum proposed the Professor, the Professor proposed Maria, and Maria proposed the People. The People remembered to propose Captain, who wagged his tail. All these were drank with three times three. Then the Lord Lieutenant gave Fox Huntin', and produced a wineglass in the shape of a huntsman's cap which played "The Horn, the Horn, the Noble Horn," and suddenly exploded, drenching everybody with port. The Professor gave The Supposed Continuator of Ingulf of Croyland. Dumbledum gave Absent Friends, which Cook refused to drink—but the others

251

had already forgiven the Vicar and poor Miss Brown, in prison, for whom they turned down an empty glass.

Finally the carol singers arrived, little boys about three inches high whose mothers had carefully brushed their hair with a drop of water to keep it down, and these sang "Oh, Come, All Ye Faithful" in trebly treble voices, until Maria cried.

What with the bells and the presents and the banners and the banquet and the trouble they had taken to meet her with welcome so far away in the snow, it was more than she could bear.

She made a speech which was mostly sobs, until she remembered to be tough, and then everybody broke into small groups, to drain a final thimble and to discuss the glorious campaign which they had fought and won together.

At this point Cook remembered that an important-looking letter had arrived the day before, with seven red seals upon it, and she delivered the same to Maria at once, in case it might contain a present.

It would take too long to explain the whole thing. To put it briefly, the letter was from Maria's solicitors. It seems that they had enjoyed a long talk with the Professor during the trial of the miscreants, and, by his advice, they had sued out a suit of *mort d'ancestre* in *trailbaston*, with collateral *praemunire* and just a pinch of *oyer and terminer*, *in partibus*, based on the document which he had discovered in the dungeon. The result was that the whole of Maria's great inheritance had been restored.

The cheers when this was understood were deafening! At least, they were nearly loud. Everybody shook hands with everybody else; "Auld Lang Syne" and "She's a Jolly

Good Fellow" were sung simultaneously; the Schoolmaster actually patted Captain; the Professor kissed Mrs. Noakes; the Lord Lieutenant promoted Dumbledum to Sergeant on the spot, and all looked forward, with hopeful hearts, as they made their way home through the snowdrifts of Christmas night, to the time when the ancient glories of Malplaquet would flourish as they had in days of yore.

So that is the end of our simple story, Amaryllis, and now it is time for you to go to bed. But, before you go, it might be best to tell you one more thing. If you take the road from Northampton nowadays, to Monks-Unmention-able-Cum-Mumble, you will pass the stone gates of a gigan-tic avenue. All the hinges are oiled, all the trees are pruned, and, if you walk up it for five or six miles, you will come to a Triumphal Arch. Out of a side door in this, there will come a seven-foot beadle in a gold-laced hat, bearing a golden staff and a brass dinner bell, to whom you should present your gilt-edged visiting card. The Beadle will rap three times with his staff, at which two under-beadles will throw the gates wide open, and he himself will ring his dinner bell like thunder, to give notice of your approach. As you wind your way up one of the five remaining ave-nues, a hundred contented-looking gardeners will look up from the spick tulip beds or from the span salvias, to touch their hats with stately courtesy. Take a peep as you pass at the one-time Wilderness, and you will see that it has once more been laid out as a wonderful Japanese garden, shown to visitors each Friday on payment of 1/- for the Red Cross, with stunted trees and little houses and Hornby trains which really run. In front of you, you will see the golden façade of Malplaquet, at the head of its shaven lawns, with every tile in place and every stone repointed.

253

A dozen footmen in scarlet and powder will rush down the steps, when you reach the North Front at last, and will deprive you of your umbrella. A dozen underfootmen, in mere striped waistcoats, will pass it up the steps, hand over hand. That will be the time to say that you have come to see Maria.

Unfortunately, however, you are quite likely to hear that she is out. Everybody will be kind to you. Everybody will give you claret cup in tumblers or champagne in buckets, whichever you prefer, but, when you ask them where Maria is, they will just seem rather stupid. The fact is that every man on that estate, and there are 365.2564 of them, is, on one subject, sworn to deadly secrecy. If Maria is *you-know-where*, they will not say a word.

But go you down past the Quincunx, Amaryllis, as you wind your long way home, and you might see a newly varnished punt, looking bright upon the water of the lake. You might even catch the flash of a skirt, or the twinkle of a long white beard, among the slender columns of Mistress Masham's Repose.

The PALACE of MALPLAQUET

Byng Obelisk

Burge Py

George II

to Vicarage

Gothick Hermitage

MALPLAQUET

The Lawn

Oriental Bridge

Chestnut Avenue

Boat House

Amateurs

Other Sea

Cascade

Quincunx
(Upper Sea)

Temple

A BLESSED WEAKNESS

Jean Vanier with an unidentified friend.

A BLESSED
WEAKNESS

*The Spirit of Jean Vanier
and l'Arche*

MICHAEL DOWNEY

1817

Harper & Row, Publishers, San Francisco

Cambridge, Hagerstown, New York, Philadelphia
London, Mexico City, São Paulo, Singapore, Sydney

To those who have taught me

FIRST EDITION

Library of Congress Cataloging-in-Publication Data

Downey, Michael.
    A blessed weakness.

    Bibliography: p.
    1. Church work with the handicapped. 2. Arche (Association) 3. Vanier,
Jean, 1928–   . I. Title.
BV4460.D68 1986   267'.182   84-47720
ISBN 0-06-062011-0

86 87 88 89 90 HC 10 9 8 7 6 5 4 3 2 1

Contents

You help us to discover that the center of the universe is the human person, as child of God, brother or sister of Jesus Christ— the human person whatever his or her mental or physical condition.

Réal Corriveau
Bishop of Choluteca, Honduras
(From an address to the International Federation of l'Arche, South Bend, Indiana, 1982.)

Introduction

Michael Downey spent three months in our l'Arche community here in Trosly-Breuil, France. During those three months he
experienced the joys and pains we all experience here: the incredible joy of discovering that we are loved just as we are and not
because we are wise and clever; the pain of touching our own
darkness and hardness of heart, our anguish and our feelings of
loneliness. Through this experience and through his reading and
theological studies Michael grew in the knowledge of how people
who are weak, poor, despised, and lonely can become instruments
of God's love and thus a source of hope. He grew in the understanding that each human being, even the weakest, is really a
person and has a gift, if we are attentive enough to see it and to
receive it; each person is capable of experiencing God's love; each
one is capable of growing in love and in human dignity.

Michael is writing as a theologian who is perceptive and
intuitive; he points out some of the signs of the Spirit of Jesus in
today's world. He shows that Jesus is calling some people today
to live the good news of the gospel as truly *good news*! But this
approach is necessarily limited because Michael lived only a short
time at l'Arche and his experience is of life in the community in
Trosly-Breuil. He is unfamiliar with other l'Arche communities
in Europe, North America, or Third World countries where the
vision is essentially the same but where the concrete reality, the
gifts, and the questions are different and open us up to a wider
world.

Michael approaches l'Arche as a theologian who has read all my writings and who is interested mainly in the spirituality of people who are fragile and poor. Therefore, he does not study l'Arche as a therapeutic community for men and women who have been excluded from society, whose psyches are thus deeply wounded, and who need competent people to help them grow toward greater autonomy. He is not there to assess where l'Arche stands with respect to various currents of thought which dominate in the field of mental retardation today. He does not seek to elaborate on the problems that l'Arche as a Christian community has to face integrated into a society with labor laws regulating the functioning of establishments for people with a mental handicap. It is not his desire to discuss all the complexities and real gifts of l'Arche, which has its roots in the Roman Catholic church but which also includes communities that are ecumenical and/or interreligious.

In today's world l'Arche has to face many questions; the road is not always clear. We have, of course, made many mistakes in the past and we will probably make more in the future. Our hope is that if we keep our eyes and our hearts focused on the weakest among us, Jesus will continue to lead us and to show us how to advance step by step.

As time goes on, we are discovering more fully the meaning of the covenant that many of us have been called to live with men and women who have been terribly rejected. Michael writes of how l'Arche continues to evolve. This book cannot then be the final word on the spirituality of l'Arche. This covenant is leading us more deeply into the mysteries that are yet to be lived. I ask you to pray that we may be faithful to this "way."

It is such an amazing reality that Jesus, our God, is hidden in those whose lives are not valued and in our own poverty. It is difficult to speak of this reality and such a privilege to be called to live it in a very small way. None of us can begin to fathom the depth of this love of our God as revealed in Jesus. He became flesh. He became the little one of Mary, a mere babe. He wept and lived the agony of the cross. The Almighty One became the helpless One in the arms of Mary and on the arms of the cross. He rose from the dead and he continues to live on in the weak and the poor who are crying out for understanding and compassion. They, in some way, continue to reveal the painful mystery of the Suffering Servant, who heals us, brings us peace, and calls us to love (cf. Isa. 53).

Michael writes a great deal about my spiritual journey. It is true that I am indebted to my own parents and my spiritual father, Father Thomas Philippe. They prepared my heart for Jesus. My studies in Aristotle certainly helped me too. Yet, it is essentially Raphael and Philippe and many others whom Jesus has used to deepen my heart, as Michael tries to point out.

Strangely enough, I do not feel I am the founder of l'Arche in the same way that other groups have founders. Perhaps I am just a catalyst or even just a voice revealing a secret, a secret we have always known theoretically in the church but one that has in so many ways remained hidden. Jesus is the poor. The poor are Jesus. He is our Savior. He continues to save us and to heal us through the poor. The essential way then is not to *do* things *for* the poor but rather to *be with* them in a covenant of love. It is to grow with them, to celebrate with them, to pray with them, to hope with them. L'Arche thus becomes a means and a channel whereby the poor can give their message to the church and to the world.

May I ask you who read this book not to suddenly decide to come to l'Arche. May I ask you rather to be attentive and caring toward those who live close to you, who are weak and lost, and to see in them their gifts and to appreciate them. By being close to them, little by little you will discover the gift we are discovering. You will discover that your heart is being opened by the gentle touch of those who are weak. This is the message that Michael Downey shares in these pages.

Jean Vanier
Trosly, June 1985

Acknowledgments

The twenty-first year of any life is momentous. It is a time of looking back and of being grateful for what has been. It is a time for lamenting what might have been and for what has gone wrong. Above all, it is a time of looking to the future, to possibilities and to what might be.

This book has a long past. It was born of a desire and a struggle to blend a concern for the handicapped and the marginalized together with a pursuit of wisdom through the study and teaching of theology.

The first fruits took the form of a doctoral dissertation completed at The Catholic University of America in 1982. Gerard Austin and Paul Philibert helped bring it to light. So did John Ford. David Power, director, mentor, guide, friend, and colleague, believed in the value of the work of Jean Vanier and l'Arche, and my own, when few others did. To them I shall be forever grateful.

The work in its present form was written while I was teaching at Mont-des-Cats, a Cistercian monastery in the north of France, and in Los Angeles, where I have been professor of theology since 1982 at Loyola Marymount University.

These two poles, the "contemplative" and the "academic," come together in the lives of two persons whose love, support, and dedication have guided me each step of the way: Clare Adams, Poor Clare Sister, and Robert Hurd, professor of philosophy. Clare Adams has shown me what is essential in life. Robert Hurd stood by me in difficult times when I was inclined to forget xii / *A Blessed Weakness*

that this work was written as an act of homage to the poor and wounded.

Ann Fleck read the manuscript with a keen eye for language and style. Her insights and criticisms made all the difference. She helped me to see the obvious and encouraged me to state it as such. I learned from her commitment to what is essential in the midst of the most mundane.

Irma Pazmiño, of Loyola Marymount University, typed the manuscript with accuracy and extraordinary care.

John Loudon, my editor at Harper & Row, never stopped believing in the value of this work. For this I am deeply thankful.

My family has supported me throughout it all. Each member has taught me about the ways of the heart. They know that the heart is a blessed weakness.

Finally, it is the people of l'Arche who have helped me to know firsthand something of what I write in these pages. To them I am grateful beyond the telling of it.

Ad multos annos, l'Arche!

Michael Edward Downey
4 August 1985
The twenty-first anniversary of the foundation of l'Arche

1. The Company of the Poor

The story of l'Arche is about persons in community. It is about the handicapped and the "nonhandicapped" who live together in common in the spirit of the Beatitudes. The tale is one of woundedness and suffering, acceptance and healing, tears and fears, compassion, commitment, and celebration.

In what follows, the story of l'Arche is told with particular attention to the heart, the human heart, which is the deepest and most vulnerable part of ourselves. Hurt and scorned at an early age, our hearts often get buried beneath our concern and quest for greater and greater efficiency, practicality, and productivity. Our intelligence, rather than serving the cause of love, tends to rationalize and deny the demands of love's prompting.

Mentally handicapped persons are often ill-equipped in the domain of efficiency and intelligence. They are often not very good with their hands or their heads. They frequently rely spontaneously and with a certain ease upon the heart and are richly endowed with its gifts. In its domain, the weak and the wounded are often the teachers and masters. This is the secret of l'Arche. Those in l'Arche communities have discovered this truth: God can and does communicate directly with the human heart. Thus, those who live so much out of their hearts alone are open to a privileged relationship with God.

Handicapped people are the teachers of the "normal" and the strong. With their tremendous qualities of heart and lives of faith and love, the handicapped give testimony to the truth that the privileged place for meeting with God is in our vulnerability and weakness. It is here that we are not only most open to meeting

God, but it is in fact where we are most like God. Since God *is* love, God is *most* vulnerable. Because God is love, God within us is most visible and accessible in the most vulnerable of people and at our most vulnerable times.

In this telling of the story of l'Arche it is the human person who is central. Jean Vanier often says that the person is the heart. This vision is key to the message of Jean Vanier and l'Arche and gives rise to a way of living that may be called the spirituality of l'Arche: a distinct, indeed unique, manner of living the gospel. What is life at l'Arche like?

In August of 1981, a group from l'Arche went on a month-long vacation at a little farmhouse at the foot of Mont-des-Cats. Atop the Mont, which is situated in the heart of French Flanders, sits a great and beautiful Cistercian monastery. I was fortunate enough to be part of this vacation group, which numbered about fifteen people. Our purpose in being near Mont-des-Cats was to rest and recuperate, to profit from the countryside, and to take advantage of the atmosphere of prayer that permeates the monastery.

My mind is filled with images of our group, a rather diverse and noisy crew to be found in the pews of a revered Cistercian monastery. Hard as we tried to make it otherwise, we were inevitably just a bit late for the services. To get there for prayers or for the Eucharist was something of a voyage in itself each and every day. We had a long way to go up that hill, with wheelchairs, battered bodies, and shaky limbs. Somehow we made it, that crew of ours, most days throughout the month. As much as I enjoyed the liturgy at the monastery, I was always somewhat relieved when our little ark settled again at the base of that mountain. In the little farmhouse at the foot of Mont-des-Cats, near the village of Godewaersvelde (the Flemish word meaning "field of the friends of God") some strong bonds of friendship were formed.

Being with Jean-Luc those days taught me a great deal about

what it means to be human, to be a person. Jean-Luc has some very basic limitations: he cannot walk very well; he can hardly see and cannot speak; he cannot wash or dress, feed or toilet himself. He needs care and kindness and rather constant attention. He frequently behaves in a self-destructive manner. In some quite mysterious way, I learned quite a bit from Jean-Luc, just by being at his side. Something happened in that encounter that is difficult to describe, but too deeply experienced to be denied. Perhaps what I learned most of all is that qualities of heart like those that developed between Jean-Luc and myself lie within each one of us.

I learned that, more often than not, these qualities of compassion, mercy, forgiveness, and tenderness are buried in us, deeply hidden, indeed sometimes crushed. Certain people or particular events or situations can call these qualities forth, but we often avoid them because of the pain and suffering they entail. It is curious, but many times we would rather live with our hearts atrophied, dried up, than open up to those situations and people that call us to really live. Be it in the north of France, Toronto, Erie, London, or Bangalore, l'Arche is a place where such qualities are called forth.

My visit to Mont-des-Cats came on the heels of a summer's stay at l'Arche in Trosly-Breuil. Trosly is perhaps the largest of the communities of l'Arche worldwide, and the oldest. The village is located at the edge of the Compiègne forest and can easily be missed by driving too quickly down the main artery. It is a rural village, an hour's ride from Paris, with few inhabitants. L'Arche members constitute a large part of its population. Some neighbors have welcomed the presence of l'Arche houses, others are more guarded, while still others are a bit hostile.

My time was spent in Breuil, in a *foyer* (which in French means "home") called the Vigne. The Vigne is a three-story house that sits next door to a restored medieval church. One enters the house through a courtyard, passing another l'Arche dwelling en route. At the Vigne there are five middle-aged mentally handicapped men and a varying number of assistants, as the "nonhandicapped" persons are called. There is usually a core group of three assistants, but month-long volunteers and long-term visitors often take on modest responsibilities as well. I was one such long-term visitor, and my responsibilities were modest indeed.

My arrival was during suppertime in the midst of a whirlwind of activity conducted in a language I had loved since childhood, but one I could hardly speak or comprehend. After a quick bite to eat, I joined the others in dishwashing, an enterprise one would think has a universal method, recognizable by all people in all places. Surprise—dishes are not washed the same way in France as they are in the States!

Everything I did needed correction. Every saucer, spoon, and fork seemed to find its way to the wrong place. People asked questions I could not understand because of my inability with the language. I felt helpless and quite ignorant. Even the music did not soothe. Once in bed, I thought, I could gain composure, rest, and face another day with a bit more confidence, but three to a room did not seem conducive to the kind of composure and rest I thought I needed.

In the morning I set off in a bus with the others of my house for my first day in one of the workshops in Trosly. My job was to work alongside others doing very mundane tasks: putting screws in nuts, putting tiles on top of one another, putting pictures in envelopes. Having been in academics for some time, I found such work tiresome and boring. Sitting next to Claude and Marie-Jeanne, who had been at this work for many years, I quickly found the work frustrating and quite tedious. I had very little to say because I hardly knew how to speak. Hard as I tried to listen, I could barely understand. Everything in me revolted. Later my stomach joined in the revolt when at dinnertime I learned the menu: tongue in tomato sauce. From here, there was nowhere to go but up.

Something of a breakthrough came when I recognized the bonds that were growing between and among the five men at the Vigne, the people in the workshop, the other assistants, and myself. On my part, these bonds were growing precisely because my own fragility and inadequacy began to surface in my limitations with language, work, health, and temperament. At l'Arche I became acutely aware of my own vulnerability, something I was not so very aware of in the academic world. None of the ready devices I had previously relied upon worked for me. In the experience of such vulnerability and limitation I began to realize that the seeds of the divine and the capacities of the human heart are found in weakness, not in strength.

Such a realization came to me largely because of Pascal. He had come to the Vigne perhaps ten years prior to my visit, having spent many years before that in an institution. His experience of rejection and anger is all over his face. He is a short fellow with a scruffy beard which he insists on trimming himself. Since he does not use a mirror, the job usually leaves something to be desired. Many people find him irksome and troublesome. He has a way of buzzing around while others are working, drawing attention to himself, and distracting others from getting their work done. At times he is quite unkempt and unsightly. He raises his voice to quarrel at the most unexpected and inopportune of times. Perhaps he draws attention to himself because he never received it as a child, having been rejected and scorned by parents, family, and neighbors, as many handicapped people have been.

But it was Pascal who from my first evening at the Vigne seemed to sense my isolation and my experience of limitation and vulnerability. On that first evening, as I attempted to wash the dishes, it was he who asked where I came from. "Washington" was the response, and "Washingtón" (notice the accent) is the name Pascal calls me even to this day. He would often whisper in my ear or ask questions I could not understand. But inevitably, Pascal would plant a kiss on my forehead, seeming to know of my hurt in being unable to understand or communicate with him or the others. He understood my inability to be understood and to understand.

Pascal is no saint, as anyone at l'Arche could testify (and perhaps would willingly testify). This portrait is not intended to beatify Pascal or any of the others at l'Arche. There were times when we all wished that Pascal would stop buzzing around, stop complaining, and cease arguing and distracting everyone. He was at times quite problematic and disruptive of the peace of the house. At times it was necessary to turn a deaf ear his way. But it was out of a deep suffering and across a deep wound that he reached out to me. After having been rejected and abandoned and despised for so long, he asked my name and touched me in my own fragility and vulnerability. There is something of the eternal, of the divine, in that.

A bond grew between us. It grew quite strong because it grew from the depths, from the heart. It did not grow from common intellectual interest—we are vastly unequal in terms of intellectual ability—or because of a common project to be accomplished or achieved. The bond is rooted in our basic need to love and to be loved, to know one another and to be known, to be understood and accepted in our weakness, which brings with it a kind of freedom. To Pascal, I was not a graduate student caught up in theological speculations or a highly efficient office assistant. I was simply "Washingtón," who bumbled around the kitchen and made mistakes in the workshop, who was a bit tongue-tied with most people, and who was often bewildered, frustrated, and confused. I was limited, vulnerable, wounded, like everyone else, and because of this he was able to reach out to me. When we are strong, accomplished, intelligent, and articulate, we do not appear to be in need of others or of God. When limitation and crisis set in, when the bottom falls out, as it did for me in those first weeks at l'Arche, there is room for others and for God.

Yet in that vulnerability and limitation where others meet us and where we meet God, there is darkness as well as light, despair as well as hope, and sin as well as grace. It is the heart that is revealed in our weakness, and the heart also has qualities that must be purified; it is not all sweetness and light. My heart was touched and called forth by Pascal, and I saw roots of anger, selfishness, and jealousy, in a word, an egotism I had never before glimpsed. Yet, in the face of all of this, there is an experience of hope for healing that comes through community with others and commitment to them. It is our weakness and woundedness that bond us together with others. This is our common lot. Community, then, becomes a place of pardon, both the granting and the receiving of it, and of celebration, when we recognize our vulnerability and need for others and God.

Perhaps my most frequent recollection of Pascal is of him standing by the fireplace, a good distance away from the circle of people joined for evening prayer. Pascal does not seem to be an explicitly religious person; he would rather be off smoking a cigarette than joining in the household prayer. Every now and then he would show up for prayer, and I was glad when he did. I was happy just to see him, because it was he, in fact, who revealed something of God to me. He showed me something of the rejection, the hurt, the vulnerability, the woundedness, and the fragility of God in Jesus Christ. Yet he also revealed to me quite concretely how it is precisely out of that vulnerability and woundedness that God reaches to touch and embrace us. It is in our own weakness and limitation that God comes to us, not in our strength, security, and certitude. God is powerful compassion and mercy who meets us in our weakness, our blessed weakness, the human heart. Those who respond become signs of God's mercy, compassion, forgiveness, and tenderness as they manifest these tremendous qualities of the heart.

Still rather enthusiastically puffing his cigarette, all the while flicking his ashes on the floor, Pascal chimes in as best he can to the closing words of the evening prayer, from the Prayer of l'Arche:

> Seigneur, Bénis-nous de la main de tes pauvres,
> Seigneur, Souris-nous dans le regard de tes pauvres,
> Seigneur, Reçois-nous un jour
> Dans l'heureuse compagnie de tes pauvres!

> (Lord, Bless us by the hand of your poor,
> Lord, Smile on us in the gaze of your poor,
> Lord, Receive us one day
> In the blessed company of your poor!)

2. Life Aboard the Ark

The name *l'Arche* refers to at least three different entities. First of all, it refers to the small home for mentally handicapped men that Jean Vanier began in Trosly-Breuil, France, in 1964. Second, a l'Arche community is one that has in some way been modeled on Vanier's first home. These communities exist throughout the world, and many belong to the International Federation of l'Arche, begun in 1972. Third, the name refers to the large community in Trosly-Breuil and neighboring villages that today is made up of over twenty different homes and a small number of workshops.

The word *l'Arche* is French for "the Ark." In the Old Testament it was into a large boat, an ark, that Noah gathered his family and the different species of animals to preserve them from a great flood. The ark in the Jewish and Christian traditions is symbolic of diversity, refuge, and hope.

There are many different l'Arche communities throughout the world, life at which is shaped by very different social, economic, and religious factors. Part of the reason for the rapid growth of l'Arche is its ability to welcome such tremendous diversity and encourage and create flexible structures to support and sustain this growth. Because of this diversity it is difficult to give a complete portrait of life at l'Arche, but a general one is worth a try.

L'Arche communities are small, familylike groupings who believe in the uniqueness and sacredness of each person whether handicapped or not. The gifts of each person are nurtured and called forth with a preference for the poorest, weakest, and most wounded. Dwellings are located in villages, cities, suburbs, or the countryside; sometimes they are close to the ocean. In these communities, handicapped and nonhandicapped persons share life together. The number of persons in each house varies, as does the ratio of the handicapped to the nonhandicapped. Some houses have mostly men, some mostly women; often there is a good balance. Most communities are comprised of adults but some have children. The type and degree of handicap varies. Some in a house may be explicitly religious, some not; still others may openly disavow any type of personal religious orientation.

An important dimension of life at l'Arche is work. This, too, is undertaken with the varied needs of different persons in mind. People work at what they can and what is available to make a living. Some may work in a pottery shop, others do macramé. Many of those in village and country areas do farming, while those in urban areas work in factories or office buildings. Some work at home doing household chores, and others who cannot get to the workplace have work from the outside brought in.

At l'Arche in Trosly-Breuil, a cluster of workshops in the village is the scene of the workday for most community members. There, many do iron works, tile works, pottery, or subcontract work for different local businesses. The situation at Trosly is not typical. Most l'Arche communities throughout the world make other arrangements for work because they are smaller than Trosly and do not have the cluster of workshops nearby.

Financial support and subsidies likewise vary with location and circumstances. Few l'Arche houses are totally independent of financial aid from government sources. Although all of the members of a house may be working, because of the low pay given them for the type of work they do, some outside assistance is necessary for the survival of the community. But again, the particular details of how such financial arrangements are made are decided according to local needs, circumstances, and resources.

Although life at l'Arche takes diverse forms throughout the world, a recognizable pattern is characteristic of a l'Arche dwelling. In the first place, l'Arche is a home. This is not to suggest that it is a home in the institutional sense, as when we think of a home for delinquent boys or a home for unwed mothers. Quite the contrary. L'Arche thrives because of its commitment to develop and sustain a familylike atmosphere. To attain this, such distinctions as "the helpers" and "the helped," "the carers" and "the cared for," even "the handicapped" and "the nonhandicapped" are really inappropriate to describe life at l'Arche. The community did not begin, nor does it continue, because of a commitment on the part of some to "take care of" others. This makes l'Arche unique. There have been many religious groups, government agencies, and private institutions whose purpose it was, and remains, to care for and help those in need. But l'Arche is different. In Vanier's mind and in the minds of many in the community it is the wounded and the weak who help and teach the "nonhandicapped." Thus any sort of two-class system or mentality is avoided as far as possible.

So, what can be said of a home with a familial atmosphere? There are times for rising and times for going to bed. There is the struggle to awaken, the hustle to get washed, dressed, fed, and off to work. There are the chores of cleaning and making beds, of scrubbing and washing dishes, of having someone out of work and sick in bed. There is the preparation of meals and the washing up. Folks come home from work sometimes tired and grouchy, sometimes satisfied with a day's work well done.

Meals, as in any good home, are focal points in the day. They provide occasions for being together and for sharing life. At l'Arche meals are well prepared, with lots of love. Food is ample without being extravagant. People gather around the table and say a blessing, even if it takes the form of a hearty "Bon appétit!"

The day's stories are exchanged. Sometimes the chef gets a compliment, sometimes someone refuses to eat liver or spinach (or tongue) as the case may be. Usually there is laughter; sometimes there is a fit of anger and a quick departure from the table.

At mealtime there is often a place set for a visitor. It may be someone from the neighborhood or from the workplace. Perhaps it is a relative or someone who once lived with the community but has now moved on but not been forgotten.

There are frequent celebrations in the home: birthdays, anniversaries, name days, holy days, and holidays. And if there is nothing to celebrate, members of l'Arche find or make something to celebrate. In many of the communities, one evening a week is usually set aside as a special time for the people of each home to be together. A special meal is prepared, with a fancy dessert. There are special decorations and music. In such ways, people show that they are happy to be with one another and to share life.

In most cases there is time at the end of each day for quiet reflection and prayer together. Frequently this includes a scriptural reading, a song, shared vocal prayer, and petitions. Members of the household sit in chairs or cross-legged on the floor around a lit candle or an icon and flowers. The prayer is simple and direct; at times it is clumsy. But it is their prayer, and they know that God hears them.

Actually, the extraordinariness of life at l'Arche lies in doing very ordinary things with love and care. It lies in being able to see the miraculous in the most simple events of the daily round of human existence: rising, dressing, working, eating, doing chores, sharing stories, helping each other, praying together, sleeping and dreaming.

People on the outside often tend to glorify and romanticize such persons and groups as Jean Vanier and l'Arche, Dorothy Day and the Catholic Workers, Roger Schutz and the community of

Taizé, or Mother Teresa and the Missionaries of Charity. Life at l'Arche is not to be idealized or idolized. Most people who know about the community from the inside are quick to point this out to visitors or inquirers. They recognize their limitations or at least struggle to do so in honesty.

When I first came to l'Arche in Trosly for the summer of 1981, I found many of the ideas and images I had of l'Arche from reading and hearsay needed changing. My visit enabled me to see that life at l'Arche is at times harsh and dreadful, simply because life is like that. As well as being a place for celebration and healing, l'Arche is a place where darkness and need for pardon are still present. This is because l'Arche is made up of people in community and in human imperfection there is darkness as well as light, error as well as celebration.

L'Arche began on 4 August 1964, when Jean Vanier, at the suggestion of his friend and former teacher Thomas Philippe, bought a home in Trosly-Breuil and invited two handicapped men from a local institution to live with him. Thomas Philippe was then chaplain at a large residential facility and workshop for the handicapped called the Val Fleuri. In March 1965, Vanier was asked to become director of the Val Fleuri and under his directorship the home flourished. Meals gradually became times of joy and celebration. The group began to pray together at home. Soon they began to make pilgrimages, the first of which was to Lourdes, France, in 1965. A sense of peace and joy gradually entered the hearts of the people of the Val Fleuri who, prior to Vanier's directorship, lived in an atmosphere of depression and violence.

During these early years the community was growing. Several other houses were purchased in Trosly-Breuil to begin new community homes for handicapped persons. As l'Arche flourished and its reputation spread, more room was required for the number of handicapped men and women who could not be cared for by their parents or could not find good living accommodations in institutions. Also at this time people were growing in the realization that mentally handicapped people should not be confined to psychiatric hospitals, because their needs are quite different from those of the mentally ill. Mental retardation or the condition of being mentally handicapped is quite different from mental illness, and these two different conditions require different care and attention.

L'Arche continued to grow. Valinos, a community home for women, was started in nearby Cuise-la-Motte. A community for men and women, called Merci, was begun in Courbillac, in the region of Cognac in France. Other homes were opened in various regions of France. Next, a home called Daybreak was opened in Canada, just north of Toronto, by Steve and Ann Newroth, an Anglican couple, making the ecumenical dimension of l'Arche more apparent. Further, the interreligious character of the community surfaced when, in 1970, under the inspiration of Jean Vanier, Asha Niketan, or Home of Hope, was opened to handicapped people of different religious traditions in Bangalore, India. More communities have since begun in India and a few other countries where the great majority of people are of a religious tradition other than Christian. In the early and middle seventies, l'Arche communities were begun in Erie, Pennsylvania, in Canterbury, England, in Copenhagen, Denmark, and in Edmonton, Cornwall, Ottawa, and Stratford, Canada. There are communities in Mexico and Honduras, Australia and Scotland, Burkina Faso (formerly Upper Volta) and Washington, D.C. A new community has just begun in Israel. In little more than twenty years l'Arche has grown to over seventy communities worldwide (representing nearly 200 homes).

One of the more recent developments in the growth of l'Arche has been the establishment of the Forestière at Trosly-Breuil, a home that houses ten severely handicapped men and women. None of these handicapped people can talk; only a few can walk. The establishment of the Forestière is evidence of the growing commitment among members of the community to the poorest and most wounded of society, who require very special care and attention indeed. In April 1983, the community opened more homes in nearby Cuise-la-Motte that welcome severely handicapped men and women. Furthermore, l'Arche is also moving toward the establishment of more and more communities within the poorer countries of the world. Responding to what l'Arche perceives to be the leading of the Spirit, it is moving ever closer to welcoming people who are the poorest and most wounded in our world.

Until 1972 the communities of l'Arche outside of France were totally independent of each other and from Trosly-Breuil. Then in 1972 the directors of all these communities met in Trosly-Breuil and formed the International Federation of l'Arche, a very loosely knit organization that still leaves each community free to develop according to its needs, thus allowing it to be more integrated into its own society and culture. The role of the coordinator of the International Federation is not that of a director or superior, but rather one of advisor, friend, and inspirational guide. "The Federation is not a legal structure and . . . the coordinator has no power at all in the individual houses."[1] The International Federation is an association and not a hierarchical unit. What binds the communities together on the international level is what can only be referred to as the spirit of l'Arche, animated by the belief in the uniqueness and sacredness of the handicapped person.

The common spirit of l'Arche has flourished for a number of reasons, but important among them is the fact that a good number of assistants and directors throughout the world have lived and worked for some time in the community of Trosly-Breuil, the scene of the foundation of l'Arche. While there is this common spirit animating the communities throughout the world, each community at the same time has considerable independence and, in many cases, has taken on quite a unique character. For example, Asha Niketan, in Bangalore, is the first home to be founded in the Third World. Although the director of the community has not always been Indian, efforts are made consistently to integrate the community into the society and culture of Bangalore. The spirit of the community is interreligious, with Christians and Hindus joining together in daily prayer. Community life at Asha Niketan is quite different from the community life at Trosly-Breuil, where the majority of people in the community are Christian and the Roman Catholic liturgy plays a large part in the community's life, but it is a viable l'Arche community nonetheless, providing love and care for its members.

To attempt to examine the structures of the communities of l'Arche at the local, regional, and international levels would take us down a long path that would not really help us understand Jean Vanier and l'Arche.[2] Let it suffice to say that the genius of l'Arche and of Vanier seems to be in the creation of structures flexible enough to allow for constant change, growth, and diversity. As a result, structures at the international level are constantly changing to allow for the rapid growth of the communities worldwide. Structures at every level are provisional by nature. The government of l'Arche is ordered toward encouraging a very high degree of member participation on all levels of responsibility. Attention has been given to involving the handicapped as far as possible in government and decision making. The provisional and flexible nature of the structure together with the high degree of member participation imply a certain fluctuation, one might say instability, within the structure itself. But the flexibility of the structure has a positive side as well—it can be more responsive to needs of the human person, changing to meet various needs as they arise. Such flexibility also demands greater reliance upon God's providence, beyond any structure, government, or institution.

Some suggest that it is something beyond the structure of l'Arche that is finally the only explanation for its continued survival and growth.[3] Organization and structure at l'Arche are designed to serve the aim of the emergence of the full gift of each person in relation to a community of forgiveness and celebration. It is this that keeps the community together and enables it to continue to grow on the individual, local, and international levels.

In describing life at l'Arche something needs to be said about the dimension of professional competence and care. Each community has a variety of persons with various disabilities and problems. Professional expertise in psychiatry, medicine, nursing and related fields is required, not simply desired, for the health and well-being of the community. Services of these various professions are part of much of what goes on at l'Arche, because it is essential that people be challenged to change and to develop their potential. More often than not people who provide professional services are not members or assistants within the community. Professional assistance usually comes from outside the community. Even if certain assistants are professionally competent in medicine, nursing, physical therapy, or psychiatry, it must be understood that l'Arche is not a community of professionals helping the handicapped. Though respectful and appreciative of the contributions of these various disciplines, l'Arche recognizes the debilitating effects of professionalism devoid of true human concern and compassion. Though some may have had some training for dealing with the handicapped, many have not. In many ways, all that is required of them is a lot of good will. Mistakes may be made by those without professional competence and mistakes may be made by those with it. Suffice it to say that at l'Arche there is deep appreciation for the importance of professional competence as part of the overall life of the community. But professional skills are understood as truly effective when they are found together with human concern, care, and compassion. Assistants at l'Arche may have very little, if any, professional training, but it is their concern, care, compassion, and a certain *savoir faire* (or "know-how") in dealing with the wounded and the vulnerable that is the kind of competence developed at l'Arche.

Because we live in an age that places emphasis upon practicality, sooner or later the question is bound to emerge: "Does l'Arche work?" We are interested in seeing achievements and results. Without oversimplifying the matter, it is fair to say that l'Arche does work. That is not to say that "handicapped" persons become more "normal" (whatever that might mean) as they spend time at l'Arche. Nor is it to say that the handicapped people at l'Arche are able to return to the mainstream of society after a given period with l'Arche, although this is true in some cases. It is rather to say that at l'Arche people find a place in which to grow and develop according to their own potential, to become the best persons they can be. Although there are exceptions and for some persons l'Arche does not work, it is fair to say for the vast majority of members l'Arche does work; it is successful. To cite statistics to verify this claim would be outside the limits of this work. The happiness and sense of satisfaction evident in most of the handicapped at l'Arche as well as the ever-increasing growth of the communities worldwide lend credence to the claim that l'Arche does work. Perhaps the challenge for those readers who remain skeptical or unconvinced is to visit a l'Arche community, then visit another "facility" for handicapped persons and make a judgment.

If l'Arche works, it is because of two factors. The first is that l'Arche is modeled on the family. This is the main reason it is so successful. We need to understand ever more deeply that the family is the primary social unit, the most important thing, the keystone of all human community, Christian or otherwise. Devaluation of the family kills any hope for deep and abiding relationships between and among persons and for any authentic community. L'Arche recognizes itself as a family, the family of l'Arche, and because of this it works.

The belief in the uniqueness and sacredness of each person regardless of handicap, a belief grounded in faith in a Source and Sustainer of all life, is the second reason why l'Arche works. This belief, which may not be explicitly religious in every case, is central to the way of life at l'Arche and is shaped, in large part, by the vision of Jean Vanier. Who is this man? This question is treated in the following chapter.

3. Vanier at Sea

Jean Vanier is an enormously tall man affectionately called "la grande girafe" by some at l'Arche. His back is arched and from the looks of things he does not care too much about clothes, though it would be unfair to describe him as unkempt. Like many men his age, he is gray and balding. He has an extraordinary store of energy—he is the first one out of bed in the morning, the last one to rest. Like others to whom people look for counsel, inspiration, and leadership, the most striking thing about Vanier is his quality of presence. When you are with him, his attention is given to you completely. He listens.

Born in Geneva, Switzerland, on 10 September 1928, the Canadian Jean Vanier is one of five children of the late nineteenth Governor-General of Canada, Georges Philias Vanier, and his wife, Pauline Archer Vanier. During his early school years Vanier was viewed as showing no great intellectual gifts or athletic ability but as having a very warm and attractive character.[4] At the age of thirteen while a student of the Canadian Jesuits, he applied through his own initiative and was admitted to the Royal Naval College in England. Several years later Vanier served as an officer in the Royal Navy and then went on to serve in the Royal Canadian Navy. At twenty he was already an officer on Canada's only aircraft carrier.

During his service as an officer it became clear that he would not stay long in the military. The young officer would spend many hours in prayer and frequently found himself reciting the divine office during the night watch when the ship was in harbor. In 1950, Jean resigned his commission with the navy.

The resignation from the navy brought with it the task of taking up the search for his place in life. The former military man looked into several different Christian communities that were trying to live a life of poverty and simplicity. He joined a small community called Eau Vive in France, directed by the French Dominican Thomas Philippe. Eau Vive was a community of students, lay men for the most part, situated in a poor area near Paris close to the Dominican community of the Saulchoir. At Eau Vive the students prayed together and studied philosophy and theology in order to deepen their commitment to Jesus Christ and the gospel.

When Vanier arrived at Eau Vive there were about eighty people there. Not long after his arrival, poor health required the resignation of Thomas Philippe and Vanier was asked to direct the community. The change of directorship ruptured the community's good relations with the Dominican community of the Saulchoir. Some of the Dominicans considered Eau Vive to be under their direction and were displeased that its leadership should be assumed by a layman. As a result, members of Eau Vive were not permitted to study with the Dominicans or have access to the Dominican library. This caused the departure of many of the members of Eau Vive. Most of the small number who remained with the community took up their studies at the Institut Catholique in Paris. In spite of all difficulties, the community continued for about four years.

While he was at Eau Vive, Vanier began to study for ordination to the priesthood. His intention was to serve in the diocese of Quebec. Not long before his return to Canada to prepare for ordination, Vanier was asked to leave Eau Vive by authorities of the church. This event left him uncertain, much like his experience at the time of his departure from the military. Vanier decided against finishing the preparations necessary for ordination.

During the years that followed the experience at Eau Vive,

Vanier lived more or less alone. He spent a year in retreat at the Cistercian abbey of Bellefontaine in France, and the following year was spent on a little farm. One of the final years of this period of solitude was spent in a small house in Fatima, Portugal. Shortly thereafter, Vanier successfully completed his doctoral dissertation on the moral philosophy of Aristotle at the Institut Catholique in Paris.[5] Upon completion of his dissertation in the early sixties he joined the faculty of Saint Michael's College in Toronto to begin a career of teaching philosophy.

It was not long after this that Vanier visited his friend Thomas Philippe, who had recently begun a chaplaincy for the mentally handicapped men living at the Val Fleuri, Trosly-Breuil, France. Their meeting in Trosly-Breuil was for Vanier the end of a long personal search and the beginning of an extraordinary venture. At the suggestion of Thomas Philippe, Jean Vanier bought a little home in Trosly-Breuil, fixed it up a bit, and invited two handicapped men, Raphael and Philippe, to come live with him. He christened this home *l'Arche* on 4 August, 1964. Thus was the ark set to sail.

Vanier's family and friends were surprised by this decision. Few could understand why he would abandon a very promising career as a university professor for the life he now chose. The seemingly endless search for his place in life had led Vanier to commit himself to share his life with two mentally handicapped men. The glamour of a promising military career behind him, the responsibility of directing a community of students lifted from him, the opportunity of a promising academic future put aside, Vanier decided to live with Raphael and Philippe with no clear plan or vision for the future. This simple, concrete decision was what needed to be done at the time. Vanier knew that this was something he had to do in answer to a call. It was this decision, this gesture of welcome extended to Raphael and Philippe, that sowed the seed now flowering in the communities of l'Arche spread throughout the world.

The *foyer* of l'Arche in Trosly-Breuil, the first to be christened l'Arche.

That first year was tough going. The house needed to be repaired, money was not always plentiful, and neighbors were not always enthusiastic or helpful. But help did come, some of the neighbors were very cooperative, and the ark sailed.

The following March the director of the Val Fleuri and most of its staff resigned. Vanier was asked to become its director. Having very little experience with handicapped people beyond his short time with Raphael and Philippe, he was suddenly plunged into life with thirty handicapped men. Slowly people came to help. They were few in number at first, but they came consistently. Vanier laughs a bit when he tells how ill-prepared he was to assume the responsibility of directing the Val Fleuri and breaks into a bellylaugh as he explains, complete with all the gestures, how he practiced giving injections to plump navel oranges before he felt confident enough to administer them to those who needed such medication.

As Vanier's experience with mentally handicapped people deepened, his contact with other groups of marginalized people increased as well. His "Letter to My Brothers and Sisters in Prison," written following a number of visits to the prisons of Canada, shows his concern and compassion for those who have been confined to prison.[6] Jean's contact with men and women in prison not only in Canada but throughout the world continues to this day.

In the late sixties Vanier had the opportunity of meeting many parents and families of mentally handicapped people. He became increasingly aware of their importance in the lives of their children. Along with a few other people, most notably Marie-Hélène Mathieu, Vanier founded Faith and Light, an international Christian association which has created small communities of mentally handicapped people, their parents, families, and friends, which meet together regularly for times of sharing, prayer, and celebration. This closely knit association, with 630 communities in 37 countries, has been a source of strength and support for its members. Occasionally, these communities come together for an international pilgrimage.

Yet another dimension of Vanier's life emerged during this period of the late sixties. In response to a group of Canadian priests who asked him to direct their retreat, Vanier gave the first Faith and Sharing retreat at Marylake, near Toronto, in 1968. Not wanting to give a retreat for priests exclusively, Vanier accepted their invitation upon the condition that the retreat be open to all Christians and all men and women of good will. Vanier has continued to animate the Faith and Sharing retreat movement in Europe, North America, Africa, the Middle East, and the Caribbean as well as India, Australia, and New Zealand, among others. The retreats that take place under the name of Faith and Sharing vary from large gatherings of three or four hundred people that last for four or five days to much smaller and briefer local and regional gatherings. All are welcome: lay people, priests, ministers, young and old, rich and poor. A particular welcome is extended to mentally handicapped and physically disabled people.

At each gathering of Faith and Sharing an effort is made to develop a deeper understanding of the message of the Christian Beatitudes. Joined together in a spirit of prayer, the participants attempt to discover the meaning of this message: to work as one community to break down the barriers between rich and poor, handicapped and "normal," young and old, weak and strong, prisoner and free, with a special preference for the people most wounded and rejected in the world.

Since 1969 Vanier has given conferences and animated meetings of young people in France, Canada, the United States, India, Belgium, Britain, Denmark, and Norway, among others. Often these conferences are called by the name *Katimavic*, an Eskimo term that means "a place of meeting." The aim of such meetings is to enable young people to penetrate more fully into the message of the Beatitudes and the mystery of the gospel.

In 1964, Jean Vanier, Raphael, and Philippe climbed aboard the ark. This was a small, apparently insignificant gesture, but one that turned out to draw a great deal of attention. Vanier's writings and work and the name of l'Arche are recognized today by many people of various social, economic, and religious backgrounds throughout the world. In 1971 in Washington, D.C., Jean Vanier received the Kennedy Award for his action on behalf of mentally handicapped adults. In 1973 in Ottawa, Vanier was named Officer Chancellor of the Order of Canada. Other awards, citations, and honorary degrees have been declined by him for personal reasons. Praise and recognition by politicians and university administrators undoubtedly come as a surprise to one who has chosen simply to live with the poorest and weakest of society.

In Vanier's early career we can see signs of some of the

concerns that work to fashion l'Arche. His decision to give up a military career shows early signs of his later intense commitment to peace and nonviolence. The importance of prayer in his life is foreshadowed in his faithful recitation of the divine office while keeping the night watch. The commitment to the value of community life finds early expression in his decision to live at Eau Vive. This same community allowed him to live in the evangelical simplicity and poverty that characterize the communities of l'Arche today. His seemingly endless search for the will of God in his earlier years offers a foretaste of the spirit of living with the provisional, the uncertain, which is typical of the communities of l'Arche. Finally, his doctoral dissertation on Aristotle, with its emphasis on justice, friendship, and contemplation, points out his early concern for understanding the needs and aspirations of the human person, and it is the human person, especially the poorest and most wounded, who lies at the heart of l'Arche.

Although Vanier's decisive lesson about suffering and vulnerability, anguish and rejection was learned from his experience with the handicapped, we cannot say that these were entirely absent from his life before l'Arche. It would not be unfair to envision Vanier during those years prior to l'Arche as someone at sea, looking for his proper course in life but quite unable to find it. There were the years in the navy, the time at Eau Vive, the time in Fatima. Finally there was the brief time of teaching at Saint Michael's College in Toronto. L'Arche began in 1964 after a long personal search. Vanier was nearly thirty-six years old at the time. From one perspective we might say that Vanier did not succeed at any of the things he had done before l'Arche, or at least they did not succeed in making him happy. The events that happened in his life, some of which were very painful, and the sense of not being able to find his place in life until age thirty-six, the wandering from this thing to that—all give the impression that when Vanier speaks of suffering and vulnerability as the occasion for growth and hope, he is speaking of something he knows from his own experience. Perhaps l'Arche was born because everything else that Vanier had tried to do or tried to live did not work, had not been successful. He was available in 1964 because he had not yet found his place, his course in life. Would it be too strong a statement to suggest that he found acceptance and affirmation of his own weakness, insecurity, and suffering in Raphael and Philippe in a way that he had never experienced before? It is Vanier's own struggles, uncertainty, confusion, and rejection that he shares with the men and women of l'Arche and that teach him the wisdom that the seeds of the divine in the human heart are found in weakness, not in strength.

A brief story may serve to throw light on this point. Several years ago, while driving across town to hear Jean Vanier speak at Georgetown University, a few of the Little Sisters of Jesus of Charles de Foucauld told me of the close bonds between their own community and the community of l'Arche. Some of them, one of whom was in the back seat of my little blue Pinto, had come to know the Vanier family while in Canada. While in Canada it seems that this Sister was constantly receiving requests from the Vanier family for prayers for Jean Vanier, who during his twenties and early thirties seemed unsure of what to do with his life. He seemed to them to be wandering, floating, drifting, a bit lost. "He certainly seems to have found his way," I suggested with obvious admiration. "We have not stopped our prayers, though," one of the Sisters assured me; she added that in their prayers they are mindful of all of the communities of l'Arche throughout the world.

Imagine for a moment the frustration and embarrassment of Canada's "first family" when one of the sons seemed to be doing nothing with his life, roaming from this thing to that, from one place to the next, seemingly unable to make up his mind. And imagine the curiosity and confusion surrounding the decision of the son of one of the most celebrated figures on the national and international scenes not to go on for ordination when he was so close to it. What must it have been like for the parents of this man in his mid-thirties with a doctorate in philosophy to learn that, after all the searching and moving from this thing to the next, he was going to settle in an obscure village in France with two mentally handicapped men?

Stories about this time in Vanier's life, a period spoken of very little, show something of the struggle and pain he has experienced. The truth embodied in l'Arche is something Vanier has lived himself and has learned to share with others, as they have shared their struggle and pain with him. And the truth is this: the divine life within and the capacities of the human heart are found in weakness, not in strength.

The early life of Jean Vanier, the influences upon him, and what he considers important all help us to understand what kind of person he is and what he has done. Perhaps no more should be said of the man, because attempts to give a living portrait of him frequently wind up making him seem like a guru or a living saint rising above the affairs and concerns of daily life, and this is certainly not the case.

His concern is for the people of his community in the first place. The people of l'Arche he refers to as "my people." This does not mean that they are his possessions or that he is their leader, but rather that they belong together, that they are responsible for one another, that his home is with them. But his care and concern move to embrace all of those who, like his brothers and sisters of l'Arche, live lives of simplicity and great suffering. These include prisoners, little children, the elderly, people of the Third World, indeed all of those who live in situations of distress, crisis, and vulnerability. Like the handicapped people of l'Arche, such persons often remind the "normal," healthy, and robust of the basics of life: the need for acceptance and love, the need to create and to find meaning in life. Such persons and situations are a further revelation of what Vanier has discovered in his own community: that each person, no matter how wounded, has great dignity and the capacity to enrich others. The communities of l'Arche, to which he gave birth, are a proclamation that salvation comes through the little and the forgotten, the weak and despised, the wounded and rejected of the world. Vanier has chosen these, and his manner of life, the choices he makes, and the way he relates to himself, others, and the world manifest his predilection for the weak of this earth whom God has chosen to confound the wise.

It is the handicapped who, in their love, have revealed Jesus to Vanier. He has learned much from them and is deeply indebted to them. They have shown him what it means to live in simplicity, to love with great tenderness, to speak the truth in love, to forgive, to welcome openly, to recognize weakness and know the need for God, to be trusting and confident in troubles, and to accept woundedness and hardships with love.

If our portrait of Vanier has given the impression that Vanier is someone rather above the rest of us, a guru or saint, then it is inaccurate and dishonest. Vanier makes mistakes and has hurt other people. He is not above reproach, and he knows and admits it. Maybe it would be best to say that the qualities in this portrait of Vanier constitute what he hopes to become rather than what he has already accomplished, but it is also true that the key to understanding another is to know what he or she hopes and strives to become.

The vessel Vanier commanded during his days as a naval officer has most probably been sold for scrap, but the little ark that Vanier set to sail with Raphael and Philippe in 1964 is still afloat. Having weathered many a turbulent storm, the fragile little ark appears to have a long course yet ahead.

4. Something to Learn

To understand who Jean Vanier is and what he has done it is also important to take into consideration the key persons and events that have gone to shape his life and the person he has become. Of course, Raphael and Philippe and the many men and women of l'Arche who love him deeply have influenced him beyond the telling of it, but first, let us turn to those persons and events that appear to have had the strongest and most lasting influence upon Vanier and through him upon the way of life at l'Arche. These include Jesus and the gospel, Vanier's father, Thomas Philippe, the study of Aristotle, and his encounter with India and the Third World.

Of all influences upon Jean Vanier, it is the person of Jesus and the message of the gospel that are most important. He often tells the story of how at l'Arche they rarely refer to Jesus Christ, or Christ, or the Christ. Most often only the name Jesus is used. He says that this is because of the very personal, intimate relationship that the handicapped have with Jesus. This tells us something of Vanier's own relationship with God.

Vanier writes that he began l'Arche as a response in Christian faith:

I began l'Arche in 1964, in the desire to live the Gospel and to follow Jesus Christ more closely. Each day brings me new lessons on how much Christian life must grow in commitment to life in community, and on how much that life needs faith, the love of Jesus and the presence of the Holy Spirit if it is to deepen. Everything I say about life in community . . . is inspired by my faith in Jesus.[7]

But Jean Vanier's reading of the gospel and its importance to him go back much further than the foundation of l'Arche. It was his original inspiration and has remained his consistent source of inspiration, even as his vision and understanding have matured. Vanier grew up in a home with parents of deep Christian faith. Their influence upon his own faith development is perhaps beyond measure.

Although our focus in what follows is on the importance of Vanier's father, the importance of his mother cannot be underestimated. It is simply that Vanier has written and spoken of his father in a way that he has not of his mother. So when we speak of his father's influence upon him we can be sure his mother and other family members are represented as well.

Shortly after his father's death, Vanier wrote *In Weakness, Strength*, a short book about his father's spiritual life.[8] The spiritual values of which Vanier speaks in this work tell us not only about his father's spiritual life, but also about those of his father's values that Vanier himself cherished and that no doubt had an effect upon him.

Georges P. Vanier, nineteenth Governor-General of Canada, died on 5 March 1967. Jean Vanier was thirty-eight years old at the time. Most significant is that in writing about the life of his father, Vanier made no attempt to give an account of the worldly successes and accomplishments of this internationally recognized figure. This has been the task of Robert Speaight.[9] Vanier, rather, describes the spiritual life of his father. This in itself indicates that the most important things about the late Governor-General to his son were his spiritual qualities or values and not the spectacular awards and military decorations of a war hero who walked with the high and the mighty. It is in the domain of the spiritual that Georges Vanier is remembered by his son.

Georges Vanier was, aside from being a fine soldier, statesman, and public figure, a deeply religious man, but he was by no means an outspoken preacher or an evangelical witness as these terms are commonly understood. He spoke very little in public about his faith in God. A deep respect for others was the source of his discretion concerning his own faith.

Georges Vanier's early religious training had a marked Jansenist thrust that emphasized fear rather than love. At the urging of his wife, he attended the Good Friday service in 1938 at which the Scottish Jesuit Robert Steuart preached. Upon hearing the sermon, Vanier realized the importance of love instead of fear in Christian life.

From that day, Georges Vanier's spiritual life began to flourish. The Eucharist took on a central role, as his growing desire to have the eucharistic presence in the chapel of his residence makes clear. He became an avid reader of books on spirituality, most especially those by the Carmelites Teresa of Avila, John of the Cross, and Thérèse of Lisieux. Pauline Archer Vanier had long been attracted to Carmelite spirituality. It was she who introduced her husband to the Carmelite spiritual sources and to the numerous Carmelites with whom Georges Vanier corresponded after his "conversion" in 1938 until his death.

He constantly tried to reach a proper balance between an active public life filled with the heavy responsibilities of a government official and his deeper, inner life developed through the inspiration of the writings of the mystics and men and women committed to the life of prayer and contemplation. Georges Vanier sought the direction of spiritual masters in a domain with which he all too easily admitted his unfamiliarity.

Georges Vanier was an intelligent man, it is true, and was graced with the common sense to know his own limitations, yet he was not by any stretch of the imagination a great intellectual. Furthermore, "he had an instinctive horror of the complicated and of theological discussions."[10] Because of this he sought direction from those spiritual masters whose writings, he believed, did not treat lofty and abstract matters. His spiritual life was one of "simplicity and humility . . . love and respect for all men flowing from his personal love and experience of Jesus Christ."[11] Here we can see the influence of the writings of Charles de Foucauld, especially during the later years of Georges Vanier's life as his firm commitment to justice expanded into a simple and sensitive love for all people, regardless of nation, race, or class.

When we look to the life of Georges Vanier a bit more closely, we see that certain Christian themes deserve our attention because their traces are found very clearly in the life of Jean Vanier and l'Arche. These include God's strength in human weakness, the importance of perseverance, spiritual simplicity, providence, Mary, the primacy of love, and unity.

Beneath the aura of the outstanding military hero, decorated soldier, eloquent statesman, and family man and father, we see in Georges Vanier the deeper reality of a man who suffered enormously. Perhaps the most obvious example of this suffering was his own physical handicap. The amputation of his leg, a consequence of an injury while at war, caused him significant pain and continual discomfort. Especially during his later years, walking even the slightest distance brought him to the brink of exhaustion. However, suffering was in no way an obstacle in his spiritual life, but rather its very foundation. The infirmities he suffered enhanced rather than diminished his faith. His weakness and his infirmities caused him to be truly humble when confronted with the numerous tasks, responsibilities, and honors given him. In a letter dated 26 August 1960, he wrote: "I feel that only in weakness can I glorify God."[12] In his inaugural speech as Governor-General on 15 September 1959, Georges Vanier stated publicly: "In exchange for His strength, I offer my weakness."[13] The clear perception of the link between his own profound human weakness and the strength and mercy of God was one of the foundation stones of his spiritual life.

In the midst of many responsibilities and physical sufferings, it was necessary for Georges Vanier to make a constant effort to develop in the spiritual life. It is sometimes difficult for us to imagine that constant struggle and striving are necessary for someone who meets with a great deal of success in life, as Georges Vanier apparently did. We are inclined to believe that the spiritual life develops naturally, as it were, with great ease and with little or no effort. This was not the case for Georges Vanier. The duties of state, the rigors and joys of family life, the discipline of a regular life of prayer, and the constant suffering due to his physical handicap called for vigorous effort and patient perseverance on his part. There can be no question that to preserve his faith Georges Vanier was required to be extraordinarily courageous and persevering in dealing with the numerous obstacles life presented to him. Perhaps the secret of greatness is to recognize an obstacle as an opportunity.

Although he walked with the high and the mighty, the strong and the powerful, Georges Vanier had what might be called a simple faith, the faith of a little child. Jean Vanier tells of an occasion when he was filled with excitement because of an important theological discovery and went to his father to share the insight, only to be reminded of his father's genuine disinterest in such matters. Prior to the religious experience of Good Friday 1938, his faith did not play an important role in his life. After this experience of recognizing in Jesus Christ the God of love, he saw his whole life and all of reality in a new light. It was this personal relationship with Jesus Christ that was the foundation of his faith. So consuming was this relationship that "he felt no need to be clouded with unspiritual considerations or fine points of doctrine or dogma."[14] He felt a strong attraction to children, especially toward the end of his life, and when with children, he himself became like a child. It appears, however, that his spiritual life was not marked by that sort of "childish" immaturity and irresponsibility that sometimes find their way into the lives of some who aspire to simplicity in the spiritual life. The challenges of daily life, the seemingly cruel and harsh physical sufferings, and the many responsibilities of a political figure of Georges Vanier's stature would not allow such leisurely flights into the world of spiritual fantasy.

Georges Vanier had inscribed upon his coat of arms the words *Fiat Voluntas Dei* ("God's Will Be Done"). By choosing these words he made known, publicly and officially, the deep motivation of his life. In all that he did he desired to conform his life to the will of God. He had a deep sense of God's abiding presence in human life, not only in the sacramental life of the church, but also in the ordinary events of daily life. He believed that the will of God would be made known in such ordinary events if one simply knew how to wait for it. Jean Vanier writes: "This confidence in Divine aid, and his wish to have his own will conform to God's, sometimes complicated life for us all. His natural temperament was to put off making decisions."[15]

Looking over his personal history toward the end of his life, Georges Vanier was able to see the active presence of God at each step along the way. It was his deep faith in God's guidance at each moment that enabled him to wait patiently for God in the ordinary events of daily life, even as those most dear to him urged him to be more decisive as he waited for God's will to be made clear.

Among the various symbols on the coat of arms of Georges Vanier there is a small holm oak. This little tree is a representation of the one at Fatima, Portugal, which is the location of one of the more widely known apparitions of Mary. On his official coat of arms Georges Vanier gave witness to his love for her. It is clear from his correspondence with the contemplative men and women religious of his day, especially the Carmelite nuns, that it was important for him to be close in spirit to those he thought were living a deep and personal relationship with God. He had a deep respect and affection for those he felt were close to God.

This is the secret of his love for and devotion to Mary. For Georges Vanier it was Mary who had lived closer than anyone else to Jesus, and in faith he held that it is she who remains closest to him. Jean Vanier writes: "My father felt that by approaching Mary lovingly, he would be sanctified, that she would bless him, that she would help him love Jesus and become humble with the heart of a child."[16] In loving the one closest to Jesus, Georges Vanier grew in love for those who in every age seem to have a deep and abiding attraction to and affection for her. He frequently made pilgrimages to the Marian shrines of Lourdes and Fatima where the poor and the lowly gather to honor Mary, the mother of tenderness and compassion. Georges Vanier, who had access to some of the most famous and powerful of his day, saw in each visit to these places an opportunity to walk with those who were truly close to God. In visiting Lourdes he considered it a privilege to be able to bathe in the waters with the poor, the ill, and the wounded. It is often the simple and the poor who are drawn to the tenderness and compassion of Mary. It was because of his own conviction that he was indeed one of the "little" ones and his earnest prayer to become more so, that Georges Vanier recognized in Mary the silent and compassionate one who was closest to Jesus in his moments of weakness, vulnerability, and littleness: in the crib in Bethlehem and on the cross at Calvary.

Every true Christian finds certain aspects of the gospel message more attractive and nourishing than others. This personal attraction, which is often not even a conscious choice, results in as many different lived spiritualities as there are people who live the gospel message. But in the life of every Christian the reality of love enters the picture if that life is authentically Christian. For Georges Vanier love was the central and most important reality of Christian life, as his own words testify:

Of all the attributes of the spirit, the greatest is love. . . . May our lives therefore be founded on love, and hallowed by prayer which is love's expression.

We all need love—to give and to receive. It has been said that a mystic is a man who has fallen in love with God and that the first step to that state is prayer. We all have to fall in love with someone—why not God? And through him— with our neighbor.[17]

The primacy of love in Georges Vanier's life was true not only of his relationship with God in the quiet moments of prayer, but also of his relationships with other people. Testimony after testimony bears witness to the extraordinary ability he had of making each person he met feel that he was a personal friend. Catherine de Hueck Doherty wrote at the time of Georges Vanier's death: "He would give . . . the greatest gift one person can give to another, the gift of attentiveness, the gift of being a listener, of truly being approachable to any person's need."[18] "He managed to convey this impression for the simple reason that it was true, every human being was precious to him."[19] He and his wife had a great gift for receiving and welcoming friends, and this heritage of hospitality continues to this day at the home of Pauline Vanier in Trosly-Breuil, as many a visitor to l'Arche can attest to.

It appears that aside from the gift of friendship, Georges Vanier had the rare gift of being a true leader. By this is not meant the ability to command an army or the capacity to issue authoritative orders to one's subjects. Rather, a true leader is one who has the extraordinary ability to call forth from others the very best they have to give. As Vanier notes, his father "had the rare gift of making another aware of his own worth or capabilities."[20]

As his years went on, he opened himself more and more to a wide variety of people in need. Not only was he attentive and receptive to those closest to him in the official residence and those in high government positions, but with increasing intensity "he wished to follow Jesus in his love for the poor, and in his dealings with them he showed a wonderful sensitivity and tact."[21] Toward the end of his life he wanted to become the universal brother to all people Charles de Foucauld wrote about. And like the life of de Foucauld, the life of Georges Vanier is marked by an increasing awareness of God's special love and predilection for the poor as seen in Jesus of Nazareth. As a result of his personal relationship with Jesus, Georges Vanier was moved to love those who were closest to Jesus while at Nazareth: the poor, lowly, infirm, and insignificant. We might say that the intense love of God born in the heart of Georges Vanier grew in such measure that during the later years of his life he loved without bounds, as if with the very heart of God.

The deep longing to become a universal brother that Georges Vanier felt was shown in his strong conviction about the need for unity. He was certain that the primacy of love itself called for unity. He worked untiringly for unity not only among the Christian churches, but among the various groups within the Canadian people. Likewise, he worked for harmony among the numerous political factions of his time. By establishing an institute on family life he hoped to bring about reconciliation and unity within the primary social structure. In every realm he was a peacemaker, a reconciler, alive with a desire for unity, that deep and abiding unity that can only come when one is fully united with God.

Especially toward the end of his life this deep and abiding thirst for unity seemed to consume him. As Governor-General, Georges Vanier made it clear that he would be happy to participate in worship in churches other than his own. When he did participate in other worship services people had the sense that he was doing more than discharging an official duty. By participating in these various religious services and in his dealings with a wide variety of people, he showed himself to be someone so close to God that he could find the divine presence not only in the people and religious services dearest to him, but also in each and every event and circumstance of human life. Each facet of life was an opportunity for God's revelation and presence.

In these Christian themes that played an important part in Georges Vanier's life we get a glimpse of some of the things that later become features of Jean Vanier's own life and work. For example, the contrast between fear, which was emphasized in Georges Vanier's religious training before his conversion in 1938, and love, which was paramount in his life after that time, is dealt with by Jean Vanier in his work entitled *Be Not Afraid*, which is essentially a treatment of the dynamics of love and fear.[22] His father's distaste for heavy theological discussions and horror of complicated matters as well as his desire to grow in childlikeness and simplicity show a tendency to value the simple and the human, an approach that later aided Vanier in his attempt to build communities that join people endowed with intellectual ability with people sometimes severely limited in mental capacity. The primacy of love and the concern for the claims of justice are values appreciated and retained throughout Jean Vanier's own life and work. His father's deep attachment to and affection for his own religious tradition coupled with an openness to the truth within other religious traditions is reflected in Jean Vanier's own growing commitment to the primacy of the human person irrespective of religious and cultural differences. The interplay between the active and contemplative dimensions of his father's life helps us to understand the importance of the struggle that Jean Vanier and the communities of l'Arche face anew each day in the effort to strike a balance between prayer and active service. Finally, the theme of weakness as one of the foundations of his father's spiritual life as well as his increased awareness in old age of God's special preference for the poor cast light upon Jean Vanier's own attitude toward what is primary and basic in the spiritual life.

While at Eau Vive, Jean Vanier came to know the French

Dominican Thomas Philippe, and their friendship, mutual respect, and admiration have grown ever since. Many suggest that l'Arche cannot be understood unless Thomas Philippe and Jean Vanier are seen as two sides of a single coin. Thomas Philippe views himself as a poor country priest, a shepherd, and Vanier as more of a prophet. Both the priestly and the prophetic are essential to the life of l'Arche in the mind of Thomas Philippe. If Vanier is viewed as the founder of l'Arche, Thomas Philippe deserves to be understood as cofounder.

While living in Trosly-Breuil during the summer of 1981, I quickly learned that many view Thomas Philippe as the spiritual father of the community. Like many others, before arriving at l'Arche I had heard only a little about him. Some perceive him as a sort of guru, whose following is increasing with each passing year. People come to l'Arche from nearby villages and from far away regions of France for his advice in spiritual matters. The annual retreat he gives in August draws people year after year from Britain and the United States, as well as from other countries more distant still. His lectures and conferences as well as his writings are beyond the counting. At l'Arche I saw a young woman of the community sitting in the library day after day pecking away at a manual typewriter, trying to organize and categorize some of his writings. The process will continue for a long time to come. There is not much that he says at l'Arche to individuals or groups that is not tape-recorded or written down in one form or another.

At the Ferme, which is a sort of spiritual center at l'Arche, there is a little chapel. Most days of the week Thomas Philippe is the principal celebrant of the community's Eucharist. Upon entering the chapel for the first time I was struck by its rugged simplicity and, in some strange way, by its beauty. Once a barn, this simple place of prayer bears little resemblance to the French churches and cathedrals I had seen in history books as a child, and which I had long dreamed of visiting. In the chapel there are a few pews, a crucifix, a statue of Mary, and a centrally located altar. Recently, a new icon depicting Jesus, Mary, and Joseph was placed above the tabernacle of the sacrament of the Eucharist. Joseph, who is so rarely depicted in iconography, has became increasingly important in the spirituality of Jean Vanier and l'Arche. The icon was painted by one of the Little Sisters of Bethlehem, a new contemplative community in France, and presented to the community at Trosly-Breuil. Its brilliance seems to set the rugged, barnlike chapel alight.

With long white robe and heavy black rosary dangling from beneath his vestments, Thomas Philippe sits at the altar from the beginning to the end of the liturgy. Having turned eighty on 19 March 1985, his age prevents him from standing for long periods. His presence is magnetic. Most of those present for the liturgy sit or squat on the floor. The Dominican's high-pitched, shrill voice rings through the air. With one hand often over his heart he speaks to the community about the gospel of the day. Rarely does he omit mentioning in his homily the place of the poor in the church and the role of Mary. Often he speaks of those figures in the history of the church who have had great devotion to Mary: Bernadette Soubirous, Maximillian Kolbe, Louis Marie Grignon de Montfort. These are given as examples of the life of poverty and simplicity in accord with the gospel. Scattered regularly throughout the homily is Philippe's urgent and passionate insistence: we must pray very, very hard to our Lord and the Blessed Virgin.

The liturgy proceeds in a rather traditional manner. The chapel is tranquil, quiet, hushed. A sense of reverence and adoration pervades the chapel more than a sense of service or celebration. Philippe elevates the sacrament of the body and blood of the Lord. Voices ring out at random: my Lord and my God!

The style of the liturgy at l'Arche in Trosly-Breuil has been criticized now and then, as has Thomas Philippe for giving homilies that are much too long and abstract for the mentally handicapped persons present. Vanier, aware of these criticisms, maintains that although the handicapped men and women may not understand Philippe's words and concepts, they are able to "sense his vibrations—the vibrations of a holy man, someone very close to God." This is much more important, according to Vanier.

Vanier himself picked up more than just vibrations from Thomas Philippe. Although he may describe himself as a poor country priest, Thomas Philippe has a strong background in philosophy and theology. While it might be argued that he is not a philosopher or theologian, it remains true that his wisdom and spiritual insight have been shaped by his philosophical and theological background, which was strongly influenced by the thought and writings of Thomas Aquinas. Vanier himself claims that in the domain of spirituality no one has influenced him more than Thomas Philippe. Until rather recently Vanier continued to take some of the informal courses Philippe gives the people at l'Arche. Much could be said about Thomas Philippe's teaching and spirituality,[23] but let us concentrate on the themes that appear to be most important to him, because these also find a very important place in the spirituality of Jean Vanier and l'Arche.

Three aspects of the gospel are central for Thomas Philippe. First, in his reading of the gospel he gives great attention to the role of Mary. Many dimensions or qualities of her life could be accented in the discussion of her role in the history of God's people. One could, for example, treat Mary as the model of faith or as the perfect example of femininity or womanhood. But the Dominican highlights the value of the hidden, mysterious, discreet, and unassuming life of Mary, and of Jesus. He sees Mary as the one who stayed very quietly by Jesus' crib at Bethlehem, tending very humbly to his quite ordinary needs. It was she who stayed with him during his years of growth and maturation at

Nazareth as he undertook the quite ordinary tasks of a worker. Finally, it was Mary who stood near him at the cross when nearly everyone else abandoned him. She did so quietly, silently, compassionately.

Next, Thomas Philippe emphasizes the role of agony or suffering. He points out that Jesus underwent a tremendous amount of agony and suffering in life, most especially in the garden of Gethsemane and while on the cross. Aside from the deep and excruciating physical pain, he felt the pain of loneliness and separation, especially because of the rupture of his loving communion with his mother. Our communion with God necessarily implies suffering and agony as well. It is only through an acceptance and sharing in the suffering and agony of the cross that our final destiny is reached. From this vantage point, he sees in a positive light those undeniable and unavoidable realities of anguish and suffering that are part and parcel of the human condition.

The third element of the gospel important to Thomas Philippe is the centrality of the Beatitudes. They are, for him, the gospel message in a nutshell. The evangelical values of poverty, simplicity, lowliness, and meekness permeate much of his preaching and writing. The original statement of the purpose and aim of the community of l'Arche, which was drawn up jointly by Jean Vanier and Thomas Philippe, stresses the primacy of the Beatitudes in Christian life. The charter later officially drawn up by the community maintains the priority of the Beatitudes in the life of l'Arche. Poverty, simplicity, humility, meekness and singleness of purpose are some of the values we find in the message of the Beatitudes.

One additional keystone in Thomas Philippe's teaching that has certainly influenced l'Arche is that God reserves for God alone the wisdom of the heart. That is to say that God can and does communicate directly with the human heart. It is the heart that is the dwelling place of God and the place where God is met.

Thus those who live so much from their hearts alone are open to a privileged relationship with God. This concept is central to life at l'Arche and unlocks its secret. It reveals simply and clearly that it is the mentally handicapped people of l'Arche who have been and remain the community's most constant teachers.

Many people who know of Jean Vanier and l'Arche are unaware that he has a doctorate in philosophy. Vanier does not speak much about it himself. Some who are aware of it are quick to dismiss the importance of his doctoral work on the moral philosophy of Aristotle. "That was before," they say, "before he learned what is really important." But the story of Vanier and l'Arche cannot be told without reference to this part of Vanier's background. He himself recognizes how influential Aristotle has been in his own development. He maintains that his study of Aristotle provided him with the tools for clear thinking. We could say that his study of Aristotle went to shape the *how* of his thinking more than the *what* of his thinking, but Vanier does hold as important some of *what* Aristotle taught as well. With a focus upon natural law, human activity directed toward a goal, knowledge of God, and love of others, Aristotle's moral philosophy provides a certain framework within which the Christian message can be heard and understood. Vanier sees the value of Aristotle's moral philosophy, even if he clearly favors a Christian interpretation or implementation of it. In recognizing the value of Aristotle, Vanier gives early signs of a later tendency to attempt to see the truth and value of other philosophies, religions, and points of view while faithfully holding on to the unique affirmations and claims of Christianity.

The moral philosophy of Aristotle aided Vanier in the development of some important ideas. Significant among these are his understanding of justice, friendship, and contemplation. It was the uniqueness and brilliance of Aristotle to recognize these as the highest activities of the human person. No one before him had given as much attention to their importance and to the way in which all three are attained. We can see throughout Vanier's later life a constant awareness of their importance. The founding of the community of l'Arche shows Vanier's desire to establish justice by organizing life toward the common good. Life at l'Arche shows signs on the one hand of the constant tension between the claims of justice, through which we order the affairs and activities of daily life toward the common good, and on the other the claims of contemplation or prayer, through which we strive to know God. The pursuit of justice and the search to know God in prayer, when shared with another or others, is the highest form of friendship. The communities of l'Arche can be said to be animated by these three values, although in most cases they have a specifically Christian interpretation. The parts of Vanier's dissertation where he treats these three notions contain, in a nutshell, some of the most important dimensions of the vision and the life of the community of l'Arche. Paragraphs of his dissertation wherein he summarizes the importance of friendship, justice, and contemplation read like he is describing the community of l'Arche.

Part of Vanier's dissertation argues that Aristotle is the author of both the *Eudaemian Ethics* and the *Nichomachean Ethics*. The question of whether Aristotle was the author of both was seriously debated at the time Vanier was writing his dissertation. Vanier tries to show that Aristotle was the author of both by pointing out how a consistent, continuous line of thought runs through both works. In this way he shows that they are not in opposition to each other. Likewise, we need to see that there is no opposition between the work and thought of Jean Vanier before l'Arche and his work and thought after its foundation; there is a thread that runs throughout.

There is at least one major difference between Aristotle and Vanier, though, and this is the absolute primacy Vanier gives to love. He sees love as the highest and most perfect activity of the human person, precisely because it reflects the nature of God (cf. 1 John 4:8). Because of the importance of love, revealed most perfectly in Jesus, Vanier thinks that the moral philosophy of Aristotle has been surpassed by the message of the gospel. Happiness and human fulfillment, for Vanier, are not attained primarily through friendship, justice, and contemplation, as Aristotle maintains, but by love, through which we participate in the life of God. Any time Vanier makes use of the concepts of friendship, justice, and contemplation, they are all colored by the primacy of love.

Meeting Raphael and Philippe and the other handicapped men and women who came to l'Arche later was a turning point in

Jean Vanier with Raphael.

Vanier's life. His life is marked in an unmistakable manner by this interaction. It is impossible to understand him and his vision of the human person if we do not appreciate how he views the handicapped and what he has learned from them.

Although his father was handicapped as a result of the amputation of his leg, Vanier had little or no contact with physically or mentally handicapped people prior to August 1964. He writes that, "before Philippe and Raphael joined me at l'Arche, I had never met handicapped people."[24] Naturally he came to his first encounters with mentally handicapped people with the prevailing view of them as individuals with arrested development who had not much ability to deal with life or take personal initiative. As the months passed after the beginning of l'Arche, he began to respect the possibility for human growth in the handicapped person. His personal experience with the handicapped people in Trosly-Breuil caused his understanding of them to change.

Vanier named his little dilapidated house l'Arche, the Ark, like Noah's ark. He envisioned it as a home of hospitality and refuge for mentally handicapped adults who would come to find care, respect, and comfort in their distress and affliction. From Vanier's perspective, the mentally handicapped are victims of a twofold affliction. First, there is a dysfunction in the brain or nervous system that presents an obstacle to the proper development and functioning of the mind. But handicapped persons are even more deeply afflicted by the rejection and discrimination experienced in family, school, and society. This second affliction often causes them to live in a state of anguish and depression. Even those handicapped people who in younger years may have had the advantage of special classes or a special school are frequently placed in a large institution when they become adults. It was from one such institution that Jean Vanier felt called to retrieve Raphael and Philippe, offering a bit of relief from the affliction of rejection.

In his life with handicapped people, Vanier began to discover that even in their deep affliction they tend to show forth marvelous gifts of friendship, joy, and compassion. He quickly found out that those whose mental capacity is limited frequently have tremendous qualities of heart. After the beginning of l'Arche he saw that those who have little or no ability with the head or hands rely much more on the heart, thereby increasing its capacity.

The word "heart" is used by Vanier in its rich biblical sense and is not meant to express mere sentiment or emotion. He does not see the heart as being at odds with the intellect, our capacity for rational thinking. Rather, the word "heart" describes the source of all physical, emotional, and moral life as well as the energies of the will. The heart is the central, unifying source of all personal life. It is the place where God resides.

Shortly after its foundation it was becoming increasingly clear to Vanier that l'Arche was not simply a haven of hospitality and refuge for handicapped people. It was emerging as a community of reciprocal respect and affirmation among its members. One of the first things that Vanier did after taking over directorship of the Val Fleuri was to allow the mentally handicapped residents to come and go in the village. Prior to this the residents were kept behind locked doors. The neighbors were not very enthusiastic about this abrupt change in policy. Vanier now recognizes that perhaps a bit more caution and preparation might have been in order, so that the neighbors could have had the chance to adapt to the adjustment he had made.

He began to see that each person is called to progress toward the full development of his or her potential, no matter how limited. Additions to the community came, and it became necessary to take on employment to earn a living. In accord with the original aim of l'Arche, work, productivity, and efficiency, important as they may be to the growth of any group, are seen as secondary to human and spiritual progress. For Vanier, this kind of progress is rooted in receptivity, respect, and a profound desire

to see each person in the community achieve the fullest development possible.

L'Arche began in order to offer solace and consolation to those
in misery who had been afflicted by the double wound of mental
retardation and social rejection. Vanier began to see that there
was no way of relieving the handicapped from these afflictions
apart from taking them out of the institutions in which they had
been placed. But as time went on, he became convinced that this
was not enough. The more burdensome affliction of rejection could
only be soothed by acceptance and affirmation of handicapped
persons as equals, as friends.

In 1964 there were plenty of institutions designed to provide
care for handicapped people. Highly efficient, organized, and
often well funded, they did indeed care for needy people. But the
very survival of such institutions depends upon their residents
remaining always in need of care and upon the administration
and staff offering that care. From the beginning of the first home,
Vanier envisioned l'Arche as providing something different, something institutions could not offer because of their very nature,
but he was not exactly sure what the "difference" would be. After
living with the handicapped people, though, he realized that the
difference would be in reducing, in cutting down as far as possible, the distinction between the caring and the cared for in an
effort to eliminate the rejection felt by the handicapped. This
breaking down of barriers became, and remains, the precise challenge of l'Arche. To many an observer this may appear to be an
impossible ideal, but it is the very basis of the community: the
"normal" accept life with the handicapped and identify with them
to the fullest extent possible without denying the responsibilities
given to them because of their sound mental ability. This vision
unites the communities together in friendship, in a common belief
in the unique value of each individual, regardless of handicap,
and in a common desire to create authentic community.

Vanier discovered that offering consolation to people deeply hurt by rejection necessarily required becoming one with them and identifying with them in their affliction by and through commitment. If one remains the helper, healer, or comforter, the other must necessarily remain the one helped, the one sick, the one comforted. When we discover the true gift of the one to be consoled, such barriers and distinctions begin to fade away.

He began to see that we need to learn from them and to be like them, while still acknowledging the responsibilities that a sound mental capacity places upon us. Handicapped persons show a simplicity of spirit, affection and a spontaneity to show this affection, honesty and directness, an openness to life, people, and God, the ability to make others, even strangers, feel welcome and at home, a real concern for what is essential in life and in persons, deeply felt joy in the midst of suffering, a desire to give joy to others, a knack for living in the present without undue and useless anxiety about past or future, and a capacity for marvel. Often they are deeply endowed with wisdom, a gift that enables them to recognize the miraculous in the quite ordinary.

In his experience with handicapped people, Vanier realized that those whom society rejects are often richly gifted—sometimes even more gifted than so-called normal people. As a result of this awareness, Vanier gradually began to see the radical equality of the handicapped with the so-called normal and therefore the radical equality of all people. Such an awareness is at once humbling and liberating, for through this awareness we are better able to accept ourselves and others. Each of us is nothing more or less than a child of God who one day will have to let go of everything in absolute poverty and return to God at the moment of death. Once we identify with those who bear the signs of death by their visible suffering, we begin to be free from the fear of death. The suffering, the handicapped, who are different, are no longer a threat from which we run away in fear. Rather, these people, precisely because they are different, become a source of enrichment that can release great creativity. To enter into the world of the afflicted and to become one with their suffering is to discover the very simple truth of human existence: humanity is, and always has been, one.

Contrary to popular opinion, handicapped people are capable of making much progress, especially in the domain of the heart. It is precisely within this domain that the handicapped offer a gift to the world. Through the gift of the handicapped to the world the so-called normal learn something of the nature of their own person. This is crucial. What is most important in the human person, what is fundamental and most basic to each and every one of us, is not intellectual ability, reason, or productivity. Rather, what is fundamental to the human person lies in the domain of the heart. This we learn from the mentally handicapped and others in situations of limitation and vulnerability, especially little children. Because of their intellectual inability, the mentally handicapped live primarily at this more basic, fundamental level. After coming in contact with them Vanier gradually shifted his attention away from the person as the knowing and willing individual we find in his dissertation on Aristotle and began to speak of the human person in terms of the more basic and fundamental reality of the heart.

In 1970, a l'Arche community was opened in Bangalore, India. This was the first l'Arche home to be opened in the Third World and the first to be situated in a predominantly non-Christian milieu. Asha Niketan, Home of Hope, welcomes handicapped persons of differing religious traditions to share a common life.

During his visits to India around the time of the opening of Asha Niketan, Vanier became acquainted with the life, writings, and tradition of Mohandas K. Gandhi. He found in Gandhi a man whose aspirations were strikingly similar to his own, though

Gandhi was from a different religious tradition. The influence of Gandhi upon Vanier and through him on the communities of l'Arche is quite strong. Vanier's words in the preface of *Eruption to Hope*, written after his return from India, point this out:

Whilst in India, I learned to love Ghandiji [*sic*], feeling that he is one of the great prophets of our times. His deep love for the underprivileged, especially the untouchables; his desire to identify himself with them; his openness to the spirit of God in order to become an instrument of His Peace; his desire to unite men, particularly those of opposed religions; his universal heart; his deep desire to bring peace into the world; his vision of poverty and riches; his own poverty; all these attracted me deeply.[25]

Vanier saw in Gandhi a man who appeared to follow the spirit of the Beatitudes. In Gandhi, he found someone who was able to bring him closer to, and not separate him from, Jesus, the preacher of the Beatitudes. The gentleness, tenderness, and meekness of the Beatitudes, which provided the very rationale for the community of l'Arche at its foundation in 1964, seemed to have a striking similarity to the patience, peace, never ending goodness, and above all *ahimsā*, the philosophy of nonviolence, of which Gandhi spoke. Of this similarity of spirit, Vanier writes:

Gandhiji [*sic*] taught me to love Jesus more and gave me a desire to make my life more like His, especially in this domain of a struggle for peace and universal brotherhood. And this struggle can only be won by using the means of the Spirit: those of love, of gift of self, of gentleness, with no aggression or violence.[26]

In the writings and tradition of Gandhi, Vanier also found someone who deeply attracted him because of his love for the poor and marginalized, his commitment to justice through nonviolence, and his deep awareness of the imbalance of the world's goods and resources, which keeps the world divided. For Gandhi, the rich have an overabundance of goods they do not need. Therefore, these goods are wasted, while millions starve for want of things. If each retained only what was needed, no one would be in want, and all would be content. If the rich would keep their own property within moderate limits, the hungry would easily be fed. But this is not the case.

It was through insights of Gandhi such as these that Vanier's vision of the world began to take a new shape. Gandhi helped him realize more and more the terrible divisions that exist in society between rich and poor, handicapped and nonhandicapped, and the many races and classes. Neither Gandhi nor Vanier advocates a violent revolution. But, for both, a violent revolution may occur unless individuals and countries choose to work toward a universal community by means of love, the gift of self, and gentleness, with no aggression or violence. For Gandhi, this is referred to as *ahimsā*; for Vanier it is the spirit of the Beatitudes.

There is an increasing need for men and women committed to the Beatitudes, who, like Gandhi, are prophets of peace walking gently but firmly between the divisions of the world. Such prophets of peace call unceasingly to the rich to dispossess themselves in order to find love and compassion, while at the same time they call forth the richness of the gifts of those suffering, miserable, and poor. Such men and women live as Gandhi lived: between two worlds.

For Vanier what is so striking about Gandhi is that he embraced the untouchables, the poorest and most despised of all Indian people. Those who were fit only to do the most menial of tasks were those with whom Gandhi chose to share his life. An influential man with a certain prestige and position, Gandhi did what he could to change the mentality that defined people as untouchables. He used all the means at his disposal to bring about this aim, but, above all, he chose to live in solidarity with them. Gandhi called these people the *Harijan*, which in Hindi means "the children of God." He did not believe that the untouchables were a necessary part of the real tradition of Hinduism, that is to say that a despised, rejected, and poor class was part and parcel of the very nature of Hinduism. Rather, Gandhi viewed these poor and despised people as infinitely valuable. Vanier writes:

> Gandhi adopted an untouchable girl; he worked as the untouchables worked, cleaning latrines every day. He identified himself with the untouchables in such a way that whenever he went to the cities he would always live with them. Ministers and Ambassadors who wanted to see him would have to go into the slum areas where the untouchables lived.[27]

In such activities and in such concrete gestures lie Gandhi's appeal and importance for Vanier.

The awareness of the divisions in the world and of the real obstacles to universal justice and friendship have been consistently important for Jean Vanier, but they appear more and more frequently in his life and writings after his contact with India and the writings and tradition of Gandhi. His contact with India helped him to find in a person of a different religious tradition his same aspirations for a community of justice and friendship that guards the rights and dignity of the human person, no matter how lowly or despised.

The means to building this community of justice and friendship, for Vanier as for Gandhi, lies in love, the gift of self, gentleness, and nonviolence: the spirit of the Beatitudes.

Through his contact with the people, society, and culture of India, Vanier's concern for the handicapped widened and took on more universal dimensions. It is not simply handicapped persons who are fragile and vulnerable. This is true of all the people of the world and is most visible in what has come to be called the Third World. Yet as handicapped people are teachers of the strong and robust, so we are only gradually beginning to see that those of us of the "First World" must learn to listen to those of the Third.

We are all shaped by our past. Key persons and events in our lives contribute to making us who we are. In trying to understand Jean Vanier, we have looked into a few areas of Vanier's past. What we have uncovered is that the person and gospel of Jesus Christ were his initial inspiration and have remained most important throughout his life. In his early years, his own family, particularly his father and mother, were extremely influential, especially in the formation of his spiritual values. In young adulthood, we see Thomas Philippe as a most influential figure. Often overlooked, the study of Aristotle, especially the philosopher's understanding of justice, friendship, and contemplation, helped Vanier to think through some very crucial questions and provided him with some key insights. But it is the pivotal event of meeting Raphael and Philippe in 1964 that crystallized the message of the gospel for Vanier and provided the possibility for living its message quite concretely. For this was the definitive revelation of Vanier's vocation, in light of which his whole life and thought must be seen. In Gandhi he found someone of a different religious tradition who shared his vision of the human person and confirmed his understanding as having universal appeal and validity.

What is this vision of the human person? This question is addressed in the next chapter.

5. The Heart Knows

In this chapter we will look to the central insight, the motivating principle, of l'Arche communities. This central insight is that the person is the heart. Understanding basic human needs is the key to understanding the heart. Attention to human needs helps us to understand the dimension of the human person that is most basic or fundamental and that is experienced in the encounter with the handicapped and the vulnerable. The concern for people's needs for love, life, and knowledge leads to an understanding of the affective core of human nature. This is the deepest, most fundamental reality of the human person and that which is transformed by the Spirit dwelling within. By looking to the heart we uncover basic human needs and the significance of vulnerability and of the desire for communion in love.

Jean Vanier says that the person is the heart. A strange use of words! Many contemporary spiritual leaders speak and write about the heart, but they often mean something quite different when they use this term. We must not think that Vanier refers to the sentimentality of Valentine's Day cards or popular tunes; we must see very clearly and carefully what he means when he speaks of the heart. Even though the heart is mysterious and impenetrable, the place where God resides in each of us,[28] we must try to penetrate this mystery. It is not enough to say that there are qualities of heart such as compassion, tenderness, forgiveness, celebration, and unity; we must search out the reality from which these qualities stem.

There is a basis or core within the person that needs to be nurtured at the beginning of everyone's life and that we as adults often lose touch with. Vanier writes:

Behind all the barriers built up since childhood, there is the pure and innocent heart of a child where the gift of God resides. This heart is capable of receiving and giving love, of living in communion with another person and with God, capable of being a source of life for others. In the designs of God, it is the heart which is meant to inspire all human activities.[29]

Vanier sees that when we, the so-called normal people, are in situations of distress or crisis and our vulnerability is revealed, we are most in touch with the base, the core of our existence— the heart. For Vanier, "often . . . suffering is accompanied by a new experience of God in the depths and vulnerability of the heart of the person."[30] When in touch with this we are able to recognize the importance of the essential values of freedom, truth, friendship, and justice and to live in accord with them. Vanier gave a great deal of attention to these concepts when doing his study of Aristotle, but they take on a new tone for him in light of the gospel, which is of singular importance for him, and when they are understood as being rooted in the basis he calls heart.

We must not overlook the fact that in his formative years Vanier was exposed to a certain theological tradition as well. Although he is not a theologian, his thought has strong roots in traditional Roman Catholic theology. Three facets of this theology are important in understanding what is meant by Vanier's statement "the person is the heart." The first is the use of the term "heart" in Christian spirituality. Second, there is the work of Thomas Aquinas and other theologians of the Middle Ages on the deepest and most basic core of the human being. Third is Thomas Aquinas's teaching on the gifts of the Spirit.

When Vanier speaks of the heart, he is referring to what others in the history of Christian spirituality have attempted to describe using the same term or another closely related term, "affectivity." Affectivity, from the Latin *affectus*, describes that in us which is open to attraction from outside ourselves. It refers to that in us which is open to be moved, touched, lured by another.

The affective dimension, or affectivity, is not mere sentiment or emotion. It is the deepest part of us, which yearns, longs, thirsts for, and makes possible communion in love with others and God.

"Heart" occurs frequently in the Bible and in Christian writing (*leb* and *lebab* in Hebrew and *kardia* in Greek). The word is used in the Scriptures ten times to refer to the physical organ of the heart, but it is used more than a thousand times to describe the root or source of diverse personal functions. In this early usage "heart" meant the whole, total person; the individual at this time was not understood as a being with the separate faculties of intellect and will, but as a unity. The heart, from this perspective, was not associated with the will, affections, or emotions *as opposed to* reason or the intellect. It was looked to as the single root of all thought and wishes and of the moral and religious life.

This integral view of the person was maintained by the thinkers of the Middle Ages. Though they did distinguish between the intellect and will, associating the heart with the will, they did not see them as working independently of one another. They still had a vision of the human person as unified.

In the Middle Ages it was Bernard of Clairvaux (d. 1153) who gave considerable attention to the dimension of the heart. The Latin terms *cor* ("heart") and *affectus* ("affectivity") became linked with one another for Bernard. Love and affectivity, especially as these play a part in contemplative prayer and union with God, were very important for Bernard, and it is with the heart that he associated the dimensions of love and affectivity. Love and affectivity are at the matrix of personal life, the heart. Though Bernard spoke most about the way of the heart in prayer, spirituality, and union with God, there were others, especially in the twelfth century, such as Aelred of Rievaulx and William of St. Thierry, who gave attention to this dimension of the Christian spiritual life.

In line with this twelfth-century understanding of the heart is the Franciscan tradition, especially the writings of Bonaventure (d. 1274). In the same current of thought as Bernard, Bonaventure saw aside from intellectual contemplation a kind of contemplation he calls sapiential. This second type of contemplation is an affective perception of God through the gift of wisdom: it is through love that we reach what our intellect cannot. It is precisely by letting go of all workings of the intellect that we are transformed by God.

The use of the term "heart" is especially prominent in French writings on spirituality beginning in the seventeenth century. Here the most noteworthy figures are Bérulle and his followers, Francis de Sales, John Eudes, and Claude la Colombière. We might also note such movements as the devotion to the Sacred Heart of Jesus as part of this trend. During this period we begin to find the prominent view that the intellect and will are separate faculties and operations and the heart is associated only with the will. The wheels were thereby set in motion for a view that sees the intellect and will opposed to one another. Because of its own particular inclinations the will was seen as superior to the intellect. The will moves toward what the intellect cannot reach.

Because of this separation of the faculties of the intellect and will, "heart" no longer refers to a whole reality, that which is most basic in us, and the human person is seen as a divided creature. Jean Vanier and l'Arche retrieve the early sense of the word, which is unitive and which describes an inclination or disposition that resides at the deepest level of our being.

A second element to consider in understanding Vanier's use of the term "heart" is found in the scholastic tradition, the tradition of Thomas Aquinas (d. 1274). This view holds that there is a fundamental, original, primitive, radical impulse toward the good within all of us.[31] It is the most basic and deepest drive within us, one that is deeper than our powers of thinking or our powers of choosing. This radical impulse toward the good and the true at the root of our being is present throughout our life. It is very important to all human understanding and to human action as well as to the spiritual life, because it is that within us which longs for completion and fulfillment and with which all thought, choice, and action must remain in touch throughout our whole life.

The third consideration is found more explicitly in the theology of Thomas Aquinas—his teaching on the gifts of the Spirit. The gifts are given by God through the Spirit who dwells in our hearts. These gifts—wisdom, understanding, knowledge, piety, counsel, fortitude, and fear of the Lord—dispose, help, or enable us to be responsive to the prompting of the Spirit of God who has been poured out into our hearts. They help us to act spontaneously and without hesitation when moved by the love in our hearts. Through the gifts of the Spirit we may be moved to act in ways that seem to go against reason and rational deliberation, but it would be more true to say that action under the impulse of the gifts of the Spirit goes beyond the perfect use of reason. Such actions are born out of a sensibility for the things and the ways of God, an instinctive feel for the mystery of God dwelling within us. Recall the words of Blaise Pascal: "The heart has its reasons which reason cannot know."

All three of these notions convey insight into the understanding of the human person as constituted at a deep and fundamental level and in a mysterious way by an intuition, instinct, or impulse of love. The term "heart" is used to describe this most basic and fundamentally important dimension within us, because the person is an affective being. This means that the person is open to attraction, to be acted upon by another—especially by God dwelling within—and to be drawn into relationships and communion with others. Our affectivity is that in us which is touched, swayed, drawn, indeed lured by something or someone other than ourselves. Our knowledge, understanding, and judgments are given a direction by our affectivity when this is developed properly.

Although we have been concentrating on the positive qualities of the heart, it can also be ambiguous, even disordered and unruly; a place of great darkness and of sin. An encounter with the anguish and suffering of a handicapped, weak, or vulnerable person often stirs up in us a great deal of fear which can bring about hatred and anger and even the desire to harm the weaker person. We are shocked to find ourselves capable of such evil. If it is true that the riches of the heart are revealed to us by the handicapped, the weak, and the vulnerable, it is just as true that their anguish, anger, and suffering may trigger our own darkness and capacities for evil. The heart needs to be shaped by the action of the Spirit and the action of the Christian community in which we experience the effects of love in our life. Molded and developed properly, the heart becomes the basis for contemplation, communion with Jesus in his mysteries, and for active life, serving others.

In his writings and at the retreats and conferences he gives, Vanier does not speak about Thomas Aquinas or discuss his understanding of the gifts of the Spirit. His style is very simple and direct. But an examination of these notions helps us to see the richness of insight and depth of perception that underlie the vision of the person as the heart.

When speaking of the heart, it is common for Vanier and the people of l'Arche to focus on basic human needs and their fulfillment. Their understanding of human need is based upon experience in which a sense of vulnerability and weakness is strong and affectivity and communion with others are of the greatest importance. It is to the understanding of human needs, then, that we must look now in order to throw light upon understanding the person as heart.

In grade school we learn of the fundamental needs for human life—food, water, shelter, and clothing. But as years go by, we learn that there are other needs as important as these material needs. We have needs for life, light, and love. The need for life is tied in with a need for freedom and creativity. We cannot really live unless we are free. The need for light refers to our need for knowledge or truth. But it is our need for love that is most basic and fundamental and unless this need is fulfilled, our search for knowledge, truth, and freedom will be in vain.

Most basically we need to love and to be loved, and this is obvious in the earliest stages of our life. From the very first moments of life, in the exchange of touch with the mother, the child shows the need to be loved and to love. This same need is very apparent in handicapped persons, especially the mentally handicapped, who, because of the vulnerability and dependency of their existence, often must rely on the constant assistance of other people. As a result, they are in a position of being open to receive love from other people. Vanier says about the handicapped: "Their open natures are made for communion and love."[32]

But in the case of the handicapped person, as in the case of the little child, the dynamic of love is not one-sided; it is a "two-way street." The child and the handicapped person need not only to receive love but to give love in return. In the smallest responses of the little child to the touch and presence of the mother there is a kind of reciprocity, a give and take, of love.

A child, born into a deeply united family, discovers his own value through the loving presence of his parents. He gains confidence in himself, discovering that he is a unique being, infinitely precious, because his parents treat him that way. He knows that everything he does, good or bad, touches the heart of his mother. If he does something good, she is happy and laughs; if he does something bad, she is unhappy. Whatever he does provokes profound emotion in the hearts of those who love him. He is not treated as an indifferent being.[33]

It may be useful here to point out that Vanier expresses disagreement with a prevalent thesis among psychologists that claims the child is always egotistical, seeking only the fulfillment of his or her own needs but not really capable of loving in return.

According to Vanier, a little child can really love, trust, enter into a deep relationship of communion with his or her parents.

Handicapped people need to know that they are not just the recipients of love, affection, and affirmation, but that they can give love in return to make others joyful and happy. The handicapped who are loved and thus enabled to love in return grow in the awareness of being able to give and do other worthy and good things. But if handicapped people only receive love and are not seen as persons who from the start can give and do good and worthy things, then the love given them only frustrates growth. Such half-love does not recognize that love worthy of the name affirms and accepts the person's need and right to give. About the handicapped person's relationship with another, Vanier writes:

> This relationship of the handicapped person with another person can and must be a relationship of dedication, which expresses itself firstly in a genuine and profound confidence in the other person and which, thereby, implies the handicapped person's gift of himself. Secondly, this relationship expresses itself in the desire of the retarded person to bring pleasure to the other person, to make him joyful, through gifts, actions, or an attitude of affection and compassion. The mentally handicapped is capable of a profound and genuine loving relationship, one in which the spirit of self-giving is much more significant than any acquisitive instincts. This loving relationship expresses itself through signs and gestures which may have little or no intellectual content, but which are nonetheless, very real in their witness of profound love. [34]

What is said of the mentally handicapped person and the child can also be said of the human person in general. The need for love is the underpinning of all other needs and action and must be recognized as the most important value in all personal and social life. Speaking about world problems, Vanier points to this need in order to explain the gravity of the world situation and the means by which it can be changed. Looked at in light of the gospel, this need for love is also the need for God, who is love. The need for love can be met provided we recognize our own vulnerability. Finally, this need can be addressed if we learn to live a life that is both simple and authentic, giving greater importance to the values and the wisdom of God than to the values of this world.

The need for life is related to our needs for security, good environment, work, and a sense of belonging. That is to say that we need all of these to live and to live freely. To these the need for authority is closely linked. But all of these must be seen in relation to our most basic need for love. Our work, systems of authority, and all the rest should be at the service of love.

The human person needs security, which is provided through proper and balanced relationships, a healthy and warm place in which to live, and the chance to earn a living through some sort of employment. Through community life, the quest for the satisfaction of these human needs is shared with others. These needs must be met so that the person may grow and develop in freedom. Unless they are met, the person is fragmented and disoriented and often acts in strange and bizarre ways. Sometimes the frustration is seen in a prolonged state of depression or boredom. But, if we are secure, if we belong and have roots with others in a warm and wholesome environment and contribute to our daily living by work, then we can rest having found our place: we belong, fit, and feel secure.

The need for life is related to the notion of community. For many, community fulfills the needs for security, good environment, and work: one belongs with others in a community. In a community one lives with people who have more or less put down roots there. Even though there is a certain amount of flexibility in the commitment and stability of its members, it is nonetheless important that some members see the community as somewhere where they live permanently. Within the community the basic need for security is met. This is especially important in the case of handicapped persons who come to the community fearful of, yet yearning for, belonging, precisely because they have often passed in and out of so many short-term relationships with doctors, nurses, and specialists in a wide variety of hospitals, clinics, and institutions. How much deeper the longing for security is in those whose need for it has never been met. How important for the handicapped person to come into a situation where people understand themselves to be at home and who invite others to make a home with them.

A good environment is essential to the quality of life. One of the primary purposes of l'Arche is to establish lifelong homes for adult mentally retarded persons. Attempts are made to make these homes places of warmth, joy, celebration, and welcome. The decor found in the home is crucial to the well-being of those who live there.

I will not speak of those requirements which are obvious—an element of beauty in the home, decorative colours, furnishings, lighting. All these things have a great importance which you already realize. We must give to our mentally handicapped an element of beauty, a home warm with intimacy, the possibility to make a fire in a big fireplace. We must make the homes hospitable and harmonious, a place where the retarded can feel at home.[35]

A home is not an art museum; it is a place that nourishes human relationships. The decor of the home is both functional and beautiful. Cleanliness is maintained, but a certain amount of disorder is to be expected, because all people are not neat and orderly by temperament. Chaos can be fertile! Meals are modest, but well prepared and sufficient without being extravagant. Further, the mealtime is the high point of the day in the home, when people come together to share, celebrate, and relax. Heavy discussions and debates are avoided at the table as they often tend to cause tension and disharmony within the group. How easy it is to get indigestion when folks sit around the table talking about all the world's problems.

Because we participate and live in the created universe, the kind of environment in which we live has an effect on personal growth and development, and we need a good environment within which to grow. Vanier says:

> Environment can stimulate in our heart either the desire to give and to share and to be compassionate, or the desire of the ego to dominate, to subjugate others, to possess as a sign of our "greatness."[36]

Conversely our surroundings reflect our psychic, emotional, and physical well-being. A home in constant disarray, for example, where there is always loud noise and heated debates, where meals are not well prepared, and where the furniture and decorations are gaudy or in bad taste says something about the temperament, dispositions, and personalities of the people in that house.

We must work in order to live. Through employment, we share in creative activity and meet the requirements for daily living. Because the human person is a being of flesh and bone, we cannot live without the things of the material world. Just as the environment is important because of the unbreakable link between the human person and the created, material world, so too in work our links with the created world are forged as we shape and re-create the material world so that it might serve our needs.

Through work we gain a sense of ability, dignity, and worth. If we are able to do, to make, or create something good and beautiful, our grasp of self improves. In being able to provide for our needs, in not having to rely on someone else for each and every necessity, we gain confidence and assurance. By working, we gain a certain independence and sense of responsibility which, especially for the handicapped person, is of extreme importance in personal growth. Granted, there are limits to the independence the mentally handicapped person can achieve and the very desirability of rugged independence, especially of the sort often advocated in contemporary circles, must be questioned. Nonetheless, the handicapped person in particular and all people in general must be encouraged to move toward a healthy sense of independence and freedom. Such independence and freedom can only grow if we are able to re-create and cooperate with the material universe upon which we depend for existence.

Because the fulfillment of these needs for security, work, and good environment is a joint effort in community, some kind of authority is necessary. If a body of people is to function properly, it needs someone to whom to listen; someone whose word commands attention.

At l'Arche, a person in authority is there less because of any legal right or responsibility than because he or she has the charisma, the gift of being a good leader. Vanier believes:

The role of authority can only be understood if it is seen as one of the many gifts or ministries which we need to build community.[37]

The leader, the one who has authority, is recognized by the group or community as one who, precisely because of his or her gifts, is able to call forth and nurture the gifts and strengths of each person in the community. Knowing the strengths and weaknesses of each one, the leader should have the ability to draw out the positive dimensions of the people in the community by affirming them and helping them to develop their very best qualities, and so strengthen the common life. Because of the ability to draw forth the very best from each member, the good leader brings about unity and harmony within the group. Authority should serve this end.

Through her or his exercise of authority in service of the corporate body or community, the good leader attempts to bring about the fulfillment of the basic needs of all members. Knowing the temperament and disposition of each person in the community, the leader is keen enough to detect when someone is moving toward the edges of the community, which can result in the frustration of the need for belonging. But some have greater need for distance and solitude than others, a need that must be respected as well. In short, the leader must be able to perceive when someone is having a true problem with belonging or when someone by nature simply "needs more space."

The leader, through a prudent and watchful eye, should be able to gain a knowledge of the likes and dislikes of all members and provide the environment and opportunities for work suited to each individual. One person likes to work with clay, while another hates it. Should the second person be required to work in a pottery workshop? Likewise, one person prefers to live in a house of ten, while another simply cannot bear eating meals with more than four or five. Are the needs of this second person for a healthy and supportive environment being met? Someone who prefers farm life cannot be thrust into the midst of an urban factory and be expected to grow and develop. When legitimate basic human needs are satisfied, the members work together to bring about the harmony of the community or group.

The role of the person in authority, then, is to assure that the community, or the corporate body, is a place where people can grow. Authority is seen as a service that by its very nature is meant to strengthen and build up the body and each individual in it. Central to the proper use of authority is respect for the freedom and independence of each person and appreciation and affirmation of the gifts each one offers in pursuit of the vision and ideals of the community. The leader must above all be mindful of the freedom of each individual and of his or her own way of working for the community's *raison d'être*, for, when all is said and done, the ideal of a group should never take the upper hand over the human beings who pursue it. Vanier is firm on this point:

"Community can never take precedence over individuals."[38] The proper use of authority aims at bringing about balance between the importance of ideals and the importance of the people who pursue them. Good authority, a good leader, helps us grow in freedom and in love of those with whom we live and work, without whom we cannot satisfy the most basic and elementary human needs.

The need of the human person to know is what is referred to by the phrase "the need for light." Vanier writes: "The need for an all-encompassing and universal knowledge runs very deep [even] in the small child."[39] Although it was not established primarily as a therapeutic center, a unique and very important approach to learning has emerged at l'Arche. This has developed as a result of commitment to three goals. L'Arche is to be a community, a family where each person has a sense of belonging. It is to be a place of healing. Finally, it is to be a place where people can learn skills and grow in competence.

Vanier proposes that the knowledge of self and others leads to the knowledge of God. The pedagogy of l'Arche is not educational method or curriculum. Nowhere would we find a manual of teaching objectives or a series of lesson plans. Rather, the distinct way of learning emerges from a belief that personal identity—the truth about oneself—is known through the experience of the other, who reveals truth, meaning, and love to us. Each person asks, on some level and in some way, the fundamental question: Who am I? Each person wants to know who he or she is, where he or she fits into the whole scheme of reality, and what, in the long run, his or her personal destiny is. These questions are answered provisionally through the experience of the other: mother, father, friend, foreigner, poor, handicapped, God. It is not scientific or theoretical knowledge that is of interest here, but personal knowledge, personal answers to the basic questions of human existence. Even the most severely, profoundly handicapped person, who may not even be able to articulate a question about human existence, meaning, or value, needs to know that he or she is loved, is of infinite worth and value, capable of doing good things, and able to give joy. In this regard Vanier says:

Let us make no mistake, the mentally retarded, such as [*sic*] the young child, though he may not have rational ability, has, nonetheless, a profound thirst for knowledge.[40]

What is distinctive in the vision of Vanier and l'Arche is that it is through the experience of others in situations of crisis, distress, vulnerability, weakness, and woundedness that the ultimate truth and meaning of every life is revealed. Ultimate knowledge and truth are gained in situations of vulnerability, especially in encounter with those who bear very visibly the signs of death in their bodies or in the moments of agony and suffering in any human life. Such encounters give rise to the startling truth: in weakness we are born. This truth, which is of vital importance in human existence, is only grasped in the face of suffering. Often we spend much of life fleeing from this truth. Only when brought up short do we accept the truth of the radical dependency and fragility of all existence, especially our own. In such situations we have a way of knowing what is important, meaningful, and true and what is not. In experiences of vulnerability, the normal, healthy, and strong individual gets a glimpse of the truth that each and every person is weak and fragile and at root dependent upon others and the ultimate other of God. Deep communion with God does not take place at the level of reason or intellect. Rather, as the tradition of the mystics reminds us, union with God occurs at the fundamental base and core of existence: the heart.

Knowledge of self makes possible the knowledge of God. We come to know and accept the truth of God as one who is filled with mercy and compassion for the weak, for the wounded, and for all of those who call upon the divine name. What we know to be true is that God is tender, gentle, forgiving, reconciling, and joyful rather than harsh and fearsome. The meaning, destiny, and fulfillment of human life is realized in the measure to which we live lives of love, mercy, compassion, forgiveness, and tenderness—qualities of the human heart that at the same time reveal the truth about God. The handicapped and wounded, who bear the signs of the neediness of us all, remind us that we meet God not in our strength and security, but in our vulnerability and weakness. It is there where we are most open to meeting God and most like God. Because God *is* love, God is *most* vulnerable.

God's grace and attraction touch the human person at the most vulnerable points of existence. Response to this movement in our hearts leads us to compassion, joy, celebration, and forgiveness. The heart is that which can be attracted, touched, moved, acted upon. It is called affective, able to be affected, inasmuch as it is drawn and does not move under its own power. Those who act from the heart, moved by God to compassion, become signs of God's love and tenderness. This is the significance of the affirmation that the person is the heart. Created in the image of God, a God who is all love and compassion, we act in harmony with our nature when we manifest the qualities of the heart that are revealed to us in weakness, not in our strength. The seeds of the divine life within and the capacities of the human heart are found in weakness. A blessed weakness this human heart!

6. The Configuration of Hope: Pardon and Celebration

In the previous chapter we focused upon the central insight, the motivating principle, of the communities of l'Arche: the person is the heart. In this chapter we look to the kind of life generated by this central insight, a kind of life characterized by suffering, relationship, covenant, forgiveness, and celebration. The next chapter gives attention to elements of the gospel that support and sustain this life. These are seen in light of the call of l'Arche to create familylike communities within which all may grow (the work of justice), to build deep relationships founded on love, truth, and freedom (the nature of friendship), and to cultivate a life of deep prayer in union with Jesus and his Spirit (contemplation). Life at l'Arche is in many ways a profoundly contemplative life. Prayer draws the people of l'Arche back to, and nourishes faith in, the seminal vision of the person as a being with a heart wherein God abides.

L'Arche is a place where there is deep suffering. The physical limitations and the social rejection the handicapped experience are wounds the community is there to ease. Though there are exceptions, the handicapped people at l'Arche seem joyful and fulfilled, and most will testify if asked that, next to being with their family, they prefer life at l'Arche to the institutional situations from which they have come.

The fact that many handicapped are and will always remain

dependent upon others is a source of great suffering. Because of this dependency, many are unable to marry and have a family and this causes them deep pain. The inability to marry is often seen by them as the obstacle that definitively separates them from the "normal" world. Often they are strengthened by seeing those who choose celibacy; to see that some people freely choose this way of life makes it seem less a curse.

It is not only the handicapped at l'Arche who suffer. The assistants are moved by a deep empathy for the suffering of the handicapped, suffering they cannot alleviate. They also suffer from sheer fatigue. Days at l'Arche are long, the tasks many, the moments of silence and rest few. Although the assistants are encouraged to take time for themselves, they frequently give their free time willingly to a person or task in need of attention. Some of them suffer from indecision, being unsure of whether or not to commit themselves to l'Arche. Is the fragile little ark worthy of a commitment of the rest of one's life? This indecision is particularly acute among those who are unmarried. For many of them, the commitment to l'Arche entails a personal choice for celibacy, which brings its own kind of suffering. Committed celibacy is never an easy way of life, but those who choose the celibate life at l'Arche take a path that does not even carry with it the kind of recognition given to the commitment of the consecrated religious. Because of this, it may be far more difficult.

Many of the assistants feel the pain of having nothing to give to the people and the community but the gift of self. They are not doctors, nurses, or educators. They have no designation, no title, no prestige. In many ways, in this they are like the handicapped people. There is also the suffering the assistants bring with them to l'Arche. That is to say that l'Arche attracts some who are fragile and delicate, people who cannot cope in "normal" society. These people find in l'Arche a refuge and the hope and possibility of healing. Finally, there is the insecurity of the provisional nature of the community. The assistants are offered little stability, permanence, or guarantee. They receive the love and affirmation offered by the community, but due to the nature of the community, indeed of life itself, things keep changing and moving. This can be a source of suffering, especially as the assistants grow older.

This suffering of the handicapped and the assistants is the basis for the unity and solidarity within the community; it is this that binds them together. The handicapped have an extraordinary ability to recognize and accept their handicaps and to know their poverty. In this they are the teachers of the clever and the strong who, precisely because they are clever and strong, attempt to conceal their essential poverty. For the assistants at l'Arche it is often a great source of suffering, but also of great joy, to recognize their poverty and to admit that the handicapped may be far richer than they.

This encounter with suffering, which provides the basis for unity, is not always rosy. The anguish and suffering of others often bring about the same in us; we too suffer and become anguished. The violent and aggressive emotions and sometimes actions of the handicapped force us to discover the sources of violence within ourselves. We are horrified. The wounds of the handicapped reveal our own. We come to recognize how the weak person can draw out not only what is most beautiful in us, but also what is worst. Such an encounter with the weak causes us to recognize that in the depths of our being we are part of a wounded humanity. At the same time we are called to have confidence and trust that, in spite of our wounds, we are not left alone. We can live and grow if we trust that we are loved by God.

The disclosure of our own poverty and wounds forces us to get off our high horse, to cease feeling superior to the handicapped and the weak. Such recognition of our poverty and suffering leads to the acceptance of the equality of all persons, handicapped or otherwise.

The mutual recognition of suffering brings with it a sense of deep joy, which springs from the knowledge of our need for others and for God. Frequently it is only through the acceptance of our woundedness, our suffering, that we know our need for others and for God. The acceptance of our own essential poverty is the first step in accepting or affirming a living and loving God. In a deep awareness of our woundedness there is room for joy. L'Arche, then, is a community of the poor in that they feel deep suffering and pain, but it is also a community of the poor in spirit in that they recognize their radical poverty and dependency as human beings on one other and God.

Part of the recognition of our limitation entails accepting the fact that we must die. Death is our greatest fear and the one to which all other fears are related. The handicapped, who bear the signs of death in their suffering, remind us that we too must die. Because of this, we often reject, scorn, or deny them. But here again handicapped persons are the teachers. Through their own deep suffering, the handicapped seem to have great openness and sensitivity to death. To recognize in them the mirror of our own limitation is to find a common base for a shared humanity. Again it is our weakness, our being toward death, that is our common lot. At l'Arche, this is learned from those who bear visibly the seeds of death in their suffering and poverty.

This unity, which is brought about through a recognition and acceptance of suffering and limitation, is expressed and strengthened in the Eucharist. The joy that springs from acceptance of our common lot comes to the fore in the eucharistic celebration wherein there is no distinction between persons: the handicapped and the nonhandicapped are one. The very concrete gestures and acts of the Eucharist appeal to those whose ability to comprehend concepts and ideas is limited. The rhythm of silence, music, and gesture touch very deeply those for whom verbal communication is sometimes a problem. Yet it often appears that the handicapped profit most from hearing the Word in the Scripture readings and in the homily. They seem to possess an uncanny ability to grasp the essential message of a particular reading from the Scriptures without getting caught up in abstraction and debate.

It is particularly clear in the eucharistic celebration that the Spirit of God can and does communicate directly to the hearts of those who have little intellectual capacity. This communication has been spoken of repeatedly by the great mystics who divest themselves of logical reason and even imagination in order to meet God in that direct and intimate embrace of heart to heart. Through contact with the mentally handicapped, who by nature are stripped of strong intellectual powers and the capacity for efficiency and productivity, we come to learn the implications of the truth that Jesus' privileged listeners are the poor in spirit. It is they who are endowed with a particular ability to comprehend the message of Jesus. So, to better understand the gospel imperative, the people of l'Arche must learn, the assistants from the handicapped and the handicapped from the still more profoundly handicapped, this kind of simplicity and poverty of spirit.

It is in the Eucharist that the life, passion, death, and resurrection—the paschal mystery—is remembered and celebrated. It is in Jesus' suffering and passing through death to life again that the handicapped most look to Jesus, because of the suffering and profound awareness of death that are part of their own lives.

Another source of deep suffering is related to the celebration of the Eucharist—the pain of not being able to share the same bread from a common table. In several communities, for example in North America, Australia, Switzerland, and Britain, the members do not come from the same Christian denomination. It is a source of great sorrow that these communities are able to share life, share prayer, share service, but may not partake of the one bread. Here again, we are reminded of our essential brokenness and fragility. Handicapped persons who look to the passion, suffering, and death of Jesus, confident that God will transform their brokenness, fragility, and death, serve again as a mirror that reflects the brokenness and fragility of the body of Christ, the church, and our need and hope for healing and wholeness across denominational lines.

By now it should be clear that personal relationships in community are at the core of l'Arche. Such relationships emerge from and are built upon the recognition and acceptance of suffering and limitation, our own and others'. Acceptance of others, their uniqueness, weaknesses, and strengths depends upon our acceptance of self. Others will appear threatening and fearful unless and until we accept ourselves at the deepest levels of our being. But this is the task of a lifetime. There is no one moment at which we make a complete act of self-acceptance. The matter is further complicated by the fact that, although it is true that we cannot accept others until we accept ourselves, our own self-acceptance is in great measure related to others' acceptance of us. The child who is accepted and affirmed by parents and siblings is much better equipped to accept himself or herself and consequently to accept and affirm others. The child, on the other hand, who is not accepted, who is unwanted, will have a harder time accepting himself or herself and others and will experience anguish throughout life.

The task at l'Arche is to build relationships based upon mutual self-acceptance. Assistants must be willing to accept handicapped people on their own terms and be open to absorb or appropriate the anguish, sense of frustration, and rejection that are often so much a part of the lives of the handicapped. The assistants' job is first of all not to change the behavior or mannerisms, however bizarre, of handicapped persons; it is to welcome them rather than resist them, as unique and irreplaceable human beings and to challenge them to grow. They must be allowed and helped to grow not according to any preconceived notion of what they should be, but according to their own inner music.

Rather than trying to change others and their behavior through control, power, manipulation and domination, all of which take a variety of forms, we can attempt to welcome and to integrate what in them we perceive as negative. Such welcoming, absorbing, and integration is not mere passivity. It requires that we act in such a way that life and other people are accepted on their own terms, knowing that they are deeply wounded, sometimes blocked in developmental capacities but trusting in their essential goodness, believing in their potential for growth, and contributing actively towards that growth.

Life at l'Arche often requires "tough love." My mind is filled with memories of many situations in which assistants had to be quite firm in dealing with some of the handicapped people. To the outsider, such firmness might appear quite harsh, but a deeper sensitivity enables us to see how demanding we must be in encouraging growth—the growth of others as well as our own. At l'Arche, where there is strong emphasis placed upon relationship in community, there is likewise a deep commitment to growth toward greater autonomy and clarity of self-identity. This requires the constant challenge to continual growth. A good rule of thumb in the domain of challenge and growth is that we have no right to expect any more from others than we demand of ourselves.

It is a hard thing to accept others and to affirm and contribute to their growth. In relationships with mentally handicapped persons, it is easy to relate to them as "handicapped." When we do, they are boxed in, so that real growth is impossible. Sometimes we box them in precisely because we so desperately need to be needed. Some of us need helpless persons. Under the guise of helping or assisting them we keep them in a situation where they will always need us. We need to be freed from our tendencies to dominate and control others, tendencies that prohibit us from calling them forth from the depths of their being and prevent them from listening to and living by the promptings of their own hearts.

The real work of the assistants at l'Arche is to absorb the anguish and suffering of the handicapped and to help create with them a community of mutual respect and genuine friendship. This requires the gift of self and compassion, two of the keystones of l'Arche. To respond to the handicapped through the gift of self and deep compassion, whereby we accept our deep woundedness and suffering and that of others, entails a recognition that help comes from elsewhere—from others in community and God.

True human relationship demands commitment. At l'Arche, where human relationships in community are viewed as the heart of the matter, commitment is a necessary element. But the duration and degree of commitment varies. Some come and commit themselves to l'Arche for a year or two; others for a summer. Still others view l'Arche as their permanent place in life, but live their commitment day by day. Some come to l'Arche with their minds made up to commit themselves for an extended period of time, only to find after a very brief time that l'Arche is not for them, and so they move on. With the constant come and go of people at a place like Trosly-Breuil, the rather provisional nature of the commitment of some at l'Arche is apparent. Again it is the genius of l'Arche to allow for and support structures and situations wherein commitments of varying degrees and duration can be welcomed as vital to the life of the community.

Just as the duration of commitment varies, so does degree. Some commit their professional services to the community, but not much more. This is rare, but it does occur. Some at l'Arche, Trosly-Breuil, have committed themselves to l'Arche as a spiritual home, to profit from the quiet, the austerity, the spiritual guidance of Thomas Philippe, and the liturgical life of the community. These people may have little or no sustained contact with the handicapped or the life of the broader community on a day-to-day basis. But the bulk of people at l'Arche are committed on a full-time basis, with the sort of total gift of self that is characteristic of marriage or religious consecration. Some of these are married, but most are unmarried and see l'Arche as primary to their sense of belonging and identity. Still others are members of different religious orders or are ordained, yet they live and work in l'Arche and view it as the community to which they are committed in a definitive way. There are others who live alone in nearby apartments or small houses because of a more contemplative bent, and these people are not part of the "daily round" at l'Arche, but understand themselves and are understood by the communities to be deeply committed to l'Arche. Finally, there are some who are actively part of daily community life, and are strongly committed to l'Arche in every aspect, save faith and worship.

Although it is true that a variety of commitments, both in degree and duration, exist at l'Arche, there is an increasing awareness of the importance of putting down roots in the community in a permanent way. There is the recognized need for a central core or inner circle of assistants who assure an element of stability for the life and spirit of the community. And continuity and stability are provided by the handicapped who have been at l'Arche since its inception and who will most likely be members of the community until death. These are the real cornerstones, the foundation of the community. They are in it for good, providing the stability and continuity essential to any true family or home.

In speaking of this central core of persons at l'Arche who understand themselves to be irrevocably linked to one another at l'Arche, it is important to look at the notion of *l'Alliance*, the Covenant, which is vital to life at l'Arche. The word "covenant," of course, refers to the bond or union brought about between God and the people. In the Old Testament we read of God's gracious action on behalf of the people, through which they were liberated from the bonds of oppression and invited to accept the bonds of commitment and fidelity to the God who saves and who requires that they love God and one another.

At l'Arche the reality of covenant emerges on all levels. Most basically, a bond exists between and among members of a given home. More particularly there is the bond which needs to be nurtured and strengthened, day after day, between the assistants and the handicapped. Then there is the deep bond that exists between God and the people of God—the church—which is expressed in the Eucharist. People at l'Arche recognize a deep connection between themselves and other Christian communities, not just l'Arche communities. This deep bond between God and the people of God is celebrated and hoped for in the Eucharist.

Of particular importance is the covenant that some of the assistants "announce" at the end of a retreat. The term "announce" is used to emphasize the fact that the covenant is not something the assistants make or initiate. Rather, the covenant is offered, given by God in and through the people of l'Arche, who are bonded to one another by God's mercy and providence. To accept entering into such a deep covenant with God and God's people is not to "make" a covenant, but rather to proclaim or announce in word and deed what it is that God and the Spirit are doing in one's own life and the life of l'Arche. To announce the covenant is to make explicit the deep bond that already exists between God and the people and to strengthen the bond in so doing. Increasing numbers of people are announcing the covenant. This occurs in a ceremony during the celebration of the Eucharist and is prepared for by an extended period of silence and retreat. It is important to note that announcing the covenant is not a pronouncement of religious vows. Perhaps it would be better to understand the covenant as a reaffirmation of one's baptismal commitment within the context of a community of the poor and wounded who recognize that God has called them together through mercy, making them responsible for one another as God's people.

With the wide variety of commitments—from visitors who

give a summer vacation to l'Arche to the handicapped who have made l'Arche home for the past twenty years to the young assistants who announce the covenant and understand themselves to be committed to l'Arche in a permanent way—l'Arche is composed of a great variety of people. With the diversity of participants, the communities represent the plurality of elements in the church and as such are examples of the universal Christian community. L'Arche is comprised of lay women and men, religious and priests, people who are married and those who are single by choice or circumstance, widows and young families. There are believers, nonbelievers, and those who are not sure. Some lead lives of active service, while others are decidedly more contemplative. Joined together in one community are Catholics and Protestants, traditionalists and progressives, old and young, rich and poor. In some cases, there are those of different religions under the same roof. This great diversity of persons, rather than being viewed as an obstacle, is seen as a great gift; it emphasizes the uniqueness and irreplaceability of each person and challenges all to cherish it. It gives cause for celebration.

Jean Vanier has described l'Arche community as a place of pardon and celebration.[41] We are each a great and glorious mystery, but because of the anguish, darkness, and selfishness that reside in us, we stand in need of forgiveness by others and God. L'Arche is a community wherein the need for forgiveness and the granting of it shape the very heart of the life. Here again, l'Arche is like a family. What mother would not forgive her child for a wrongdoing if the child recognized the wrongdoing and brought it in sincerity before her judgment? What brother would not forgive a sister?

Part of the task at l'Arche is to enable persons to recognize their need for forgiveness. How difficult it can be to recognize our need for pardon! How much more difficult to accept pardon when it is offered! Sometimes we would rather live burdened and bound by the weight of our selfishness and anguish, in a word egotism, than accept the liberation and healing that comes when we are forgiven by others and God. Such healing and liberation overflow into deep and joyful celebration.

Celebration at l'Arche is not an occasion of compensation for deep suffering. Rather it is a natural outpouring of the flow of everyday life. Joy born of deep suffering is nourished by moments of celebration. There seems to be an intimate connection between suffering and celebration. People who suffer deeply often more readily recognize the necessity of celebration. Where there is great suffering there is the possibility of great celebration. To speak of celebration in such a way is not to equate it with "party time" or dissipation. Rather, celebration properly understood is the acceptance of life in an ever growing recognition that it is so precious. Life is wonderful and precious because it can be enjoyed, tasted, and treasured, but it is precious all the more because one day it will be gone.

To speak of celebration at l'Arche is to recognize that the whole community is a place of celebration. But it may be useful to look at the three focal points where celebration comes to the fore: the home, the chapel or place of worship, and the vacation or pilgrimage. At l'Arche there is always something to celebrate, and most celebration goes on in the home. If there is nothing to celebrate, people find something to celebrate. There are the special celebrations of Christmas and Easter, birthdays and anniversaries, weddings of neighbors and members of the community. There are feast days and name days, holy days and holidays. Aside from these major celebrations there is the more ordinary, daily rhythm of celebration, which constitutes a true liturgy of life at l'Arche. To speak of a liturgy of life is to recognize that persons, families, and groups have accepted and recognizable ways of engaging and enjoying themselves in the events and activities that are important to them. At l'Arche this includes regular get-togethers with visitors, the daily evening meal, the weekly evening at home with the members of the household, common prayer, and for many the Eucharist.

The home is a world of symbols and symbolic communication: the type of foods prepared, the way the table is set and the food served, the decorations displayed, the music played, the furnishings used. The liturgy of life finds a focus in the evening meal, the one time of the day when all are together. The saying or singing of grace, no matter in what form or to what tune, helps convey something of the sacredness of the encounter. Meals are long. Each one at the table is given the chance to share the joys and/or frustrations of the day. Visitors are always given a warm welcome and place of honor. The person who invited the guest introduces her or him to those seated at table. Then the questions begin! "Where are you from?" "Do you like the English?" "The Germans?" "Do you like to smoke?" "What's your favorite sport?" "Do you like to garden?" "Do you like so-and-so?" It is a whole array of seemingly unrelated questions, but all are asked because of a sincere interest in the guest and a desire to extend a deep and warm welcome. The home is a place of security and belonging, and visitors are invited to share in the riches of the hospitality.

This is one of the most striking dimensions of life at l'Arche. Here you have small groups of persons who attempt to live in familylike community, yet visitors are always coming and going. Sometimes perfect strangers show up for a weekend or a week or two. It is amazing that such persons are welcomed and received into the homes, sometimes without previous notice. More striking still is the openness and the genuine receptivity to such visitors on the part of the handicapped who might be expected to shun or mistrust newcomers because of a past history of only short-term relationships. These people, sometimes abandoned and scorned by others, do nevertheless seem to possess an extraordinary generosity in welcoming others into their lives, even though there may be "nothing in it" for them. There is something of the divine and eternal in the openness and willingness to welcome and be vulnerable even though others may choose not to respond in kind. In their vulnerability and love, the handicapped participate in the life of God who is love. Precisely because God *is* all love, God is *most* vulnerable.

Two important aspects of celebration at l'Arche are worthy of note. First, it continues no matter how deep the suffering. Perhaps it would be truer to say that it intensifies as the suffering is recognized and appropriated. Second, it flows very easily into prayer. But before we say our prayers, to the dishes!

Dishwashing after a long and leisurely meal is a continuation of the liturgy of life. There are no dishwashing machines at l'Arche, Trosly-Breuil. The shared enterprise of clearing the table, scraping the plates, loading the sink with cookware, serving plates, and utensils for twelve or fifteen is a real community builder. Everyone who is able helps. Comments are exchanged, jokes are told, complaints are passed. Just as folks are bonded in the eating, they are bonded in the cooking and the cleaning up. It has always struck me that those Christian communities that do not share the daily tasks of cooking and cleaning, shopping and washing have very little spirit of community in them. While it may be true that the family who prays together stays together, it is also true that the real stuff that brings and keeps a family together is made up of the small details of daily, ordinary, simple, mundane life. Again, l'Arche works as a community because it is modeled on the family, and in most families throughout the world doing the dishes constitutes part of the business of life.

Evening shared prayer follows dishwashing. Prayer is simple, direct, straightforward. Not everyone participates. A candle is lit or an icon or picture of Jesus or Mary placed in view. Scripture is read aloud. Prayers are spoken. God listens.

Two particular evening prayer periods live on in my heart.

Community members gather for prayer in the *foyer* of Valinos, near Trosly-Breuil.

Chantal, a middle-aged handicapped woman who is a convert to Christianity, has been deeply hurt by the rejection and antagonism of her mother. During my time at l'Arche the mother came to visit once. She brought candy and wine and flowers for the household. Her charm and grace were quite winning, but she refused to communicate with her daughter. She spoke with the assistants, the other handicapped people and visitors, but she ignored her daughter. She greeted her daughter upon arrival and bade her farewell; other than that, there was no exchange.

But that evening at prayer, Chantal spoke the same words she had been heard to speak every single evening since arriving at l'Arche. The words echo in my mind to this day: "Lord, for my parents, especially Mother, I pray to you."

The second memory is a bit amusing. After several weeks at l'Arche, I was asked during the evening prayer to read the Scripture passage from the French Bible that the men and women of the Vigne had given to me during my own birthday celebration just a week or so before. If anyone needed evening prayers, I did! After several weeks in the community, I was still stumbling and searching for words—and now I was being called upon to read aloud for the benefit of others. Thank God it was not one of those readings about Hananiah, Azariah, and Mishael. But even a simple reading about the vine and the branches in another language was a chore.

Alain, the member of the Vigne who requires the most care and attention, was seated in the chair across from me. He has difficulty communicating with others; his speech is very poor. I struggled so hard during those months to understand what he was saying. When I took up the book to begin the reading, Alain seemed relatively inattentive. But as I read, fumbling on every line, stuttering and massacring that beautiful language of the angels, Alain hung on every word that came from my mouth. His gaze was fixed. He recognized in my search for words his own deep and lifelong struggle, and I was able, if only for a moment, to experience deep solidarity with him in his pain.

Because of the depth and the intensity of suffering and its acknowledgment, there is a deep sense of communion that is supportive and liberating. Suffering touches us at the depths of our existence. Because this is so, communion built upon a mutual recognition and acceptance of suffering is a real communion of persons. This person-to-person encounter is a joyful experience that finds expression in moments of celebration, be they the special feasts of Christmas, birthdays, or anniversaries or the ordinary celebrations of mealtime, evening prayer, the Eucharist, or dishwashing that go to shape the liturgy of life at l'Arche.

A second focal place where celebration comes to the fore is the chapel, church, or place of worship. It is in the prayer of the community at the Eucharist that their unity based upon a common awareness of poverty and suffering is most manifest. But their Eucharist is a celebration, a simple expression of deep joy in personal communion, which invites an individual out of the abyss of anguish and self-centeredness. It is a call away from the fear of death, which is implicit in all pain and suffering.

In celebration, at least for a brief moment, people are set free from anguish and selfishness by being taken up in something beyond themselves. Brief though this experience may be, celebration makes manifest the desire and possibility for a final and complete emancipation in a feast that is without limit and without end. Celebration of its very nature is an experience of liberation that is a hope and promise of fulfillment in an eternal celebration. This is, of course, what is ritualized in the celebration of the Eucharist. There is, then, an important connection between the celebration that goes on in the home and the liturgical life that goes on in the place of worship, at the heart of which is the celebration of the Eucharist.

Liturgy at l'Arche is simple and solemn, yet spontaneous. There is always some kind of commotion going on: a small spat in the corner, someone arriving late in a wheelchair, an altar server vesting minutes before the eucharistic prayer, or an outburst of joy and delight. There is always some type of music, as music is a normal part of any celebration. At Trosly-Breuil, the liturgy is ordinary and traditional, largely due to the fact that the chaplain, Thomas Philippe, desires to be faithful to the directives of church hierarchy and to keeping l'Arche united to the universal church in communion with the pope and bishops.

By the standards of contemporary liturgical studies or sacramental theology, the liturgy at l'Arche would most likely not be called "good liturgy." But clearly, folks at Trosly-Breuil and beyond come to the chapel to worship God in sincerity and truth, and for them the liturgy is quite satisfactory or at least does not seem to present any obstacle to their prayer and worship.

What is particularly striking is the extraordinary quality of attentiveness or presence of persons to one another, making the presence of Christ celebrated in the Eucharist all the more compelling. This is evident from the lively participation in the liturgical music and the tender glances, reaffirming touches, and handshakes that people give each other during the course of the Eucharist. Personal presence is perhaps most obvious in the passing of the peace, or the kiss of peace, just before communion. Maurice, one of the most faithful and trustworthy altar servers, whose pipe leaves his mouth only while eating, sleeping, or serving at the altar, will walk the entire length of the chapel to pass the peace to a visitor, someone quite sick, or a friend, patting heads and giving little pecks on the cheek on the way back to the altar. The commotion continues during the reception of the Eucharist at communion. Nearly everyone in the chapel receives the Eucharist. There are people in wheelchairs and people with braces on their legs. Some walk with difficulty, while others need to be carried. It's a motley crew in the singing, in the serving, even the sitting and standing, but they place themselves before God in their place of worship, knowing that God sees them and blesses them just as they are.

After the liturgy each day, people gather in the courtyard outside the chapel. Notes are exchanged, plans are made, acquaintances renewed, quibbles had (there are some). But this daily informal gathering that seems to follow the liturgy naturally shows the natural connection between liturgy and life. This small impromptu gathering takes on an air of festivity and lightheartedness, especially after the liturgy on Sunday. Celebration stems from communion in a shared enterprise, shared vision and values, as well as in a mutual sharing of suffering and deep joy.

The small courtyard gathering each day after the Eucharist shows the way in which such communion of persons in suffering and joy is at the heart and soul of l'Arche in its liturgy of the Eucharist and its liturgy of life. The Eucharist leads quite naturally to the continuing celebration and the air of festivity of the courtyard, while the festivity and celebration that are at the heart of each home overflow almost spontaneously into prayer. There is no separation between the "holy" and the "worldly," the "sacred" and the "secular." Life is one. God has embraced us in our woundedness and suffering. In acknowledging and accepting our suffering and that of others, there is great joy and cause for celebration. Nothing escapes God's grasp. There are grounds for hope.

The experience of communion at community worship is grounded in hope and is a wellspring of hope. We try to avoid or deny our woundedness, pain, loneliness, and anguish when there is no hope for transcending, passing beyond them in some measure. Only with a profound hope of transcendence can our woundedness and limitation be accepted. Hence belief in a Source and Sustainer of life is vital. Christians express faith and hope in transcendence through the Eucharist, which is the memorial act wherein the mystery of Christ's passage through death to life is remembered and his presence among us celebrated. Acceptance of limitation becomes possible by identification with the passion, suffering, and death of Jesus in the hope and promise that we, like him, will pass through death to new life.

In the celebration of the Eucharist, barriers and divisions between handicapped and nonhandicapped are broken down. Suffering and joy are expressed in a profound sense of communion between persons who are all equal before God. Because suffering and woundedness lie at the deepest level of the person, the heart, the sharing of suffering and woundedness leads to encounter and unity, real presence, at the deepest level of being. Such an experience of encounter and real presence, particularly during the

Eucharist, is itself an experience of transcending one's woundedness and limitation. In such deep personal communion there is a recognition of a present reality that gathers the individual and group together into the memory of the suffering, death, and resurrection of Jesus, confident that God is coming. The Eucharist is the occasion for celebrating not just a future event, but the presence of God in Jesus Christ alive in the communion of persons who are gathering in his memory.

In many ways it is the vacation or pilgrimage, the third main form of celebration at l'Arche, that captures the whole heart and soul of l'Arche. Vacation is an important dimension of life at l'Arche and often takes the form of a pilgrimage to Rome, Lourdes, Fatima, or some other place revered by faithful Christians. The pilgrimage is both a time of rest and relaxation and a profoundly religious experience.

My month-long vacation in the foothills of Mont-des-Cats, described in the first chapter, was one such pilgrimage. Our time was characterized by a sense of adventure, freedom, and providence. It was an opportunity to live in the present moment with a sense of abandonment and unpredictability. Perhaps it would be best described as an experience of living with the provisional, day by day, trusting that God would provide enough for each day. Most of us have had experiences of God taking very special care of us in particular circumstances, seemingly against all odds. I shall never forget my experience of insecurity and uncertainty when the fifteen of us, some of whom could not walk or talk, set off in a minibus for a cottage at the foot of a mountain crowned by a monastery whose name I had never heard, to say nothing of my inability to pronounce it. But our little month-long vacation-become-pilgrimage was a time of great freedom and adventure. We did not live "hand to mouth," but we did have to count our francs to make ends meet. When problems emerged, as when someone got sick or hurt or had a seizure, we had to draw upon the know-how of those with the practical skills, surrendering each day and leaving the rest to providence. Our journey up and down the mountain, wheelchairs and all, amazed me beyond the telling of it. I learned how important it is to live with the essential, the basics, in simplicity and confidence, trusting in God's mercy and compassion. With this confidence comes a certain freedom.

Frequently the place of vacation or pilgrimage is one of the Marian shrines. Often Christians of very simple and direct faith are more attracted to Jesus the child at Bethlehem and Jesus on the cross at Calvary than to other areas of the life and preaching of Jesus. The vulnerability of the baby and the suffering of the crucified speak so very clearly to those who possess a childlike faith and suffer a great deal. There is likewise a great attraction on the part of these people to Mary, the mother of Jesus, the mother of compassion, who cared for him tenderly at his crib and in his childhood and stood by him in compassionate solidarity during his suffering, passion, and death. Historically, Mary has appeared to the children, the poor, and the lowly, be it to Juan Diego at Guadalupe, the children at Fatima or Bernadette Soubirous at Lourdes. Visits to Marian shrines are popular with the communities of l'Arche because they understand Mary as mother of the little, lowly, wounded, and weak to be their mother too.

The sick and the invalid often visit the Marian shrines with hope for healing and strength in suffering. Crutches and wheelchairs left behind in the churches and chapels of these shrines pay tribute to her through whose intercession healing has been granted. Seeing them touches something very deep in the handicapped people of l'Arche. And encounters with others in wheelchairs or on stretchers call forth tremendous compassion and make their suffering seem somewhat lessened in the face of the suffering of someone else. They seem to possess a marvelous ability to reach out and help someone else, regardless of how deep and wounded they themselves may be. Long after the pilgrimage, it is the handicapped people of l'Arche who pray for this or that person

met at Lourdes or Fatima. Faced with those less fortunate, they
quickly forget themselves and their own difficulties.

Perhaps one of the richest gifts to come out of the experience
of the vacation-pilgrimage is a deep awareness of l'Arche's own
esprit de corps, which comes to the fore as l'Arche members reach
out and touch others they meet on the road. If it is true that the
handicapped persons have remained the constant teachers at l'Arche,
it is also true that the most severely handicapped are the teachers
of those less handicapped. Such awareness has grown as l'Arche
has journeyed on its pilgrimage these past twenty years.

Pilgrimage and vacation, then, might be looked to as a
ritualization or crystallization of the celebration that permeates
the whole life and spirit of l'Arche. The following remarks then
may serve as a conclusion to this chapter, which has looked to
suffering and forgiveness as the basis for relationship, understood
as a covenant, that gives rise to joyful celebration.

Using the image of pilgrimage helps us to see l'Arche as a
fragile, wounded group of people who are on the road, on the
journey together. With the risk and insecurity that fragility implies, l'Arche communities are forced to live in absolute surrender
and dependence upon one another and upon the Source and Sustainer of life. Such reliance is undertaken in a remarkable simplicity, confidence, and faith that refuse to separate the holy and
the ordinary, sacred and secular, prayer and active service, worship
and washing. Birthdays slip into worship, worship blooms into
festivity and courtyard celebration, and the pilgrimage-vacation is
at once a religious event and a good time. At root, what is at
issue here is the sanctity of every dimension of human life, a
value that is all the more apparent when one lives the basics, the
essentials. It is often only when suffering and death are faced
squarely, by choice or circumstance, that one is able to live the
essential and recognize life's precious quality. Life is to be accepted and celebrated in a posture of abandonment, which springs

from a recognition of personal and communal woundedness and poverty, and from an acceptance of the sacred mystery of life itself.

To celebrate life in the face of the woundedness of the human condition is to taste the first fruits of liberation and to announce with one's life, for self and others, a belief and a hope that are grounded in the sacredness of life and in the irreplaceable and undying worth of the human person.

7. L'Alliance

Each Christian and each group of Christians select, sometimes quite unconsciously, certain themes or elements of the gospel as more important than others. As these elements become taken in or embodied by individuals and groups, they give rise to different Christian spiritualities; they shape different forms of Christian life. What Dorothy Day considered vital and essential in the Christian gospel was different from what most Cistercian monks, tucked away in monasteries large and small throughout the world, think is primary in Christian living. We see in the Cistercian tradition a strong attachment to the gospel elements of the hidden life or the heavy emphasis upon the biblical theme of seeking God's face. These do not have the same importance in the life and writings of Dorothy Day and the Catholic Workers. Day's own reading of the gospel led her to see the all-important value of love shown in direct active service to the poor (corporal works of mercy) and the importance of community. What results from these two different selections of gospel themes are quite different, though not conflicting, approaches to living the gospel of Jesus Christ. Though each is very different from the other, both are equally valid and authentic expressions of the message of Jesus Christ.

The life that results from this personal selection of gospel elements may be referred to as the spirituality of a person or a group. In the past, and in many contemporary circles as well, the term "spirituality" has been associated with different levels, degrees, and methods of prayer, flights into mystical frenzy, and transportations into seventh heavens of all sorts. Often when the term "spirituality" is used, images of long vigils, never ending fasts, and hairshirts and ghostlike faces for the greater glory of God are brought to mind. Properly understood, spirituality has to do with the Spirit in persons. It is a question of a living, pulsating, vibrant response of the whole being to the message of Jesus Christ. Spirituality is concerned with the total development of the human person under the sway of the Spirit, the experience of the draw of God's love.

The question, then, about the spirituality of Jean Vanier and l'Arche can be posed this way: how do these people live the message of Jesus Christ? What in the gospel nourishes and sustains their way of life? Which elements of the gospel do we see evidenced in their living?

At l'Arche people are extremely active. There are many things to be done in a day. On my visits there I have often wondered how, and if, people found time to relax, recuperate, and refresh. There is always a whirlwind of activity at l'Arche, yet people seem to manage to find time in each day for that heart-to-heart meeting with God. It is a tough thing to work out a balance between prayer and activity, but it is apparent that the people of l'Arche attempt to stay in touch with the Source of life greater than themselves in the midst of their activity. How do they manage to strike the balance between the two? What is the key to overcoming the great gap that exists for so many between the life of action and the life of prayer or contemplation?

The key is the vision of the human person that lies at the core of l'Arche community. Recall that the human heart is understood as the deepest level of our being; it is open to communion with others and at the same time the region where the Spirit of God resides in us. The human heart, then, becomes the focus for finding God and the root of all our actions under the influence of the Spirit within. With this understood, there is no reason to see ourselves in terms of different capacities or compartments, with actions, thoughts, and prayers stemming from different parts of ourselves. Attentiveness to God (prayer) and service to those in need (action) are rooted in the same source.

As we have seen, this vision of the person as the heart is colored in large measure by an understanding of human needs. To speak about the heart is to speak in the same breath about our needs. We all need to love and be loved, to know others and to be known, and to live freely and allow others to live freely. There is a connection between these basic human needs and certain actions by which these needs are met.

Through the pursuit of justice, or in acting justly, we try to satisfy the deep need to live and let others live freely. People do not truly live in an unjust society or in a community shot through with injustice; they simply exist. Through justice, we hope to assure the members of a community or society a place in which they can live freely, a place in which they can grow. Real growth occurs where there is respect for the freedom and maturation in independence of each person and where the needs for security, a good environment, congenial work, and a sense of belonging are fulfilled. We simply cannot live if we do not have these. Since the satisfaction of these needs takes place through cooperation with others within the community or society, each and every one must act justly in order to bring about a place within which all can grow. At l'Arche the leader and community members are all seen as responsible for bringing about and maintaining an environment within which all may grow and develop in true freedom.

Our need to know, or the need for light, is met in part through contemplation. Most people feel that the contemplative life is out of their reach. It is for monks and nuns. But contemplation is not a primarily intellectual or rational act through which the mind gazes upon or penetrates the mystery of God's eternal being. Rather, because for the Christian God is love made known in the experience of vulnerability and dependency, God is known or contemplated through love. Speaking of the way to union with God, the great Spanish mystic John of the Cross tells us: "Love knows."

In the mystery of the incarnation God embraces and accepts human weakness and vulnerability by becoming a little child. This God becomes one with the concrete, the human body and the human condition. Through the incarnation, God shows a special care and favor for the poor, wounded, weak, suffering, and those in agony and crisis. For the Christian, God incarnate in Jesus lived life close to the weak and the wounded. Consequently we can know God through a manner of contemplation different from that envisioned by Aristotle and the Greek philosophers; that is to say, in fulfillment of the words of Jesus: "Anyone who welcomes one of these little children in my name, welcomes me; and anyone who welcomes me welcomes not me but the one who sent me" (Mark 9:37). We are able to be in touch with, to know, to contemplate God through very simple means. From this point of view, contemplation is achieved in contact with the body and with created reality, not in the avoidance of or passing beyond these. It is a way of knowing that includes the total self, not just the intellect or reason. This knowledge of God is given in the encounter with weakness and woundedness, which is precisely what is embraced and accepted in the incarnation. The God of love, precisely because of love, dwells in weakness and vulnerability and therein is encountered and known. If we understand contemplation in this way, then growth in the life of contemplation happens to the degree that we love, accepting and affirming the presence of the divine dwelling within a human heart that is weak, wounded, vulnerable, and dependent.

At l'Arche this most important need for love is met through the activity of friendship. In friendship we share with another the fruits of contemplation and the quest for justice. By giving attention to human affectivity and needs, the people at l'Arche are better able to understand the conditions of real friendship and the possibilities for its growth in terms of heart, care, woundedness, healing, and support.

Friendship, justice, and contemplation are rooted in love, which is seen in compassion and openness to the wounded and the weak. Love is of the highest value because it reflects the very nature of God. It is the highest activity of the human person and colors the activity of justice, contemplation, and friendship.

Based upon the primacy of love, friendship becomes possible between persons vastly unequal in human capacities. Rooted in love, the activities of justice are carried out in a unique manner at l'Arche, since in the quest for the common good the needs of the weak and wounded have a primary place. Knowledge given in contemplation is itself based on love, since it is rooted in the heart and looks to the weak and vulnerable, to the mystery of Jesus in the weakness of his infancy and hidden life, and to his agony and passion for the revelation of God. Friendship, justice, and contemplation are activities performed under the movement of God's Spirit and are linked to the mystery of weakness, vulnerability, and poverty.

All of this does not mean that intellectual resources are not used in the community of l'Arche. Alongside the activities and qualities of heart, there remains the need to use the head as well to achieve the goals of community motivated by love.

The community of l'Arche, then, may be said to be one in which the style of life is marked in some measure by friendship, the pursuit of justice, and contemplation or prayer—all rooted in the centrality of love abiding in the human heart. But life at l'Arche has a specifically Christian character. Three important elements of the gospel appear to be consistently sustaining and nourishing in the life of the community of l'Arche and give form, a certain distinct and recognizable shape, to this life of friendship, justice, and contemplation: the hidden life at Nazareth, the agony and passion of Jesus, and the Beatitudes.

It would be a mistake, however, to think that l'Arche members would describe their lives in terms of friendship, justice, and contemplation and the gospel themes of the hidden life, the passion and agony, and the Beatitudes. The spirituality of l'Arche has not been spelled out; it is not a written agenda that members read and explicitly follow. Life at l'Arche is vibrant, growing, fragile, and provisional; it is always changing. But if we attempt to analyze it, this is the pattern that consistently emerges. Holding these various elements together in a noble tension through a way of life directly focused upon the singular significance of the handicapped person, constitutes a form of Christian living that is unique in the life of the church. It is in this sense that we speak of the spirituality of l'Arche.

Human life for most people consists of a very ordinary and routine sort of existence. The great majority of people are not called to do great things, just a lot of little things. The thousand and one small details of human existence—the making and eating of meals, the washing and drying of dishes and clothes, the feeding and clothing of children, the daily grind of employment—make up the lot of most of us. The lives of Jesus, Mary, and Joseph were given to many of these same ordinary and routine realities. What has been called the hidden life of Jesus, or the mystery of Nazareth, makes us see the ordinariness and dailiness of human existence in a new light, for it was precisely in the midst of daily routine that Jesus lived and grew to maturity and wisdom. He was plunged into the heart of the human condition, and through his participation in it he emerged as the chosen and beloved One.

The life of Jesus at Nazareth, a hidden and quiet life with Mary and Joseph, very close to the poor, shows us that holiness, wholeness, and sanctity are attained not through great and earthshaking acts but through little concrete acts of love and the ordinary affairs of human life. At l'Arche there is increasing attentiveness to the holy family at Nazareth. More particularly, the communities have been looking to Joseph, Mary's husband, as a source of inspiration for their own calling. In the Christian tradition Joseph is understood as the one entrusted with and responsible for the growth and nurture of the family. Joseph is charged with the care of Jesus in particular, even though according to Christian tradition he is not related to him by blood. Likewise, those at l'Arche are entrusted to care for one another and to be responsible for challenging one another to grow and to do good. Like Joseph, they are called to strengthen and build a family, a home, even though they are not related by blood. This family is not of their own making, as it were, but is a gift and a challenge from God, as was the family of Joseph.

Attention to the very humble and ordinary things of life and living in loving fidelity to them discloses the message of the holy family at Nazareth. In our own day there is much to be learned about doing little things with great love and care. The attainment of human fulfillment and happiness is not to be found outside the daily routine, but in our fidelity to it.

A second gospel element important in the spirituality of l'Arche is that of the agony and passion of Jesus. Jesus experienced the agony of physical pain and discomfort as well as the agony and anguish that result from separation, alienation, loneliness, and rejection. Such anguish and agony are part and parcel of every human life. Agony resulting from alienation, a broken relationship, or loneliness enters most human lives at one point or another. So does physical pain and loss. Agony and suffering are part of the human condition. It is precisely because Jesus participated in the human condition and did not avoid the pain of death by crucifixion or the pain of separation from those he loved that there is the possibility of giving positive value to this apparently negative dimension of human existence. It is not through the avoidance of agony and suffering that human fulfillment and

Elizabeth and Hélène

perfection are attained. Rather, growth and human happiness can come about through the willful acceptance of these harsh and dreadful realities, if we trust that God's grace can transform them.

In the experience of encounter with the handicapped, Vanier perceived something of human poverty, brokenness, woundedness, and suffering. These were the despised, the outcast, the marginal, and the persecuted. Yet in spite of all the tragedy and anguish they had experienced, these people showed a marvelous ability to love, to give tenderness and kindness, and to be compassionate;

they seemed to be exceptionally gifted with the qualities of heart. Vanier also saw many of the same qualities of heart in "normal" people in situations of distress and vulnerability.

What he experienced with handicapped people and others in positions of vulnerability he saw reflected in the Sermon on the Mount. Not only did he perceive in these people the mourning, poverty, suffering, and persecution of which the Sermon on the Mount speaks, but he also saw reflected in the Beatitudes something of the blessedness, peacefulness, happiness, indeed beatitude he had experienced with them. He saw expressed concretely in the lives of the handicapped of l'Arche the values the Beatitudes exalt, and as a result the Beatitudes became the foundation for the rationale of the community and the backbone of its unique way of living the gospel. Perhaps nowhere else in the gospel are the values of Jesus so clearly opposed to those of contemporary Western culture as here, yet they represent the truth of the human person. Trying to live these values in the wide variety of cultural, societal, or religious settings constitutes the unique challenge of l'Arche. In the handicapped, we see the suffering and persecution of which the Sermon on the Mount speaks, but also we see that it is such people who are the blessed, happy, and privileged ones of God exalted in it. Vanier writes:

The handicapped person comes close to God through his handicap, his poverty, and then close to the immense love God has for him. You just have to read all the prophets, the whole message of Jesus and the prophets of other religions to discover that God is close to the little one. And God will be close to us to the degree that we open our hearts to his love, that we recognize our poverty and not our capacity, that we discover that it is not above all by our acquisitions and intelligence, or by the acquisition of professional capacity that we will get close to handicapped people. We will get close to handicapped people when we become conscious of our own fears, of our prejudices, our own fear of death, our own need of God. Then, because we believe in the love of God, we will become the real brother of the handicapped person.[42]

Perhaps there is no clearer statement than the Beatitudes of the central Christian truth that each and every human person, no matter how lowly, sick, poor, or suffering, possesses a unique worth and dignity. Further, it is precisely those who suffer, are persecuted, poor, and lowly who are exalted and called blessed.

Vanier and the communities of l'Arche are profoundly aware of the dimension of mystery in the human person. Likewise, they are concerned with the mysterious quality of the gifts of the Spirit and the Spirit's indwelling as well as the dimension of mystery in Christian faith and revelation. Life at l'Arche is shaped by this profound sense of both God and the human person as mystery. The infancy and hidden life of Jesus, his agony and passion, and the Beatitudes are all within the domain of mystery precisely because as Christian revelation they lie outside the area of philosophical reason, properly speaking. Sharing in the agony and passion of Jesus through woundedness or weakness, seeing value in the ordinariness and dailiness of life in recognition of the hidden life of Jesus and his family, or acting in line with the message of the Beatitudes is possible only because of the mysterious activity of the Spirit. Further, the Spirit's dwelling within the human person in the secret recesses of the heart, moving us to participate in Christ's mysteries and in the activity of the Beatitudes, is in itself a most ineffable mystery and gives the dimension of mystery to the human person.

Not all l'Arche communities are motivated by specifically Christian principles. We have already noted some of the challenges of the l'Arche communities whose members are not Christian or that are located in a predominantly non-Christian environment. Be that as it may, l'Arche communities throughout the world have been founded under the influence of a man whose vocation and inspiration have remained fundamentally Christian throughout his life. The gospel elements of the hidden life, agony and passion, and the Beatitudes have had impact upon the communities whether they are predominantly Christian or not. Likewise, although Vanier himself does not speak of l'Arche communities as places of friendship, justice, and contemplation and the communities may not speak of gospel themes in the precise configuration presented here, they are nonetheless evident in life at l'Arche throughout the world.

The understanding of God and the human person that we find at l'Arche and the kind of gospel living that results lead to some very simple but important practices in the domain of the spiritual life. The first of these is meeting God in Jesus in quiet prayer. Since God is known as a mysterious presence, it is necessary that we meet God in quiet, tranquil prayer. Vanier writes:

. . . we must become people of contemplation. If we do not nurture our deep emotional life in prayer hidden in God, if we do not spend time in silence and if we do not know how to take time to live from the presence and gentleness of our brothers and sisters, we risk becoming embittered. It is only to the extent that we nurture our own hearts that we can keep interior freedom.[43]

It is necessary to stress this point because the communities of l'Arche are quite active and lively and therefore run the risk, as do all active communities, of overlooking the fundamental spiritual origin and orientation of their life. The practice of quiet prayer helps us to penetrate more deeply into the mystery of God in the heart of our own vulnerability and in that of others.

The second practice is that of the celebration of the Eucharist. We discover more clearly the presence of God in our wounds and others' when we share in the sacrament of the body and blood of Jesus. The real presence of Jesus in the Eucharist enables us to experience his hidden presence in ourselves and others in our poverty, weakness, and woundedness. In this sense, we can speak of Jesus in the sacrament of the Eucharist and in the sacrament of the poor. In faith he is really present in both. The presence of Jesus in poverty and woundedness leads us to the mystery of the banquet table of infinite love: the Eucharist. Fed, we return to find this divine presence in the faces, hands, and hearts of the poor.

A third practice is related to the second. If we are to really encounter Jesus in the celebration of the Eucharist and in the sacrament of the poor, then we must prepare for and prolong this encounter. We do this by spending time in the heart-to-heart meeting with Jesus in the Eucharist, even outside the eucharistic liturgy itself, by silent adoration before the reserved sacrament of the Eucharist.

The spirituality of l'Arche, then, may be described as a way of life in a community that attempts to live the message of Jesus Christ in his hidden life, agony and passion, and in adherence to the Beatitudes. At the same time, this message of Jesus is lived with attention to the importance of friendship, the pursuit of justice, and contemplation or prayer. All of this must be seen together with the dimensions that touch the heart and soul of l'Arche treated in the previous chapter: suffering, forgiveness, relationship, covenant, and celebration. Realizing the essential woundedness and vulnerability of their own existence and that of others, the members embrace the radical poverty of all human life and witness to it in the simplicity and poverty of the lifestyle of the community. Since it is in our poverty, woundedness, and vulnerability that our own truth and the reality of God are revealed, the poorest and most wounded in the community hold pride of place. In their person is disclosed the poor and wounded Christ crucified who is served in the flurry of seemingly endless activities of the community and who is contemplated in times of quiet prayer and in celebration. When all is said and done, the concluding words of the Prayer of l'Arche best express its spirituality:

> Seigneur, Bénis-nous de la main de tes pauvres,
> Seigneur, Souris-nous dans le regard de tes pauvres,
> Seigneur, Reçois-nous un jour
> Dans l'heureuse compagnie de tes pauvres!

> (Lord, Bless us by the hand of your poor,
> Lord, Smile on us in the gaze of your poor,
> Lord, Receive us one day
> In the blessed company of your poor!)

8. The Branch of an Olive

The message l'Arche offers is of value to anyone trying to live the gospel. Perhaps what is most important about the spirituality of l'Arche is its ability to include the reality of human vulnerability and suffering in an overall vision of Christian life shaped by the self-emptying and suffering of Jesus Christ and by the Beatitudes. If we find that the spirituality of l'Arche offers us insight about the living of the gospel, we must take what is offered on its own terms. Nowhere and in no way do the people of l'Arche suggest that they are offering a contribution to Christian spirituality or to theology. The writings of Jean Vanier and the members of l'Arche do not present an orderly and airtight treatment of the human person or of spirituality. L'Arche dwellers are people who are simply trying to follow the gospel. In one sense, their message is quite simple and available to all those who would choose to live by it, in whatever circumstances they find themselves. One need not join a l'Arche community or visit one to profit from and live something of the spirituality of l'Arche. Its message is for the church and for the human community, not just for the community of l'Arche itself.

What is the message of l'Arche? In the final analysis it is about the sacredness and dignity of the human person. L'Arche simply means a new type of family life, at the heart of which is the wounded person to whose well-being everything is geared. L'Arche is a way that leads to an encounter with God. The mystery that is revealed at l'Arche is that the poor and wounded lead us directly to the heart of God. The belief that underlies life at l'Arche is that we cannot walk with God unless we walk with the poor and the wounded. To walk with the wounded and the weak means to walk with God. In short, the message of l'Arche is that the seeds of the divine and the capacities of the human heart are found in weakness. This is the cornerstone of l'Arche. Related to this central message are other insights that may be of help to those who try to live the gospel. Let us look at these insights, so that we, all of us, may profit from the wisdom of l'Arche by living something of its spirituality, each in our own situation in life.

First of all, in the spirituality of l'Arche the concept of the human person or the notion of what is valuable in the human being is very large; it makes room for a wide variety of people, especially the weak, wounded, and vulnerable, and others often left out of the scope of our regular concern. Today, more than ever, there is a need for an understanding of the person that is not based upon intellectual promise or rational ability, what one can accomplish with the head and the hands. This tendency to define the person exclusively in terms of the ability to think, decide, and act productively is all too obvious and has terribly destructive consequences. Those who see the person from this point of view have a great deal to learn from Jean Vanier and l'Arche, whose all-inclusive vision of humanity, with special attention to the poorest and most wounded, commands respect. To live the message of l'Arche requires that, in the first place, we see and relate to persons, all persons, differently.

If we look at the importance that Jean Vanier and l'Arche attach to their own experience, we discover how important it is to pay attention to our own human experience. The first and fundamental word God speaks to us is through our humanity. The way of life at l'Arche does not result from principles and ideals conceived in the abstract. Rather, in the concrete experience of suffering, vulnerability, and crisis, the people of l'Arche perceive something of the spiritual dimension of the human person.

They get in touch with aspects of the human spirit in these situations that are often unknown otherwise. All theories of personality development and all philosophical explanations of human nature fade into an embarrassed silence when confronted with the stunning truth about the person that is learned from experience and that is lived in the communities of l'Arche. Like them, we need to constantly look to our own human experience and consult our own inner depths for the truth about ourselves, others, and God. We need to see our own weaknesses, our own fragility, and vulnerability as the very place where we encounter God. We need not try to bypass what is ugly in us on the way to union with God. It is precisely in what is ugliest in us that God embraces us.

Among the truths about the human person that the people of l'Arche learn through experience, the following deserve special attention because they form the core of Vanier's contribution to contemporary spirituality and to our own effort to live out the gospel. First, the weakness and fragility of the human situation is the focus for the revelation of the presence, strength, and power of God. Second, when we recognize the woundedness and weakness of the entire global situation, we realize the need to work toward a universal human community according to the spirit of Beatitudes. Third, this unity will only be made possible when there is common recognition of everyone's woundedness and need for communion and will only be accomplished through love. We strive for this unity by being compassionate, which is a reflection of the compassionate love of God, who gives strength in human weakness by sharing in the fragility and suffering of the human condition. God meets us in our need.

Another strength that Vanier and l'Arche offer to contemporary spirituality and to those who try to live the gospel is the unified vision of the human being expressed in the term "heart." Rather than denoting one faculty or source of human activities among others, "heart" refers to the basis, core, or foundation of the person. The term "heart" expresses the dynamic unity of our total being, which is capable of being affected or attracted, especially by God's presence in the weak, little, suffering, and vulnerable. Such a view of the person around one central axis of the heart allows for the unity of both our experience and faith as well as our action and contemplation. Instead of having to locate contemplation or prayer in one source and active service or ministry in another, or faith in one faculty and experience in yet another, we can speak of all these realities being encompassed by the dynamism of the attraction of God's love, which touches our hearts in interaction with others. We can put a final nail in the coffin of spiritual schizophrenia, thanks to some of what can be learned from l'Arche. Prayer and active service need not be compartmentalized. Contemplation of Jesus in his mysteries (prayer) and direct service of those in need (action), even if it be the changing and washing of diapers, are rooted in one source, the heart, the deepest level of our being, the place where the divine lives in us.

Another contribution is the importance Jean Vanier and l'Arche attach to human relationship and to community. Recent currents of thought in the social sciences, philosophy, and theology all give evidence of the singular importance of our relationship with others in the human community. We have simply missed the point if we overlook the fact that absolutely everything Jean Vanier has spoken and written about since 1964 has as its context common life with others in a familylike community of pardon and celebration. The human being without others exists in a void. No one can live a Christian life or a deeply spiritual life alone. We need others on the way.

Yet another contribution to contemporary spirituality is the emphasis on human needs and affectivity. L'Arche's concern is with basic human needs, with communion of persons, human

Marie-Noëlle (left) and Mimi

vulnerability, joy, suffering, celebration, reconciliation, and compassion. In this understanding of Christian life there is tenderness, touch, ecstasy (sexual or other), pleasure, embrace, the
meeting of eyes and hearts, tears, and fear.[44] We all long to caress
and be caressed, to hold and to be held, to bathe and be bathed
in love. We need to be comforted and cared for as well as to care
for others and offer comfort. Above all, we crave compassion: to
be met and embraced in the weakness, fragility, brokenness, and
tragedy that enter every one of our lives and that are transformed
by the graceful and compassionate embrace of Jesus in his incarnation, passion, agony, death, and resurrection. All of these

notions show a concern for the place of human needs and affectivity in the spiritual life. This is a most important contribution, we might say corrective, to those views of the Christian life that focus almost exclusively upon the intellectual or rational abilities or upon the will of the person. God's grace and attraction touch us and lure us from the inside out, as it were. God does not simply speak to our mind, but to our heart, which is our total self.

A final insight from which we can profit in our attempt to live the gospel is the Christ-centered vision of the human person at the root of l'Arche. Each one of us is a mystery because we share in the mystery of Christ. This demands infinite respect for the dignity of each individual. For Jean Vanier and l'Arche, everything, most especially the human person, is unified around the central axis of the mystery of Christ.

The contributions Jean Vanier and l'Arche offer to contemporary spirituality are many; the real challenge is to see how we can profit from their insights in our own attempt to live the gospel given the many diverse situations we find ourselves in. Concretely this means giving attention and time to those persons whom contemporary society seems to view as waste, residue, or "rents in the veil": the elderly, Third World people, prisoners, little children, the abandoned, the poor and forgotten. It means that our most precious possession, our time, will be demanded of us. Elderly people need those who are willing to take time with them, even if it is simply to watch the soap operas together. Little children need time in learning how to tie shoelaces or button a dress. Time is the one thing we do not seem to have enough of; it is often the most precious gift we can offer to another.

L'Arche can teach us about how to live our lives in an authentic, true way. This is because those at l'Arche have an uncanny ability to focus on what is essential in life. What we see at l'Arche is the recovery of the essential values of the dignity of the human person, the importance of human relationships, the need for a home, a familylike atmosphere, and attention to the basic human needs to love, to know, and to be free. At l'Arche we glimpse the truth of how we really need to challenge others to grow. This challenge sometimes requires "tough love," which means being more than a mutual admiration society—a pat on the back here, a kind and gentle glance there. "Tough love" requires that we be demanding of the other for his or her own growth, health, and well-being.

Life at l'Arche is simple and ordinary, but it is a life of intense personal relationships, modeled on the family. There are deep bonds between and among members of the family of l'Arche. Such bonds emerge from deep needs and entail the members' responsibility for each other. The heart is a place of woundedness, darkness, great joy, and compassion, but is also the place in us where we recognize our responsibility for others. Such bonds are built upon the recognition of our uniqueness and suffering and that of others. Such mutual recognition helps to overcome the barriers that separate us, handicapped from "normal," old from young, weak from strong, one color or sex from the other, so that we can celebrate life together. Such unity and celebration require that we recognize the wound deep in each person's heart and the capacities for great love and growth that are cultivated as we learn to recognize our need for one another and God and our responsibility to them.

L'Arche is countercultural in that its values run counter to those prevailing in society. Our contemporary society has so little time for the little and the weak. Strength, power, and achievement are the key words. The strong survive. Articulate voices advocate "mercifully" eliminating the "waste of society" or terminating the "rents in the veil" before they get burdensome. Cool, measured, and calculating minds argue that in some cases abortion may be morally justifiable, lending support to those whose abortion-on-demand platform amounts to nothing other than massive genocide. We tend to be pragmatists; we are interested in what is practical, in what works. But one has to wonder whether the ultimate criterion for our choices is practicality or convenience. Is the concern for "mercifully" eliminating the sick and the suffering, the fragile and the weak really anything other than putting out of sight those we do not want to see or spend time with or money on, because we are afraid that we might get a chance to see through them to something real?

The ultimate question here is one of a human way of life focused upon the essentials of love, creativity, truth, and freedom versus the road of technology with its values of convenience, comfort, consumption, and competition. Now technology is not necessarily opposed to a truly human life; it can advance it. But the deeper meaning of human existence is obscured by technology's unbridled quest for efficiency. The two great horrors of our age, the holocaust of the Jews at the hands of the Nazis and the imminent nuclear holocaust, bring about a tremendous crisis of vision and a crisis for hope. Even if one does not accept that the world will end in nuclear war, the possibility of nuclear annihilation still has an effect on the contemporary psyche. Both holocausts, one fact, the other possibility, are the fruits of the spirit of the technological age and its unbridled quest. Part of the horror of the holocaust, the deaths of six million Jews together with millions of others—Poles, Slavs, gypsies, handicapped, homosexuals—is the efficiency with which the whole thing was accomplished. The willed, efficient, systematic attempt to annihilate whole groups of people took place in one of the most advanced cultures in history.

The joy of l'Arche springs from focusing upon the opposite of convenience, comfort, consumption, competition, and efficiency. As a countercultural movement it lends to the building of a new culture. This new culture would strive for the essential in human life, which is uncovered through simplicity and acceptance of the reality of suffering and fragility. L'Arche is built upon those values the contemporary culture seems to work against, but they are the only values that matter in the long run: family, love, truth, freedom, and the dignity of persons. It is built upon the desire to fulfill basic human needs. Emerging from the commitment to the basics and essentials is an understanding of what it means to be human. Valued over all else is the interpersonal, the giving and receiving of love, the affirming and being affirmed as a person.

What we can learn from l'Arche is that we need to create conditions that support full human existence, conditions that permit us to live at the level of our most basic needs. We need to create environments that keep us from buying into the false needs that technology and consumerism tell us are ours. They would have us confuse our wants with our needs. We need love, truth, and freedom, not a two-week vacation at Lake Tahoe or a body like Raquel Welch or Robert Redford.

The technologically based consumer- and convenience-oriented society, rather than providing us with more freedom, which is its claim, takes our freedom away. We are bound by our wants and fleeting desires, which we have been seduced into believing are our needs. Whatever moves us toward greater simplicity is a movement toward greater wholeness and humanity. Contemporary society and culture seem to do just the opposite.

This emphasis on comfort, convenience, and efficiency, which has gotten to the point where these have become almost absolute, makes suffering seem the greatest evil. It must be avoided at all costs. But to flee suffering and to ignore death's claims is to flee reality. The inability to face suffering causes barriers between people. Contemporary society seems bent upon the denial of death. Bonds are created when suffering is accepted as the common lot of two people and the entire human community. Whatever leads to an honest acceptance of vulnerability, suffering, and death leads to more freedom to live life and to accept others. Boredom, listlessness, and escapism are the results of attempting to flee the facts of our humanity: in weakness we are born. Brief periods of strength and success, good health and prosperity may obscure the truth of our existence. In the end, we all must surrender everything into the hands of the Source and Sustainer of all that is. Such surrender requires that we recognize our vulnerability and limitations—our weakness. Otherwise we come to the end of our lives resentful and "go out kicking."

The spirituality of l'Arche can be for us a way of living the truth of human existence and the paradox of the gospel: in weakness is our strength. It can be the occasion for accepting the uniqueness of each one of us, our vulnerability and poverty, and the freedom to be ourselves. To accept our own poverty and to identify and be in solidarity with the lowly and the weak, the wounded and the marginalized, the little child and the old lady, is to be rid of the fear of rejection which plagues us all in our very competitive world. To be in compassionate solidarity with the lowest, the littlest, the forgotten is to recognize that we have nothing to lose. If we are in compassionate solidarity with those who, according to the dictates of society, are at the lowest rung of the ladder, then we have little or no fear of being rejected or of losing face. There is no lower for us to go, there is nothing that can be taken from us, there is no prestige to be lost.

Such compassionate solidarity has political ramifications. To stand in solidarity with those rejected by society is a political and social witness that can engender life for our troubled world. In living by the spirit of l'Arche we must recognize that we are called to struggle as those in Africa, Central America, Northern Ireland, and Poland struggle. Living the spirituality of l'Arche requires that we live in solidarity with all of those throughout the world who are oppressed, discriminated against, tortured. It means standing with those who live in fear, those who struggle and pray for justice and the coming of God's reign.

The handicapped, the elderly, the marginalized, and the weak have little sense of competition. These people call the healthy and the robust to a life of sharing, where individuals are valued for themselves in their uniqueness. There is, we learn from them, no need to conform—we are already one in our fragility and in our being toward death. The more we move toward a deeper sense of our oneness with others, especially those whom society rejects and whose merciful extermination is advocated by many, the more we will discover wholeness and fullness of life. The challenge for those who do not live in l'Arche communities is to opt to live as much as possible in compassionate solidarity with all victims: the handicapped, prisoners, battered women, victims of injustice. Such compassionate solidarity does not require that everyone go live at a house of the Catholic Workers or at a l'Arche community or volunteer time with the Missionaries of Charity. It is rather to choose to see ourselves as one with the wounded and the weak, for this is what we are, and to take their side and allow their perspective and experience to shape all our experience, understanding, judgment, and actions. It is to understand ourselves to be one of them and consequently to allow ourselves to be changed by them. It is to engage in the struggle against the prevailing values of society, to say yes each and every day to the weak and wounded in our midst and to the littleness of our own life. The struggle requires that we not give in to the temptation to greatness, to the lure to do great things. It is to accept doing small, seemingly insignificant things. Such a life entails the acceptance of the consequences of going against the tide, the fact that we may be subject to the same rejection, scorn, and discrimination experienced by those poor, wounded, and marginalized with whom we live in compassionate solidarity. Sometimes friends do not understand or offer support. Often support does not come from the local church. We are criticized and ridiculed. But standing firm in our beliefs can be an opportunity for growth.

To live something of the spirituality of l'Arche is to approach every person we meet with absolute respect and reverence, believing that in this person, especially the poorest and most wounded, God dwells. It is, finally, to recognize ourselves to be what we are. All our experience, understanding, judgment, and actions are different as a result of such recognition. And we are brought to our knees by the awareness that we, the healthy, strong, robust, wise, and efficient, have been taught and will continue to be taught by the little child, by the victim, by the wounded, by the outcast. It is to recognize that up until this point, we have known and done very little. It is to see that God's grace slips through the cracks and reaches to the lowest and basest regions of human existence, working in hidden, secret, ineffable ways. It is, finally, to penetrate something of the truth of the fullness of God's life in the crucified Christ.

Living in fullness is as much a gift as life itself. We can choose to live more fully or we can choose to simply exist—there is a difference. We can learn from l'Arche that we must look in different places for the fullness of life than we have heretofore thought. The fullness of life does not come from increasing the accomplishments of head or hands. Real life is lived from the heart.

We must look to the heart. Despite what the billboards and the TV ads say, the good life, the full life, does not come from sipping the best brandy or eating at the finest restaurants with "the beautiful people." Again we must look in different places, to the cracks and the dregs, to the fringes and the margins, to the "rents in the veil." By looking to the edges and the cracks, we glimpse that it is there that the quest for a truly human life continues in our terrible age, a time in the history of humanity that seems hopelessly bent on self-destruction.

To live the spirituality of l'Arche right where we are is to recognize that the edges are the center, the bottom of the rung the most important, that what we perceive as ugly and repulsive can be an invitation to great beauty. It is a call to risk, but also to the security of faith in others and in the Source and Sustainer of life. It is a summons to deep interpersonal relationships with one another for the very practical reason that we need one another as members of a family need one another. We are responsible for one another. Those who live the message of l'Arche learn that the human heart is what matters in life. They learn that weakness binds and that "strength" divides, that weakness is a blessed thing we can celebrate because it has been accepted and embraced by God becoming flesh. The weakest members of family, community, and society are our teachers. We must listen to them, the wounded prophets of the heart. In them we have access to the unfathomable mystery of God's loving vulnerability. Since God *is* love, God is *most* vulnerable. To participate in the life of God, the God revealed in the self-emptying of Jesus, is to recognize, accept, and celebrate our vulnerability.

In telling the story of l'Arche we focused on the handicapped person as the teacher of the wise and robust. This is as it should be. The handicapped person is the message of l'Arche. But it is also true that the assistants are at the core of l'Arche as well. Learning day after day what the weak and wounded offer as a gift to humanity, the assistants at l'Arche attempt to be faithful to the secret of God's dwelling in human vulnerability. Their lives are a proclamation of this good news, this message of l'Arche. As we draw to a close, let us look to the life of one of the assistants at l'Arche.

When I telephoned Marie-Annette at l'Arche from Paris to arrange my visit to Trosly-Breuil, she told me I'd be arriving at a very difficult time. The evening of my intended arrival had been set aside for the people of her *foyer* to be together. She had some hard news to tell them.

Marie-Annette, a lovely young woman in her mid-twenties

with sparkling eyes and an ear-to-ear smile, hails from Brittany, in the northwest of France. To anyone visiting or living at the Vigne these past years, Marie-Annette's dedication to the people of her *foyer* has been apparent. Quite simply, her life has been given to those of the Vigne, and this gift has been manifest in the untiring and selfless activities that comprise the daily round of life at l'Arche: rising and washing, working and playing, listening and praying, and working again long after the others have gone to rest. She smiles a great and beaming smile with patience and gentleness when she is asked why she works so hard or where her energy comes from and if she gets enough rest. "It's nothing," she assures this questioner and with confidence and security beyond measure insists that she has received much more from l'Arche than she has ever given.

The life with the people of her *foyer*, especially the five mentally handicapped men who comprise the heart of the Vigne, as well as her commitment to Jesus Christ maintained through prayer, are her sustenance and nourishment. Her vivacity and energy, to say nothing of her enthusiasm, appear to be endless and effortless. Had she entered it, the professional world would have had a gem, but she did not. Instead she decided to become part of the world of the poor and wounded, the marginalized, the handicapped. In the *foyer* of the Vigne she was opened to the world of deep suffering and celebration that is life at l'Arche.

Not long ago she announced the Covenant, *l'Alliance*, with God in the presence of some brothers and sisters of l'Arche. Responding to an invitation, a call from God in Jesus Christ, she gave her life to these people. She is responsible for them, and they for her; they are her people.

But all during her time at the Vigne, Marie-Annette felt another pull, a deep and abiding call to live the message of Jesus with people poorer still than the handicapped men and women of her own country. On the evening of my arrival in Trosly-Breuil,

Marie-Annette was to tell Richard, Pierre, Marcel, Jean, Jérome, and the others that in a few short months she would be leaving France to go to Israel with the hope of beginning a l'Arche community there, God willing. She would go alone.

The responses to her news were mixed. Some seemed deeply distressed by the news of her departure, while others seemed to have a sense that she would remain with them in the spirit that binds the family of l'Arche throughout the world. Others seemed concerned for her health and safety. Still others appeared to be relatively unaffected by the news. After the meeting of the *foyer*, I sensed a feeling in the house unlike any I had ever known during my previous visits. In a few short months Marie-Annette would not be living at the Vigne, and she would be missed.

The story of l'Arche is a story of people in community. It is a tale of woundedness and suffering, acceptance and healing, of compassion, commitment, forgiveness, celebration, and common life. Marie-Annette and the people of her *foyer* are the story of l'Arche. Worlds apart from them in terms of their abilities, talents, and intellectual capacities, this bright and beautiful young French woman has made a home, given her heart, and shared her life with people who, for all intents and purposes, are useless, undesirable, without worth or dignity in the eyes of many of her contemporaries. They have given much more to her than she to them, she maintains with her characteristic gentle firmness. Her time has come to leave them, but the roots and bonds that have grown between and among them, deep within their hearts, will remain. *Partir c'est mourir, un peu.* To leave is to die a little.

Driving to the train in Compiègne for my departure from Trosly-Breuil, Marie-Annette assured me with a great confidence that she would not go to Israel on her own, but rather would be carried there by God and by the prayer and support of the l'Arche communities and their friends throughout the world. In her story we glimpse something of the history of l'Arche: a call to community with the poor and wounded and an ever deepening hunger

to be close to the poorest, most wounded, most despised throughout the world. Her life and the lives of others in the community
manifest the message of l'Arche for the church and for the world:
the seeds of the divine and the capacities of the human heart are
found in weakness.

As the train began to pull away from Compiègne, Marie-
Annette looked at me graciously and offered her farewell. "I am
not sure where, or when, or how, but we will be together again.
Of this I am sure." Deep from within my heart's memory came
words from the Prayer of l'Arche that could not find their way to
my lips:

> Seigneur, Bénis-nous de la main de tes pauvres,
> Seigneur, Souris-nous dans le regard de tes pauvres,
>   Seigneur, Reçois-nous un jour
> Dans l'heureuse compagnie de tes pauvres!
>
> (Lord, Bless us by the hand of your poor,
> Lord, Smile on us in the gaze of your poor,
>   Lord, Receive us one day
> In the blessed company of your poor!)

Conclusion

In the beginning we saw that Jean Vanier christened his little home l'Arche, the Ark, like Noah's ark. For Jews and Christians the ark is a symbol of refuge, diversity, and hope. It was in an ark that Noah carried precious cargo—life, two of every kind of living thing. The promise of future life, of long life, was made by God to Noah, his wife, and all those on board. Preserved from the destruction of the great flood which had wiped out all living things because of humanity's choice to continue to do what was evil, life as we now know it is the fruit of those on board the ark. God created us good. Humanity chose to do evil. The story of Noah's ark is a way of communicating the truth of the destructive power of evil and chaos and God's never ending promise of deliverance. Even though humanity chooses evil, God's judgment is a hopeful promise. But the promise of deliverance from chaos and evil, from the destructive forces that threaten to annihilate us, is always made by God quite concretely and responded to quite concretely by a few. The promise may ultimately benefit everyone, but it is always offered to a certain person or group and accepted at great price by that person or that group. On board the ark of Noah were the man himself, his wife, their children, and two of every kind of creature. It seems a lot. But they were such a small group when considered alongside the whole of creation. The point is that through this ever-so-small group, from this precious cargo, salvation and promise are offered. Life continues through them.

The Ark of Jean Vanier is in our own day a symbol of refuge, diversity, and hope. Through it God has done and is doing great things. In the message of l'Arche there is offered promise and hope in our terrible age. Nuclear war threatens us with the destruction, annihilation, and termination of everything and everyone that we have ever known. It signals the end of everything as we know it. The two great symbols of evil in our age, the holocaust of six million Jews and others at the hands of the Nazis and the imminent nuclear holocaust, bring about a crisis of vision and a crisis of hope for us and for our children. To what future can our children look? What can they hope for? In what or whom can they trust?

The story of l'Arche is about persons in community. It is a tale of woundedness and suffering, acceptance and healing, of compassion, commitment, forgiveness, celebration, and common life. As such it holds out a vision and a hope built on these values, these qualities of the heart. It holds out a vision of the future in which every dimension of life, personal, communal, religious, and political is shot through with the values of the heart. It inspires hope, not in a future brought about through yet more strength, efficiency, competition, and domination, but in a future built on mutual respect, reverence for the dignity of each individual, and attention to the weak and the wounded, the marginalized and the forgotten.

It is not a question of building families, communities, and personal relationships upon such values while leaving the corporate, national, and international political machine to run its destructive course. It is rather to see that such political machines are comprised of persons and can be changed by them. Such change comes about as the riches of the heart are unlocked in each person. This begins in families, communities, and personal relationships, but it does not end there. The point is to see that beginning with the family, personal relationships, or communities modeled upon the family is to begin with the most basic social structure and thus to affect every level of society from the bottom up.

In these pages we have followed l'Arche on its journey. We have watched its launching and have glimpsed its course of travel over these twenty-one years. We have seen the reason for its launching and the vision that guides its course. We have seen its source of inspiration and the power from outside itself that helps it move and progress. We have gotten a peek at the diversity, the great suffering, and joy of the life on board.

The key to Noah's ark unlocks the Ark of Jean Vanier. What we see is that the life on board, the precious cargo, is itself the vessel of God's saving promise. We shift our gaze from the Ark to the cargo within, the human person, weak and fragile, open to attraction and communion with others and God, as the bearer of God's hope and promise. We see finally that since God *is* love, God is *most* vulnerable. Those who live from their hearts alone are the clearest signs of God's presence and promise in our terrible age.

Notes

CHAPTER 2

1. Jean Vanier, "Federation, October 1973: Introduction" (Paper presented to a meeting of the International Federation of l'Arche, 1973, mimeographed), 18.
2. Michael Downey, "An Investigation of the Concept of Person in the Spirituality of l'Arche as Developed in the Writings of Jean Vanier" (Ph.D. diss., The Catholic University of America, 1982), 16ff., offer a treatment of the structures of l'Arche.
3. Bill Clarke, *Enough Room for Joy* (New York: Paulist Press, 1974), 67.

CHAPTER 3

4. Bill Clarke, *Enough Room for Joy* (New York: Paulist Press, 1974), 30. A reference to Robert Speaight's description of the young Jean Vanier in Speaight's biography of Georges P. Vanier entitled *Vanier: Soldier, Diplomat, and Governor-General*.
5. Jean Vanier, *Le bonheur: Principe et fin de la morale aristotélicienne* (Paris: Desclée De Brouwer, 1965).
6. Jean Vanier, "Letter to My Brothers and Sisters in Prison" (n.d., mimeographed).

CHAPTER 4

7. Jean Vanier, *Community and Growth* (New York: Paulist Press, 1979), xi; see also 35–36.
8. Jean Vanier, *In Weakness, Strength* (Toronto: Griffin House, 1975). Text first published 1969.
9. Robert Speaight, *Vanier: Soldier, Diplomat, and Governor-General* (London: Collins, 1970).
10. Vanier, *In Weakness, Strength*, 21.
11. Ibid., 4.
12. Ibid., 19.
13. Ibid., 18.
14. Ibid., 22.
15. Ibid., 25.

16. Ibid., 32.
17. Ibid., 41–42.
18. Ibid., 36.
19. Ibid., 39.
20. Ibid., 40.
21. Ibid., 45.
22. Jean Vanier, *Be Not Afraid* (New York: Paulist Press, 1975).
23. For a more detailed analysis of T. Philippe's thought see Michael Downey, "An Investigation of the Concept of Person in the Spirituality of l'Arche as Developed in the Writings of Jean Vanier" (Ph.D. diss., The Catholic University of America, 1982), 31ff.
24. Jean Vanier, in "Letters of l'Arche," no. 8 (Winter 1974/75): 10.
25. Jean Vanier, *Eruption to Hope* (New York: Paulist Press, 1971), preface.
26. Ibid.
27. Jean Vanier, *Followers of Jesus* (New York: Paulist Press, 1976), 26.

CHAPTER 5

28. Jean Vanier, "The Spiritual Needs of the Handicapped" (n.d., mimeographed), 1. Text in hand is a reprint from "Letters of l'Arche," no. 7 (Summer 1974): 24–27.
29. Jean Vanier, *Man and Woman He Made Them* (New York: Paulist Press, 1985), 37.
30. Ibid., 48.
31. Here I refer the reader to the scholastic notion of *voluntas ut natura*. The similarities between this notion and the contemporary usage of the term "heart" have been treated by M. D. Chenu in "Les Catégories Affectives dans la Langue de l'Ecole," *Le Coeur,* vol. 29 of Etudes Carmélitaines (n.p., Desclée De Brouwer, 1950), 123–128.
32. Vanier, *Eruption to Hope* (New York: Paulist Press, 1971), 42.
33. Ibid., 26.
34. Jean Vanier, "Lifelong Homes for the Adult Mentally Retarded" (n.d., mimeographed), 5–6.
35. Ibid., 16.
36. Jean Vanier, "To Build So All May Grow," *Habitat* 19, nos. 3/4 (1976): 5.
37. Vanier, *Community and Growth* (New York: Paulist Press, 1979), 126.
38. Ibid., 24.
39. Vanier, "Lifelong Homes for the Adult Mentally Retarded," 9.
40. Ibid.

CHAPTER 6

41. Jean Vanier, *Community and Growth* (New York: Paulist Press, 1979). A translation of his work *La communauté, lieu du pardon et de la fête* (Community, Place of Pardon and Celebration). This work, along with Ch. 7 of Bill Clarke, *Enough Room for Joy* (New York: Paulist Press, 1974), has influenced the present treatment of the notion of celebration.

CHAPTER 7

42. Jean Vanier, "The Spiritual Needs of the Handicapped" (n.d., mimeographed), 3. Text in hand is a reprint from "Letters of l'Arche," no. 7 (Summer 1974): 24–27.
43. Jean Vanier, *Community and Growth* (New York: Paulist Press, 1979), 77. See also "Letters of l'Arche," no. 8 (Winter 1974/75): 12–14.

CHAPTER 8

44. Jean Vanier, *Man and Woman He Made Them* (New York: Paulist Press, 1985). In this recent work Vanier explores the relationship between affectivity and sexuality.

For Further Reading

BOOKS IN ENGLISH BY JEAN VANIER

In Weakness, Strength. Toronto, Canada: Griffin House, 1969, 1975.
Tears of Silence. Denville, NJ: Dimension Books, 1970.
Eruption to Hope. New York: Paulist Press, 1971.
Be Not Afraid. New York: Paulist Press, 1975.
Followers of Jesus. New York: Paulist Press, 1976.
Community and Growth. New York: Paulist Press, 1979.
I Meet Jesus. Quebec, Canada: Editions Anne Sigier, 1981.
  (Released in the United States by Paulist Press)
Man and Woman He Made Them. New York: Paulist Press, 1985.
I Walk with Jesus. Quebec, Canada: Editions Anne Sigier, 1985. (Released in the United States by Paulist Press)

BOOKS IN ENGLISH ABOUT JEAN VANIER AND L'ARCHE

My Brother My Sister. Sue Mosteller. New York: Paulist Press, 1972.
L'Arche Journal. James H. Clarke. Toronto, Canada: Griffin House, 1973.
Enough Room for Joy. Bill Clarke, New York: Paulist Press, 1974.
The Challenge of l'Arche. With introduction and conclusion by Jean Vanier. Ottawa, Canada: Novalis, 1981. (Released in the United States by Winston Press)

OTHER MATERIALS AVAILABLE IN ENGLISH FROM:

L'Arche International
c/o Daybreak
11339 Yonge Street
Richmond Hill
Ontario, Canada
L4C 4X7

OTHER MATERIALS AVAILABLE IN FRENCH FROM:

L'Arche Internationale
Trosly-Breuil
60350 Cuise-la-Motte
France